OF BLOOD

AND FIRE

OF BLOOD
AND FIRE

BOOK ONE OF
THE BOUND AND THE BROKEN

RYAN CAHILL

Of Blood and Fire

Book One of The Bound and The Broken series

Copyright © 2021 by Ryan Cahill

First edition: March 2021

ISBN 978-1-8383818-0-6

www.ryancahillauthor.com

Cover Design by Bookscovered.co.uk

Illustrations by Aron Cahill

To Séamus, for always fuelling my imagination.
To Mam and Dad, for teaching me to love stories.
To Amy, for not killing me.
To lovers of Fantasy all over the world, this is for you.

By Ryan Cahill

The Bound and The Broken

The Fall

Of Blood and Fire

Contents

PROLOGUE

Beams of pale moonlight drifted through the forest canopy as Kallinvar pushed his foot against the Urak's lifeless body, turning it over onto its back. Its leathery grey skin was latticed with a motley collection of scars and fresh wounds. He curled his lip with indifference. He had long ago lost count of how many of these monstrosities he had sent to the void.

There had been a battle in this forest, between men and Uraks. Most of the dead were men. Young men. Judging by the spread of the bodies, the Uraks had lured them into a trap. The Knights had arrived too late to stop the massacre.

"Brother Captain, one of them is alive."

Kallinvar raised his eyebrow and nodded for Brother Tarron to lead the way. *He must be the one. The Grandmaster said we would find the last Sigil Bearer here.*

Brother Ildris and Sister Ruon already stood over the man's body. Their brilliant white cloaks sat still across their backs.

"He is alive?"

"Yes, Brother Captain. Though, he is not long for this world."

Kallinvar nodded. He pushed past his companions and knelt beside the man. He was young. He had seen twenty or so summers at most. His shoulders were broad and his muscles were dense. Had he been on his feet, he would have easily been looking down at Kallinvar, and Kallinvar was no small man. But he wasn't on his feet. He was lying on the flat of his back, with a deep wound in his gut. Kallinvar was surprised he was still alive.

"I—" a cough cut the man's attempt at speech short, blood spluttering up over his lip.

Kallinvar placed his hand on the man's chest. "Easy. Do not speak. I am going to ask you three questions. Answer with a nod or a shake of the head. Do you understand?"

The man nodded.

"The duty of the strong is to protect the weak. Do you agree?"

The man nodded without hesitation.

"No decision is straightforward. Black and white do not exist. We live in a world of ever-shifting grey. Do you agree?"

The man paused only for a moment, then nodded.

Kallinvar locked eyes with the man. "If we save you, are you willing to forgo your past life and everything that holds you to the person you are now? Are you willing to bear the Sigil of Achyron? To follow his creed and serve The Warrior until the day you are taken from this world?"

Kallinvar saw the look in the man's eyes. Uncertainty. That was good. A lesser man would jump at any chance to save his own life. One should not simply wish to live. They should wish to live in a way that they deemed to be right. That distinction was the separation between men.

"Let it be known that if you take the Sigil of Achyron and betray his creed, the life will be stripped from your bones in the most painful way that you could imagine. It is not an easy cross to bear. Will you accept it?" Kallinvar didn't allow his eyes to drift from the man's gaze. The measure of a man's intent was in his eyes.

"Yes," the man choked, more blood sprinkling from his open mouth.

"Very well. Brother Tarron, the Sigil." Kallinvar didn't have to wait long.

"The last Sigil, Brother Captain."

Kallinvar turned and reached out to take the Sigil. "Thank you, Brother Tarron."

He ran his gauntleted fingers across the Sigil's smooth surface. It was made of a strange metal with a greenish hue. Forged by Achyron himself. It was shaped in the symbol of the Knights of Achyron: a downward-facing sword set into a sunburst. "This will hurt, Brother," Kallinvar said to the man. "But pain is the path to strength."

Kallinvar held the Sigil out in front of him, just above the man's chest. He rested his other hand on his shoulder. "Are you sure?"

The man nodded, his eyes half-glazed over. He was close to the void. *So it will be. All the Sigil Bearers have been found. The Knights have been restored – and before the Blood Moon.*

Kallinvar pressed the Sigil into the man's leather cuirass,

over his sternum. It shimmered, as if reflecting the light from a thousand stars. The acrid smell of burning leather drifted up to Kallinvar's nose as the Sigil melted through the man's armour.

It was followed by screams.

CHAPTER I

Ölm Forest

The Glade - Spring, Year 3080 After Doom

Calen's fingers slipped snugly into the worn grooves on the wooden practice sword's handle. His shirt stuck to his chest and sweat matted his dark brown hair to his forehead as he flowed from one form to the next. He squinted as the orange glow from the rising sun sprayed over the crest of Wolfpine Ridge.

His father had given him the day off from the forge so he could go hunting in Ölm Forest. But he hadn't been able to take advantage of the extra time in bed. With The Proving a little under two weeks away, Calen couldn't remember his last good night's sleep. Instead, his brain preferred to pick tirelessly through everything that could go wrong, rather than allowing him to dream. Practicing sword forms settled his mind. He focused on his breathing, filling his lungs with the brisk morning air, while the trill of birdsong floated along the breeze.

The familiar sound of heavy paws bounding towards him pulled Calen out of his concentration. A weight crashed into his chest, knocking the wind from his body and sending him soaring back onto the damp, dew-coated grass.

"Faenir, get off me, for the love of the gods!" Calen yelled as Faenir's coarse tongue bombarded his face. He could swear the wolfpine was smiling. "Every damn morning…" Calen playfully shoved Faenir aside and tussled the ash-grey fur on the crown of his head. At four summers old, Faenir still behaved like a two-month-old pup. Although, standing on all fours, the crest of his spine reached as high as Calen's chest, and he was nearly seven feet long from tail to snout.

Faenir's nose twitched as the aroma of fresh-baked bread wafted enticingly through the kitchen window and out into the garden. "Yeah, yeah, come on. I'm late, and all you ever think about is food." Calen snatched his bow and quiver from where they rested against the side of the house and slung them over his shoulder. He stepped up onto the porch and made his way into the house.

The kitchen was scrupulously clean, as it always was. There was not a speck of dirt or food to be found on the oak floorboards, and the long, L-shaped countertop on the far side of the room was wiped to a sheen. Calen's mother, Freis, stood over the worn but sturdy kitchen table in the middle of the room, grinding herbs in a clay bowl. Her sleeves were rolled up past her elbows, and her golden-grey hair was tied back with a piece of tired old string. The sweet, honey-like scent of Cretia's Breath mixed with

Bluebottle drops tinged the air. *The base for any good healing salve*, Calen remembered his mother saying.

Calen pointed to the greenish-grey paste in the bowl. "Is someone sick?"

"Mara Styr's young one has a bit of a fever. I told her I would go to see her at midday," Freis answered. "Should you not be gone?"

Calen spotted the warm, crisp loaf of bread by the windowsill. "Aye, I'm leaving now."

"Could you pick some more Cretia's Breath and Mullder for me while you're in the forest? I've used up the last of what I have." Freis didn't look up from the clay bowl as she spoke.

"Sure." Calen shuffled over to the windowsill, careful not to step on the creaky floorboard that had been the cause of more than one red mark on his backside. He snapped off the end of the loaf without making a sound and wrapped it in cloth, then shoved it into the leather sack he had left in the kitchen earlier.

"When should we expect you back?"

"Be back around sunset!" Calen shouted as he flitted out the back door, Faenir howling after him.

The cool morning breeze rolled over Calen's face as the sun continued to rise over Wolfpine Ridge. Amidst the usual aromas of the grazing animals and the metallic twinge from the forge that permeated the village, a slight yet unmistakable scent of lavender always seemed to float in the air around Calen's home. Lavender was essential for a variety of herbal remedies, Freis always said, but Calen was sure that she just liked the smell.

He heard the hustle and bustle of the village as the traders from Milltown set up in the market square; the giddy anticipation for the Moon Market was evident. The constant squeaking of axles and clip-clop of horse hooves provided a soft background noise to the buzzing conversations as traders pitched their antiquated tents. Even at that early hour, Calen saw a bard – dressed in all manner of audacious reds and yellows – regaling a group of captivated children.

"And then," the bard said, puffing his chest out and rolling back his shoulders, "the mighty Fane Mortem smote his enemy across the ramparts."

Calen rolled his eyes as he passed, not caring to listen to anymore. The villagers of The Glade had no love for Fane or his Lorian Empire. They were many months' travel from the capital in Al'Nasla, and Fane's taxes robbed them of what little coin and food they had. Most of his father's shipments went north, and the empire paid half of what the weapons and armour were worth, if they paid at all. That didn't stop the travelling bards from spinning their stories. It didn't matter though; the children would learn the truth of it soon enough.

Calen weaved through the market square, dipping and twisting between the growing throng of people. A young, spindly trader sauntered through the crowd ahead of him, carrying a set of tent poles with all the grace of a three-legged donkey. He would have separated Calen's head from his shoulders had he not been watching the young man cautiously for the past twenty feet.

Ducking nimbly under the swinging poles, Calen made

for the edge of the square. With a thud, he felt as though he had walked into a stone wall.

"Young Master Bryer." Erdhardt Hammersmith was a behemoth of a man, with a chest like two oak barrels and tree trunks for legs. His long grey and white hair was tied up into a ponytail. His bronzed, lightly-leathered face betrayed his years. He was the village elder and head of the village council. Calen had been on the wrong end of his usually long temper on more than one occasion, with no small thanks to his friend Dann. "Your father tells me you are off on a hunt today."

"Yes, sir. I'm on my way to meet Dann and Rist now by the edge of forest. We'll be back before the Moon Market kicks off." Calen wore as innocent a grin as he could muster while he attempted to shuffle his way around Erdhardt's wide base. A hand rested on Calen's shoulder, firm but gentle.

"I hope that you are leaving Faenir at home this time?" Erdhardt raised one eyebrow in a quizzical gaze. "The last time you boys took him hunting, he came back in a frenzy, and Master Pimm's chicken coop hasn't been the same since."

A loud crash, followed by angry shouting, sounded behind Erdhardt's shoulder. Two traders had collided, and there were apples strewn all over the ground. Erdhardt glanced over at the raucous scene. "I must see that these *children* don't leave each other black and blue. Stay out of trouble, Master Bryer."

Erdhardt strode off towards the two squabbling traders, his booming voice resounding through the square. Calen didn't wait for him to change his mind. He darted off, dipping between two pitched tents and bounding over the low wall that marked the edge of the market square. Relief washed over him as his feet hit the ground on the other side of the wall.

Calen couldn't help but laugh at the image of Faenir squeezing through the tiny door of the chicken coop. *Those chickens didn't even lay many eggs.*

As he slogged through the long grass, the chirping of the blackbirds droning in his head, he made out two figures perched on a fallen tree at the edge of the forest.

"About time you showed up. We've been here for days!" called Dann, dropping down off the trunk of the tree. The hood of his dark green robe fell down over his shoulders, exposing his short, messy blond hair.

Dann Pimm was only a few inches shorter than Calen, with a lean frame that belied a surprising strength. "How are you?" Dann asked warmly, embracing Calen. "I see we don't have Faenir with us today. I think Father will be glad of that after the last time."

"Yes, but we might miss his keen nose when we get lost in this forest tracking *your* deer," Rist called, striding over towards the two young men. "Nice of you to join us, Calen. Dann hasn't shut up all morning." Rist pulled Calen into his chest and clapped him on the back.

"Don't pull him too tight, Calen. Our Rist seems to get skinnier by the day."

"Oh, piss off, Dann. At least I can read," Rist sniped. He shoved Dann away, then reached behind his neck to tie up his shoulder-length brown hair.

"Hey, I can read. I'm just not as much of a bookworm as you are," Dann laughed, playfully shouldering Rist. The corner of Rist's mouth gave a disapproving turn.

Calen strode past the pair, who were still exchanging insults, and started off towards the edge of the forest. "Come on, you two. Keep up, will you?"

Dann trotted up beside Calen. Along with his yew bow, two short planks of wood with curved ends, reinforced with steel bands, were hung over his shoulder. "Did you really need to bring your bow, Calen?"

Calen's glare did nothing to the mischievous grin that painted Dann's face. Dann never missed an opportunity to turn someone's handle and wind them up.

"I rarely like to agree with Dann, but is there really much point?" Rist asked as he caught up. His long, measured strides made up the distance with little effort. "I mean, I've literally seen you miss a barn door. That cat died, Calen."

Both Dann and Rist broke out in fits of laughter. Calen tried his utmost to ignore them, focusing instead on the forest ahead. There wasn't much Calen could say; as irritating as it was, they were both right. He wasn't much use with a bow, and it had turned into a bit of a running joke. He was far happier with a sword in his hand, but he couldn't hunt deer with a sword.

Ölm Forest was as vast and dense as any in Epheria. Calen felt the world change around them as they entered the outer rim of the ancient woodland. The raw, woody smell of time consumed the forest; centuries of fallen leaves and snapped branches incensing the dense air. Spongy star cap mushrooms littered the damp forest floor; the clusters of the vibrant yellow and blue fungi were striking against the lush green and venerable umber brown of the trees. Calen felt the firm spring of the ground give way to the soft, pliable forest floor, carpeted with leaves in every colour, moist from yesterday's rain. *Good. Tracking should be much easier after the rainfall.*

"Dann, you're sure we'll be out of here in time for the celebrations later? I've been waiting to hear Therin's stories for months now." Calen heard scurrying squirrels leaping overhead, then that familiar crack as their small, nimble bodies landed on the arthritic boughs of the towering trees.

"Without a doubt. I was tracking a herd of deer earlier this week. I think if we carry on in this direction for an hour, then we should pick their trail back up again. They won't have strayed too far from the river."

As they ventured deeper into the twisting, tangled heart of the forest, it came to life. A constant birdsong resonated through the woods. Hares and rabbits scuttled through the thick tendril-like roots that laced the ground. Every once in a while, they heard the deep rumbles of animals a lot bigger than the ones that scampered around at their feet. But it was the constant buzzing and droning of insects that bothered Calen. A bear or wolf, he could kill. Or at least, he could try. But he couldn't use a sword to stop the incessant noise of those bugs.

"There've been strange sightings in here recently," Rist said matter-of-factly. "I overheard a few trappers the other day arguing about some creature that ran them out of their camp."

"Sure, whatever it is, throw it into the mix with the bears, wolfpines and kats, and The Proving is going to be all kinds of fun," Dann said, his voice thick with sarcasm.

About an hour passed as they worked their way through the dense, lush forest. Ahead of them, the trees fell away into a wide-open glade. It sloped down on either side towards a languid stream that flowed through its centre.

Calen knelt by the river, breathing in the fresh air, unfiltered by the dampness within the thick of the forest. The burbling of the river relaxed him. There was something about the way that it melted into the back of his mind without him noticing. But as he listened, a noise drifted into his ears. Something in the distance – a low rumbling, snapping, and cracking of twigs and fallen branches, rising to a crescendo. Dann and Rist seemed not to hear anything. They knelt by the river a few paces up, probably arguing as per usual. "Dann, how far into the forest did you say the herd of deer should be?"

"Ah, maybe an hour or so more." Dann took a swig from his waterskin. "There's a larger stream farther in, and they usually don't come this far out. It's too close to the village."

Calen stood up slowly. The rumbling noise was getting louder. The birds around them chirped frantically as they jettisoned from the trees in flock. Calen caught Dann's eye. He could hear it now too. Dann bounded over towards Calen, drawing his bow and nocking an arrow.

"How many of them were there?" Calen whispered, unsure why he felt the need to lower his voice.

Dann didn't get the chance to answer. The bushes on

the opposite side of the glade shook; the cracking of branches and stomping of hooves surrounded them. A tremendous stag, about eight feet in height, burst through the copse of trees on the other side of the glade, only stopping long enough to acknowledge the existence of the three hunters. Its powerful, sinuous horns caught Calen's eye. As the stag came crashing towards them, more erupted from the trees. Four, nine, twelve; he stopped counting.

A piercing whistle zoomed past Calen's ear. Dann's arrow plunged into the right eye of the lead stag, killing it instantly. Its gargantuan body cascaded down the slope of the glade, slamming into a nearby fallen tree before being swallowed by the stampede. Both Calen and Rist loosed their own arrows into the onrushing herd. If they hit anything, it was impossible to tell, as the arrows disappeared into the blur of deer. The herd was nearly upon them.

Dann nocked another arrow.

"Get down!" Calen screamed.

Rist immediately threw himself behind the large boulder to which Calen had pointed, but Dann was lost in focus. His eyes narrowed as he found his target. He let his arrow fly just as Calen collided into him, sending their two bodies crashing to the ground behind the boulder.

In a daze, Dann whipped his head around to glare at Calen for ruining his shot, but seemed to catch sight of his rucksack being trampled into nothingness where he had just been standing. He glanced at Calen and nodded.

After a few minutes, when they were sure that the stampede had passed, they emerged from behind their guardian boulder.

"Well… fuck me. That was close," Dann said.

"You nearly got killed, Dann!" Rist snapped.

"Pfft… *You nearly got killed, Dann,*" came the mocking reply as Dann knelt to look at the body of the large stag he had shot through the eye.

Calen's heart still pounded in his chest as he surveyed the glade with a pensive gaze. It was a mess of upturned earth and broken branches. A shiver ran up his spine at the sight of the mangled body of a fawn that lay trampled on the opposite side of the glade, the snapped shaft of an arrow protruding from its neck. "Something spooked them good…"

Rist rested against the trunk of a tree, then slid to the ground with a sigh. "Maybe a bear?"

"I don't think it was a bear. Come and look at this," Dann called, waving his hand up in the air, a tremble in his voice. When Calen and Rist reached Dann, he was stooped over the corpse of the stag, tracing his hand along a vicious, wide-open gash that ran the length of the animal's ribs.

"Gods…"

"What could have done that?" Calen asked.

"I have no idea," Dann admitted, pursing his lips. "But the cut is far too clean to be a tooth or claw. It's marked down to the bone…"

"What are you saying?"

"I'm not sure," Dann said. His hand probed the edge of the wound. He let out a sigh. "Whatever did it, I don't think we should stick around any longer than we have to."

CHAPTER 2

The Gilded Dragon

By the time they emerged from the thick of the forest, the sun had already begun to set along the dusky horizon, but The Glade was still visible by the plumes of greyish-white smoke that gently rose from chimneys, and the warm glow of tallow candles that illuminated the cloudy glass windows of the houses.

Calen stopped to breathe in the fresh air and gaze over the familiar sight of the village in the distance. He tilted his head back and rolled his shoulders, cracking his neck to relieve some of the ache that had set in. The return journey had taken them a lot longer; they had taken turns hauling the stag, which was no simple task considering its size.

Dann had removed its entrails to reduce the weight and strapped it to his makeshift sled. It was quite a handy contraption. The two planks of reinforced wood were locked together with two bridging slats and secured with handmade bolts. The deer was then strapped to the planks with roughly cut rope, which was strung through small metal loops on the upper edge of the planks. It made it a lot easier to haul the deer and caused less damage to the fur. It was quite a bit of effort, but it was worth it to get the massive animal back in one piece. The size of the stag meant there would be meat for all their families for quite a while. Anything they didn't eat, they could sell.

The Moon Market's festivities were well under way by the time the boys approached the outskirts of the village. The buzz of excitement echoed through the valley; roars of laughter and awe as storytellers from Gilsa and Camylin wove their fanciful tales could be heard amidst the constant hum of the cheerful, melodic music being played around campfires. The Moon Market was the biggest festival in the villages. It occurred every cycle, when the moon was at its fullest. Traders, entertainers, and bards from all across the western lands gathered in the market square of The Glade to flog their wares, commune with old friends, and share in the festivities.

The town guards nodded as the boys trudged along, each on the brink of collapse from exhaustion. Calen heaved the body of the stag behind him on the sled.

"Just in time, boys," Ferrin Kolm, one of the guardsmen, remarked, drawing his gaze towards Calen. Ferrin had been one of Haem's best friends. His face was warm and friendly, spotted with freckles. The skin on his lips was cracked from the frosty night wind. "Gods, that's a nasty one," he said as he caught sight of the gash that ripped along the side of the stag. "You boys all right?"

Calen nodded. "Aye."

Ferrin's mouth twisted as he and the other guard, Dalmen, exchanged a sideways glance.

"Will we see you both in The Dragon later to hear Therin?" Calen asked, changing the subject. He liked Ferrin, but they were already late and he had no intentions of getting caught up in any conversations that might make them even more so.

Ferrin gave a weak smile. "Aye, we shall see you there, young Bryer. We change over shortly."

The boys said their goodbyes and carried on. They kept to the edges of the village to avoid trudging through the crowds. Even then, they drew the odd glance from a drunken traveller or two who had gotten lost in the moonlight.

When they got to Dann's house, there was not so much as a flicker of candlelight to signal that anyone was home. "Father must already be down at The Dragon," Dann mused. "We can leave the stag hanging out back. It's cold enough tonight that it will keep till morning."

The others nodded. Calen would have agreed to whatever Dann had suggested. He was cold and tired, and they should have been at the inn already.

It was difficult for the boys not to get caught up in the excitement as they made their way towards The Gilded Dragon, weaving through the crowd with ardour. The streets of the village were packed to the brim. Drunken revellers traipsed about, arm in arm, not heading anywhere in particular. Groups of young men bellowed songs of summer as starlight illuminated the streets.

As Calen, Dann, and Rist made their way into the middle of the village, the large, stout structure of The Gilded Dragon came into sight. Built from long, thick beams of spruce, the inn was one of the largest buildings in the village. It was also one of but a few buildings in town to possess a second storey; from which a thatched canopy extended outward. Under the canopy, there was a raised deck with a central staircase that formed the entrance to the inn. The top of the staircase was framed on either side by two ornate wooden dragons. Each scale was carved with masterful precision, and their tails coiled tightly around the balusters atop which they sat. They seemed alive, as if ready to tear, limb from limb, anyone who would do the inn harm. Lasch Havel, Rist's father, commissioned them from a passing craftsman many summers ago. He was so thrilled with the finished pieces that he promised the craftsman free accommodation and mead for life. The man has made frequent visits back to The Glade ever since, and Lasch has stayed true to his word.

As they ascended the staircase, Calen heard the tumultuous hubbub of the drunken crowd within. The familiar sound was oddly pleasant to his ears.

The doors to the inn swung open abruptly. For a moment, Calen smiled, eager to join the celebrations within. Then Kurtis Swett and Fritz Netley came stumbling out onto the deck. *Arseholes.*

The two young men guffawed, shoving each other back and forth. "Anya is only waiting for you to take her, Kurtis. I don't know why you're waiting. I would have her in a heartbeat!" Fritz teased, stumbling a little and taking a deep slug of mead from his tankard.

"You will keep your filthy hands—" Kurtis stopped mid-sentence as he saw Calen, Rist, and Dann standing in front of him. A scowl spread across his face. "What do we have here? Has Mother allowed the children to come and have a drink?"

"Get out of the way, Kurtis," Dann snarled, attempting to push past the two young men.

As he did, Fritz rushed towards him and shoved him in the chest with two hands. "Whoa, now. Don't you speak to us like that, you little piece of shit." The smell of mead wafted from his breath. Fritz was bad enough sober. Alcohol only made him worse.

Fritz manoeuvred himself to shove Dann a second time. Calen leapt forward, balled his hand into a fist, and caught Fritz across the cheek with his knuckles. Calen couldn't keep the look of shock from his face as Fritz touched his forefingers to his tender cheek. "You are going to regret that!" Fritz shouted, his eyes narrowing into a glare.

"Regret what, might I ask?" queried the calm, smooth voice of Lasch Havel, who had appeared as if from nowhere, standing between the young men and the door to the inn. Lasch was not a tall or imposing man, but he was highly respected in the village. His hair was tightly cropped and grey. A thick scar ran from his left eye into the obscurity of his fierce blackish-grey beard. He cut a particularly intimidating figure, with the sleeves of his mead-stained shirt rolled up past his elbows and his bar cloth draped over his shoulder. Despite his usually charming demeanour, he was well known as a man one did not cross.

"Ehm… nothing, Master Havel. We were just turning in for the night. Fritz here is feeling a bit ill," Kurtis said, looking down at his feet. Fritz scowled at him out of the corner of his eye. The two young men shuffled off down the stairs as quickly as their feet could take them, not daring to look back over their shoulders as they disappeared into the crowded streets.

"Aye, safe home, you two," Lasch called down after them, more than a hint of sarcasm in his voice. He cast his eyes over the three in front of him. "Come on in, you three. Therin is about to begin." He turned to Rist, raising a cautionary eyebrow. "Rist, remember, your mother needs you up early tomorrow to help with the house."

"Yes, Father."

Lasch nodded, gesturing Rist into the inn. A smirk spread across his face as he saw Calen stroking the knuckles of his right hand. He placed his hand on Calen's shoulder and raised an eyebrow.

"He deserved it," Calen said sheepishly, shuffling his feet on the floor.

"Aye, no doubt he did." Lasch let out a deep chuckle as he shoved Calen through the doors of the inn.

The interior of The Gilded Dragon was equally impressive as its exterior, especially around the time of the Moon Market. Calen was immediately greeted by throngs of people, buzzing about and attempting to squeeze onto one of the many tables strewn about the main floor. Many tried to balance tankards of mead in each hand, protecting them from the flailing body parts of the other patrons. The warm and enticing aroma of Lasch's fresh-baked bread mingled with the sweet, honeyed scent of the famous Gilded Dragon mead. It made his stomach rumble.

The room was bathed in a soft yellow glow, which emanated from the beeswax candles that were dotted all around. The bar stood along the western wall; a long, solid oak countertop that stretched from one side of the building to the other. Behind it were massive wooden casks, each several feet taller than Calen and filled to the brim with Lasch's homemade mead. They were bound with wrought iron hoops, and a tap was inserted along the bottom of each.

A raised wooden stage sat against the eastern wall of the room, roughly six feet wide and pushing about four feet out from the wall. This was where the bards, storytellers, and performers stood as they entertained the crowd.

Just as Calen reached the edge of the crowd surrounding the bar, Rist pushed through the swell of bodies, extending his arm outward to hand Calen a large tankard of mead. "Drink it slow. I nearly lost an arm in that madness," Rist said, throwing his free hand over Calen's shoulder.

"It's your family's inn," Dann said as he emerged from the crowd behind Rist. He choked down a large mouthful of mead. "Why do you even queue in the first place?"

Rist rolled his eyes with a sigh. Dann shrugged towards Calen in response.

"I think I saw your dad over this way, Calen." Rist set off, pushing his way through the crowd.

"A little sensitive sometimes, isn't he?" Dann said. He clinked his tankard off Calen's, and they both took a deep gulp of mead before following Rist into the crowd.

Calen soon spotted the broad outline of his father. Vars Bryer was a lean but powerful man. His thick, broad shoulders were earned from years of working with the hammer and anvil. His short brown hair was flecked with specks of grey, and a muscular jaw carefully outlined his face, slightly leathered from the flames of the forge.

As if sensing Calen approaching, Vars turned his head and stood up in one fluid motion, pulling his son firmly into a warm embrace. "It's good to see you, Calen." Vars's tough, no-nonsense exterior often melted away when it came to Calen and his sister, Ella. Even more so since they lost Haem. His eyes scanned Calen's body up and down, searching for any cuts or bruises. "How went the hunt?"

"Actually, something—" Before Calen could finish his sentence, the tumult that had filled the room only seconds before dissipated into a wave of hushed whispers.

A tall, thin figure stepped up onto the stage. His face was obscured by the hood of his long heavy cloak, which looked as if it had seen all four corners of the world. Coloured a mixture of muted browns and greens, it was scuffed all over and covered in dirt and clay. Despite this, it seemed tough and truly unscathed by time, giving off an air of immortality.

As the whispers droned off into an unerring silence, the man pulled his hood down onto his shoulders. His fine silver hair was tied back over his ears and up into a ponytail, which emphasised his sharp youthful facial features. He had a narrow jaw, high cheekbones, and supple milk-bottle skin. His ears, soft and thin, tapered off into a point at the end. It was almost impossible to determine how many summers he had seen.

Elves were rarely seen west of Wolfpine Ridge, or in

the world of men at all for that matter. Therin was the exception, and his stories were legend. People travelled for some distance just to hear the whispers from his silver tongue. Rumours floated around The Glade that he was older than the empire itself and had witnessed those legendary tales unfold with his own eyes. He was the villages' worst kept secret.

"It has been some time since I have visited these lands." The elf's calm and subdued voice seemed to fill every crack and crevice of the room. "Much has changed," he muttered, almost to himself as his eyes searched the crowd. "It is my great pleasure to have returned!" he roared as he threw his arms wide open.

A rapturous applause erupted throughout the room.

"Settle down, settle down," Therin said, gently pushing his hands in a downward motion, a wry smile forming at the corner of his mouth. "Tonight, my friends, is special. Tonight, I tell you the story of how the ancient city of Ilnaen was obliterated from existence. Bands of fire and destruction spread from the centre of Epheria to the foothills of Mar Dorul and the Lodhar Mountains, forming what is known to us elves as the Svidar'Cia – The Burnt Lands." Therin surveyed the room, his gaze greeted only by awe and wonderment. "*Tonight*, I shall tell you the story of the fall of The Order and the birth of the Lorian Empire – the *true* story."

Growing up, it was a special thing for Calen to hear Therin's stories of a time when all the races roamed the lands freely. The beautiful ornate elven cities, the mighty giants, and the heroes of old. But most of all, he adored hearing of The Order and the noble Draleid who protected Epheria, fighting fearlessly astride massive dragons – some as big as houses. The stories told by some of the other bards were decidedly different.

"Fane Mortem…" Therin allowed the name to sink in. "The Emperor of Loria was once but a young mage, rapidly rising through the ranks of The Order. Born to a noble family inside the city walls of Al'Nasla, it was not long before his Spark was noticed. By the age of six, he was sent to the city of Ilnaen to train with the legendary mages of The Order. There was no greater honour among magic wielders in the kingdom of Loria. To be chosen to practice your craft alongside the ancient mages of the elves and giant clans was a rare thing indeed, and it was no mistake they chose Fane, for his Spark was both raw and powerful."

Therin paused, taking a long, deep drink of mead from his tankard.

"However," he said, as he dragged his sleeve across his mouth, wiping the leftover droplets from his lips, "he did not take kindly to the company of others. He preferred solitary study. Fane confined himself to the darkest corners of the illustrious Ilnaen Library, where he researched the histories of all magic, from the archaic magics of the Blodvar and the mythical human druids to the twisted ways of the Urak shamans. By the time he was only twenty summers old, Fane was considered one of the most powerful human mages in The Order – and the most ruthless."

Therin cast his gaze over the crowd. His voice adopted a deeper tone.

"Fane slowly became enamoured with power, as most

in his position do. He was driven by his need to test his abilities and to prove his strength. He challenged other mages to duels, binding them by honour to accept. But Fane did not simply want to beat them; he wanted to break them."

Therin crouched down at the edge of the stage. He went silent for a few moments, his eyes closed, locked in concentration.

"Fane was not content with just reading of the archaic magics of the past. He wanted to feel them, to wield them. He delved into the minds of his opponents, warping and twisting them to his will, pushing at the boundaries of convention. He wanted to prove that he was without equal. Although most in The Order did not approve of his methods, there were those who stood in awe of him. In every task he was set, Fane returned successful. In every battle, he was victorious. And with every victory, his following grew."

Opening his eyes and rising to his full height, Therin glared into the onlooking crowd. His all-knowing eyes glowed an incandescent orange as the candlelight shimmered across his face. His sequin-silver hair sent light dancing across the room, illuminating the faces of the awe-struck villagers who packed the inn like grains of rice in a sack.

"However," Therin's voice boomed, "there was one who openly challenged him at every turn, unyielding: the Archon of the Draleid, Alvira Serris." It was as if a gust of wind had somehow entered the room at the mention of her name. The candles flickered, and every hair on Calen's body stood up. He glanced at Dann and Rist to his right, then at his father to his left, all of whom were entranced, their eyes fixed on the elf.

Therin placed his tankard on the stool to his right.

"She was strong!" He gracefully swept across the stage, curling his arm and tensing his bicep towards the crowd. "And quick-witted." He tapped his index finger sharply against his right temple. "She could wield a blade like a gust of wind sweeping leaves off the forest floor, such was her skill and grace." Therin swung his arms from left to right, as if slicing a sword through the torso of an unseen enemy. A lash of air seemed to follow the arc of his arms. Calen's hair was blown off his face, and with it, he thought he heard the shrieking wail of a blade as it cut through the air.

What is in this mead? Calen stared into the mellow liquid, his mind seemingly playing tricks on him.

Therin took a deep, longing breath. Calen saw a sense of pride on his face as he described Alvira. It was as if she were his closest friend or a long-lost lover. "But even she, in all her wisdom, could not imagine the depths of Fane's ambition."

Suddenly, the light in the room seemed to dim, as if swallowed by the shadows. The only thing that Calen could see clearly was Therin, now perched on the stool that had previously held his tankard. "Through his unwavering dedication to the pursuit of knowledge and his raw magical Spark, Fane's magical abilities far surpassed his peers', but it was not enough. Fane was enamoured with the Doom at Haedr. The sheer power required to cause such an atrocity was almost romantic in his unique mind. This kind of power was everything his wildest dreams had imagined, but he did not know—" Therin's words dropped to a captivating whisper. "He did not know the poison that is blood magic."

Gasps of shock and muffled whispers followed as people searched the room for the presence of empire soldiers, as if the simple utterance of the words "blood magic" could summon them through walls.

"Hush!" Therin boomed, his voice like unbottled thunder. An absolute silence fell across the room. Nothing could be heard but the beating of hearts and hushed breathing. Therin folded his arms, a look of disdain in his eyes. "In his relentless, unwavering search for power, Fane heard whispers of a shaman that resided in the mountains of Mar Dorul, revered among Uraks for his knowledge and skill with blood magic.

"The journey from Ilnaen to Mar Dorul took only a few weeks, but Mar Dorul is a vast landscape, devoid of life and leaf. Its ominous peaks, as ridged as a dragon's back, seem to pierce the sky itself. It could have taken years to search, but to Fane's surprise, the shaman was waiting for him in plain sight, where the Naiwell Woods met the snaking legs of the mountains. Nobody truly knows what happened on that mountain, but Fane left Mar Dorul that day a different man than when he entered.

"Upon his return to Ilnaen, he spent two years spreading the seed of corruption within The Order, meticulously selecting those he considered weak of mind. He whispered in their ears, promising them their deepest desires, preying on their darkest fears. His serpentine words of power and glory twisted their minds and bent their will. Men, elves, and even giants succumbed to his malevolent manipulations." Therin's voice dropped to a melancholy requiem. "Most fatally, however, he wormed his way into the minds of many Draleid. He told of how The Order was corrupt and how it needed to be destroyed from the ground up and reformed. He picked at their minds, planting the seeds of betrayal."

Calen thought he saw a fire begin to burn in Therin's almond eyes.

"Among the Draleid that turned to support Fane's cause was one of the most powerful in The Order: an elf by the name of Eltoar Daethana. He was the First Sword of Alvira Serris and bonded to the largest dragon in all of Epheria: Helios." Therin stood from his stool, his mouth set in a hard line and a longing in his eyes.

"It was the year 2682, after Doom, on the eve of the Winter Solstice, when Fane's plans were set in motion. Once he gave the orders, his followers silently murdered the guards on duty at the castle walls. They moved with ruthless efficiency, using knives and magic to quietly send the guards into the void. As planned, when the Blood Moon was at its highest point in the sky, the traitors opened the gates of Ilnaen. Urak war horns were heard for miles. Under cover of night, nearly a hundred thousand had gathered close to Ilnaen. Never before had a single force of Uraks so large been assembled."

The room was consumed by silence. Not a whisper was heard while Therin wove his engrossing tale.

"The Order never stood a chance. Betrayed from within and surrounded on all sides, they were butchered as they slept. The Draleid and their dragons were slain in the ensuing chaos. Alvira was betrayed and murdered by Eltoar, one of her closest friends, who was twisted by the deceitful machinations of Fane's lies." Therin's voice caught in his throat as pain cut its way through his face.

"Fane stood atop what is now known as the Dead Tower, surveying the madness he created. He watched the city smoulder from a safe distance. And from his perch, Fane sent a message to all those still loyal to The Order. With the twisted, dark magic behind him, he unleashed a magical detonation of fire and wind that eclipsed even the Doom at Haedr. The flames engulfed Ilnaen in seconds, spreading to the foothills of the Lodhar Mountains in the west, and Mar Dorul in the east. They raged for days, fuelled by the power of blood magic. Whatever deal Fane had made with the Urak shamans did not protect them; their usefulness had ended. When the flames finally died out, all that was left was stone and ash."

The absence of sound in the room filled Calen's ears.

"Fane returned to Al'Nasla and assumed power over the Lorian Kingdom. King Eric was burned alive by Helios as Fane took his place on the throne. Eric was a conspirator in The Order's tyranny, or so proclaimed Fane. Over the ensuing months, Fane and his followers rooted out and eliminated those who remained loyal to The Order. The temple at Dracaldryr was laid waste, as was the giant city of Ölmur. Nearly all the dragon eggs perished in the carnage, and those that survived were hoarded away in the vaults of Al'Nasla. Not one has hatched to this day.

"The Order had fallen; Ilnaen, Dracaldryr, and Ölmur

were nothing but rubble. Fane laid waste to elven and giant cities across the length and breadth of Epheria. Though, he dared not attack the elves in Eselthyr or Caelduin. He knew the forest of Lynalion was laced with wards and traps, laid over a millennium, but he also knew that he need not fear them. Their fabled protectors – the Draleid – were dead, their dragons slain, and their power broken. The elves would not dare emerge from Lynalion, not in force. They could not face the might of the newly formed Lorian Empire. The giants were all but eradicated, and the dwarves burrowed themselves in their mountain kingdoms. He had won."

The room erupted in a thunderous cacophony of cheers and shouts – more for the weaving of the engrossing tale than its conclusion. The dark oak floorboards creaked and groaned as the crowd fervently stomped their feet and clapped their hands. Amidst the celebration, Calen thought he glimpsed an emptiness in Therin's face, an unequivocal sadness. A moment later, it was gone. He bowed, grasped his mead with one hand, and made his way off the stage, disappearing into the mass of people.

"Well, brother, I think that was his best yet!"

Calen nearly jumped from his seat as a pair of hands clapped down on his shoulders. "Ella, get your hands off me!" he groaned, swatting her away as if trying to bat a fly.

"Get over here," chuckled Vars. Rising from his seat, he pulled his daughter into a tight embrace.

Both Dann and Rist had made more than a few comments about Ella over the years. Most of it was teasing. They enjoyed winding him up and watching him lose his temper. But at twenty summers, Calen was acutely aware that there were more than a few young men in the villages vying for Ella's attention. She had the same blue eyes as Freis, and her hair was the same colour their mothers' must have been when she was younger, a shimmering golden-blonde.

"Come on, Calen. I owe you a drink from the last Moon Market." Ella tugged at Calen's hand, dragging him towards the crowded bar. "Your hunt went well?" The crowd seemed to part around her as she glided through the mass of people. Calen followed in her wake, and they managed to arrive at the time-ravaged wooden countertop with surprising ease.

"Yeah, but we found…" Calen's voice trailed off as he caught a young man staring Ella up and down with a wanton look in his eyes. Calen did not recognise him, but he had the sallow skin and brass nose rings of Salme. Calen glared at him before he turned back to Ella, who had just collected two tankards of mead from Lasch with a grateful smile on her face.

Ella laughed as she noticed Calen's change in demeanour. She gently placed her hand on his cheek. "A little protective, brother? Don't you worry. I am well able to take care of myself," she assured him. "I think you might have someone more interesting to talk to anyway." Ella nodded over Calen's shoulder. She pushed both tankards of mead into his open hands, taking advantage of his surprise to slip away into the crowd.

Anya Gritten's ember-red hair tumbled down over her slight shoulders, highlighting the gleam in her emerald eyes.

Just like Calen, Anya had seen nearly eighteen summers. She had a slight, svelte build. Her high cheekbones, dotted with numerous freckles, framed a face that had often left Calen searching for words. He had always had a soft spot for Anya. Maybe a little more than a soft spot.

She waved at him as she approached.

"That was amazing, wasn't it?" Anya always smelled of sweet flowers; her mother, Verna, was a soap maker as well as a village council member. This night, Anya smelled of cherry blossoms.

Calen wanted to say something witty, but his mind went blank. All he could manage was a muffled "Mm-hmm" as he offered Anya the second tankard that Ella had given him. He made a mental note to thank her later.

"Aw, thanks, Calen," Anya said, scrunching her shoulders together. "I don't know what it is about him, but when he tells his stories, they always feel so *real*. I do hope he comes back soon. My Pa said that he saw Dann, Rist, and you dragging a gigantic stag through the gates earlier. That's great!"

Calen struggled to suppress a slight swell of pride in his chest. "Well, there was a bit of luck, but—"

Dann came stumbling in on top of them. He wrapped an arm around each of their shoulders, and a gleefully drunk smile spread across his face.

"Are you talking about the stag? Not like Calen had anything to do with that. He couldn't hit a barn door if—" Dann let out a groan as Calen jammed an elbow into his ribcage. "What? I was just telling Anya—" Another swift elbow to the ribs ensured Dann never finished his sentence.

Anya started laughing. Calen thought he noticed a smile sent in his direction, although that was interrupted by Dann losing strength in his legs and nearly taking Calen with him. Calen grabbed tightly onto Dann's hip, righting him as best he could.

"I think it's probably best if I get this idiot home," Calen said, apologising with his eyes.

"Hey—" Dann let out a loud hiccup. "Don't you call me an idiot."

Calen said his goodbyes to Anya, then found Vars and Rist to let them know that he was bringing Dann home. He made his way out of the inn with Dann wrapped around his shoulder, using him as a walking stick. "You have terrible timing, you know that?"

Dann didn't even look at Calen. Not that it would have mattered if he did; his eyes were barely open. With a hiccup, he drew his mouth up into a dopey grin.

Calen couldn't help but laugh. "Just try not to fall over, yeah?"

The streets of The Glade ·were dimly lit by the gentle glow of candle lights emanating from the windows of the surrounding homes. Celebrations from the Moon Market had died down a bit, although the hum of nearby music and drinking could be heard from within The Gilded Dragon and from the campfires of the travelling merchants who had set up at the edge of the village.

As he glanced upward, Calen caught sight of the full moon resting in the darkness. Its pearlescent hue gave the sky an ethereal look.

Something heavy crashed into Calen's side, sending

him and Dann spiralling to the ground. Calen's back ached as he pushed himself to his knees. He tried to shake the dizziness out of his head.

"So, you two little shits think you're funny, do you?" Calen recognised Fritz's voice in the darkness. He tried to stand up, but a boot crashed into his chest, knocking the wind from his lungs. A pair of hands grabbed him on either shoulder. A hard punch to his jaw sent stars flitting across his eyes. A second punch drew blood; he felt it trickling down his cheek. "Thought you would take me off guard with that punch, did you, Bryer?"

A third hit landed on his cheekbone. The strength in Calen's legs gave way as he fell to his knees. He heard blows being thrown beside him. No doubt, they were laying their boots into Dann's chest while he lay there, drunk.

"I think you boys need to learn your place," said a deeper voice. *Kurtis.*

Blow after blow landed into Calen's chest. A pair of hands held him upright. He was beginning to lose consciousness when he heard a low grumble. The grumble rose into a steady growl, joined by the slow padding of feet as it got louder. A gust of air blew by Calen's face, and the crashing sound of wooden barrels being smashed to pieces filled his ears. A loud snarl was followed by shouts.

"It's the fucking wolf! Get him off me!"

Calen felt Faenir's snout nuzzle against his temple, followed by a low whine. Then darkness.

CHAPTER 3

Ella

Ella weaved through the crowd in The Gilded Dragon. She pushed open the door of the inn and pressed onward into the brisk night air. As the door closed behind her, the cheers of merriment dimmed and turned to echoes. There was a still serenity in the night, occasionally broken by drunken chants of merchants, but only for seconds at a time.

Ella adored the Moon Market. The storytellers, jugglers, and merchants gave the village folk a feeling of excitement and adventure, a taste of what lay beyond their small circle. There was so much to see, so many places to go. She knew she could not stay in The Glade forever, and Rhett knew that too. She had never known anyone like him. Ever since Haem's death, he had always been there for her. He was her rock.

She said she would meet him by the outer edge of the town, by the large green tent with the golden trim and a snow-white cap. It skirted the low wall of the market square, where the merchants had pitched.

Ella heard the crunch of freeze-dried leaves beneath her feet as she made her way through the streets. She cursed herself for not bringing her long cloak as she rubbed her hands up and down her arms. As she turned the corner around Iwan Swett's butcher shop, the white cap of the tent came into sight, followed by its murky green canopy.

"I was worried you had decided to stay warm by the fire." Rhett smiled as he strode over to Ella, not waiting for her to come to him. He was tall compared to most in The Glade, with a strong chest, thick arms, and jet-black hair that was uncommon around the villages. Rhett Fjorn's parents had come from Berona when they were only teenagers, to build a new life for themselves.

He traced his fingers along her cheek. The callouses at their tips felt rough against her skin, but not in an unpleasant way. There was something uniquely comforting about the feeling.

She gazed up at him, taking a moment to admire how handsome he was, then placed a gentle kiss on his lips. "There are other ways to keep warm." Ella gave him a wry smile before wrapping her arms around him.

"Really?" he said with a laugh. He pursed his lips and shrugged. "I can't think of any."

"Oh go away, you," Ella said, giving him a half-hearted shove.

Rhett laughed at her again. Small creases formed at the corner of his eyes as his smile grew wider. He always did that – smiled with his eyes. He bit the corner of his lip as he held her gaze, only for a moment, before taking her hand and leading her back towards the village streets. "Come on. A group of merchants at the southern edge of the village told me they will be playing music long into the night."

"Okay, okay." Ella tried to add a disapproving tone into her voice, but it was not an easy task.

"I'll miss this," Rhett said, gazing around. He laughed as his eyes rested on the comatose body of Marlo Egon, an empty tankard of mead in his left hand. "Every time," he chuckled.

"I know, but we still have plenty of time. We won't leave till after The Proving, and that's not for a few weeks." She nestled her head against his shoulder. "As soon as we are set up in Berona, we will come back to visit, and we can leave notes to make sure they won't worry."

Rhett's lips pulled to the corner of his mouth as he let out a sigh. He kissed the top of Ella's head and pulled her closer to him as they walked. She knew that he wanted to start a life with her in Berona, but he was unsure about leaving this way. They didn't have a choice, though. Her father would never let them just leave. He would never forgive Rhett.

"Rhett, I—"

A deep growl came from down one of the side streets, followed by shouting.

"Get him off me!" came a shrill voice.

Rhett gave Ella a look that she knew meant for her to stay where she was. He took off around the corner without a moment's hesitation.

"Ella!"

She hurried around the corner after him. Two young boys were strewn out on the floor. Rhett knelt beside one of them with his hand slipped under the back of his head. A greyish-white wolfpine sat curled up beside the boys, blood lining its mouth.

Ella's eyes narrowed as she stared at the wolfpine. "Is that Faenir?"

The wolfpine lifted his head at the mention of his name and padded over to Ella. He rubbed his back against her leg with a low whine.

"It's Calen and Dann," Rhett said with a hushed voice.

Ella dropped down beside him, worry coursing through her veins. "Rhett, is he okay? What happened to him?"

"They've been beaten pretty badly. I couldn't see who it was. Faenir must have chased them off." Rhett placed his hands on either side of Ella's cheeks. "Ella, look at me. He is okay. He's unconscious, but he's okay. Ferrin is only around the corner. He told me he was going to The Gilded Dragon after his watch was done. Go, bring him back here so he can help me carry the boys home." She began to protest, but he immediately stood up to go check on Dann.

The wind nipped at Ella's face as she ran. The cold air burned in her chest. *He's going to be okay.*

Ferrin was exactly where Rhett had said he would be, standing outside the inn, mead in hand.

"Ferrin!" Ella dropped her hands to her knees, panting as she dragged air into her lungs. "You need to come – now!"

"Whoa, Ella, calm down. What's wrong?"

"It's Calen and Dann. They're hurt. Rhett told me to come and get you."

Ferrin's expression changed in an instant. He shoved his tankard of mead into the hands of the merchant he was talking to, who took it without hesitation. "Take me to them."

"Okay, we have this from here," Rhett said when Ella and Ferrin bounded into the side street. "You need to go now, ahead of us. I will come and see you tomorrow." Rhett placed a kiss on her forehead and turned back towards Calen.

"I'm not going anywhere. Calen is hurt—"

"Ella, what happens if he wakes up and sees the two of us here? Do you want to explain that? To him – to your father?"

Ella's shoulders dropped. She sighed. "Please get him home safe."

"I will. Don't worry. Now please hurry home. It's getting cold out."

Ella sighed, pinching her lips together. He was right. Calen would probably understand, but her father? No, that would not be a conversation so much as it would be a screaming match.

She reached up onto her tiptoes and planted a soft kiss on Rhett's cheek. She didn't say anything as she turned around the corner, onto the main street. She slipped her hands in her pockets and tucked her chin down against the top of her chest.

The walk home didn't take long, but her heart pounded with every step. She eased the front door of the house open, careful not to elicit the creak that always came when it was opened too slowly. The smell of lavender twisted around the smoky aroma of extinguished candles as she tiptoed through the kitchen, stepping deftly over the creaky floorboard beside the kitchen table. Her mother was a light sleeper.

With a hushed sigh, Ella slipped in between the crisp

sheets of her bed. She didn't toss or turn. She just lay there. She knew there would be no sleep for her until she heard Rhett and Calen at the door.

CHAPTER 4

Like Father, Like Son

Calen felt the tenderness in his bones. It had been a week since he and Dann were attacked by Kurtis and his idiot friends, but the bruises persisted. He told his parents that they had gotten in a fight with some drunken traders and that it was all a misunderstanding. There was more than a hint of suspicion in his mother's eyes. He thought about telling them the truth, but there was no need to cause any more tension in the village, especially with The Proving coming up.

He nocked an arrow. The glaring sun caused him to squint. He took a deep breath as he drew his string back, trying to clear his mind, as his father had taught him.

"Morning, Calen."

With a *whoosh*, the arrow sliced through the air and disappeared into the thicket behind the wooden target. Dann chuckled. Calen sighed as he greeted his father.

"I just hope young Lina Styr isn't still picking berries in those bushes," Vars chimed, a cheeky smile spreading across his face. "It's time for sword practice. I figured you would enjoy a break from the bow."

Vars reached down and unfurled a bundle of cloth on the ground, then tossed Calen his wooden practice sword. It was a hand-and-a-half sword, with blunted edges. Calen twirled the sword around in his right hand, gauging it, getting used to its weight and balance. He knew them like he did the finger grooves that had been worn into its handle. But it was habit.

He barely had a moment to react as the blow came in, just above his shoulders. He turned it away shakily; the collision of swords jarred his arm. Without a chance to take a breath, the first strike was followed by an unrelenting flurry of attacks. It was all he could do just to keep Vars's blade from marking his hide.

He grimaced as one strike hit his ribcage, which was already a little worse for wear. Another connected with his hip, then his shoulder. Calen knew that he couldn't keep on the defensive for long. Pressing forward, he shifted his feet, driving his sword straight towards Vars's abdomen. He felt the wind rush from his lungs as Vars's knee collided with his unprotected chest.

Calen sat on his knees, desperately attempting to re-capture the air that had just been forcibly removed from his lungs. Vars grasped his forearm and dragged him to his feet.

"I've told you a hundred times, don't expose yourself like that, even if you're sure of a killing blow. Haem would have—" Vars cut himself off. A look of regret crossed his face. "Again."

Calen stroked a newly emerging bruise on his hip as Vars tossed him a waterskin. He knew by the burning sensations striped across his body that there would be more bruises to follow.

"Is there something on your mind, Calen? You seem distracted today. I should not have connected with that last one." He spoke matter-of-factly, but there was a tenderness in his voice.

"I'm okay. I guess I'm just a bit nervous about The Proving. It's only a few days away now... I'm not ready." Calen took a deep drink from the waterskin, his eyes never leaving the ground. The silence seemed to go on for an eternity.

"Haem was nervous too, Calen." Vars ran his eyes over his son's face with a note of caution. "The night before The Proving, I found him throwing up in the grass out back. He was a nervous wreck. Worried about failing. Do you know what I told him?"

The air caught in Calen's throat.

"I told him that the sun will set, and it will rise again, and it will do so the next day and the next. The gods are in charge of such things, but it is by our own will that we pick ourselves up when we fall. He would be proud of you, Calen, as I am." The words seemed to hang in the air as

Calen handed the waterskin back to Vars. "We should get back to practicing."

His knuckles were white as he gripped the hilt of the practice sword.

Haem...

The sun was near setting when Vars placed the practice swords into their cloth wrapping, tying it off with a worn piece of string. Every muscle in Calen's body ached. His shoulders stung with a dull, pulsing throb, and new cuts had sprung up across his body from the many times he exposed himself. Even so, he wore a grin. He had landed a few blows – strong blows, by the way his father rubbed his fingers along his ribs. Calen knew he was a fine swordsman for his age, but Vars was the best in all the villages.

Vars was eighteen summers, working as a blacksmith apprentice, when High Lord Rayce Garrin rose to power in Varsund and turned his eyes towards the plains of Illyanara. The Lorian Empire had never paid much attention to the petty squabbling of the Southern lords, only stepping in if one seemed to gain too much power. The fighting was an easy way to "cull the herd."

When the Varsund War broke out, being a young man with a sense of adventure in his bones, Vars answered High Lord Castor Kai's call and rode to Camylin with a group of other young men from the villages and joined up with the Illyanaran army. The Varsund War lasted eight gruelling years. Calen had heard the stories many times over. The devastation was far reaching. The soil was fed with the blood of over-eager youths from the fields of Oberwall all the way to the Argonan Marshes. Towns and cities burned, fields were salted, and bloodlines were erased. Through it all, Vars survived.

He never spoke much about it to Calen, but it was well known across the villages. "A captain of the Illyanaran army,"

Calen had heard Jorvill Ehrnin say once. His father was well thought of in The Glade, and his words were always considered. Even Erdhardt Hammersmith gave ground when Vars spoke, and Calen rarely saw the village elder heed counsel at all.

"Calen, I didn't mean to upset you when I—"

"I know," Calen cut in. "I'm sorry."

Vars rested his hand on Calen's shoulder. A warm smile spread across his face.

"Well, how are we? Not too sore, I hope, after beating each other senseless with sticks?" Calen had not noticed Dann until his hand clapped down across the middle of Calen's back, igniting a tenderness from the earlier sparring session. He swatted away Dann's hand. "Get off me, you ass."

Calen's anger was met with a mirthful laugh. "How is he doing, Vars? I hope better than the bow. I had to go pick that arrow out of a dead squirrel earlier." Dann laughed at his own joke until a swift hand cracked him in the back of the head.

"Do you ever shut up?" asked the stern voice of Tharn Pimm, who seemed to appear out of thin air. He winked towards Vars as Dann rubbed the back of his head, muttering to the wind.

Dann's father was a handsome man of average height, with short blond hair. His frame was wiry, but the muscles that rested on it were dense and used to hard work.

Dann began to complain, but a stern look from Tharn made him think otherwise. Calen found it difficult to suppress a grin.

"How goes the training, Calen?" Tharn asked. "I was watching with Jorvill from the edge of the training field. I don't think I've seen anyone land as many strikes on Vars in a long time."

Vars raised his eyebrows.

"Well… ever, to be honest. You have a fine sword arm on you." Calen saw Dann getting ready to make a smart comment, but the words never made it to his lips. "Unlike this loudmouth over here. He's not too bad with that bow of his, but Achyron himself will need to bless him if a boar gets close enough to smell him. Look after him in there, Calen, and try not to let him do anything *too* stupid." Tharn wrapped his arm around Dann's neck and knuckled his hair playfully as he led him away towards the village. "I will see all four of you for supper, in about two hours. Vars? Ylinda has been preparing the venison all day."

"Aye, we shall see you then."

Dann muttered in protest as the pair ambled away, Tharn's headlock still in place.

Vars stared at Calen out of the corner of his eye, an approving look on his face. His father often did that when looking at Calen or Ella, and he always seemed to have a semi-vacant look in his eyes when he did so, as if he were in a faraway land.

"Dad?" Calen wiped the sweat from his brow that had condensed with the cool evening air.

With a momentary look of sadness, Vars's eyes snapped back to the real world. His expression shifted, as if melancholy had never touched his face. "Yes, sorry. Let's get going. Best not be late, Calen." He turned away and started for the village, the bundle holding the practice swords gripped neatly under his arm.

They walked in silence for a while, side-by-side, across the practice fields and into the village streets. With the Moon Market over and the peddlers and performers now on their way to the far reaches of Epheria, The Glade had transformed back to its natural calm and relaxed atmosphere. People floated through the square, going about their business in a lackadaisical manner as dusk settled in.

Mara Styr was in a world of her own. She packed up the stall outside her shop, in her typically haphazard manner. She threw carrots, leeks, potatoes, and onions unconcernedly into one big woollen sack before dragging it through the shop door, not so much as flinching when the sack cracked off the doorframe with a thud. The hard-earned lethargy of a hard day's work was evident in every motion.

Aela Hammersmith nodded at Vars and Calen as they passed across the main square. There was a warmness in her smile as she fastidiously tucked away her jewellery display. Each necklace was placed into its own tiny wooden box and topped with cloth before the lid was placed on.

Calen found it strange to picture her and Erdhardt together. He was easily twice her size, and he was as gruff as she was beautiful. Her dark opal eyes were mirrored by her chestnut brown hair. The softness of her facial features had led many a traveller to mistake her for a woman twenty years her junior. Calen didn't let his eyes linger too long.

The imposing figure of Rhett Fjorn emerged into the square from a side street. He wore the deep blue of the town guard, with a worn metal breastplate across his chest.

His raven-black hair was swept back off his face by the wind. By all definitions, he was a handsome man; even Ella seemed to swoon after him.

He directed a cautious smile in Calen's direction, then gave a stiff nod to Vars, which was returned with a thin-lipped grimace. With that, Rhett ducked down another street on the opposite side of the square, disappearing as quickly as he appeared. Calen sensed a coldness emanating from his father as Rhett vanished into the night's cloak.

Calen felt sorry for Rhett. He had been Haem's closest friend, and he was a genuinely honourable man, kind to a fault. He was the only one who returned two years before, when Haem led a group of men to force the Uraks back through Ölm Forest and into Wolfpine Ridge. He was half-dead when he crawled like a lame animal through the trees at the edge of Ölm Forest and into The Glade. His arm was broken in two places, and his clothes were soaked in the blood of the men he had grown up with. Vars had nearly spat on him when he was finally conscious enough to recount his story to the village council. "You should have brought Haem back or died with him!" Calen remembered him screaming, his face red with pain and wrought with anger. Rhett had just stared at him, his eyes sunken holes of despondency, his lips unable to form words.

Haem and Rhett had been inseparable since they were kids, brothers bonded by time instead of blood. Deep down, Calen knew that Haem's loss burned as deeply in Rhett as it did in himself.

He had always sensed that Vars knew his words were

entirely misplaced, but that he did not have the strength to take them back, so he continued to treat Rhett as if he had swung the sword himself. It weighed heavily on him.

"Have you seen Ella today?" Calen asked, trying to pierce the ice that surrounded his father. Ella always brought a glow to his father's face, no matter the time or place.

"She went out with your mother this morning to help her gather some herbs. Verna had asked for your mother's help with a sick peddler. She's not sure if he'll see the next moon."

They continued to make small talk as they made their way back to the house. The dark mood lifted further from Vars's shoulders with each footprint they left in the dust.

CHAPTER 5

The Proving

"Quiet now. Quiet! Settle down."

Erdhardt Hammersmith's booming voice carried through the market square, staving off competition from the deafening buzz that was synonymous with large crowds and a bit too much mead. Many new arrivals had made their way into The Glade over the past few days, and many more would arrive through the night.

Erdhardt stood on a newly erected wooden stage that looked out over the market square; his huge frame made the thirty-foot-wide stage seem something more akin to a large podium. He waited for the noise to die down as the crowd turned their gaze upon him. There were three or four hundred people packed into the market square. Entire families came to celebrate the young men proving themselves – and to join in the celebrations afterward. "It is my honour to welcome you all to our village. Food and mead will be provided to all, as much as it takes to fill your bellies and warm your hearts!"

The crowd erupted in a chorus of cheers.

Rist caught Calen's attention and rolled his eyes in Dann's direction. Dann raised his tankard in the air, roaring his appreciation at the sky while his free hand was wrapped around the waist of a young woman from Ölm, evident by the way her hair was braided at the back in twisting knots. Rist and Calen had decided that they would steer clear of mead for the night. The Proving was going to be difficult enough without starting the day with drums banging in their heads.

"As you all know," Erdhardt continued, "for centuries, the young men of the villages, in their eighteenth summer, gather here on the edge of Ölm Forest to take part in The Proving. They will spend three nights in the depths of the forest with only a knife and a bow. For these are the two things that will ensure they never go hungry. They must show that they understand how to survive on their own before we can allow them out into the world. So it has been, and so it will be. We go in groups – never less than two, and never more than four – to forge bonds that will last a lifetime; for no weight is too heavy when shared. But listen closely. Do not take this lightly. Ölm Forest is a dangerous place at night, and there are larger things than wolfpines that roam its depths. It has claimed the lives of many."

There was a momentary silence. The earlier ruckus died down as the crowd was swept up in Erdhardt's ominous words. "As such, it has long been the case that each group must return with the pelt of a predator. You must stand against what you fear – and conquer it. Only then will you pass The Proving, for everything you seek lies on the other side of fear. However, the group who returns on the fourth morning, after the third night, with the pelt of the most dangerous predator will be announced as the victors of The Hunt, and they will, of course, receive the victors' purse.

"For tonight, drink heartily, eat well, and warm yourselves by the fire. Take advice from your fathers, better advice from your mothers, and laugh with your siblings. Tomorrow, you enter the forest as boys and return to us as men."

Erdhardt raised his tankard of mead in the air, which was mimicked by the crowd. Those without tankards raised their closed fists. Calen felt a surge of pride flow through him as he crunched his fingers into a fist and thrust his hand into the air. A fire burned in the pit of Calen's stomach as Erdhardt spoke the blessings of the gods.

> *"May The Mother embrace you,*
> *and The Father protect you.*
> *May The Warrior guide your hand*
> *and The Maiden guide your mind.*
> *May The Smith keep your blade sharp*
> *and The Sailor see you to safe shores."*

The sun had not yet risen above the mountains to the east, but Calen couldn't sleep. He stared off into the distance while he ran his knife over a small whetstone, again and again.

"How sharp can a knife be?" Calen hadn't heard Ella come into the kitchen.

Ella glared at Calen as he mimicked her, in as high-pitched a tone as he could reach.

"You know that I can hear you, right?" She stepped out onto the porch, nudging Calen's shoulder with her own as she sat down beside him. She handed him some bread and cheese, which he took with a half-hearted smile before returning his gaze to the hazy distance.

"Sorry," Calen sighed, shrugging.

Ella let a few moments pass before she spoke again. "You're thinking about Haem, aren't you?"

The knife stopped moving back and forth across the whetstone. Calen hadn't even noticed that he was still sharpening the knife. He turned his head to answer Ella, but once he met her gaze, he immediately dropped his eyes to the floor, the air puffing out of his chest. He felt the soft touch of her hand at the side of his cheek as she slowly turned his head back up toward her face.

"He would be proud, Calen. I might not say it to you often, but *I'm* proud. You're my brother, and you are a pain in my backside most of the time, but I *am* proud of you." She pulled him into a hug, wrapping her arms tightly around his shoulders. "Come on, let's go inside and have tea with Mam and Dad. Put your knife away until you're in the forest. It can't get any sharper."

With that, she brushed the crumbs of bread off her dress, stood up, and walked back into the kitchen. Calen was sure that there would never come a day when he would understand Ella. One minute, she mocked him; the next, she told him she's proud of him. He hoped all women weren't like that.

He tossed the last of the bread and cheese into his mouth, sheathed the knife, and placed it back into his satchel. He then followed Ella into the kitchen, careful to put the whetstone back onto the shelf by the door.

Freis and Vars entered the kitchen not long after the sun had crested the mountain. The morning light caused Calen to wince as he shuffled in his chair.

Vars knuckled Calen's head affectionately. A warm smile rested on his face as he looked out at the rising sun and back towards Calen. There was an anxiety in the way Freis shuffled about the kitchen, pouring everyone deep mugs of Arlen root tea.

"You know I hate Arlen root tea," Calen protested, his nose scrunching up into a ball at the earthy smell wafting from the mug.

"Calen Bryer, you are about to go into a dangerous forest for three nights. It will be cold, dark, and wet. There are animals in there with teeth and claws. Arlen root will keep your mind focused. I am your mother. *Drink* your tea."

Calen glared at Freis' back while he choked down a mouthful of poison that masqueraded as tea. Vars exchanged a look with Ella, and they both broke out in laughter, much to Calen's annoyance.

"Okay, once we've all finished this delicious tea," Vars said, another laugh escaping him as Calen shot him a dirty look, "we should get going. The Havels will most likely be there already. I'm not so sure about Dann. I would say Tharn had to drag him out of bed this morning. Talked the ear off that poor Ölm girl last night before he passed out."

That brought a smirk to Calen's face, which was swiftly wiped away by another mouthful of tea.

By the time they had gathered themselves and set off towards the edge of Ölm Forest, the streets were alive with people. The sound of children playing blended with the spring birdsong, which crashed against the roll of wheels as traders moved their carts into position, trying to sell off the last of their wares. The Proving always brought a din of excitement with it to match the tense anticipation that hung in the air.

Every so often, someone stopped Calen to wish him well and exchange a few words with Vars and Freis, commenting on what a fine young man Calen had become. He would have enjoyed the compliments had it been a different day. As it was, he nodded and thanked them, his mind busy on other things.

"Okay, you head on, and I'll meet you at the forest," Vars said. "I figure I should probably check in on Tharn and Dann, make sure they are all set and ready to go. You know what they can be like."

"Okay, dear." Freis kissed him on the cheek and continued to shuffle Calen and Ella through the streets.

Once they made their way to the edge of the town, after being stopped for a pat on the back and a well-wishing smile every ten paces, the rest of the journey to the meeting point didn't take long. There were hundreds of people at the edge of Ölm Forest, gathered from all across the villages to witness the young men begin The Proving. The small red flag perched atop a wooden podium was meant to mark the meeting point, but it wasn't much use hidden in the throngs of people.

"Calen, Freis, Ella, over here!" Ca¹
ognised Elia Havel's shrill voice anyw   £
easily-excitable woman. Her chestnut bro,
back in a neat ponytail, highlighting her high c.
and wide smile. Elia's bubbly demeanour was a cont.
Lasch's stoic nature. Maybe they balanced each other out.
It was hard to think what Elia would be like on her own if
this was her balanced out.

Elia pulled him into a tight hug, her slight frame capable
of quite some strength when she was excited. "Oh, Calen,
you boys are all so grown up. Look at you! You've lost all
that baby fat." Calen winced as she pinched his cheek, the
sincere smile never fading from her face.

"Elia, I—"

"And you've gotten so tall! You're almost as broad as
your father now!"

"Elia, you only saw me yesterday," Calen snapped, pushing away her probing hands. Her smile momentarily curled
into a frown.

Calen and Rist exchanged a brief nod before Elia's attention turned to Freis.

"How are you this morning, Freis? Excited to see our
young boys become young men? Our Rist is terribly
excited as well. Aren't you, sweetie?" Elia turned her giddy
smile towards her son, an expectant look on her face.

Rist rolled his eyes. "Yes, Mother…" he huffed, a touch
of exasperation in his voice. He aimed a mocking smile at
Calen, then whispered, "She's been like this all morning. I
know she's happy, but by the gods, I wish she could be
happy in a less annoying way."

'I'm in great spirits this morning, Elia. Thank you," eis said. A disapproving look let Calen and Rist know that she had heard what Rist said. "It is indeed a proud day for every one of us. Where is Lasch? I would have expected him to be here already."

"Ah, he is talking with Erdhardt, arranging everything for the festivities. Extra mead from Milltown, some fish from Salme, and I've heard rumours that Thorvan might be arriving with his light sticks," Elia said in a hushed whisper. "And Vars, is he on his way?"

"Aye, he went to check on Tharn and Dann. Ylinda was out early this morning to pick Myril berries to dye her clothes, and you know what those two are like when left on their own."

Elia raised an all-knowing eyebrow. "Oh, I do, all right. They would sleep right through the entire Proving if left to their own devices."

"There they are now," Ella said, an amused tone in her voice. It didn't take long for Calen to see what had amused her.

Vars, Dann, and Tharn were slogging their way through the crowd. Vars led the way. There was a gingerness in his step and a tentative smile flickered across his face, which threatened to turn into a laugh. Tharn's mouth was set into a deep scowl as he marched ahead of Dann, turning his head around every few seconds to look behind him, as if he expected Dann to vanish into thin air.

Dann trudged along behind the two men, dragging his feet through the grass as if lifting them to walk was more effort than he could manage. The mead-induced lethargy was evident with every strained movement. His eyes were sunken into deep wells, while his hair and clothes looked like he had slept in – and then been dragged out of – a bush. He let out an exaggerated sigh when they finally stopped in front of the group.

A mocking laugh escaped Rist's mouth. "Dann, you look fantastic! You must have slept all night!"

Dann snarled, his eyes narrowing and nose scrunching. It seemed all the effort he could muster. His usually quick tongue had deserted him.

"Now, now, boys. Leave Dann alone. Although the hammer pounding inside his head is probably punishment enough, I'm sure Tharn has given him a tongue lashing for the ages," Freis said with a raised eyebrow. Tharn simply furrowed his brow and let out a frustrated huff of agreement. "Now that we are all here, how are you boys feeling? Have you everything you need?"

"Well, all they're allowed to bring is a knife and their bows. So, if they forgot anything, then they have more to worry—" A slight raise in Freis's eyebrow let Ella know to end her sentence there.

"Yes, I've got everything," Calen said.

"Me too. I double-checked before we left the house," Rist answered.

Tharn elbowed Dann in the ribs, which brought about a sharp grunt.

"I've got everything," Dann coughed.

Tharn reached into a sack he had slung around his back. "I almost forgot. These should fit perfectly. I only finished them the night before last." From the sack, he pulled two leather belts, handing one each to Rist and Calen.

Calen ran his fingers over the belt. It was a rich umber brown, smooth to the touch and sturdy. Every stitch was neat and as close to perfect as could be. Tharn was widely known as one of the best tanners and leather craftsmen in all the villages. He could have easily sold the belts for two or three silver marks a piece to a trader heading for Gisa or Argona.

"Thank you, Tharn. I don't—" Calen started.

"Nothing needs be said, Calen," Tharn said. "We are family, the lot of us. Look after each other in there."

Calen nodded, immediately fixing the belt around his waist.

The idle chat continued for a while; they discussed what weather to expect over the next three nights, where the boys should set up camp, and other details that they had gone over a hundred times before. Calen's attention was waning when the crowd shifted towards the podium.

The leaders of each of the seven village councils had assembled atop the podium. Four men and three women, with Erdhardt at their head.

"It is great to see you all here, gathered in such numbers to see our young men off on their rite of passage," Erdhardt said. "This has long been a tradition in the villages, and I am proud to see it continue."

Erdhardt stepped back into line with the other elders, giving them each a chance to make a short comment. Each spoke of pride, tradition, and honour; their words mimicked those of the one who spoke before them.

"It is time," Erdhardt said, when each of the elders had said their piece. His voice rose above the chattering crowd. "Can all the groups please say their goodbyes and then move up to the brazier?"

Calen turned to his mother and father and instantly had the wind knocked out of him as Freis pulled him into a hug so tight that it could have been used to incapacitate a bear. When she finally released him from her clutches, Calen found himself staring at his father. Vars simply placed his hands on Calen's shoulders and pressed his forehead gently against Calen's. "I love you, son." He placed a kiss on the top of Calen's forehead, and no further words were exchanged.

"Try not to starve yourself in there," Ella said. "And remember not to let any poison Tharin leaves touch your skin."

Calen laughed. "Love you too, sis."

He slowly paced backwards, then turned around. Dann and Rist joined him once they had said their own goodbyes.

"I genuinely wish my mother had even a tiny bit less energy." Rist laughed. Calen responded with a laugh of agreement while Dann only grunted. "Rough night, Dann? Maybe four or five too many meads?"

"Oh, curse you, Rist. I had planned on going to bed a lot earlier. It was only meant to be one drink."

"It's always only one drink with you," Calen said.

The boys continued to joke together as they approached the brazier that marked the start of The Proving, nodding and saying hello to those they recognised along the way. Calen noticed Kurtis, Fritz, and Dennet Hildom about a hundred paces upward along the line. He felt a slight pulse of anger swell in his chest. He took a few long breaths and focused his attention back towards his friends, who were exchanging insults at their usual pace, with a few delayed responses from Dann. Calen shook his head as he watched the pair of them.

A horn sounded behind them, followed swiftly by a flaming arrow shot overhead, streaking smoke behind it. The arrow landed firmly in the large brazier filled with oil-soaked wood. With a *whoosh*, the brazier erupted in a burst of flames.

"The Proving begins," Erdhardt called out.

All along the line, young men advanced towards the forest. Some took a bit more time than others, but eventually followed the lead of those before them.

"Well," Calen said, letting out a breath that he had held in since the arrow ignited the brazier, "I suppose we'd better get going."

Rist responded with a quick smile and a nod, swinging his bag over his shoulder. Dann grunted. Calen had a feeling that was the most conversation they were going to get out of him today.

"We should try to find a stream as soon as possible to fill our waterskins," Rist suggested.

Calen nodded; his eyes fixed on the treeline. As they reached the edge of the forest and made their way through its outer rim, Calen felt the familiar weight in the air with every breath he took. The dense moist air pressed down into his lungs. After about half an hour of walking, he began to acclimatise to the sensation a little – but not enough for his liking.

"It's so strange," Rist remarked, inhaling deeply.

"What do you mean?" Calen replied as he stumbled over the unearthed root of a gargantuan tree.

"It's just odd how hard it is to breathe in here. The other woodlands around the villages don't seem to have the same effect."

"Well, Therin always tells of how the giants ruled these lands and used magic to build this forest. He said that they used to sing to the trees and that they could create entire groves in just weeks. Maybe it's magic?"

"Surely you can't believe those fairy tales, Calen?" There was a mocking look on Rist's face.

Calen frowned. "You can't really think that all the legends are lies? All Therin's stories, just spun on a wheel to entertain people? The Bards always talk about the Circle of Magii in the North, even the ones who call The Order traitors. Are they *all* lying?"

Rist shrugged. "Maybe?" He pulled his mouth up into a frown. "I don't know, maybe there is magic somewhere far away from The Glade – and I'm not saying there is – but I can only believe what I can see. Not what some travellers tell us because they want our coin."

"Oh, will you two shut up?" Dann groaned. "You're hurting my head. There should be a stream about half an hour's walk east. If you can be quiet until then, maybe some water might be able to uncloud my head." Rist and Calen laughed at Dann's sudden outburst, but agreed to follow him through the dense foliage as he led the way.

It didn't take long before they heard the burbling of a small rivulet through the constant haze of forest sounds.

Calen stopped, closed his eyes, and took a deep breath. If he focused, he could pick out each of the sounds on their own. The sweet chirps of small birds as they went about their day, oblivious to the world outside their own. The buzzing and clicking of the thousands of insects that ruled the forest floor. The cracking and snapping of branches broken under the weight of rabbits, deer, and the occasional kat flitting between the trees.

"Calen… Calen!" Dann's voice pierced through the wall of sound. "Will you stop daydreaming? I'm thirsty, and we need to get to the cave before it gets too late. We don't want to be wandering through here in the dark."

Calen opened his eyes, let out a soft sigh, and jogged after Dann and Rist. The few deer who were drinking at the rivulet when the boys arrived disappeared into the brush almost as soon as Calen laid eyes on them. Dann and Rist knelt down at the water's edge and dipped their water-skins in. A welcome silence replaced their usual back and forth as Dann continued to mope over his foggy headache.

"Well, so far, so good," Calen said as he hunkered down beside Rist and dipped his waterskin into the rivulet. "No wolfpines in sight, none of the kats have taken a liking to us, and we haven't eaten any poison berries."

"I like the positivity," Rist replied, "but we have a long way to go yet."

The sunlight waned as they made their way through the forest. Calen's stomach ached. He had eaten nothing since that morning, when Ella had given him a morsel of cheese and bread. And judging by the fading light drifting through the canopy, that was quite a few hours ago. Dann took down a pair of rabbits with his bow as they hiked through the trees, but that would not be much meat to split between three of them.

None of the animals seemed to pay them much heed at all as they traipsed their way through the forest. They spotted the occasional kat watching them from a distance, but they never came too close. According to Dann, they were only young, which worried Calen a little. Those "young" kats were already nearly the same size as Faenir. They hadn't seen a single wolfpine either, which Calen wasn't exactly disappointed about. The wild ones were not as friendly as Faenir was.

Dann seemed to have recovered from the mead-induced body ache that had plagued him earlier in the day, and slowly, he became less brusque.

"How long until we reach that cave, Dann?" Rist called out from a couple of feet behind the pair in front.

"Shouldn't be more than a half-hour at this rate," Dann called back.

Where to camp had been a topic of discussion many times in the days leading up to The Proving. They needed somewhere that had shelter from the elements but was also close to a water source. Having a source of water nearby was crucial. Not just for drinking; it would also be the easiest way for them to find dinner without having to go too far. There were fish in the river, and deer or rabbits needed water just as much as they did. A bit of patience, and they would be far from hungry over the next few days.

"I can see it just up ahead," Dann called, picking up his

pace. He gave a short shrug to his right shoulder to shift the two rabbits that dangled there into a less precarious position.

Calen lifted his head from the forest floor and saw the trees open up slightly into a rocky clearing. A stream meandered through its centre; it was quite a bit larger than the rivulet they had stopped at earlier, but its pace was far more lackadaisical.

On the other side of the stream, Calen saw what they had come for. The mouth of a small cave, nestled into the jagged rock face, smothered by the dense forest around it. It could easily have been missed by someone who wasn't looking for it.

Without a word, Dann leapt from the bank of the river, landing deftly on a rock that stuck out above the surface of the water. "Tonight is going to be cold enough without our clothes being wet," Dann shouted back when he caught Rist raising an eyebrow at him. Rist looked at Calen and shrugged. With Dann at the lead, they made their way across the stream, hopping from rock to rock.

"Ah, fuck!" Calen yelled as his foot slipped on the slick surface of a flat stone covered in green and brown moss. It was all he could do to stop himself falling headfirst into the water. He let his shoulders sag and resigned himself to slogging the rest of the way through the languid stream. The smirk on Dann's face only made it worse. When he reached the other side of the stream, Calen kicked out at the air as he tried in vain to shake the water out from inside his boot. He should have known Dann would make it look easier than it was.

The cave itself only stretched back into the rock face about twenty feet, which suited Calen fine. He didn't want something sneaking up behind him from the depths while he slept. The walls were overgrown in patches, thick with green moss and small purple flowers streaked with crimson veins. There was an unpleasant aroma wafting into Calen's nose that he couldn't quite place.

"Well, it's not the palace of Al'Nasla," Rist remarked as he brushed a pile of stones away with his foot, "but it's not that bad. Cleaner than my room – it even has flowers." Rist reached up and plucked a purple flower from amidst the moss.

"Don't touch that!" Dann roared. He smacked the flower straight out of Rist's hand in a blur of motion.

"Why did you do that?" Rist cursed, caressing the now reddish mark on the back of his hand.

"That's Purple Ember. If you had held it any longer, your hands would have felt like they were on fire," Dann sniped. "Did you not read about it in those books of yours?"

Rist glared at the back of Dann's head.

"You two are like children, I swear to the gods," Calen laughed. "But seriously though, Dann's right – don't touch those flowers."

Rist scrunched his upper lip and took a step away from the wall of the cave as he eyed the purple flowers askance.

Calen had to suppress a laugh as he looked at Rist. "Okay, Dann, can you hold the fort while Rist and I gather wood for the fire before the night sets in? I want to see if I can find any useful plants and herbs as well. They could come in handy."

Dann was already lying down on the packed dirt, his head propped up against a rock. "Sounds like a plan to me, Calen. Consider the fort held." He closed his eyes as he pulled his bow up to his chest and dragged his quiver to within arm's reach.

Calen started to protest but surrendered to the reality that Dann probably still had a better chance of putting an arrow in a would-be attacker in that position than Calen did with his eyes open, standing up straight. As much of an idiot as he could be at times, it was like he was born with that bow in his hands.

Rist just shrugged at Calen and nodded towards the forest.

The juices from the rabbit tumbled down Calen's chin as he sank his teeth into the leg, eager to get the meat off the bone and into his rumbling stomach. He used his sleeve to wipe away the brownish-yellow beads glistening from the firelight.

With a bit of luck, Rist had got the fire going just before the sun had set. Calen had never mastered the trick with a knife and a rock, not that it mattered as long as his belly was full.

"You know what, Dann? You're a bit of an ass, but you sure know how to cook rabbit," Rist said matter-of-factly as he picked the bone clean with his teeth. Calen never cared too much for rabbit meat. It was usually dry and tough, but he was not going to complain.

Dann let out a snort, sending pieces of half-chewed rabbit spraying across the fire, which drew a chorus of laughter from Rist and Calen.

"You okay there, Dann?" Calen laughed, coughing as he attempted to suppress the waves of laughter.

"Fuck off," Dann choked, taking a deep breath inward to settle himself. When they were finished, Dann gathered all the bones and threw them into the river. "We don't want any kats or wolfpines strolling in here, looking for the meat that used to sit on those bones."

Calen felt sleep creep up on him. With his belly full and the fire pulsating heat throughout the small cave, it was all he could do to keep his eyes open. He pulled his coat tighter around himself and shuffled down into the dirt. It wasn't the most comfortable place to sleep, but he found it incredible how a hot meal and a warm fire could make hard clay feel like a goose feather mattress.

He saw Dann and Rist's eyes drooping as well. A bit of sleep was well deserved for the three of them.

Calen awoke to the sound of what he thought was someone rummaging through one of the bags. His eyes were stuck together with crusty flecks of sleep, which he rubbed away with the back of his hand.

"Dann?" he whispered, his voice still hushed with tiredness. His half-awake eyes saw a shape at the other side of the smouldering fire, near Rist's bag. *We must have all fallen asleep without putting out the fire.*

A low rumbling sound, interrupted by the occasional muffled snort, came from whoever it was at the bags – or it could have been Dann snoring. Calen heaved himself upright; the fatigue from the day's trek made it a greater task than it should have been. He rubbed his tired eyes again, pushing his fingers into the creases and dragging them down his face as if to pry open his lids and bring his vision back to normal.

"Rist, what are you doing?" Calen sighed. The embers of the fire provided little light, and darkness still covered the mouth of the cave, obscuring the forest from view. Calen's mouth bunched up into a frown, frustrated by the lack of response. "Rist, what—"

Calen leapt to his feet, stumbling backward. The figure huddled over Rist's bag turned its body sideways, allowing Calen to catch sight of the immense shadow that it cast across the wall of the cave. "Rist! Dann! Wake up! There's a fucking bear!"

The blood drained from his face as he saw the hulking figure of the bear for the first time in the dying firelight. Its thick, blackish-brown fur was mottled with tacky dark patches of dirt – or blood. It was hard to tell. It had a dished face, with short roundish ears. Eyes as black as jet. Teeth of alabaster and claws that dwarfed Calen's fingers.

Calen saw Rist leap from his sleeping position, shaking his head back and forth as he processed what was happening. There was a look of pure horror on his face when the bear raised itself on its hind legs, its head scraping the jagged rock ceiling of the cave. It had to be ten feet tall.

A roar erupted from its now open jaws but was cut short by a sharp *whoosh*, followed by a heavy *thunk*. The turkey feather fletching of one of Tharn Pimm's arrows now jutted from the bear's chest. The roar that the bear had initially intended paled in comparison to the visceral thunder that now crashed forward from its open mouth. With it came a spray of spit and phlegm, accompanied by an abusive waft of rotting flesh.

Slumping its upper body close to the ground, the howling bear swept its hulking shoulders towards Rist. Its thick muscular neck collided with his sternum in a crash, launching him backwards into the darkness.

Whoosh.

Another arrow now protruded from the bear's right shoulder. Calen didn't even remember seeing Dann get to his feet. Yet, there he stood, bow raised, the string drawn back to the corner of his mouth, which was a thin line of concentration. He squinted to see in the bleak light.

The bear let out another earth-shattering roar. The natural acoustics of the cave amplified the sound, and Calen and Dann both winced as their ears drummed with pain.

In that moment, the bear charged, its solid, burly legs carrying its gargantuan body at a pace that Calen could not believe. He pulled his knife from its sheath as the creature careened towards him. Another arrow sank into its shoulder. The sound was drowned out by the crashing stones and lumps of clay lifted by the bear's feverish charge.

Dann threw himself out of the way, crashing into the wall of the cave. Calen wasn't so lucky. He swung his knife as the top of the bear's skull caught him in the shoulder, sending him spinning to the hard ground. A searing pain shot through his torso.

As the bear lifted its head, Calen caught sight of his knife, buried to the hilt in the animal's neck. It lurched to the right as its feet staggered. Both the knife and the arrows had wounded it badly, and the wounds were taking their toll. Its movements were slow; each careful step towards Calen seemed to take all of its energy. Calen's heart pounded in his chest as the enormous creature got closer. The bear's now wobbly legs heaved its towering frame by sheer will alone. With little warning, the bear collapsed. The ground shook with the impact, plumes of dust occluding what little light there was.

It took a lifetime for Calen to drag himself to his feet. The aching pain running up the right side of his body distracted from the pain everywhere else. He found Dann standing over the crumpled frame of the bear. Its sheer size still struck fear into Calen. It was still alive, its breathing slow and laboured. Each breath was heavy, rasping, as the bear attempted in vain to drag air into its collapsing lungs.

Dann pulled an arrow from his quiver and wrapped his fist firmly around the shaft. Even in the frail light, Calen saw his fingers turning white from the grip. He lifted the arrow and, with a grimace of regret, drove it straight through the soft tissue at the side of the bear's head. The breathing stopped.

Dann hunkered down onto his knees and placed a hand on the fur of the bear's neck. "Better it was quick," he sighed heavily, his shoulders drooping.

There was a weighted silence in the air. The only sounds were the creaking of branches and the whistling wind, accompanied by the chirping of crickets. His shoulder would hurt in the morning. In fact, it already did.

"Guys," Rist called, "is it dead?"

Calen couldn't stop his hands shaking. He heard Dann sigh, and although he couldn't see through the darkness that had grown stronger as the fire dwindled, he could tell that he had thrown his eyes up to the heavens.

"Yes, Rist, the bear is dead." Calen frowned as he looked towards Dann's slumped silhouette.

"Okay, good," Rist said. His voice was shaking, and Calen could hear the dryness in his throat. Rist must have pushed a log into the fire because it spat embers into the air, and the cave became a little brighter. He was fully visible now as he stood by the fire. Dried blood and dirt were matted into his dark hair. His coat was covered in clay and dust, and a few rips and tears raced down his left sleeve. In his hand was the skull of a deer – young, judging by its size. It was blotched grey with dirt and picked clean of flesh.

"I'm not going back to sleep."

CHAPTER 6

More Than Bears in the Woods

I still think Anya will dance with you on Feast Night,"
Rist said as he pulled his knife up the length of wood
that rested across his lap, tapering it into a point at the
end.

"Leave it, Rist. We are just friends," Calen said, his cheeks
reddening. Rist and Dann exchanged a look. Dann tilted his
head and raised an all-knowing eyebrow, laughing.

Calen tried his best to ignore them as he held the sharp-
ened end of his own makeshift spear just above the flames
of the fire that sat in front of them. That was a trick his
father had taught him long ago. Baking the tip of a wooden
spear made it lighter and stronger. The thick pole of wood
was about six and a half feet long, and just under two inches
in diameter. He would have felt far more comfortable with
a sword in his hands, but given the circumstances, the spear
would do just fine.

They all sat just in front of the cave mouth. Even with
the bear dead, there was not a chance any of them would

sleep in there again. A few feet away, the bear's pelt hung between two trees, stretched as wide as it could go. Dann had spent most of the morning and early afternoon skinning the bear with the utmost care and concentration. He made a point to open the ears, nose, and lips to remove all the excess fat. Without access to salt, he needed to ensure that as little moisture as possible remained to prevent the skin from rotting. Moving their camp out of the cave for the night had the added bonus of avoiding the damp air produced by the moss, and the evening sun was just warm enough to dry the hide without damaging it.

"So, tell me again, why are you bothering to preserve the pelt?" Rist asked. A sharp *tssk* escaped him. He pulled his finger up to his mouth to suckle on a thin stream of blood that trickled down his thumb – the result of his over eager knife work. He threw a dirty look at Calen when he noticed the smirk on his face.

Dann was splayed out on the ground, head propped up on a thick log, chewing on a long piece of grass. He stared off into the surrounding forest. "Well, after we bring it back, we'll be declared victors of The Hunt. I can't see the others bringing back anything bigger than this monster." Dann tilted his head towards the bear pelt that was suspended in mid-air a few feet away. "After that, there is no sense in letting it go to waste. Father could easily make a masterpiece out of a pelt like that. The gods know we could use the coin."

Rist let out a mocking snort. "Last night, you were all upset it was dead, and now you want to turn it into a coat?"

"Yes, Rist, I was upset that an incredible creature died.

Slowly, and painfully, for no reason, and I was the cause."
Dann's reply was curt, his eyes still lost in the haze of the
forest. His jaw clenched.

"Incredible creature? For no reason? Dann, it was
going to kill us. Like, dead. Snap, gone—"

"You did what you had to do, Dann," Calen interrupted.
He gave Rist a look as if to say, *please give him a break.* Rist
seemed to understand, giving a soft nod in reply.

Dann pulled his eyes away from the depths of the forest
to look towards Calen. There was a heavy expression on
his face. Calen hadn't noticed the purple rims developing
under Dann's eyes, nor the slumping of his shoulders
throughout the day. But when he thought back, he realised
that Dann kept to himself most of the morning and afternoon, with few words passing his lips. Considering Calen
once witnessed Dann have a drunken conversation with a
tree, the silence should have raised some flags.

"Calen, I've never ended a life before without there
being a real reason. I hunt deer, rabbits, fish… so that we
can eat. To survive. That bear was hungry. It came back
and found us in its home. We – *I* killed it. I know it would
have killed us if I didn't kill it first, but… it's not the same."

"I get it, Dann," Calen said. *I get it.*

Calen tossed another log onto the fire. A soft sigh
escaped him as he sat back down onto the spongy trunk of
the fallen tree he had been perched on.

They sat in silence as the evening drifted away and the
night settled around them. The sounds of the forest provided
a soothing chorus as the day's birdsong was replaced by the
soft burbling of the stream as it meandered through the

forest, the crackling and snapping of the fire as it consumed the flesh of the wood, and the ever-present buzzing of insects as they went about their nocturnal business. Every so often, the howl of a wolfpine broke the tranquil blanket of familiar sounds, drawing sudden jerks from Calen, Dann, or Rist as they spun around to make sure that the bear hadn't risen from the dead.

"Guys... I think we may have a visitor," Rist squeaked.

Calen opened his eyes. A large kat, about the same size as Faenir, skulked around the rim of the fire. Its spotted brown and silvery-black fur caused it to blend in and out of sight with the forest backdrop. Its tapered ears pointed straight up towards the sky, giving the impression that it was always paying attention, always listening. He had never seen a kat up close before. The dazzling yellowish glow in its eyes was hypnotising. The two tufts of fur that draped down past its shoulders on either side of its head gave it a wizened look.

Calen reached for his bow, careful not to make any sudden moves, stretching out his fingertips to wrap around the grip.

"No," Dann hushed. He was already standing up by the fire, his hand pointing at Calen but his eyes fixed on the kat.

Without a sound loud enough to be heard above the leaves rustling in the wind, Dann made his way over towards the leftover fish they had caught and cooked that morning. It was splayed out on a smooth flat stone by the fire. He stayed low to the ground, with his knees bent and his arms raised slightly in the air, spread out to either side. His eyes never left the kat.

The kat's gleaming yellow eyes returned Dann's fixed gaze. An unintelligible purring emanated from its muscular throat.

The kat took two steps around the fire, towards Dann, slow and deliberate. Its head lowered as its back arched. The muscles rippled on its hind legs. The purring deepened, dropping into its chest.

Dann's eyes narrowed. He turned to face the kat. The light from the fire flickered shadows across his face. He opened his palm and tossed the fish up into the air, to the other side of the fire.

The kat flexed its muscular legs momentarily, then launched itself into the air. The patterns on its fur shimmered in the mixture of moon and fire light as it twisted and turned its torso mid-flight. It seemed to hang in the air for an eternity, as if weightless. It snatched the fish out of the air with its mouth in one smooth motion before landing, without any discernible sound, on the other side of the fire.

The kat bit the fish clean in half, letting the other half fall to the ground. Once it had finished eating what it had bitten off, the kat bent its head down to the ground and picked the second half of the fish up with surprising care. Its eyes locked on Dann again.

The kat padded over towards Dann. Stopping in front of him, it lowered its head and, in almost a tender manner, placed the second piece of fish down on the ground at Dann's feet.

A soft purring noise reverberated from its throat.

"What in the…." Rist whispered.

Dann reached down for the fish, careful not to move

with too much haste. The kat's head turned, staring with intense focus into the darkness obscured forest. It didn't move, but the hackles on the back of its neck, all the way down its spine, stood upright. The soft purring changed into a deep, chesty rumble. Calen listened intently, trying to hear whatever the kat had heard.

Snap.

The sound of a thick branch splitting under the weight of something heavy. An arrow flew out from amidst the trees, slicing through the fire and planting in the ground where the kat's leg had been.

Calen had not even seen the kat leap. Its reflexes were quicker than his eyes could follow. In one bound, it propelled itself clear of the camp and was gone, back into the forest.

"Who's there?" Dann yelled. His bow was already drawn, aimed in the direction the arrow had come from.

Rist grasped the shaft of his spear with both hands, surveying the surrounding forest. His head jittered from place to place as he searched for any other would-be attackers.

Drawing his eyes away from where the kat had leapt into the abyss of trees, Calen snatched up his makeshift spear in one hand and bounded over towards Dann.

"Guys, I think—" Rist was cut short as a second arrow shot through the trees. Though it was impossible to follow the flight of the arrow in the darkness, a howl from Rist let both Calen and Dann know where it had landed. Calen's heart dropped into his stomach. He turned to see Rist standing by the fire, his spear rolling along the ground and the shaft of an arrow protruding from his left leg.

"Rist!" Calen and Dann leapt to Rist's side, stabilising him as he stumbled.

"What the fuck are you doing, Fritz? You could have killed him!" came a familiar voice. *Fritz Netly?*

"Shut up, Dennet. I would have gotten it if they hadn't scared it off."

Three figures emerged from the copse of trees. Calen could only make out their silhouettes in the pale moonlight. One was larger, with thick, broad shoulders. He was flanked on either side by two smaller figures. "Calen, we didn't mean for Rist to get hurt, I swear it," the taller figure said. The voice was deep, familiar. Something clicked in Calen's head.

"Kurtis? What the hell do you think you're doing? You shot Rist!" Calen lunged towards Kurtis, raising his spear as he did so, his shoulders and arms tensing.

"Whoa! Don't take another step, Bryer, or I'll put an arrow in you too." One of the smaller figures drew his bow and aimed it straight at Calen's chest.

"Fritz…" Calen muttered, a scowl spreading across his face.

He turned his head, just for a second, to check on Rist and Dann. They were on the ground, Dann cradling Rist's head on his knee. It looked like he had managed to remove the arrow, but Rist's breathing was heavy. Calen's muscles tensed as the rage burned through him. He wanted so badly to rip the smirk off Fritz's smug face.

"Careful now… He'll be fine, but I can't say the same for you if you even think about coming near me," Fritz said. He drew his bowstring back a little farther to make his point clear.

"Fritz." Just one word from Kurtis. The meaning was clear: *You're going too far.* Fritz just glared back at him. That absent glare always unsettled Calen; the way Fritz's eyes never seemed to be looking *at* you, but *through* you. As if everyone was simply an obstacle to what he wanted. A grin spread across Fritz's face as he looked past Calen. Something had caught his eye. *The bear pelt.*

"What do we have here?" Fritz said, the firelight flickering across his face. "That looks like the perfect payment for costing us that kat. Dennet, take it down."

"That's ours!" Rist coughed. The pain was evident in his voice.

"No, it's *ours*," Fritz said.

Dennet cut the ropes that kept the pelt strung up between the trees. Then he made his way over to join Kurtis and Fritz, struggling as he heaved it over his shoulder. The clouds overhead had moved on and released more moonlight. Calen could see their faces more clearly now. Kurtis bit his bottom lip as he watched Fritz, who examined the pelt in the firelight, running his hand over the rough fur and the part-dry skin. "Not a bad job at all. This beast must have been huge. A good kill. You idiots must have gotten lucky," Fritz said. "Thank you very much. There is no doubt we will be declared victors of The Hunt when we bring this back."

"Burn you all! What is wrong with you?" The venom in Dann's words burned like a hot knife through his voice.

"It's simply being smart, Dann. You scared off our kill, so we take yours. Fair is fair," Fritz said. He had that same cold, calculating look in his eyes. "Now get out of here."

"You think we're leaving?" Dann roared, still cradling Rist's head in his lap.

"Yes, I do. I'll be nice. Take a minute to gather your supplies. Then start walking towards the mountains. If you're not gone in five minutes, I will show you how serious I am. I will follow you for a while, to make sure you keep walking."

Kurtis looked like he wanted to protest, but a sharp look from Fritz stopped him in his tracks.

"Okay, we'll go," Calen said through gritted teeth. A wicked grin curled at the corner of Fritz's mouth.

Dann stared at him, his mouth agape. "What are you doing?"

"Rist is hurt, Dann. We need to get him away from these assholes and make sure he's okay. That's more important than fighting with these three. Can you get him to his feet? I'll carry the bags."

Dann replied with a resigned nod.

Calen gathered their supplies, and Dann got Rist to his feet with a few bouts of protest. They made their way towards the edge of the clearing, in the direction of Wolfpine Ridge. Calen noticed what he thought was an apologetic look in Kurtis's eyes.

"Keep walking until the sun starts to rise," Fritz called after them. "I'll know if you don't."

They trudged through the dense forest in silence, exhaustion in their bones. Calen carried the bags while Rist used a combination of Dann and his spear as walking sticks. Every once in a while, Calen checked behind them for any signs of Fritz following them. He thought he saw something a few times, but he couldn't be sure. It wasn't worth finding out.

As the sun crested over the top of the mountain, a small rivulet came into view about thirty or so feet ahead. Calen hadn't heard it as they approached. With fatigue causing a slight throbbing in his ears, he was finding it hard to focus.

"This is ridiculous," Dann said, his voice a mixture of tiredness and irritation.

Calen sighed. "We need to stop at the water. We need to drink and take a look at the wound. We can't leave it too long, or it might become infected."

Dann nodded. Rist grunted.

After they sat for a while in silence and filled their bellies with water, Calen rolled up Rist's trouser leg to inspect the wound.

"The arrow went clean through," Dann said. "I broke the head off on the other side and pulled the shaft out. He was lucky." Dann dunked his waterskin into the rivulet as he spoke, sighing with exhaustion.

"Lucky?" Rist said, coughing. "How, by the gods, do you consider this lucky?

"Well, you didn't bleed much, which means the arrow didn't hit anything important. The arrow came through, which meant I could pull it out. Otherwise, it would still be in your leg. And it hurt just enough to shut you up for the last few hours," Dann said, grinning to himself.

"I swear, I'll put one in you if you don't wipe that grin off your face," Rist snapped.

"Should have left the bloody thing in," Dann said, shrugging.

"Will you two shut up?"

Both Dann and Rist jumped a little, taken aback by Calen's abrupt and irritated tone.

"Rist, Dann just pulled an arrow from your leg, hauled you to your feet, and dragged you here." Rist hung his head, ashamed. "Dann—"

"Yes?" His tired face gave its best impression at a cheeky grin. Calen wasn't in the mood for it.

"Stop being an asshole."

Dann opened his mouth but didn't argue. Calen reached into his bag and pulled out some of the herbs and plants he had gathered the other day, while he was looking for firewood. He mulled over the different options, trying to remember exactly which ones his mother had said were good at stopping infection.

Two, he knew immediately. Cretia's Breath and Bluebottle drops. He pulled them out and set them down on the rock to his left. He muttered to himself as he sifted through the rest, "Mullder, docleaf…" None of them were as good as brimlock sap. But they would do.

When he had picked out all the ones he needed, he used a rock to grind them into a paste. He added some water from the rivulet to get the consistency he wanted.

"These herbs will act as a poultice. It should keep infection at bay while the wound heals," Calen said, still grinding away at the plant mixture. He noticed a hesitant look on Rist's face. "It's that or we cauterise it with fire. Dann, could you get a fire going?"

The colour drained from Rist's face. "Let's go with the plant thing."

"Good choice!" Dann choked, coughing up some water in between bouts of strained laughter.

Despite the multiple protests and gasps of pain, it didn't take long for Calen to apply the poultice to Rist's leg. He tore a strip off Rist's shirt to act as a bandage once it was dried in.

"We should get going." Dann dragged himself to a seated position. "We're going to have to walk through the night and all tomorrow morning just to make it back in time."

Calen's stomach rumbled. "Can we eat something first?"

"I second that," Rist said.

Dann sighed. With a grunt of exhaustion, he got to his feet. "If you can get a fire going. I'll go and see if I can find something to eat. Some food and rest might not be a bad idea before we get moving."

Calen had just managed to get the fire going by the time Dann re-emerged from the trees, the limp body of a beaver slung over his shoulder. There wasn't going to be much food to go around.

"We eat, then we rest until the sun passes the peak of that mountain." Dann winced as he pointed up towards a craggy peak in the distance. "Then we need to move."

"Agreed, Rist?" Calen said.

Rist grunted, a grimace twisted on his face.

The sun had already begun to set when Calen, Dann, and Rist started the long hike back through Ölm Forest. The combination of a warm meal and exhaustion meant they had rested far longer than intended.

"Well, we're not going to pass The Proving. But given what's happened so far, I'm pretty happy just to be going home without an arrow wound in my leg." Dann's attempt at humour was met with a swift kick in the ankles from Rist.

"Too soon." There was a no-nonsense tone in Rist's voice, but Calen noticed a smirk just lingering on the corner of his mouth. Dann managed to catch himself before falling and thought better of complaining, but something caused him to stop in his tracks.

"Dann—" Dann's raised hand cut Calen short. He squinted as he stared into the dense brush.

His voice was a whisper. "There's something…"

Calen thought he could hear it. The rustling of leaves. The snapping of branches. The thumping of heavy feet. A small puddle of water in front of them rippled at regular intervals.

In a flash, a wolfpine burst out of the trees about ten feet ahead of them. Its fur was mostly a greyish-black, mottled with streaks of dark blood. The wolfpine stared straight at them. Something was wrong. It was large, less than half a foot smaller than Faenir from nose to tail. But it was not large enough to cause the ripples in that water.

"Oh, for the love of the gods! This is getting ridiculous! Can't we just catch a bre—?" Just as Rist was about to finish his sentence, a massive axe with a half-moon blade followed the wolfpine out of the trees, swinging through the air with a ringing metallic whistle. The axe blade was massive, nearly the width of the wolfpine's belly to the crest of its back, with a smooth translucent gemstone set into its surface. It crashed straight into the creature's ribcage and, with a howling whimper, lifted the wolfpine off its feet. The sheer force carried it through the air and slammed it into the trunk of a nearby tree. Calen didn't need to look to know that the animal would not be getting back up. He felt his grip on the spear involuntarily growing tighter as fear made itself at home in his bones.

Dann was in the middle of nocking an arrow when two creatures emerged from the trees near the body of the wolfpine. An unintelligible noise came from Rist's mouth.

A thousand thoughts ran amok in Calen's head, none of them able to make sense of the other. He had to squeeze his hands around the spear even tighter to stop them from shaking. *Uraks.*

They were human in shape, but the larger of the two was easily over seven feet tall. Its shoulders were heavy and broad, and its dense muscles rippled with every movement. Its ashen-grey skin was thick and rough, almost like it was made of leather. Of everything, its sharp, angular face was the least human. The pale skin made it seem almost bereft of life, while its thin bluish lips curled back to reveal a yellow set of sharp, vicious teeth.

It wore no shoes of any description, but battered pieces of plate mail covered its legs, secured with thick straps of leather. Its chest bore no such protection; the exposed flesh was crisscrossed with half-healed wounds and scars of battles long past. What struck Calen the most, though, were its eyes. The irises were as red as blood, and the pupils were long and sharp, like those of a kat. He had never seen one up close before.

The smaller of the two Uraks looked similar to its companion, although it was around a foot shorter, and its skin had more of a brownish hue to it. Like the larger one, it wore no shoes but bore a ragged iron chest plate and vambraces to match.

It only took a couple of seconds for the Uraks to notice Calen, Dann, and Rist huddled together a stone's throw away with dumbstruck looks on their faces. Wrapping a thick grey hand around the shaft of the axe buried in the crumpled heap of the wolfpine, the larger of the two shouted something at the smaller one. Its voice was harsh, like stones crashing down the side of a mountain. Calen could not understand anything it said.

Without hesitation, the smaller Urak charged towards the group at a pace that Calen would not have thought possible, given its size. It swung a jagged sword over its head, unleashing a guttural howl. The charred-black sword was nearly four foot long, with a translucent gemstone set into the blade, just above the crossguard.

Calen heard the familiar whistle of Dann's arrow only half a second before he saw it jutting out just above the armour on the creature's chest. It did not slow it down. Within seconds, it was upon them.

Rist was the closest one to it. Twisting out of its way, he jabbed his spear straight for the creature's legs. He missed by the thickness of a hair, then took a backswing from the pommel of the beast's sword. It struck him right in the chest and sent him tumbling into the base of a tree. He didn't move.

Calen roared. His pulse was like fire in his veins, fear

driving him on as much as anything else. The Urak evaded the first jab of his spear with alarming ease, but found Calen just as well equipped to dodge its return strike.

When Dann planted a second arrow, this time in its abdomen, the creature erupted in a frenzy of flailing swings. Calen lost his footing. Tripping over a loose stone, he went crashing to the ground. Smelling blood, the creature lunged after him. In a panic, Calen heaved his spear up into the air behind him, turning as he fell, eroding every last bit of strength he had left in his body as he did.

As the Urak lunged downward at Calen, it was trapped by its own momentum, helpless as the spear plunged straight through its exposed neck, spraying blood down over Calen. The weight of the creature as it collapsed pinned the spear into the ground, leaving both suspended in mid-air above Calen. Its piercing red eyes, void of life, still somehow burned with anger as they stared through him. A putrid smell of rotted flesh wafted from its open mouth, nearly emptying the contents of Calen's stomach.

Calen didn't have long to catch his breath. A blood-chilling roar erupted from the remaining Urak. It bounded across the forest floor, axe in hand. Branches and plants crumbled beneath its powerful legs as it covered the distance between them with ease. By the time it reached them, a number of arrows jutted from its unarmoured chest. Enough to have killed a man twice over.

Dann attempted to nock another arrow, but the creature caught him with a vicious kick to the chest. Calen thought he heard a crunch as Dann's knees buckled, and he fell to the floor in a heap.

His mind was racing. Every fibre in his body burned in a symphony of exhaustion and pain. He didn't know if Dann or Rist were alive. Neither of them moved.

The massive Urak placed one hand on the body of its fallen companion. Then, with a terrifying display of strength, it yanked the limp corpse free from the spear as if pulling a splinter from a block of soft butter. Blood fountained over Calen as the creature held the corpse above him. Then it tossed it to the ground a few feet away, without even looking to see where it landed. There was no sense of loss on its face. No sobbing, no whimpers.

Calen's heart pounded like hammer on anvil. Slow, methodical thumps echoed in his ears.

The creature's chest lifted and dropped in heavy breaths. Its mouth twisted into what could almost be called a grin. Its tongue dripped thick beads of saliva down its jagged teeth. The massive half-moon blade glittered in the pale moonlight, a mix of beauty and misery forged in steel.

With its gaze fixed firmly on Calen, the Urak whispered something in its guttural tongue before raising the axe above its head with both hands. Its horrid red eyes burned into Calen's skull. Time slowed down as the blade fell. Calen saw what it did to the wolfpine, and he would fare no better.

The panic in his heart gave way to a sudden sense of acceptance. He had always heard that your life flashes before your eyes in the moments before death. It's what all the bards and storytellers said. How they truly knew, Calen wasn't sure. It was not as if they had fought in the wars they sang of. It didn't matter either way. He didn't have long to look back on, but he would like to see Haem's face again.

A blinding light filled the space around the hulking shape of the Urak, a flash as bright as the sun. Calen heard someone screaming, shrieking, as if the very noise was burning their throat from the inside out.

The axe never fell.

The massive creature dropped to its knees, the ground shaking as it did. Its arms sagged down to its sides. The axe rang out harmlessly as it fell from the Urak's lifeless fingers.

Swaying where it knelt, it collapsed on its side with a heavy thud. Smoke and the repugnant smell of burning flesh filled Calen's nostrils as it wafted back and forth in the wind, emanating from a horrid scorch mark on the creature's back. The previously ashen-grey skin had been melted and disfigured into an oozing, pitch-black liquid.

Calen retched as the smell hit the back of his throat. Coughing violently, he peeled his eyes away from the charred remains of the Urak that had attacked him, searching for whatever had brought that behemoth to its end. He squinted to see. The mixture of smoke and exhaustion stuck his eyes together.

"Rist?"

CHAPTER 7

Seeing is Believing

Rist dropped to his knees. Exhaustion ached throughout his body. His legs felt like reeds in the wind, and he didn't have the strength to keep himself upright.

He had been knocked unconscious when the smaller of the two creatures caught him in the chest. When he came to, all he saw was that beast standing over Calen, that monstrous axe raised over its head. Something just took over. He felt a fire burning in his chest, moving up through his arms, and searing pain consumed everything as the fire moved. *What did I do?*

Beads of sweat cascaded down his forehead. His shirt was stuck to his back. The smell of charred flesh permeated the air, causing his stomach to turn. He held his hands out in front of himself, turning them over and back again, trying to find something, anything. There wasn't a single mark on them. Nothing.

"Rist?" Calen's voice was weak and tired, but it dragged Rist out of his own head.

Looking up, he saw Calen on the ground a few feet from him, propped up on his arms. His clothes were ripped and torn, decorated generously with blood. Beside him were two large bodies. One was soaked in blood, with a gaping wound in its neck. The other was a charred, crumpled mess of burnt flesh and smoke. With a sudden retch, he vomited on the ground.

"Rist!" Calen's voice pierced through the fog in his mind. Rist was finding it hard to focus on anything. He was exhausted, as if the energy had been leeched from his bones. His thoughts danced through his head like girls at the town square, paying him no heed, always just out of reach.

Calen stood over him now, struggling to carry the weight of his own body. "Rist, are you okay? Did you see what happened? It was standing over me... that axe..." Calen glanced at the axe, lying on the ground by the body of that monster, its wicked half-moon blade slick with blood from the wolfpine. "I thought I was dead..."

Rist took a deep breath, attempting to collect his thoughts. "I'm okay," he sighed. "Dann?"

Panic spread on Calen's face. He sprinted to Dann's side as fast as his legs could carry him. He collapsed to his knees beside him, more from exhaustion than by choice, by the looks of it. "Shit, Dann... Dann? Dann, please be all right!"

Rist pulled himself to his feet, wincing as he stood upright. His entire body was battered. The wound in his leg burned brightly. In the panic, he had forgotten about it; fear had concealed the pain. Now, as his heart settled, the pain came rushing back like a rockslide. *First a bear, then an arrow, then… Uraks.*

He looked over the bodies of the fallen creatures. They were almost human, if not for the greyish leathery skin, the red eyes, and the jagged yellow teeth.

He turned his focus back to his friends. Calen had his hand at the back of Dann's head. Dann's eyes were closed.

"Dann! Wake up!" Calen shook him back and forth, gently at first, but more aggressively when he got no reaction. For a moment, Rist's stomach sank.

Dann's eyelids flickered. "Ugh… stop shaking me. Curse you. What happened? Did I get it?" Dann's voice was hoarse, as if waking up from a long nap. *Thank the gods.*

Calen collapsed backwards, dropping Dann's head as he did. Dann let out a sharp groan as his head cracked off the tree trunk.

Rist needed to sit down. He *needed* to sleep. He felt like he could barely hold his eyes open.

"Curse you, Calen," Dann groaned, rubbing the back of his head. His eyes fell to the bodies of the two creatures, lingering on the larger, its back a muddled mess of melted skin. "What…. what happened?" Fear laced his voice.

"I don't know," Calen said. "One minute it was standing over me, its axe raised up over its head. Then there was a flashing light, so bright I could barely see. Then… it collapsed. Dead. That wound on its back."

Rist nodded. "Yeah, I woke up to Calen calling me. Both of them were on the ground."

A pang of fear rushed through his mind. Had Calen seen what he did? What *did* he do?

Dann nodded and exhaled loudly. They sat in silence for a few minutes. The sounds of the forest echoed in the background.

"We should probably get moving," Dann said, a steely look on his face. He pulled himself up to a seated position. "If we're going to carry one of these guys with us back to The Glade, we need to start moving now to get there before the sun sets tomorrow." Dann's words hung in the air for a second.

"Bring one of them with us?" A look of disbelief crossed Calen's face. "Why in the void would we want to bring one of them with us, Dann?"

Dann shrugged. "Well, nobody will believe us if we don't, and they need to know they are out here. And it's our chance to pass The Proving – and become victors of The Hunt. Nobody is bringing back anything worse than these guys. Uraks, Calen!"

Calen said nothing. His mouth tightened into a thin line.

"But… what are they doing here? Uraks haven't been seen anywhere near The Glade in at least two years, not since—" Rist saw the look on Calen's face and didn't finish his sentence.

"I don't know, but for whatever reason, they are here," Dann said. "We need to bring one back. Well… maybe just the head?"

Rist couldn't hide the look of surprise on his face. "The head?"

"Well, I figure the entire body is probably too heavy for us to carry – or even drag. We could fit the head in one of our bags. Kind of just makes sense, really." Dann spoke with a matter-of-fact tone; it was clear that he had already decided this was the best course of action. He had always been that way. Once a decision was made, Dann Pimm's mind was like stone.

Dann got to his feet without waiting for a reply. He hobbled over to the two corpses; his hand held to the spot on his chest where the Urak had kicked him. Rist glanced over towards Calen, who had remained silent during the entire discussion. Calen always withdrew into himself when anything to do with Haem was mentioned. Uraks definitely fell into that category.

"Are you okay?" Rist placed the palm of his hand on Calen's shoulder and lowered his head to look him in the eyes.

"Yeah... Yeah, I'm fine." Calen shrugged off Rist's hand and got to his feet, making his way over to Dann. Rist sighed, sitting there for a moment before standing up and joining the others.

"Which one?" Calen said.

"Huh?"

"Which head are we taking?" Calen's voice was cold, void of emotion.

Dann didn't seem to notice. He folded his arms as he pondered. "Well, I'm thinking the smaller one. I don't think the bigger one will fit in any of our bags, and I don't fancy holding a bloody head in my arms the entire way back to The Glade."

"Okay. Well, get it done, and let's get moving, then." Calen didn't wait for a response. He just walked away and sat in silence on a nearby log.

Dann turned his head towards Calen and then back towards Rist, unfolding his arms. "What's his problem?"

Rist raised a questioning eyebrow. "You don't see how fucked up this is? Not to mention… Haem?"

"Oh…"

"Well… Get it done," Rist said as plainly as he could. Then he turned and walked over to join Calen on the log.

They sat there listening to the forest until they heard the loud thump of metal sinking into flesh. Calen winced at the sound. Rist felt his stomach lurch again. A grunt was followed by another thump. A few moments later, Dann stood in front of them, blood seeping through the fabric of his bag.

"Didn't really think that through," he said with a shrug.

"You never do," Rist said.

As they set off into the forest, Rist looked back at the bodies of the Uraks. The axe, now wet with fresh blood, lay beside the headless body of the smaller creature. The gemstone set into the axe blade seemed to give off a red glow as the twilight sun faded over the horizon.

His eyes dragged over to the body of the larger Urak and the gaping wound of seared flesh on its back. The unnerving sound of crackling skin still wafted through the air. He looked down at his hands once more.

What did I do?

CHAPTER 8

I See You

The orange glow of the setting sun drifted through the canopy as they approached the edge of the forest near The Glade. They had walked through the night and straight through the next day. They were late; they should have been back in The Glade that morning. Calen's legs burned, struggling under the weight of exhaustion. His clothes were torn in more places than he could count, and his body was painted with enough cuts and bruises to last a lifetime. He wanted to sleep for days.

Up ahead of him, Dann trudged through the gradually thinning undergrowth. His bag dangled over his shoulder, stained red with dried blood. Rist lagged a bit behind. Calen had a feeling his leg was giving him a lot more trouble than he was letting on. "Nearly there now, Rist."

Rist's response came in short bursts, separated by sharp huffs of exertion. "I'm not tired. Are you tired? I could keep going for days. I bet Dann is tired. Dann, are you tired?"

Dann chuckled up ahead. "Not long now, Rist."

Blisters had formed on Calen's feet at some point over the

last few hours. The grinding pain was a constant reminder as his feet rubbed against the inside of his boot. He grimaced and kept walking. *I'm getting a new pair of boots.*

In the space of just a few minutes, the forest began to thin out. The ground regained a firm spring, and the heaviness in the air dissipated as the trees peeled away. When they emerged from the forest, the cool breeze that swept across Calen's face was almost enough to drag a smile out of him – almost.

As soon as Rist was out of the forest, he collapsed in a heap on the ground, like a puppet whose strings were cut.

"Rist!" In a panic, Calen bounded over to where Rist lay motionless in the grass. When Calen reached him, he was lying on his back, staring up at the sky, a hazy grin on his face.

"I'm fine," he said with a satisfied sigh. Closing his eyes for a moment, he inhaled deeply and smiled from ear to ear. "I wasn't sure if we were ever going to make it out of that forsaken forest. It's nice to look up at the sky and not see branches and leaves."

Rist's focus waned for a second as he stared at his hands, covering every inch of them with an intense gaze. Relief poured through Calen. He allowed himself to collapse down beside Rist. They lay there for a minute, just staring up at the unobstructed blue sky.

"Are you two nearly done?" Dann said. "Because it looks like someone has noticed we're back."

Calen dragged himself into a seated position, looking out over the fields, squinting in the fading light from the sunset. A few hundred feet to the northwest, five horse riders were galloping towards them. As they drew closer, Calen could make out the riders. Leading the group were his father and Erdhardt, with Lasch, Tharn, and Jorvill Ehrnin galloping alongside them.

As the riders reached the young men, Vars slung his leg over the saddle and slid off the horse in one smooth motion. He crashed straight into Calen, embracing him so tightly that Calen thought he might actually break a rib.

"I thought maybe…" The words escaped Vars's mouth as nothing more than a hushed whisper.

Calen pulled his father into a tighter embrace, deciding the pain was worth it. "I'm okay."

Lasch and Tharn embraced Rist and Dann in a similar fashion. After they had all made their greetings, Erdhardt spoke up. "It is good to see you boys – men – back safely. We feared the worst when the sun sank into the ocean, and you had not emerged from Ölm. The last of the groups arrived back hours ago." His eyes passed over Calen, Dann, and Rist one by one. Despite the scarcity of light, Calen knew he was taking in everything: the torn clothing, the cuts, the blood. They must have looked like they were half-dead. "What has happened?"

The boys all exchanged a look with each other, agreeing with a nod.

"The story might take a while," Calen said, unable to hide the hesitation in his voice.

"Take the time you need. The truth is what is important." Erdhardt folded his arms across his chest, a sombre look in his eyes.

Calen let a small sigh slip out before diving into the

events of the last few days. He left out what had happened to the larger Urak. He didn't really know what had happened after all, but Rist had been acting funny since, despite what he had said. They didn't push as to how it actually died, and none of them noticed when Calen moved swiftly onward. The group of men listened intently to Calen, exchanging a few looks between them from time to time. A gasp escaped Lasch's mouth when Calen told them how Fritz had shot Rist in the leg with the arrow.

Dann chimed in occasionally, mostly just to elaborate on his own feats of heroism, which received more than its fair share of glares from the men. Rist, for the most part, stayed mute. His eyes appeared slightly glazed over, as if lost in deep thought.

When Calen finished, there was a brief silence. Just the chirping of crickets accompanied the pale moonlight as the twilight sky gave way to the night. Erdhardt spoke first. "Are you sure, Calen? Uraks haven't been seen here in at least two years, not since—"

Dann cut him short by thrusting the bag into his arms, a little more forcefully than would usually be considered respectful. Erdhardt did not chastise him. He simply opened the bag and took a long look at its contents. His face twisted into a resigned frown. He passed the bag back to Vars, who had much the same reaction.

"Very well," Erdhardt finally said, unfolding his arms and nodding as if only to himself. "Join us on the horses and let us return to the square. The councils – and everyone else – will be eager to hear what you have told us."

As the horses approached the tents in the market square, crowds formed around them, eager to hear whispers of what trouble they had run into that caused them to be so late. Calen noticed a few of the other young men that he had seen near the brazier on the first day. By the look in their eyes, they had already started celebrating the conclusion of The Proving.

Erdhardt led the group on horseback through the forming crowds and directly to the feast tent, where they dismounted.

Ferrin Kolm stood guard at the entrance. The warm smile on his freckled face turned to a look of concern as he spotted Calen and the others. Erdhardt called him over as they approached. "Ferrin, please find Iwan Swett, Tarren Netley, and Jon Hildom for me. Ask that they make an audience with the council in this tent before the hour is out."

"Yes, Master Hammersmith, I will do now." Ferrin nodded, taking another worried look at Calen and the other boys.

"Thank you, Ferrin. Also, please ask them to bring their sons."

Ferrin tilted his head as if to question why, but he thought better of it and simply nodded before heading off into the crowd.

Satisfied, Erdhardt turned back towards the group. "Come, boys. Let's get you some food and water. Vars, would Freis be able to look at Rist's leg?"

Vars nodded. He paused to give Calen's arm a gentle squeeze before disappearing in the same direction as Ferrin.

"I think it best we go and let our families know the boys have returned safely. We do not want rumours reaching them first," Lasch said.

"Aye, you're right," Tharn said. "I believe they are over near the campfires, enjoying a song or two. We'd best head over and return swiftly." With that, the two of them were gone, leaving only Jorvill and Erdhardt to lead the boys into the feast tent.

The tent was massive, easily a hundred feet long and nearly just as wide. It seemed even larger inside than it was outside. The bone-white canvas of the tent was supported along the walls by massive wooden supports, with thick lengths of rope binding everything together in knots and loops. The bulk of the tent was taken up by rows of long wooden tables and benches. Brilliant white sheets were draped across each table, contrasted by rich emerald-green cloths that marked where people should be seated. Regardless of how tough the year had been, no expense was ever spared for The Proving.

According to Jorvill, the feasting had been postponed when the boys never returned that morning. At present, the only occupants of the tent were the villages' council members, who all sat at a long, elaborately-dressed table at the other end of the massive tent. The table itself had to be about twenty feet long, large enough to fit the councils of all seven villages. They were so engrossed in conversation that they didn't notice the tent's new occupants.

"You boys take a seat. We'll be back in a minute," Erdhardt said, gesturing for Jorvill to follow. It only took a few minutes before Erdhardt and Jorvill returned, carrying baskets full of bread, cheese, and meat. Three women followed behind them, carrying large tankards of mead and buckets of water. Erdhardt and Jorvill tossed the baskets onto the table. Dann caught a small roll of bread in mid-flight as it bounced free from the impact.

"Well, eat up. You must be starving," Erdhardt said. He accepted the tankard of mead one of the women offered him. "My thanks, Meera," he said with a short bow of his head. She gave him a polite smile and returned his nod, then flitted away to carry out what was most likely a hundred other tasks before the feasting began.

They ate in silence, almost choking on their food as they shovelled it into their mouths like hungry dogs. Calen felt a pain in his stomach as he ate, but he couldn't stop himself from eating more. Food had been scarce on the return journey. They dared not stop too long in any one place for fear of losing too much time, and when they did, they were often too tired to think about much else, other than lying down.

Vars was the first to return, with Freis, Ella, and Faenir in tow. The wolfpine did not stand on ceremony; it dodged past Erdhardt and bounded towards Calen in one massive leap, knocking him clean off his chair. There was a warm rumble in his throat as he nuzzled his nose into Calen's chest.

"Faenir, get off—" Calen stopped short of finishing his sentence, instead wrapping his arms around Faenir and pulling him in tightly.

"Ahem."

Calen looked up to see his mother staring back down

at him, unimpressed. He shoved Faenir aside, much to the wolfpine's disagreement. Calen got to his feet, patting down his shirt with his hands as if he would somehow be able to brush away the dirt and blood stains. Freis looked him up and down, horror etched on her face at the sight of him. She pulled him into a fearsome hug. His ribs complained, but Calen didn't say a word. He just closed his eyes and welcomed the comforting embrace.

"I'm just glad you're okay," Freis said. She pulled out of the hug and gave him a loving smile. Her eye lingered for a moment, betraying a momentary flash of intense sadness. It was one that Calen knew well; the knowledge of loss, and the fear of its return. Puffing out her cheeks, Freis turned to Rist, to examine her new patient. "Now, I hear you got yourself into all manner of trouble out in that forest. Let me take a look."

Rist protested as Freis fussed over him, examining him from head to toe. She turned back to Calen, her lip turned up in a half-smile. "You *do* listen." She held up the strip of Rist's shirt that had been wrapped around his leg. It was slightly damp and mottled with the greyish-green poultice that Calen had made. Calen couldn't help but swell with pride. *Of course, I do.*

Ella nodded to Calen. "I'm happy you didn't die," she said, her tone flat. Calen couldn't help but cough out a short laugh. Ella gave him a quick hug. "I'm glad you are back."

"Me too. I didn't know you cared."

Ella gave Calen a sly wink before joining Freis in her inspection of Rist's wound.

Not long passed before Tharn and Lasch returned, with the rest of their families in tow. Elia and Ylinda directed glancing smiles at Calen as they rushed to fuss over their own children. Ferrin was the last to enter the tent, and with him came Iwan Swett, Tarren Netley, and Jon Hildom. Anger burned in Calen when Fritz, Kurtis, and Dennet crept in after them.

Calen didn't see Dann stand up. "You have some nerve coming in here after what you did. I'll put you down where you stand if you take one step further. I—"

Erdhardt raised his hand in the air. Even Dann knew that meant for him to shut up. "I will have none of that, young Master Pimm. They have been brought here in the interest of fairness. We cannot simply take your word on what has happened."

Dann's face was incredulous. "Our word? Rist has an arrow wound in his leg. Do you think he shot him—"

Erdhardt glared at Dann. "Sit down. *Now.*"

Dann did as he was told. Erdhardt was a fair man with a warm heart, but even Dann's stray tongue knew its limits.

Erdhardt turned, opening his arms to the group. "Now, if you will all join me, there is a matter that we must discuss. I have asked the councils of all seven villages to hear this matter. I trust there is no disagreement with this?"

"Aye, I should think not," came a low but clear response from Tharn Pimm. Mumbles of agreement followed. A few muffled grumbles came from Iwan Swett, but he did not argue. Taking one last sweep across the group with his eyes, Erdhardt nodded and gestured for everyone to follow him. He made his way to the long table at the end of the tent.

The chattering from the village council members died away gradually as the group approached, turning to silence as soon as they noticed Calen, Dann, and Rist. The silence remained as Erdhardt and Jorvill made their way around the table and took their seats next to Verna Gritten. Calen couldn't help but think of how alike she and Anya looked. Were it not for the slight evidence of time's touch at the corner of her eyes and mouth, and the odd streak of grey in her hair, they could have been sisters.

As seemed to always be the way, it was Erdhardt who spoke first. "Now that we are all gathered here, Calen, can you please tell aloud what you told us earlier, when we found you at the forest's edge?"

It took Calen a few seconds to realise that he was expected to speak next. He was suddenly aware that every set of eyes around the table were now fixed keenly on him. He cleared his throat and took a step forward. *Well, here goes nothing.*

Once more, Calen recited the story of their time in Ölm Forest. Concern and anger flickered across people's faces. Kurtis and Dennet looked at their feet the whole time, not daring to raise their eyes. Calen thought he saw a grin on Fritz's face, but it was hard to tell from the corner of his eye.

A few unintelligible murmurs passed between some of the council members, which Calen tried to ignore. Anger was replaced by shock at the mention of the Uraks. Even the council members who had shown little interest until that point now sat to attention with perked ears. He once again left out how the larger Urak died, crediting its kill to

Dann's arrow, to which Dann raised an amused eyebrow. Calen was short of breath when he finished. Relief flowed through him as he spoke the last words. Almost as if he were no longer there, the group broke out in a commotion, none of it aimed at Calen.

"Uraks, this close to the villages?"

"That can't be. We would have heard something by now," said a rat-faced man from Talin.

"One of the other groups would have seen them. This is ridiculous—"

"There will be order!" Erdhardt's voice filled the empty tent as he slammed his hand down on the wooden table. The squabbling council members were quick to quiet their tongues. He continued, "There are two things we must establish here. The first is the truth of the altercation between these two groups of young men. The second is to decide what our course of action is regarding this Urak sighting."

A thin man with greyish-white hair was the first to speak. Judging by his clothes, he was from the village of Pirn. The thick brown and cream cloth from which his shirt and trousers were cut was common there. "How, may I ask, are we even to be sure as to the truth of this sighting? It could simply be children making up stories. There hasn't been an Urak sighting in these parts for over two years."

Dann scowled. "Children?"

Erdhardt glared at Dann. His eyes were like steel. Dann turned his face to the floor like a chastised dog. Erdhardt pushed his chair back, got to his feet, and lifted his other hand in the air. In it was Dann's drawstring bag, stained dark with dried blood. He turned the bag upside-down and dumped its contents onto the table, then sat, arms folded.

The group erupted in a frenzy of shouts and roars, mixed with yelps of shock as the Urak's head rolled along the table. It came to a stop in front of Kara Thain, the village elder from Erith. Calen remembered her speaking before The Proving. Her eyes were a piercing ice blue, stark against her dark brown hair, which was slightly greying and tied up in a ponytail. Her beauty was not lost behind her stern expression.

She was one of the few not contributing to the chaos. She was observing. Her eyes flitted between the council members and the Urak's head, unblinking. But it was clear to Calen that behind those icy eyes, she was deep in thought.

"Well… are you lot done?" Erdhardt asked after the shouting had persisted for a touch too long.

"What is the meaning of this, Erdhardt?" demanded a slightly plump lady with oily skin and thinning blonde hair. A deep scowl was set on her face.

"The honesty of these young men was questioned," Erdhardt said. He did not attempt to hide the glare he directed at the thin man from Pirn. "Here is your proof that there were Uraks in Ölm Forest."

It was Jorvill who spoke next. "What are we to do, then? How are we to know how many more, *if* there are any—"

"There are more." Kara's voice was soft, but there was a firm undertone. The council members paused to listen, as they did when Erdhardt spoke. She exchanged glances with the two other members of the Erith Council, as if seeking their blessing before continuing. "Until now, we were not sure if the reports were true. They mostly came in from the likes of hunters and trappers, or the occasional peddler. However, over the past few weeks, the reports have increased in number, and now this." Kara wrapped her fingers around the rotting skull, holding it up in the air. "This is the first shred of solid proof we've seen." The council members exchanged a few murmurs. Kara raised her voice a little, enough to quieten the chatter. "It could be nothing. There were only two, Calen?"

Calen nodded.

"Well," Kara continued, "we know there are Urak clans that call Wolfpine Ridge their home, this is not news to us. We haven't spotted any since the attacks a few years ago, but that could simply be luck. We always knew that they would raid again, eventually."

"But you said the sightings have been increasing in number," said a man with a chest as thick as oak barrels. His arms were the width of Calen's head. His head was bald from front to back, and he had a number of brass rings in his ears and his nose, as was common among the seafaring folk of Salme.

"Yes, I did, Baren. And that is something we should keep an eye on. For now, in Erith, we will put the village guard on alert and perhaps look to erect a long-overdue palisade wall. To all those here who counsel villages along the base of Wolfpine Ridge, I would recommend you do the same."

"Aye, I believe this to be a sound course of action."

Erdhardt folded his arms across his chest and nodded.

"Aye," the council elders of Milltown and Talin said.

"Although we lay not along the edge of Wolfpine Ridge, the villages are one. Our unity is our strength, and should you need it, the village of Ölm will come to your aid."

"As will Salme," said the barrel-chested sailor, Baren.

"And Pirn," said a small raven-haired woman with streaks of grey.

"Many thanks to you, friends. Your words warm my heart," Erdhardt said. "Now that is settled, we have the matter of the altercation between these two groups of young men."

"With all due respect, Hammersmith, both of these groups are of your village. It is an issue for The Glade, not an issue for this council," said the thin man from Pirn.

Erdhardt cocked an amused eyebrow. "Not an issue for this council? This happened in The Proving, a rite of passage for all in the villages." There was a rumble of agreement throughout the group. The thin man from Pirn folded his arms across his chest with an irritated grunt, but he did not argue. Erdhardt nodded. "Okay. Kurtis, Fritz, Dennet. Tell us what happened."

"It was an accident," Fritz said, not waiting for the other two to speak. "I was aiming for the kat, but it was so dark."

Dann barely attempted to suppress a snort.

Ignoring Dann, Erdhardt raised a questioning eyebrow. "And can you explain why, instead of correcting your mistake and tending to the injury you caused, you instead pushed them farther into the forest? And stole the bear pelt?"

"They scared away the kat. That was our kill. We only took what was due to us! And we couldn't trust them to not try and take it back, sir. I did what I thought was smart." The silence that followed Fritz's words was only broken by the sound of Erdhardt's fingers drumming on the table.

"This is The Proving," Erdhardt said, lifting his gaze from the table. "It is meant to throw young boys into the harshest of environments on their own and show them what the world can be like, to forge them into men. To test their skill and their character. Sometimes, the honourable path is not easy, and the easy path is not honourable. This is a lesson that must be learned – and I think it has been. From the point of view of this council, I do not feel any further action needs to be taken. If you will all agree, I believe this to be settled."

There was a quick haze of chatter before a chorus of "Aye" was heard from all members of the council. Calen felt a flare of anger when he saw the smirk spreading across Fritz's face.

"We are settled, then," said the barrel-chested man from Salme, as he rose from his seat.

"No," Erdhardt said. "In the view of this council, the matter is settled, but from the view of The Glade—" Erdhardt looked between Jorvill and Verna, who both nodded. "This is not over. For tonight, we will celebrate The Proving." Erdhardt's eyes locked on Fritz, Kurtis, and Dennet. "Tomorrow, we will revisit this."

Kurtis and Dennet nodded, only lifting their eyes from the ground momentarily. Fritz, however, protested. "That is not fair! You said it yourself. This is The Proving—"

"Shut your mouth, boy," Tarren Netly, Fritz's father, said while giving him a firm slap across the back of the head. "You'll be lucky not to get a lashing."

Tarren was a tall man with a grizzled beard and a stern jaw. He was not known for his soft touch. Calen couldn't help but feel sorry for Fritz. Tarren had seemed to become even colder when Fritz's two brothers died. They died with Haem, pushing the Uraks back through Ölm and into Wolfpine ridge. In a different world, it might have brought Fritz and Calen together. But that world was not this one.

Erdhardt eyed Tarren and Fritz with a grim look as he pushed his chair back and rose to his feet. "I will send word that the feasting is to begin shortly and that the victors of The Hunt are to be announced. All of you who took part in The Proving, we will give you an hour to clean yourselves up and prepare for the feast."

A few filthy looks were exchanged between the two groups of young men as they made their way out of the tent, but no words. None were silly enough to risk incurring Erdhardt's wrath.

"Do you want me to go back with you?" Vars asked as they stepped out into the brisk night air.

"No, that's okay. You all should stay. Start your celebrations. I can go clean up by myself," Calen said with a weak smile. He did not want Freis and Vars fussing over him, and he could do with at least a few minutes on his own. If he could survive The Proving, then he could survive the walk home.

"Don't be too long," Freis said, cupping her hands on either side of Calen's face and placing a kiss on his forehead. "I've left some clothes out for you."

"I won't. I'll be back as soon as I'm ready – and thank you." Calen turned to Dann and Rist, "I'll see you two in about an hour?"

"You think I'll miss the opportunity to get some free mead? I'll need it after what those idiots got away with," Dann said, a scowl on his face.

"They didn't get away with anything, Dann," Rist said, stuffing his hands into his pockets. "Have you ever known Erdhardt to let anyone get away with anything? He said he will revisit it tomorrow. For tonight, can we just get drunk?"

"Agreed," Dann and Calen said together.

Calen felt a sense of relief as he stepped into his room, collapsing onto his bed with a sigh. He lay there for a few minutes, allowing his aching body to sink into his mattress. If it were up to him, he would have lain there all night. *If* it were up to him.

With a sigh, he dragged himself to his feet, scrubbed the dried dirt and blood from his skin, and began to dress in the clothes his mother had laid out. The trousers were a simple pale brown, secured at the waist with dark wooden buttons. The shirt was a pearlescent white, the front opening coming down to his collarbone. Finally, he pulled on a warm coat before stepping out into the chilly night air.

The feast tent was an entirely different spectacle upon Calen's return. It was a cacophony of sound. Every table was packed from one end to the other. Serving girls glided between drunken revellers, ducking and diving under flailing arms, somehow never spilling a drop of mead or dropping a morsel of food. The cheery mead-induced conversations warmed Calen's ears. If he could go the rest of his life without hearing the incessant noises of insects, he would be the happiest man alive.

Music blended with the din of merriment. Travelling bards ambled about between the tables, carrying lutes, harps, or the occasional flute. Their garb was as flamboyant as Calen had come to expect. Wildly ornate coats accented vibrant shirts and trousers, each one more extravagant than the last. Some wore wide-brimmed hats with feathers of all shapes and sizes pluming from the top. Others had beards that draped as low as their waistline, twisted in plaits and coloured with dyes.

"Come on, then. Let's get some food in our bellies," Dann said, appearing beside Calen. "Oh, and some mead." He clapped one hand down on Calen's shoulder; his other hand snatched a tankard of mead from the tray of a passing serving girl. Nothing ever seemed to faze Dann. No matter what happened, he was always back to himself before anyone could tell any different.

"For once, I'm with Dann," Rist said, emerging from behind the flap of the tent, a stiff limp in his walk. He looked like a different man after cleaning the matted dirt and dust from his face.

Calen laughed and nodded in approval. His body ached, and exhaustion still held him firmly in its grasp, but the scene before him gave him a renewed feeling of vigour.

"You clean up well."

Anya was beautiful. Her ember hair rolled down the side of her face. It was striking against her flowing green dress, decorated in a white floral pattern. The scent of honeysuckle drifted through the air around her.

Calen's voice caught in his throat. He wanted to reply, "So do you," but his lips wouldn't listen to his brain. He couldn't help but be angry with himself. He had just faced a bear and two Uraks, yet he couldn't bring himself to speak when Anya stood in front of him.

"Come on, lover boy. We have to get to our table," Dann said, wrapping his arm around Calen's shoulder. Calen wanted to give him a swift elbow to the ribs, and he would have done if he hadn't seen Anya blush.

"Dance with me later?" As soon as the words left Calen's mouth, his heart sank into his stomach. He wanted the ground to open up and swallow him whole.

"Find me after we eat," Anya said. The dimples on either side of her mouth creased as she smiled. Calen felt like leaping into the air. His heart raced as Dann turned him around and walked him into the crowd.

"Smooth," Dann said.

They caught up with Rist and made their way through the chaotic celebrations, over to the table where their families sat. When they arrived, Vars stood up and pulled Calen into a tight hug. He stepped back for a second and gripped Calen by both shoulders, beaming at him.

"My boy… You will always be my boy." Vars's eyes gleamed. "Come on – I'm sure you're starving."

"And thirsty!" Tharn Pimm extended a tankard of mead,

placing it almost forcefully in Calen's hand. Calen couldn't stop his smile from spreading ear to ear as he looked around the table. The Havels, the Pimms, his mother and father, Ella. Family.

He joined Dann and Rist at the table, grabbing greedily at the wide assortment of food that was laid out in front of him. Even after eating earlier, his stomach still rumbled. The hours passed as they all ate and drank, telling stories and tales of days long gone. It was a welcome change from the cold nights in the forest.

Vars was deep in a story about when he and Lasch were young and stole a chicken from Old Master Pimm's coop when Dann leaned in close enough so only Calen could hear, and whispered, "You think maybe, you might have somewhere to be?"

"What do you... oh." A nervous knot twisted in Calen's stomach as he remembered his conversation with Anya. "She probably doesn't even—"

"Get out of that seat right now and go find Anya." A grin crept across Dann's face as he grabbed Calen's hand and looked him dead in the eye. "You got this – now go."

Calen took a deep breath inwards, steeling himself. "I got this." *I do not have this.* He saw Rist nod at him as he stood up, a knowing smile on his face.

Calen tentatively pushed his way through the throng of people that filled the feast tent. Everywhere he looked, people danced and sang, and in every corner of the tent, bards played a different song. How was he meant to find Anya in this madness?

He recoiled as a chill shot up his right arm. "Fuck sake,"

he said, feeling the damp patch on the sleeve of his shirt. "You just have to get it in your mouth—"

"Looking for me?" The sweet scent of honeysuckle hit Calen before he heard the words. Anya stood in front of him, her hands clutching at the corners of her green floral dress. Calen's voice caught in his throat at the sight of her. *Gods damn it. Say something.* "Ehm… I was." *Say something better.*

"I hope you came looking for that dance." Anya raised an eyebrow as she gave Calen a cheeky smile. Her freckles always stood out when she smiled like that. "There's a bard over there," she said, nodding her head towards the other side of the tent, "apparently her music is beautiful, if you wanted to…"

"Let's go!" Calen said, jumping at the opportunity before she changed her mind. "Lead the way."

Calen couldn't stop the smile from spreading across his face – or the shiver from running through his body when Anya took his hand. For some reason, pushing through the crowd again didn't irritate Calen the way it had before. They didn't speak as they made their way over to the other side of the tent. But that suited Calen just fine – he had no idea what to say.

The closer they got to where Anya had pointed out, the more the crowd thinned, and the soft, melodic sound of a woman singing drifted into Calen's ears. He couldn't make out the words, but her voice was mesmerising. A rapturous applause broke out just as they reached the edge of the crowd that stood around the bard.

"She is beautiful," Anya whispered.

The woman sat on the edge of a long table with a lute in her hand, one foot rested on the cross-leg of a chair, and the other on the ground. Her skin was a dark chestnut brown, like the petals of the Dalya flowers that Calen had seen in the window of Anya's home. Her short-cropped hair was as dark as jet, and two dimples held up the edges of her smile. She wore sturdy leather riding boots, and a long purple dress pulled in at the waist by a thin leather belt. It seemed an odd combination to Calen.

Anya was right – she was beautiful.

But Calen knew better than to say that out loud. His father had warned him of that once, when they were drinking in The Gilded Dragon. *A woman can call another woman beautiful, but you can never agree.*

"Thank you," the woman said, giving a slight bow at the waist. "For those of you who have just arrived, my name is Belina Louna. I hail from the western lands of Narvona, and I am privileged to be passing through your village tonight. Now, would you like to hear a traditional Narvonan love song?"

A chorus of cheers broke out at the suggestion. But Calen thought he saw the woman smiling at him and Anya as she spoke.

"Okay, so we call this one, *On Summer Nights.*"

The melody that came from the woman's lute was slow and sweet. Calen could still hear the rumbling of the louder, more up-tempo music coming from other spots inside the feast tent, but they drifted into the back of his mind when she started to sing.

"On summer nights, when the moon paints the sky,
On summer nights, when your touch is all I know.
When the stars shimmer in the sea up high,
And the warmth of your love holds me close…"

The touch of Anya's hand broke Calen's concentration. "Dance with me?"

As if by magic, Calen's heart hammered against his chest, and he could have sworn that his forehead was slick with sweat. He nodded, unable to speak. He tried his best to smile as he took Anya's hand and moved into the open space in front of the bard. *How do you dance?*

Anya reached out and took both of Calen's hands into her own. The light from the candles flickered across her freckled cheeks. Before he knew it, they were moving. Calen followed Anya. He had danced before, but not with a woman – not like this. It wasn't as hard as he thought it would be. All he had to do was follow her feet. How did she know how to dance so well?

Calen blushed when he realised that he had been following Anya's feet so closely that he hardly looked at her face. She giggled at him, letting her head rest on his chest, which only caused his heart to beat faster. It felt nice, though – comforting. He forced his mind to relax. They swayed back and forth, their feet drifting with the music.

"On summer nights, I will hold on to your memory.
When the air is warm, I will sit beneath the old Oak tree.
For your arms, I will yearn, for your voice I will hope.
We will be side by side, again my love, on summer nights."

The crowd clapped and cheered as the lute played out the end of the song. Reluctantly, Calen lifted his head to find that five other couples had joined them in dancing. He felt Anya's head lift off his chest. *No, please stay there.*

Her green eyes glistened as she looked up at him. "That was... lovely."

"It was..."

All other sounds capitulated to the methodical beating of Calen's heart as he held Anya's gaze. It seemed as if time stood still.

"There you are!" Calen nearly leapt out of his skin as Dann clapped his hand down across his back. "Your dad said to come and get you. They're about to announce the victors of The Hunt and... shit." He muttered the last part and mouthed the word "sorry" to Calen as his eyes fell on Anya.

Calen let out a heavy sigh. Dann always had the worst timing. Calen looked back to Anya. "I'm sorry, I have to—"

"It's okay," she said. The smile on her face let Calen know that she meant it. "I'll see you after they make the announcements. Go, go!"

Calen let his head hang back over his shoulders as he and Dann walked away from Anya. "You couldn't have waited, just a minute?"

"Yeah... I'll take that one. I probably could have."

A loud clanging noise rang out through the tent as they sat back down at the table with their families. Erdhardt stood at his table, knocking a spoon off a steel tankard. The ringing resonated through the tent with surprising volume.

"It is with great pride that we look out over these tables tonight. Our boys have become young men." He paused for a second as his eyes swept through the tent. "Everyone that entered Ölm has returned to us, some with a few more scars than when they entered." His voice dipped into a sombre tone. "But they have returned. That has not always been the case."

He raised his tankard in the air. "I ask you all to join me in a toast. To all the young men who have returned to us, and to those that never did. To the young men who have passed through The Proving, and to the young women who have nothing to prove."

A raucous cheer erupted all over the tent. Calen noticed a smug look on Ella's face as she raised her cup in celebration.

Erdhardt raised his tankard slightly higher, and Calen joined the rest of the crowd in following suit. Erdhardt repeated the blessings of the gods, as he did before they entered Ölm. "May The Mother embrace you and The Father protect you. May The Warrior guide your hand and The Maiden guide your mind. May The Smith keep your blade sharp and The Sailor see you to safe shores."

The words were echoed through the tent.

"And now it is time to announce the victors of The Hunt. Those young men who went above and beyond, those who stared fear in the eyes and did not blink. This year, The Proving has provided many a surprise and many a test. You have brought us the pelts of kats bigger than I have ever seen, and wolfpines and boars aplenty. It has truly been a year like no other. However, this year has brought us something that has not been seen before. Something that has united all the councils in unanimous vote."

Each council member raised their tankards in the air in a note of agreement. The tension in the air was palpable as everyone sat in anticipation.

"A group of young men were driven through Ölm Forest, all the way to the foot of Wolfpine Ridge. They have proven themselves beyond their years, and I am proud to say that they hail from right here in The Glade." Cheers and shouts erupted from the tables where villagers of The Glade were sitting. "They returned to us from the depths of Ölm Forest only a few hours ago. With them, they brought something that not one of us on this council expected to see – the head of an Urak."

Shock and disbelief spread through the crowd like a wave.

"Settle down, settle down. The councils have spoken at length with regard to the possible Urak threat, and we have a plan of action. For now, join us one more time in raising your cups in a toast to these three young men. Calen Bryer, Dann Pimm, and Rist Havel – victors of The Hunt."

CHAPTER 9

A Game of Chance

A couple of days had passed since the feast night, most of which were a blur. After Calen, Rist, and Dann were announced as victors of The Hunt, the tent had erupted in shouts and cheers, and the mead was free flowing until the early hours of the morning. Calen's head still had not recovered from the mead–induced fuzziness he endured the morning after.

Calen winced as the morning sun sprayed through the dense clouds overhead, catching him by surprise. He was on his way to meet Dann and Rist at his father's forge. A delivery of armour and weapons had to be made to the port in Milltown, and Vars had asked him if he would make the journey. It was a perfect opportunity to visit the Milltown markets and spend a bit of their victors' purse.

When he arrived at the forge, he did not see any sign yet of Dann or Rist, but the clanging of hammer on steel emanated from within. Ducking out from the crispness of the frosty morning air, Calen felt the heat hit him like a wall as he stepped inside. He had spent an uncountable number of hours inside the walls of this forge, the sweltering air forcing his skin to rain sweat as he methodically beat the hammer down on folded steel. He never had the same love for it that his father did – nor the talent – but he enjoyed spending the time together. Ever since Haem died, he found himself in there more and more often.

Calen nodded at Kurtis, who stood in the corner, sweat streaming down his forehead as he worked the bellows. There was a grim look on his face, but he nodded back. He had taken his punishment a lot better than the other two. The night after The Proving, Kurtis, Fritz, and Dennet were called before the council. It was decided that each of them should spend one cycle of the moon working for Vars, Lasch, and Tharn as punishment for stealing the bear pelt and pushing the boys farther into the forest. There was protest, but in the end, Erdhardt's word was law.

Vars stood over an anvil, hammer in hand. His chest was bare, besides the thick black cowhide apron that he wore while working. His forearms pulsed with effort from whatever it was he had just finished, and sweat dripped from every patch of exposed skin. When he saw Calen enter the forge, Vars patted invisible dust from his apron and tossed his hammer on the table beside him.

"Stay there, two seconds," he said, not giving Calen a chance to speak. He disappeared into the back of the forge, then emerged a couple of seconds later with a thick cloth bundle in his hands. "I figured it was about time that you had one you could truly call your own."

Calen took the bundle carefully into his outstretched arms, his eyes flitting between it and his father's expectant face. It was surprisingly heavy.

"Well, unwrap it," Vars said, a touch impatient, rubbing his hands back and forth over themselves. Calen felt a bit uneasy as he held the heavy cloth bundle. His father was not usually the type of man to show any kind of nerves. He peeled back the cloth as if whatever was inside might jump out and strike him. A glint of steel flashed at him from within the bundle. He let the cloth wrapping fall down around his hand, revealing a shimmering steel sword.

The blade was effortlessly smooth, sharp on only one edge, and slightly curved, not like the typical style of sword Calen was used to seeing in Illyanara. It looked as if it had been made to slice through the clouds. The polished steel shone in waves of oranges and reds as the light of the forge flickered across its pristine surface.

The crossguard was simple. Starting as a silver bar set perpendicular to the blade, its centre pierced upwards into the blade and downward into the handle like the points of a star. Its handle was wrapped in dark emerald-green leather and masterfully set, with ornate swirls and spirals etched into its surface. The pommel looked like a thick silver coin set at the base of the handle. Calen could have spent hours just looking at it.

"It was given to me a long time ago," Vars said as he gazed down at the sword. "And now it's time that I pass it on to you. It's an elven blade, better than anything I could make myself. The curve in the blade allows for smoother, cleaner strikes. Not as good at punching through armour, but if you're quick enough, that won't matter." He nodded to himself, his eyes drifting across the sword.

Calen was still in shock. "Dad… I—"

"You need not say anything. I cannot give you much, Calen, but I can give you this," Vars said with a half-smile. "Give it a swing. Feel it."

Calen took a step back, letting the cloth bundle fall to the floor. He gripped the sword tightly with both hands. The leather felt smooth against his skin.

"Hand-and-a-half," Vars said. His head followed the flight of the blade as Calen swung it with one hand, moving through some of the forms that Vars had taught him. It felt perfect in his hands. It was almost weightless, perfectly balanced.

When he looked back at Vars, he was holding a brown leather scabbard fitted with straps of green leather, similar to what the blade's handle was wrapped with. "No sense in having the sword and not being able to carry it. A gift from Tharn."

Calen could not have wiped the smile from his face even if he wanted to. He took the scabbard from Vars and fixed it to his belt, sheathing the blade. "Thank you, so much." Calen wrapped his arms around Vars and pulled him into a hug, which he held for a few seconds.

"There is no need to thank me, Calen. You have filled me with more pride than I ever thought possible. The man you have become is thanks enough." Calen held his left hand on the hilt of his new sword, unwilling to break contact with it. "Come, the cart is already loaded. Let's just take a last look over it before you head off."

Rist and Dann were waiting for them when they stepped out from the forge into the brisk morning; their breath plumed in streaks through the air.

"Ready to go?" Rist said, pulling his coat tight around himself.

"Just about," Calen replied. "We're just going to head around back and check the load before we set off."

As they turned the corner around the forge, Calen went straight to Vars's horse, Drifter. His reins were already set, and he was ready to go.

"Ready for a bit of a trip, boy?" Calen asked, running his hand along the side of Drifter's face. Drifter had been his father's horse for as long as Calen could remember, as much a part of the family as Faenir was.

"Everything looks good," Vars called from the back of the cart. "Darda will be waiting for you at the port." Vars made his way around to the front of the cart, rubbing dirt off his hands with a small cloth that he then shoved into the pocket at the front of his apron. "He's expecting you around midday. Just bring the cart up around the back, and he'll help you unload the stock. Drop off the delivery, and then you boys enjoy a good night."

"Okay, perfect." Calen cupped his hands to his mouth and blew warm air into the space between them, then rubbed them together for heat. "And again, thank you for the gift."

Vars embraced Calen. "Travel safely, and I will see you when you get back."

They finished up with some final checks, ensuring the cart was in working order. Then, with a firm shake, Calen checked that all the ropes were secure. Once they were set, one by one, they all climbed up onto the front of the cart.

"Hey. What's that?" Dann said. He pulled back the bottom of Calen's coat to reveal the sword his father had gifted him, secured within the emerald green leather scabbard.

Calen swatted Dann's hand away, pulling his coat back over the sword. "It's a gift from my father," he said curtly.

"Hey, no need to be rude. It's beautiful is all. You'll have to show me it properly when we're back for the night."

Calen nodded, twisting his mouth up into a placating smile that could have been taken as a frown. He wasn't sure why he felt uncomfortable showing the sword to Dann and Rist. He just was. Coin wasn't something that any of them had a lot of, and just by virtue of the craftsmanship alone, the sword was worth a lot. Anything with that kind of value always made Calen uncomfortable.

He took the reins firmly in both hands. Waving goodbye to Vars, they set off following the road north, towards Milltown.

The journey to Milltown was a reasonably short one and mostly downhill, only a few hours when travelling by horse and cart. They arrived just before midday, as Vars had said they would. The earlier chill dissipated from the air as the sunlight ebbed away at the blanket of cloud above.

Milltown was the largest of all the villages. In truth, it was more of a town. It was nearly twice the size of The

Glade. Most of it had to do with its small but busy port, which acted as the main supply port from the villages to Gisa. All of Vars's shipments to the North went through Milltown, on to Gisa, and then up the coast to Loria. Calen figured that was the case for most craftsmen in the villages.

Despite its size, the buildings were much the same as those in The Glade, thick and wide-set, built with trees from the outer edge of Ölm Forest. As they drew closer to the centre of the village, the bouncing of the cart let Calen know that the usual dirt track underneath had changed to cobbled stone.

"Well, that's new," Rist said. His speech was jarred as the vibrations pulsing through the cart bounced him up and down on the rough plank of wood that masqueraded as a seat.

Leading the cart down the main street turned out to be more difficult than Calen had remembered. He had forgotten how frantic it was during the big trading periods. The start of summer was one of those periods, with apricots, blueberries, and a plethora of other fruits grown in the southern regions of Epheria coming into season. The ports of Milltown and Salme were always flooded with trading vessels at that time of year, and the streets were thronged with merchants eager to flog their fresh harvests.

Calen tightened his grip on Drifter's reins. The horse was old and reliable, but scared easily. He had to swerve to avoid a woman who had stepped into the middle of the street to shout at a peddler. It would only be a matter of time before he knocked down some poor rambling child or ran over a small dog.

Even in the off seasons, the entire town seemed as if it were simply one big market. The sides of the road were lined with stalls, day traders, and peddlers. The buzz of excitement never seemed to dim. If it weren't for the ever-present, pungent waft of fish emanating from the port, Calen would almost consider it a nice place to live.

"I think Darda's building is just up here," Rist said.

The cobbled stones under the cart gave way to the wooden planks of the docks. Rist pointed to a shop on the right-hand side of the road. A heavy wooden sign hung above the doorway, featuring a large black lion above the words, *Darda Vastion Shipping*.

"And what would make you think that, Rist?" The sarcasm oozed through Dann's words as he smirked to himself.

Ignoring Dann, Calen nodded and pulled the cart down the nearest side street, narrowly avoiding flattening a small child who did not seem to have any heed for personal conservation. After Dann shouted a few choice words at the hapless child, Calen drew the cart up around the back of Darda's shop.

Darda Vastion was an abrupt man, not impolite but without any time for dawdling. It took less than ten minutes from him answering the door for the entire cart to be unloaded and double-checked for anything left behind.

"Thank you very much, young Master Bryer. Tell your father I send my thanks. His delivery is as high-quality as ever," Darda said as he shook Calen's hand.

"I will, of course," Calen replied with a smile.

"Oh, and young Master Bryer, congratulations on The Hunt. You both as well," Darda said with a shallow bow towards Dann and Rist, who were sitting up on the cart. Before any of them could reply, he was back inside his shop with the door closed. The lock clicked into place before a "thank you" could escape Calen's lips.

"Strange man." Dann's eyes were still fixed on the rear door to Darda's shop.

"Agreed," Rist said.

Calen leapt up into the front of the cart and shoved Dann aside, despite his protests. He grabbed the reins with both hands and ushered Drifter onward into a slow walk.

"Looking for a room, young sirs?" enquired a fair-haired man in a long blue coat as they drew the cart into the stable yard of The Two Barges. He was in his mid-thirties, his face dotted with freckles, with a crease at the corner of his mouth that showed when he smiled.

"Aye," Calen replied.

The group dismounted to greet the man, then retrieved their bags from the back of the cart.

"Happy to hear. Barret, see that the horse is fed and watered and the cart secured," he barked at a young boy, no more than fourteen summers. The boy nodded and set about his business, guiding Drifter over towards the blocks. "Well met, my name is Gawain, and I am the stablemaster here. Shall I take you inside to the mistress of the house? She can see to it that your rooms are arranged."

Calen nodded, shaking the man's hand with a firm grip. Calen couldn't help but think that Gawain was altogether too formal for his station. His back was stiff, and his nose was ever so slightly tilted into the air. His long blue coat was crisp, not a crease in sight. His shirt was the same, firmly tucked into the waist of his plain brown trousers.

The man led them through a short entrance corridor. A small woman, no larger than five feet tall, met them as they entered the common room.

"Afternoon," she chirped, a welcoming smile spread across her youthful face. She wore a long blue dress with white frills at the end and a white apron draped over her front. Her long braided hair was a deep brown, tied at the end with a white bow. She was quite pretty and looked a lot younger than Calen had expected, not even thirty summers.

"I am Elena, mistress of The Two Barges inn. I'm delighted to make your acquaintance. I see you have met Gawain already. We have a lovely room available upstairs with three beds, if that takes your fancy?"

"Aye, that would be perfect," Rist said.

Elena nodded, her smile never leaving her face. "Please follow me this way, and I will show you to your room. It will be five coppers a night each if that does suit you?" she said, speaking half over her shoulder as she led them through the lounge and around to the base of the stairs. A quick nod of her head let Gawain know that his presence was no longer required, and he strolled back through the entrance corridor without a word.

"That sounds fine. We'll only be staying one night," Calen said. He cast his eyes around the room. The inn seemed well-kept. The common room was large, with big round tables taking up most of the floor space. The long oak bar was set across the wall to the left of the door Calen had just walked through. It was clean, and the air was warm with the aroma of freshly cooked food – beef stew, if his nose was right.

Being so early in the day, not many people idled around. A group of four hard-looking men sat at a table on the other side of the room, talking away about some troubles out at sea. Something to do with the empire. Calen couldn't help but lean in to catch more of the conversation. But Elena shuffled them up the stairs before he could hear anything. She led them down a long tidy hallway, stopping at the room second from the end. Mistress Elena promptly opened the door and stepped inside, beckoning for Calen, Dann, and Rist to follow. "Come on now. Don't be shy. There are three beds here that I think should do you just fine. The washroom is back down the hallway – last door on the right."

The room was simple and homely, if not a touch small. A window was set into the back wall, where three single beds were lined next to each other, with just enough space between them for one person to stand. A small chair and desk sat in the right-hand corner of the room closest to the door. There was only just enough space for someone to lean back in the chair without bumping off the end of the closest bed. Still, it would do perfectly.

Calen tossed his bag down on the bed at the far left, while Dann jumped onto the bed opposite him, bouncing up and down.

"Will you be eating right away?" Elena asked, her hand lingering on the door frame.

"No, thank you, Mistress Elena," Calen said. "I think we are going to look around the markets. My father tells me that supper here is lovely though. We will be back by dark."

Elena's eyes lit up, and her eyebrows peaked in interest. "Oh, who might your father be?"

"Vars Bryer, Mistress. He's the blacksmith of The Glade," Calen replied as he searched through his bag for his woollen gloves.

"Oh, I know of him. He's a fine man." Elena paused, a smile curling at the edge of her mouth. "Your mother is a lucky woman," she chirped, and then she was gone.

"Well, she's just a big ball of excitement, isn't she?" Dann said, finally sitting still on the mattress.

"I think she's quite lovely." Rist pulled his coat tighter around himself, puffing his cheeks out. "Although, she could do with lighting a fire in this place."

Calen laughed to himself as he checked his pockets for his purse. A light jingling noise disclosed its location. He didn't think he'd ever seen as much coin in his life; he still didn't feel comfortable carrying it around. He had offered it to his parents the morning after the feast, but they had seemed almost offended. Vars just turned and walked out of the room. "Okay, shall we go to the markets? We can wander around and then meet up back here before sunset?"

The sun sank down over the docks as Calen placed an intricately woven silk scarf into his coat pocket, paying careful attention not to crease or mark it. It was a beautiful autumn red, with vines of gold and cream woven through it in the pattern of leaves blowing through the wind. His mother would love it.

He thanked the merchant and started off towards The Two Barges. He raised his hand to his forehead, protecting his eyes from the twilight glow piercing over the rooftops.

The liveliness of the town did not die down with the setting sun. Instead, it transitioned seamlessly from bustling market centre into a hub of nightlife and revelry. In the docks, the sailors gathered in sunken pits of sand, crowded in around braziers. They emptied casks of ale into their tankards as they exchanged adventure stories at the top of their lungs.

"Sunk the ship, so they did," one of the sailors said in a whispered voice, that may as well have been a shout. "Dremin said they 'ad a mage aboard. He tore it apart with magic, so 'e did. But the ones they were after got away. That's why they're 'ere!"

The other sailors leaned in close, their eyes wide open as they drank in the story. Calen couldn't help but perk his ears as he walked by. Sailors were known for their wildly ridiculous stories. Not much else to do at sea, Calen supposed, but the mention of the word "magic" always caught his interest.

"Ensure the boat is moored securely before you begin your patrol. We are not in southern lands to be marooned here. Go, and report back to me before you set off." The commanding voice boomed through the docks. It came from a man with mid-length black hair and a tightly cropped beard. He wore a battle-worn steel breastplate bearing the sigil of a roaring black lion across its width. A long coat of mail dropped down to his knees. A deep red hooded cloak was draped around his shoulders, flapping in the wind. He addressed twenty or so men who were garbed in much the same way, except they did not wear a cloak. Another man stood behind the commander, his black cloak billowing in the wind as he stared off into the distance.

They stood on the deck of a large, broad warship that appeared to have only recently arrived in the docks. Three masts protruded from the deck of the ship, jutting up into the sky, each rigged with cream-white sails. The same roaring jet-black lion on the man's breastplate was emblazoned on the middle, largest sail. *The Black Lion of Loria. What are imperial soldiers doing in Milltown?* Calen slowed his pace. The dim moonlight caused him to squint as he tried to get a better look at the group of soldiers.

There were old wives' tales that the imperial Inquisitors snuck around at night and stole children that misbehaved. His mother had often scared him witless with those stories. But Lorian soldiers were rarely seen in the villages, not in the hundred years since the Valtaran uprising. There was just no need for them to venture out that far. When they came south, it was usually a show of force to the high lords, or to accompany the emissaries.

Travelling from the North to the South of the continent, or back the other way, was difficult since the fall of The Order. The continent was split in half by the Burnt Lands and the Darkwood. Those who survived the vast wastelands in the centre of Epheria were then faced with journeying through the cursed woodland. Calen had heard more than a few stories of doomed adventurers who tried to make that journey. Nobody who ventured into the Darkwood ever came out the other side.

This made voyage by boat the only viable option for

those who wished to go from the North to the South of the continent. For that reason, the Lorian Empire seemed content to let the Southern lords of Epheria argue amongst themselves with minimal supervision, only intervening when things did not go the way the empire wished.

Calen was pulled out of his thoughts when he noticed that the man in the black cape now stood at the siderail of the ship, staring across the docks – directly at him. It was a cold unblinking stare.

Calen averted his gaze as quickly as he could, nearly tripping over a wooden crate as he darted for the nearest side street connected to the docks. His heart beat out of his chest, and he cursed himself for being so stupid. Soldiers of the empire were not known for their patience or their good will, and that was not something he wanted to test. They were none of his business.

He picked up his pace, moving as fast as he could without attracting any undue attention. He weaved his way through the streets, taking as many turns as possible without losing his way, eventually finding himself at the front door of the Two Barges inn. His pulse slowed a little as he wiped the sweat from his brow with the sleeve of his coat. He hadn't realised quite how much of a panic he had been in. He laughed out loud at himself. *Sometimes I can be such a fool. He was hardly looking at me.*

His heart was still thumping a bit harder than usual as he pushed open the door to the inn.

Farda flicked his coin up in the air, never lifting his gaze from the other side of the docks, where he had seen that boy skulking about.

He heard the metallic *whoosh* as the coin spun in the air. The flight of the coin did not concern him. He had flipped it enough to know where it would land. On which side it would land was what interested him. His eyes still fixed on the alleyway, he extended his arm out to his side and snatched the coin from mid-air. Finally pulling his gaze from the docks, he opened his palm and looked at the result. *Crowns.*

"Your lucky day, boy," he whispered to himself. *I don't usually tolerate people who snoop, but the gods have spoken.*

Plodding footsteps approached. The familiar creak of the wooden deck reminded him of how long he spent cooped up on that damned ship. He didn't turn to face the approaching soldiers.

"Sir, the ship has been checked over, and she is secured fast to the moorings. Inquisitor Rendall has insisted we start the search. Those Southern rats can't have gotten far."

There was a metallic clink as the coin flew back up into the air. Farda reached out once more and opened his palm. *Lions.*

Farda's black cloak billowed in the breeze as he pondered. He tucked the coin back into his pocket. "Good. I will be joining you."

CHAPTER 10

Where Two Roads Meet

The waft of warm air hit Calen as he walked through the doors of the inn. The honeyed aroma of mead and the oddly satisfying smell of burning wood filled his nostrils. The inn was far busier than it had been earlier in the day. All the tables were packed with townsfolk, travellers, and merchants, who traded stories and played games of dice and cards. The serving women dashed about, filling their bellies with mead and stew. A bard in the corner of the room played a lute. Well, attempted to play the lute. Failed to play the lute.

As he searched the room for Dann and Rist, Calen heard a triumphant roar erupt from across the room. He looked over to see a group of men huddled together about twenty feet from a thick sheet of wood hanging on the wall. They were dressed in furs and worn leathers, their unkempt beards marking them as strangers to the villages. They smashed their tankards off one another in celebration.

On the sheet of wood were five red circles within each other, each one smaller than the last, until the middle was a solid red dot. There, the head of an axe was buried, its handle protruding outward. Calen watched with curiosity as one of the men strutted over to remove the axe from its rest. As the man turned, Calen's eyes widened in surprise.

Dann?

Just as Calen was about to call out to Dann, a hand jutted above the canopy of heads, waving in his direction. There was a lethargy to the wave, as if the owner of the hand were not aware it was being held up in the air.

Rist was seated at a table in the middle of the room, a book splayed out in front of him. His eyes were glued to the pages, a tankard of mead in his hand. Calen made his way over and pulled out the empty chair beside Rist. He let his shoulders sag as soon as his ass touched the seat, his heartbeat finally settling to a normal rhythm.

His face must have betrayed him, as Rist raised a questioning eyebrow.

"I'm fine," Calen panted. "Just got a little overexcited is all. There are imperial soldiers at the docks."

Rist looked up, his eyes narrowing at Calen over the edge of his book. He folded over the corner of the page he was reading, then closed the book. "Here, in Milltown? Why would they be here?"

"I've no idea, but one of them may have caught me staring. I decided not to stick around."

"Isn't Dann supposed to be the one who does stupid things?" Rist suppressed a laugh. He folded his arms and pondered. "I don't think I've ever seen imperial soldiers."

"I have. Once. When Dad brought me along to a trade fair in Camylin. There were imperial guards outside the house of the Lorian Emissary." Calen wasn't eager to stay on the topic. He had heard stories of imperial soldiers. The things they did to Southerners – some of them had to be exaggerated. The stories mostly came from the likes of Valtara and Varsund, where the High Lords had rebelled or started wars. But there were a few from Illyanara. The stories made him shiver. "Dann found a few new friends?"

He tried to get the attention of a young serving girl with porcelain skin and fair blonde hair tied in a long braid.

"He's been at that for an hour or so," Rist said. "Of course, he is fantastic at it." A sigh escaped his lips before he took a deep draught of mead.

"You weren't interested in joining him?" Calen asked. He finally managed to grab the attention of the serving girl and order the mead that had been on his mind since he walked in. His throat felt like it had been rubbed with cotton.

Rist let out a soft chuckle as he peeled open his book. "No, I'm perfectly fine here with my book and my mead. *A History of Magii*. The merchant didn't want to part with it cheaply, but I managed to bargain him down a bit." He licked his finger and used it to turn the page.

"*A History of Magii*? You spend your time mocking me for believing the legends and fairy tales… and then you buy a book about Magii?"

Rist hesitated. Again, he folded over the corner of the page to mark where he had stopped reading, closed the book, and pushed it to the side. "I was curious – you know, after our conversation in the woods. Then I saw the book at the markets and figured that it would be an interesting read."

Calen only half-heard Rist's reply as the serving girl returned with his tankard of mead. He passed her two copper marks for the drink and turned his attention back towards his friend. "Sorry, Rist. I've just been thirsting for this ever since I walked in."

Calen took a strong mouthful of mead, then let out a satisfied sigh. He sat back in his chair to take a proper look around the busy inn.

Three men sat in the corner of the room. Their calm and introverted behaviour painted a stark contrast to the surrounding revelry. All wore thick black mantles that covered most of their garb, but the glow from a nearby candle caught a glint of metal on a blackened studded leather cuirass on one of the men.

"Who are those guys in the corner?" Calen asked. "They don't look like merchants – or soldiers." Calen turned his eyes back to Rist to make sure he didn't draw any more unwanted attention. Not twice in one night.

"Aye, they do not. They were here when I arrived earlier. Haven't moved much either. They just ate some food and have been sitting there, muttering to each other. None of my business – or yours." Rist stooped his head down to look Calen in the eyes.

Calen rolled his eyes, letting out a mocking sigh. "Yes, *Father*. Thank you for your wise words."

Rist responded with unimpressed silence, then returned to his book.

Calen stewed in the silence for a moment, then took a drink of his mead. "I'm going to go see how Dann is getting on. That axe throwing game seems like fun. Sure you don't fancy joining?"

Rist raised his eyes from the book for a moment. "I think I will pass on this one. For the gods, Calen, will you two please try not to cause any trouble? He's already had four meads."

Calen shrugged as he stood up, puffing his cheeks in resignation. "If he's already had four meads, you and I both know that there is no way I'm stopping trouble if he chooses to cause it." Calen slapped his hand down on Rist's shoulder as he passed his chair. Rist rolled his eyes and beckoned over the serving girl for another mead.

There was absolute silence coming from the group of travellers as Calen approached, which worried him a little. Some people should be feared when they are loud, and others when they are silent. This group seemed like the latter.

Without warning, an axe flew out of the middle of the group, soaring through the air in a series of acrobatic flips. It nestled in the target with a *thunk,* slightly to the left of an axe that had already made its home there, about an inch closer to the centre. The group erupted in a chorus of cheers and shouts.

"Having fun?" Calen asked as he tapped Dann on the shoulder.

Dann turned around, his eyes growing wide. "Calen!" He threw his arms around Calen, pulling him into a tight, slightly painful embrace. "I was beginning to think you had wandered off onto a ship and gotten lost at sea. What took you so long? I've made some friends. They have come all the way from Drifaien to sell furs and drink. In fact, I

think they might just be here to drink – and throw axes."
He pondered on his words for a moment, scrunching up
his lips in thought. "Yes, I'm pretty sure they are here just
to drink and throw axes. Mead?"

Calen was sure that Rist had missed a few meads when
he was counting. This sounded like six mead Dann.

Dann raised his tankard up in the air, clinked it off
Calen's own tankard, then took a deep draught.

"Come, I will introduce you." Dann threw his arm
around Calen's shoulder, directing him towards the heart
of the group. "Friends! Let me introduce to you my companion and brother at heart." Calen rolled his eyes; they
always seemed to require a lot of rolling when Dann had
been drinking. "This is Calen Bryer! Calen, this is Audun,
Baird, Destin, Fell, Kettil, Leif, and Alleron."

Calen held his breath as he tried to match the names to
each man. Which was easier said than done. All of them
looked almost identical – strong, rugged, and slightly dirty.
With thick beards that covered most of their faces, their
only distinguishing features were the colours of their eyes
and hair. There was not the slightest chance that he would
remember their names for longer than five minutes.

Each man responded to Dann's introduction with a
hearty, "well met," clasping Calen's hand with their own,
which Calen repeated in kind. Calen had only met a
Drifaienin man once before, a few summers back, but he
had dressed as they did, and his accent was the same. Thick
and gruff, though with a slight lilt to it.

One of them stepped forward – the one Dann had
called Alleron. He was a solidly built young man, no older

than Calen. His ice-blue eyes stood in contrast to his dark brown, shoulder-length hair, and full beard. He held an axe by the flat, at the back of the blade, the handle extended towards Calen. It was just short of two feet in length, with a smooth ash wood handle and a single hatchet blade. It was fine craftsmanship.

"Would you like to try? Dann here has taken to it like a duck takes to water." He smiled. At least, Calen thought he was smiling. It was hard to tell behind all that hair.

"Sure, why not?" Calen took the axe from Alleron. He felt its weight, trying to gauge its balance. "How does it work?"

Alleron put his hand around Calen's shoulder and turned him towards the makeshift target on the wall. "If you land the axe between the outer ring and the next ring inwards, that's one point. Two points for the next ring, and so on. Five points if you land it in the centre, like your friend did. Easy." He smirked at Dann, who laughed it off and took a mouthful of mead.

"Okay." Calen gripped the axe, tossing the weight about in his hand. "Hopefully, I'm better with this than I am with a bow. Where do I stand?"

"Over here, behind this mark on the floor," Alleron responded. He pointed to an etched line in the floorboards about two feet behind Calen, drawing a frown from the passing mistress Elena. Calen had a feeling that line was a recent addition to the inn's floorboards, courtesy of his new friends.

The group was quiet as Calen stepped behind the line and touched the tip of his left foot right up to its edge. He was going to need all the help he could get.

It was hard to focus with the background noise of the inn droning away in his ear. The click-clack of dice as they bounced off tables. The clinking of tankards as they cracked off each other. The shouts and roars of the drunken townspeople who were drowning the tiredness of a day's work in a bellyful of mead. Whatever pain that bard was inflicting on that poor lute. It seemed like it was getting louder and louder as the seconds passed, like the crow of a rooster in the morning.

"Well, come on then, Calen. You waiting on the damned sun to rise?" Dann mocked. The rest of the group laughed along with him.

Calen threw Dann a dirty look and then tensed his grip on the axe, his knuckles turning a pale white. He pulled his shoulder back and lifted the axe up over his head. Throwing all his strength forward, he launched the axe at the target.

It seemed to move in slow motion as it twirled through the air. A metallic ringing noise reverberated in Calen's ears as it did. After what felt like an eternity, the axe head buried itself in the target, just outside the outermost ring. Calen's chest sank.

Above all the noise, he heard Dann cackling. "Well, look on the bright side. At least you are better with an axe than you are with a bow. I've never seen him hit a target with a bow before," he said to the group, struggling to keep upright from the laughter.

Calen felt a fire burning in the pit of his stomach. A hand landed softly on his shoulder. "Take a minute. Breathe in and hold it. Don't let the air escape until the exact moment you release the axe and don't let your hand

drop after you've thrown it. It will drag the axe off course."
Alleron gave him a reassuring smile and handed him another
axe.

Calen nodded. He took the axe from Alleron and set
his feet behind the line once more. He took a deep breath
in and let his muscles loosen.

"Four coppers, he hits dead centre," he heard Alleron
say.

"Oh, I'll take that bet. I'll never say no to a free drink,"
Dann said, raising his tankard in the air. Calen didn't wait
for Dann to say anything else. He launched the axe
through the air, leaving his hand hanging there after he
released it, just as Alleron had said. He closed his eyes just
as he threw it. *Please, please let Dann lose this bet.*

The group erupted in a frenzy of raucous cheers that
drowned out all sound from the rest of the inn. Calen felt
his heart beating. His nerves pricked at the inside of his
stomach like small needles. He peeled open one eye, too
nervous to look with both.

The head of the axe was nestled firmly in the centre
circle, the handle suspended in mid-air. A surge of energy
seared through his body. An unintelligible roar left his throat
as he jumped up into the air. He turned to see a despondent
look on Dann's face as he stared in disbelief at the axe.

Alleron thrust a tankard of mead into Calen's hand.
"For The Warrior! For Achyron!" he shouted.

"For The Warrior!" came Calen's elated response.
They both drained their tankards down to the last drop.

"I knew you had it in you," Alleron said, beaming.
"Though, next time, try keeping your eyes open." With a

wink, he turned and strode over to Dann to collect his winnings. The rest of the group congratulated Calen the same way Alleron did.

"Not bad," Dann said when Calen walked over to where he stood, half-slouched, leaning against the wall. He raised his tankard up in the air, tipping it off Calen's in the salute that the Drifaienin enjoyed. "I'm going to have to win those four coppers back, though – either off Alleron or you."

Calen felt the mead providing him with some liquid courage. A smirk formed on his face. "Four coppers to whoever gets the best of three axes each?"

The challenge seemed to send a bolt of lightning through Dann. He immediately pushed himself from the wall and stood up straight, his eyes filling with that familiar fire. "Oh, it's on. I'm throwing first."

"Yes!" Calen roared as his axe landed firmly inside the fourth ring, two points clear of Dann's. A mischievous grin spread across his face. "Looks like it's your round."

Dann mimicked him in a mocking voice as he trudged off towards the bar to order the next round of drinks. He accidentally kicked a table and floundered into the arms of Mistress Elena, who simply smiled, patted him on the back, and then pushed him towards the bar a little harder than necessary. Calen just laughed, took a mouthful of his mead, and turned to enjoy the spectacle of Alleron and one of the other Drifaienin – he thought it was Leif, but it was nearly impossible to tell – taking the next match up.

Dann could be an ass when he wanted to be, but Calen

was acutely aware of just how lucky he was to have him and Rist as friends. Brothers, even. They never treated him any differently after Haem died. They made fun of him when he deserved it, and they called him out when he was being an ass. Others avoided him like he was a fragile egg shell, never sure of what to say to him, or if they should say anything at all. He only ever felt Haem's loss more keenly when they did that.

Trying to shake the thoughts from his head, Calen patted his hand down on the coin purse in his pocket, which jingled in response. A pang of guilt cut his smile short. He had almost gambled away enough money to buy food for a week. *It is just one night.* He took a sip of his mead and tried his best to let himself enjoy everything around him.

He peeled his eyes away from the brutal display of sheer strength in front of him to glance back at the table where Rist sat. His face was buried in that new book of his, his fingers wrapped around the handle of a tankard of mead. Rist always was more interested in the *intellectual* than he ever was with fighting or weapons, but it was strange of him not to join them on a night like tonight. He had been acting strange ever since The Proving. Calen had been afraid to ask him what actually happened to that Urak. Was there any answer that could possibly make sense?

As Calen decided to drag Rist from the table, he noticed the figure of a man approaching him from the corner of his eye.

"Would you mind if I joined you?" Calen had spotted him sitting in the corner of the room earlier. He was a match for Calen in height and build, which was rare in the villages.

Working in the forge with his father had given Calen quite a sturdy frame.

The man's long, black mantle was pulled back, exposing the studded black leather cuirass he wore on his torso. Two silver triangular pommels and black leather handles stuck straight up over either of the man's shoulders. It wasn't uncommon for men in Illyanara to walk around the towns or villages with their swords, but Calen couldn't remember ever seeing someone carry two at the same time, strapped across their back. Calen wondered how well he could use them, and how difficult it was to put them back in their scabbards. Although, the man walked with the confidence of someone who knew how to wield those weapons.

He was clean-shaven, and his hair was short and dirty blond. There was something warm in his eyes. The closer he looked, the more Calen was sure that the man could not be much older than him.

"Of course." Calen extended his hand. "My name is Calen. And yours, friend?"

"I am Erik Virandr. It is a pleasure to meet you, Calen."

Calen introduced Erik to the rest of the group, who embraced him with the kind of drunken vigour that one would expect after drinking your body weight in mead. Dann arrived back with his and Calen's drinks just as Alleron began to explain the basics of the axe game to Erik.

"Who's that?" Dann asked, eyeing Erik with curiosity as he handed Calen his tankard. He tipped the rim of his own tankard off Calen's, then they both took a long mouthful.

"His name is Erik," Calen replied. "He asked to join us."

Dann's face perked in approval. "I see. Well, hopefully his pockets are lined with coin, and he is not as good with that axe as I think he might be with those swords." Dann had mischief in his eyes.

Erik turned back towards Calen, holding an axe in a tight grip with his right hand. "Well, Calen, care for a bit of friendly competition? Kettil tells me that the common wager is four coppers to the best of three axes each, and that you are so far, unbeaten."

"Only because he is so slow at drinking his mead," Dann murmured.

Calen narrowed his eyes into daggers. Dann avoided his gaze and pretended to be distracted by something floating in his drink. There was a touch of hesitation in the back of Calen's mind as he patted his hand down on his purse again. *Just one night.*

"That sounds good to me," he said. "Has Alleron explained the rules to you?"

"He has." Erik moved the axe around in his hand, gauging its weight and balance, much like Calen had done earlier.

"Okay, perfect. Would you like the first throw?" Calen asked.

Erik shook his head. "You can throw first. I might pick up a few tips that way." A friendly smile accompanied his words as he passed the axe to Calen. Calen wasn't sure if he was being sincere or trying to put him off his guard. The man carried himself with a confidence that unsettled Calen.

Calen took the axe from Erik and stepped over to the

etched line. Once again, the tip of his foot just touching the mark in the floorboards, Calen became acutely aware of all the sounds in the inn that had fallen into the back of his mind. Mistress Elena's high-pitched voice, like the chirp of a bird on a spring morning. The drunken conversations from the surrounding tables, which had started off as intelligent discussions and devolved into unintelligible grunts as the mead continued to flow.

Then there was a sharp tapping noise of steel on steel. He wasn't sure if he had heard it at first, but it began to pierce through the other sounds, like a ray of sunlight on an overcast day. His eyes followed the path of the noise. Past the serving girl whose acrobatic talents had suddenly abandoned her as she tripped over the outstretched leg of a patron, who had long since fallen asleep, sending her tray of drinks soaring through the air. Past the group of men playing dice at the large table in the middle of the room and the one man who had just pulled a hidden set of dice from up his sleeve, his hand a blur of motion. Calen's eyes moved past these things, and settled on a small knife in the corner of the room, which was tapping off the rim of a steel tankard.

As his eyes moved upwards, his heart almost stopped. The man holding the knife was staring straight at him, watching him the entire time. Calen looked away, snapping his vision back towards the target in front of him, hoping that the man had not caught him staring. He was one of the two men Erik was sitting with when Calen had walked in, but he was alone now. Watching. Calen glanced over to-wards Erik, who was chatting with the others and had not seemed to notice anything at all.

Calen took a deep breath. As the air filled his lungs, he felt the din bubbling over, giving way to a sense of calm. He gripped the axe firmly. The rough wooden handle, cool to the touch, was coarse against his skin. Going through the motions that Alleron had shown him earlier in the night, Calen launched his first axe at the target.

Thunk.

Three points.

Thunk.

Centre. Yes – five points.

Thunk.

Three points.

The group cheered as he landed his first two axes, but their applause was rather subdued as his last axe sank into its place. Not the worst round that he had thrown all night – eleven points out of fifteen was not a bad score, but it was certainly not a great one. He handed the axe over to Erik, who had been watching intently.

"Not bad at all. It's going to be tough to beat that, I think." Erik took the axe from Calen and placed it down on the table beside him. "I'll just have to take this thing off before I throw. It's only going to get in the way." Erik undid the ties of his mantle, laying it down over a nearby chair. His leather cuirass did not extend over his shoulders or down his arms, leaving them bare, the heavy-set muscle belying his few summers.

He moved over towards the etched mark in the floor. Erik tossed the axe up in the air, letting it complete two or three full rotations before snatching it back. His eyes never left the target. Calen felt the suspense building in the group. The chatter amongst them subsided, bit by bit, until all attention was focused on the newcomer holding the axe.

Erik's chest swelled as he took a deep breath inward. He pulled the axe up over his head and unleashed it with an almighty swing. With a vicious thump, it sank straight into the centre of the target. The group erupted in a cacophony of cheers.

"Beginner's luck," Erik said, shrugging at Calen. Calen could already feel his purse being four coppers lighter. Dann grinned from ear to ear. He leapt over to the axe, grabbing it with one hand to remove it from the target and return it to Erik for his second swing. *Well, Dann has definitely wagered against me.*

Absently, Dann turned back towards Erik, his hand still grasping the handle of the axe. A look of surprise coated his face when the axe did not budge, even in the slightest. He placed his free hand beside the other and heaved with all his weight. The axe came loose like water from a spring, sending Dann flying backwards onto the ground. Calen almost felt the impact himself when Dann's backside cracked against the solid wooden floorboards. The entire group broke out in laughter, guffawing wildly at the dumbstruck look on Dann's face. Dann pulled himself to his feet with an expression that only conveyed large amounts of displeasure and handed the axe back to Erik.

"Next time, you're getting it yourself," he said, rubbing his backside tenderly as he walked back to find solace in his mead.

Erik and Calen exchanged glances, both failing to hold back an eruption of laughter.

The group quietened down as Erik readied himself to take his second throw, although Calen could still hear Kettil and Leif mocking Dann in hushed voices.

The metallic ringing sound echoed through the air. The axe landed with a crack, again in the dead centre of the target. Drunken hysteria erupted, like when the first axe landed, and some coin changed hands. This time, though, Erik retrieved his own axe. Dann stared off at the ceiling, pretending to have noticed something in the wooden rafters. Calen was definitely not going to go the night undefeated at this new game.

As Erik took another deep breath in preparation for his final throw, Calen heard that tapping noise again – the knife knocking against the tankard. He noticed Erik's head turn towards the table, but when he looked back over himself, the man was gone. Erik seemed tense, not as confident as he had been before. Without any ceremony, he launched the axe one last time, slicing through the suspense in the air.

Thud.

The flat of the axe connected with the wooden target, bouncing harmlessly onto the ground, leaving the group with stunned expressions. A few of them roared loudly, clapping their friends on the back – the ones who had bet on Calen. Alleron did the same to Dann as Dann dropped a few coppers into Alleron's outstretched hand.

"Well, it looks like you win. Four coppers, was it?" Erik said, not impolitely but with far less enthusiasm and warmth than he had previously shown. His face was un-readable as he rummaged through a small purse that Calen had not noticed before. "It was a good game. I am pleased to have met you, Calen, but I need to be on my way. I wish I could stay for a few more rounds." He passed the coppers to Calen, gave a quick nod to the group, and made his way towards the rear door. Just like that, he was gone.

"Well… that was a bit strange, wasn't it? I mean, I don't like to lose, but at least I don't storm off in a strop when I do. Cost me four coppers—" Dann shut his mouth as soon as he saw the look on Calen's face. "Sorry. I was just kind of sick of you winning." He shrugged, an apologetic look on his face. "I'm going to go check on Rist. He's had his head buried in that book so long, he's probably turned into one." With that, Dann stumbled through the inn, struggling to keep control of his legs.

Calen made his way back towards the table where he had left his drink. He had some catching up to do on Dann. He could hear Baird challenging Alleron to the next round of axes. That was a round Calen wanted to see.

Before he enjoyed the spectacle, he needed to put something in his rumbling belly. He had been so distracted he couldn't remember when he last ate. He managed to catch the attention of the serving girl who had tripped over the slumbering patron earlier. Her dress was a little damp from mead, but she was pretty. Short, with auburn hair and an endearing smile. He asked her if there was any soup and bread left, to which she gave a brisk nod and a curtsy before shuffling back through the crowd. It felt strange to have someone curtsy towards him.

As he waited for his soup, sipping away at his mead, he watched Alleron and Baird play some game with their hands to decide who would throw first. He hoped beyond hope that the bard would suffer some form of sudden, non-life-threatening but still incapacitating injury that would stop him from singing or hurting that poor, defenceless lute. The noise that came from it was almost as bad as the insects in Ölm Forest. *Almost.*

Out of the corner of his eye, Calen noticed that Erik's black mantle was still draped over the back of the chair he had left it on. Calen reached over, rubbing the material between his thumb and forefinger. It was a lot heavier than he had expected, built for warmth and comfort over long distances. Calen placed his tankard down on the table, then pulled the mantle off the back of the chair, doubling it over and draping it across his forearm. It was good quality and probably worth a fair amount of coin. If he lost something of its likeness, his father would have him in the forge day and night to work back the cost.

Taking one last draught of his mead, Calen made his way towards the stable yard door, trying his best to hold his patience as he pushed his way through the drunken crowd. When he finally reached the other side of the room, he breathed a sigh of relief as he walked down the corridor and out into the fresh air.

CHAPTER 11

An Unexpected Journey

S tep away from the cart. It is to be searched, by order
of the emperor."

Erik and his two companions stood to the right of
the stable yard door, in front of the bonnet of a horse and
cart. His two companions had their mantles drawn about
them. Their hoods covered their faces from the shimmering
yellow lights of the lanterns hung around the yard. A
group of Empire soldiers stood in a semi-circle around
them. The two men who Calen had seen on the deck of
the ship stood at their fore – the man in the black cloak and
the man in the red cloak with the lion breastplate. Red
Cloak was nearly half a foot shorter than Black Cloak, with
a wiry frame that did not make him any less intimidating.
There was a coldness in his eyes.

Erik glanced over at Calen as soon as he had stepped
out into the yard. His mouth furrowed into a frown when
he noticed him carrying the mantle. Only his eyes moved;
his body remained fixed towards the group of soldiers in
front of him. Calen wasn't the only one who noticed Erik's

glance in his direction. Almost half of the soldiers turned to see who their new visitor was, including Red Cloak.

"Get out of here, boy. This does not concern you," commanded the soldier, slightly tilting his head. "Do not make me tell you twice."

Calen's feet were glued to the ground. Every fibre of his being told him that this was not the place that he should be, yet something was stopping him from moving his feet. He simply stood where he was. His expression was the picture of calm, while inside his bones trembled. He wanted to excuse himself, step back inside, and continue drinking with Dann and Rist.

"I…" His words betrayed him.

"That was not a request, boy. That was a command." The anger in the man's voice was palpable. He drew his sword and turned, straightened his arm, and pointed it directly at Calen. "Get inside," he growled.

"He has no part in this. Leave him be. Calen, get back inside," Erik said, taking a step towards Calen.

"Erik, what are you doing? Get back over here now. He is not our problem," said one of Erik's companions. His voice was wrought with impatience. He turned to Red Cloak. "Please, sir. We are just leaving; we don't want any trouble."

The man in the black cloak let out a sigh. "I grow tired of this. We are searching all carts and wagons in the village. If you had nothing to hide, then we would already be gone. I have no qualms with spilling blood, but if you step aside now, that will save me cleaning my blade in the morning." The man's face looked tired but handsome. A long thin scar ran from just below his hairline, down over his right eye and nearly to the bottom of his cheek. His eyes were a vivid deep green, almost unnaturally so.

"We will not be stepping aside, Farda," said Erik's other companion, his voice calm and unwavering. He lifted his hands and drew back the hood of his mantle. He was a slightly older man, probably a few summers more than Vars. Flecks of white and grey peppered his short black hair; the colouring in his beard was much the same. His piercing blue eyes contrasted his leathered skin.

With inhuman speed, Farda's sword was drawn. He stepped forward, death in his eyes. The other man smiled, flashing his teeth, and pulled both his swords from the scabbards across his back in one smooth motion.

"Aeson Virandr," hissed Farda. His tone was still cold and unyielding, but his eyes were alight. "I knew it was you on that ship. You got away from me at Ilnaen. I promise you that won't happen again."

"Don't make promises you can't keep, Farda." Aeson twirled his swords through the air, his eyes never breaking contact with Farda's. Aeson moved with such effortless confidence that it almost made Erik seem like a timid mouse.

Without warning, Farda launched himself at Aeson, swinging his sword overhead. Their swords met in a crash of ringing steel that reverberated through the courtyard.

Within seconds, the courtyard was enveloped in mayhem. Farda and Aeson exchanged blows back and forth at a frightening speed. Both of their faces were void of expression, conveying no sense of anger or fear as they each attempted to find the chink in the other's defences. Their blades ricocheted off each other like metallic cracks of thunder.

Erik and his other companion fought four or five soldiers apiece, both wielding almost identical twin short swords. Erik's hooded companion was ruthless. He moved through his attackers in a whirlwind of whistling steel, weaving in and out, dodging and parrying blows without ever seeming like he was trying. One soldier struck high and charged, only to be left screaming when the hooded man glided out of the way, hamstringing him with the backswing of his blade. Then he drove his second sword through the chest of another.

Erik's fight was going much the same. He wasn't so much fighting as dancing with steel in his hands. It didn't take long for Calen to conclude that these soldiers never stood a chance.

It was at that moment, however, that another handful of Lorian soldiers charged into the stable yard from the side street, swords drawn, yelling indecipherable battle cries. They must have heard the fighting. Distracted by the new arrivals, one of the soldiers took Erik off guard. The smaller man threw all his weight into a shoulder charge that sent Erik stumbling backwards. The back of his heel crashed into the ribcage of a crumpled body, sending him tumbling head over heels onto the well-trodden, dusty ground. The soldier lunged, swinging his blade in a downward arc.

Calen's hand fell to the thick coin pommel of his sword strapped to his hip. He had forgotten it was even there. Without thinking, he pulled it from its scabbard, with a little more force than necessary, and thrust it out into the space between Erik and the soldier's plummeting sword.

The metallic clang of steel on steel let him know that he had caught the blade mid-swing before it struck its intended target.

For a brief second, Calen's eyes locked with the soldier's. His chest swelled as it filled with air, and his heart thumped in his chest. The crash of blades and the droning haze of men shouting grew louder and louder, consuming the space in his eardrums. He snapped back to attention as the soldier pulled his blade back, swinging it again, this time at Calen. Memories of training in the field with his father took over. His arms swung from form to form, blocking each strike as it came. They had names, the forms. Vars always recited them, but for the life of him, he couldn't remember what they were called.

The soldier over-reached; he was getting tired. His fingers struggled to grip the handle of his sword as he swung his blade towards Calen's side. Stepping back onto his left foot, Calen steadied his shoulders and met the soldier's swing midway through its arc, sending the blade ricocheting away from his body. He was exposed. Digging in his heels and twisting at the waist, Calen took advantage of the opening and thrust his sword forward with all his strength. He felt it sink into the soldier's belly, the leather armour giving way to the momentum as Calen carried through his strike.

Calen looked into the man's eyes. He saw surprise. Calen watched as the light in his eyes faded slowly.

Surprise turned to fear, then faded to nothing.

Calen felt an emptiness in the pit of his stomach as he pulled his sword free of the soldier's body, watching as it slumped to the ground. Lifeless. Calen stumbled backwards, a slight tremble setting into his hands.

Without warning, something hard struck him in the chest, knocking the wind from his lungs. He crashed to the ground. Another soldier stood over him, the black lion of Loria emblazoned across his breastplate, a heavy double-bladed axe held high over his head. He roared as he thrusted the axe downwards but was interrupted by the steel that slid through the side of his throat, cutting the sound off at the source.

Dann stood over Calen, his fingers wrapped around the hilt of a sword that he must have picked up from the corpse of a fallen soldier. His eyes were glazed over, and his chest rose and fell in deep, slow bursts.

"Calen! Are you okay? You need to get up." Rist's voice started off as a subdued droning noise in Calen's ear until it came through sharply as Calen became aware of his surroundings. The fighting was still in full pitch around him. Erik had gotten himself to his feet and was taking on a group of soldiers less than an arm's reach away.

Calen tried to focus as he steadied himself. "What… what are you two doing here?"

An incredulous look spread across Rist's face. "What are we doing here? You were gone so long, and then when we got to the door, we heard fighting. What are *you* doing here?"

Calen didn't respond. He couldn't think clearly. He tried to survey what was going on around them. Erik and his companion were being overrun. There were simply too many imperial soldiers. Aeson and Farda were still exchanging vicious strikes back and forth, their faces like stone. A few new trickles of blood decorated them both.

Dann half-stumbled over towards Calen and Rist. As their eyes met, Calen gave him a questioning nod, mouthing, "You okay?"

Dann paused for a second, then gave a half-hearted nod.

A hand gripped Calen's shoulder. "Calen, we need to go. We can't win this. Your friends too, *now*. Follow me." Erik rounded himself almost immediately, carving a path through the soldiers ahead of him, his two blades whistling in the wind. Calen did not have to look back. He knew Dann and Rist were following him.

He felt his heartbeat throughout his body. His hand shook as it held the slightly curved sword that his father had given him. Despite all that was going on around him, he only now noticed the intricate swirls that spouted from the guard up into the blade. The ornamentation seemed ironic on something that was made only to take life.

I just killed a man.

A flash of steel glinted in the corner of his eye. He reacted without thinking, swinging his sword to meet the incoming blow. He followed up with his shoulder, sending the man crashing to the ground.

"Dahlen, cover us!" Erik roared towards his hooded companion.

Dahlen had already reached the cart. He pulled a long-bow and quiver from inside.

Whoosh. An arrow shot past Calen's ear, the familiar *thunk* signalling its successful flight. "Run!" Dahlen loosed another arrow, and another soldier dropped.

As they reached the cart, Erik stopped. "Get in!" He shoved Calen up and into the cart, then Dann and Rist, before joining them.

"Dahlen!" Erik nodded toward Aeson, who was still locked in his duel with Farda.

"Father!" Dahlen screamed, loosing an arrow. Aeson turned his head just as the arrow slammed into Farda's shoulder. Only a grunt escaped the man's lips, which seemed more from annoyance than pain. Aeson leapt away from the wounded Farda, sprinting towards the cart.

Dahlen passed the bow to Erik, then made his way around to the front of the cart and started the horses into motion. Erik loosed arrow after arrow into the thick crowd of soldiers, attempting to clear a path.

Aeson fought his way towards the cart, dipping in and out of Calen's field of vision as he weaved through the soldiers. There was no way he was going to make it. There were simply too many men.

A loud, deep *whoosh* filled Calen's ears. It ended with an almighty thump, like an immense gust of wind cracking head-on into a tree, or a powerful wave crashing into the side of a cliff. With it, several soldiers between Aeson and the cart were thrown through the air, hurtling in all directions like rag dolls. Rist almost leapt over the rail of the cart when he saw what had happened, his eyes glistening.

Aeson charged through the gap that was created. An arrow whizzed past his head and through a soldier's eye as he leapt up into the back of the cart. "Go! Go!"

With a crack of the reins, the cart took off like

lightning escaping the clouds. The sudden jerk nearly sent Calen spinning over the back rail. As he peeked over the rim of the rail, an arrow sliced through the air near his face, tearing straight through the canvas canopy that arched over the cart.

Thinking better of another attempted look, Calen flipped himself, letting his back thump against the wooden rail. He slowly slid down until his ass hit the wooden base of the cart. The vibrations shook up through his bones as the wheels battered against the cobblestones. He let his eyes close for a second.

"Calen?" Rist's hand rested on his shoulder. "What in the name of the gods just happened?"

Calen looked at Rist with a blank stare, then tracked his eyes over towards Aeson and Erik, who were similarly propped up against the wooden rails of the cart.

Erik counted the arrows remaining in the quiver, while Aeson sat with his eyes closed. His chest rose high, held for a moment, and then dropped low. Dann sat in silence, his eyes fixed on his blood-covered hands.

"Dann?"

Dann did not even so much as blink. He held his hands out in front of himself, fingers outstretched.

Calen held out his own hands. They were caked in dried blood, congealed and cracked. "I don't know, Rist… I don't know," Calen said in response to Rist's question.

He looked up from his hands. His eyes met Erik's, who gave him a weak smile before returning to counting his arrows.

I killed a man.

A tingly chill ran down Ella's back as she stepped out into the night air. The newfound warmth of the summer days had not yet seeped into the nights. The sun had dropped over the horizon hours ago. Both Vars and Freis had retired for the night around the same time, and Calen was off in Milltown. Most likely drinking himself stupid if he was with Dann. *It is as good a night as any.*

Ella pulled up the hood of her long brown mantle. Her hands fidgeted as she adjusted the drawstrings, ensuring it was tied tight around her. She hesitated for a moment, refusing to check the contents of her bag for a fifth time. She took in a deep breath of crisp air and held it for a moment, letting the cold flow through her lungs. She released it in a heavy sigh, watching as it plumed out and upwards like smoke from a chimney.

The streets were mostly deserted. It had been a long few weeks. With The Proving and the celebrations, most people were tired enough to sleep for days. That suited her fine.

The silvery glow of moonlight splashed down over the streets, providing just enough light for Ella to see the way ahead of her. Not that it would have mattered; she could have found any door in the village with her eyes closed. The dirt crunched under her feet as she made her way through the village, the sound accompanied only by the crickets in the nearby fields and the occasional cough of someone turning in their bed.

Rhett was exactly where he said he would be; by the broken signpost at the south of the village, beside the low wall. Even by the faded light of the moon, he was the most handsome man she had ever laid eyes on. She picked up her pace, slightly skipping as she walked. A warm smile spread across his face, the corners of his mouth almost stretching to touch his ears. She loved that smile.

"You're here," she said, feeling a warmth spread through her body. She threw herself into him, wrapping her arms around him so that her hands clasped together at his back. He waited a moment, then wrapped his arms around her in return, pulling her in closer, sharing the warmth of his chest.

"Of course, I'm here," Rhett said. He craned his neck slightly to place a kiss on the top of her head, lingering for a second or two before pulling his lips away. "I would follow you to the pits of Mar Dorul. I sincerely hope I never have to, but I would."

She tilted her head upwards, resting her chin on the flat of his chest. "I know you would, as I would for you. Are you ready? Did you leave your letter?"

She saw the hesitation in his face. Rhett loved The Glade. It meant everything to him, but if they remained there, then there would be blood between Rhett and Vars. They could not be together if they remained. Maybe one day, they could return. If they were married, with children, that may soften her father's heart. *Time heals all wounds.*

"Aye, I left my letter. I think my parents will understand. Did you leave yours?"

"I did. Mother will understand. Father, I think maybe

in time. I did not tell them where we were going. I felt that was probably for the best. We can come back, in time."

Rhett nodded. Ella knew his smile was more forced than natural, and she understood. She loved him, and she hoped that she would never have to ask him to do something like this again.

CHAPTER 12

Myth and Legend

Calen had lost track of how much time had passed since they left Milltown, but the sky was still as black as jet. The only light came from the pearlescent glow of the moon as it floated into the cart through the openings in the canopy.

Aeson sat on the driver's bench, steering the horses somewhere. He and Dahlen had switched over a short while after leaving Milltown.

Calen had no idea where they were going. He had tried asking a couple of times. Dahlen responded with nothing but a blank stare, then returned to cradling the large leather rucksack he had nestled on his lap. Erik said he wasn't sure, but that his father knew, and they could all rest soon.

Dann hadn't spoken since they left Milltown. Calen wasn't sure if he had even blinked. He just stared at his hands, occasionally giving his eyes a break to stare into the emptiness of the night sky out the back of the cart.

The only actual conversation Calen had was with Rist. He explained everything that had happened before he and Dann had stepped out into the courtyard. Rist let out a short gasp when Calen told him of how he had killed the soldier only moments before. He noticed Dann looking over towards him when he got to that part, but as soon as Calen met his gaze, he went back to staring at his hands again. So, he just sat there. What else was there to do? They had to stop eventually, and then they would answer his questions.

After a while, more and more trees passed by through the opening at the back of the cart. Calen knew they had reached rolling hills when the cart swayed to and fro, tipping back and forth when they hit slopes. He was about to ask where they were when he heard neighing, echoing in the empty night. It was close by, and there was more than one horse, by the sounds of it.

"We get out here. We're leaving the cart," Aeson called back. He pulled the cart to an abrupt stop, causing all of them to jerk forward slightly. Erik nodded at Calen as he heaved himself to his feet. It was a sombre nod; there was tiredness set in his eyes.

One by one, they all piled out of the cart and into the night. Calen's breath misted in front of him as he hopped down into the open fields set on rolling hills as far as the eye could see. A light blanket of frost swept across every blade of grass, dressing them in white; rigid and crisp. It crunched under the weight of his boots. The adrenaline from earlier had worn off, and there was a slight chill setting into his bones. Calen pulled his coat tighter around himself.

About twenty feet away, beside a thicket of trees, three horses were tied to a small post that appeared to have been hastily planted in the ground not too long ago. It seemed as good a time as any to ask his questions. "Why are there horses here? Why are *we* here?"

"Because we arranged for them to be here. We can't take the cart into the woods. We didn't expect you three boys, so there are only three. We will have to go two to a horse." Aeson walked towards the horses, not waiting for a response. Erik and Dahlen followed him without hesitation, Dahlen throwing the large satchel over his shoulder.

Rist didn't move. "Wait – what in the gods is going on here? Where are we going? Why are we even here? Calen, we should be in bed, heading back to The Glade in the morning. This is madness."

Aeson stopped and turned to face Rist. A sigh escaped his lips. There was a melancholy in his eyes. "Look, regardless of the why or how, after what happened back there, those soldiers are going to be looking for you. Going back would be stupider than coming with us. We are due to meet some friends at a small camp in the forest. Come with us, rest for the night, and then decide on a clear head in the morning. Does that sound agreeable? I won't force you. In fact, I'm happy to leave you here, but the offer stands."

"We'll go with you." Dann's voice was hoarse, croaking, as if he had just awoken from a long sleep.

Rist stared at Dann, his eyebrows raised in shock. "Dann, are you seriously—"

"Rist, we have nowhere else to go. He is right. They will be looking for us. We killed people, Rist. I killed someone. Do you think the empire is just going to let that lie? 'Carry on, young sirs. All is forgiven?' Don't be stupid, Rist."

"He's right," Calen said, sighing. "We don't have much of a choice."

Disbelief set into Rist's face. His stare flitted between Dann and Calen, searching desperately for the magic words that would change their mind. In the end, he shrugged and sighed. "Who am I riding with?"

When they were all mounted, Aeson slapped the flank of the cart horse, sending it charging off into the night, towing the cart along behind it. "That should send them the wrong way," he said, giving his bay a brisk kick in the side.

Dann rode with Dahlen, and Rist with Aeson. Not much conversation arose from either group.

Erik broke the silence first. "Do you have any brothers or sisters?"

The question sat in Calen's mind, and a knot twisted in his stomach. Two years had passed since Haem's death. Had it actually been that long? The pain was as fresh as if it happened only that morning. It was like there was a hole in his chest. "I have a sister, Ella. And you?"

"It's just me and Dahlen. And Dad, of course."

"What about your mother?" There was a silence that hung in the air.

"She passed away when we were young. Consumption. It took her too fast for the healers to understand what it was."

"I'm… I'm sorry."

"It's okay. It was a long time ago." Erik cast his eyes ahead into the dark of the fast-approaching forest. There was an awkward silence as the horse trotted along. Calen didn't know what to say. What could he say? He knew what that loss felt like – it was not something words could heal.

It didn't take long before the trees swallowed them. Ölm Forest. Calen often forgot just how immensely large it was, stretching all along the western foothills of Wolfpine Ridge. It seemed to him that he simply could not get away from the place. His legs tightened around Ildarya's ribcage as the horse stumbled over a hole in the ground. *Guess you don't like the dark either, boy.*

Ildarya meant "Wind Rider" in the old tongue, so Erik said. Calen didn't doubt the name fit the horse; they moved at a fair pace considering they were riding double, yet Calen got the impression that Ildarya was not even close to pushing himself. The horse was a beast; its legs were thick as tree trunks, and its neck was sturdier than a bear's.

"Ölm Forest – not this damned place again. Are we really going in here after last time?" Rist posed his question aloud, but clearly meant it for Dann and Calen.

"Last time?" Erik said, turning his head slightly.

"Well, last time we were in Ölm Forest, we ran into a few problems." *If nearly being killed by a bear, and then two Uraks could be considered "a few problems".*

Erik's head turned a bit more. "A few problems?"

"Well…" Calen paused for a second, wondering how much he should tell. "We had a close call with some Uraks."

175

Erik tugged on the reins. Ildarya came to a sudden halt, sending Calen jerking forward, slamming hard into Erik's back. "Uraks? *You three* fought Uraks?"

"I wouldn't say we *fought* them. Truth is, I don't really know how we're all still alive, but we are."

Erik nodded, turning back to face the forest. He took in a deep breath, as if about to say something, then stopped himself. He gave Ildarya a light tap in the ribs with his heel. The horse started into motion again, picking up pace a bit to catch up to the others. "You'll need to tell us that story around the fire later while we eat."

That unmistakable thickness seeped into the air again. Calen's lungs worked that little bit harder to take in each breath. As the grass fields yielded to the spongy forest floor, the horse's hooves sank a little deeper, its steps dragging a little more each time. The crickets chirped, and Calen heard the occasional flutter of wings as a bird awoke from its slumber, but otherwise, there was silence. It was a little eerie. The forest usually seemed alive, day and night, like a bustling city going about its business in complete ignorance of the world of men. There was something in the extra silence that made the hairs on the back of Calen's neck stand on end.

He saw it in Erik too. His eyes darted from tree to tree, scanning for danger. He was much more awake than he had seemed earlier. "Father, I—"

"I know," Aeson responded bluntly. He pulled one of his swords from the scabbard across his back, holding the reins with his other hand.

Calen tried to focus, although it wouldn't do him much

good. It was too dark to see anything. The forest canopy blocked out what little the moonlight had allowed him to see until that point.

They must have vision like kats because—
Crack.

He heard the branch snapping as clearly as if it were right beside his ear. He stopped trying to see what was happening and instead listened. Listened to the deafening silence.

Crack.

"Ride!" Aeson snapped his reins, kicking his horse into a gallop. Without hesitation, Erik and Dahlen followed suit. Calen tightened his grip around Erik's waist as he was nearly thrown from Ildarya's back, the horse lurching forward into the depths of the forest at lightning speed, bounding over fallen trees and ditches.

There was a *whoosh* of air, almost entirely masked by the thunderous sound of hooves tearing chunks of sodden earth from the forest floor. Something massive flew out of the darkness and crashed into a tree only five or six feet away, sending splinters of wood flying in all directions. Shards of fragmented bark battered against Calen's raised arm as he tried to protect his eyes from being shredded.

Shouts and roars rumbled behind them, each one more ferocious, as if it were answering the last. Guttural, blood-curdling roars.

An arrow whizzed past Calen's head, a little too close for comfort. He looked up to see Dann holding Dahlen's bow, nocking another arrow. Calen thought he could see him shrug apologetically.

An Urak burst out of the bush to their right, launching

itself at Calen and Erik. Its blood-red eyes were the only thing that Calen could see clearly. It was halfway to them when an arrow plunged into its neck and knocked it straight out of the air. With a monstrous scream, it hurtled into the abyss of the night.

"Uraks!" Erik roared. He snapped the reins up and down, sending Ildarya into a frenzy of speed. The horse lived up to its name. It was all Calen could do to hold on as it bolted forward with astounding force. Most horses Calen knew would struggle to match Ildarya's speed, even if they were not riding double. Vibrations shot up Calen's back as the horse's hooves pounded against the forest floor. His muscles strained as he gripped on with his legs, his arms firmly wrapped around Erik's waist.

Just as he thought that there was no way anything could match their speed, the world started to spin. He tumbled through the air, helpless as he spun, before he slammed into the trunk of a tree. He was not sure if the cracks he heard came from the brittle bark of the old oak or the bones in his back. All he felt was pain.

He slipped in and out of consciousness. Bursts of the aching pain flared at the base of his spine. It was hard to tell whether or not he was awake; his eyes closed to complete darkness and opened to more of the same.

He heard Ildarya wailing. Whatever had hit them, the horse had taken the brunt of it. It would not survive the night. His head was pounding, as if it were being struck with a hammer, over and over. Dragging strength from the pit of his stomach, Calen pulled himself to his knees. Slowly, his eyes attuned to the darkness. As he gripped onto a vague sense of consciousness, he saw shapes.

The Urak was ripping Ildarya apart, limb from limb, as it lay wailing on the ground. The horse howled and shrieked in pain as the Uraks teeth tore into its flesh.

There was a flash of steel, followed by a spray of blood. The Urak collapsed, its head following its body to the ground. It looked like Erik had fared a bit better in the collision than he had. Within seconds, there were two more Uraks trading blows with Erik. Heavy, merciless strikes pummelled down on him like hammers pounding on folded steel. He parried, dipped, and sidestepped. The blur of motion gave Calen a renewed headache as he tried to follow it. He attempted to get to his feet, then collapsed onto his back as the strength in his legs failed him. The pain in his back seared like fire.

"Take my hand." The voice was calm and cool, with an assuring tone. It reminded Calen of Erdhardt Hammersmith. He managed to raise his head to look towards whoever it was that held that voice, half-expecting to see the village elder standing over him.

Calen's mind must have been playing tricks on him from the fall. The man in front of him was far taller than Erdhardt, taller even than the Uraks, maybe eight feet tall from head to toe. His skin shimmered a pale whitish blue in the weak moonlight. His dark hair was tied into a ponytail. Calen tried to make out his face, but it was difficult in the darkness. He was bare-chested, his body made up of thick slabs of muscle to rival any blacksmith. He wore long dark trousers that had the same look as Therin's cloak did – old, worn, but with a sense of timelessness, like they could neither burn in fire nor be torn by a blade.

To his surprise, Calen reached up and took the man's hand without thinking. His hand was warm to the touch. Calen was not sure why he expected otherwise; maybe it was because his pale skin looked like a thin sheet of ice. Something about the enormous man put Calen at ease.

Without warning, the man shoved Calen away with enough force to send him thumping back to the ground. He winced with pain as his back hit the forest floor.

Calen looked up towards the man. Tendrils of shimmering red light wound from his hand in both directions, wrapping and weaving themselves around each other, like vines crawling up the side of a house. The light was so bright it was almost blinding, illuminating everything around them in a flash. As the tendrils of light weaved around each other, the form they left behind became solid. The handle and blade of a massive, double-sided axe formed in a glowing red light, the strength of which died down as it settled into its shape.

The man hefted the axe backwards and then swung it over Calen's head with almighty force. It crashed straight into the chest of a leaping Urak, lifting the beast higher into the air. The entire blade disappeared into its flesh. The man shook the body of the Urak off the axe as if it were nothing but a splinter. Whirling around, he let go of the axe, launching it through the air and into the distance. Calen watched as it sliced straight through the head of a charging Urak and buried itself in a tree behind the collapsing body. Then it was gone, faded into the darkness faster than it had appeared.

More Uraks emerged from the forest, leaping over the

bodies of their fallen companions. They snarled and roared, swinging their heavy axes and charred-black swords above their heads in a frenzy.

The man stepped past Calen, roaring ferociously in return. He raised both of his arms in the air, as if pushing something imaginary towards the incoming monstrosities. Thick vines erupted from the ground below them, weaving their way through the air much like the red light had done. Except these did not form a weapon; they *were* the weapon.

They shot through the air faster than Calen's eyes could follow, growing thicker the farther they went. Five Uraks, five vines. Each vine found its target, piercing straight through the Uraks' torsos. The vines kept moving until each of them was buried in the trunk of a different tree, leaving the lifeless bodies suspended in mid-air. Calen's jaw hung open. He wanted to be terrified, but his head couldn't process what was happening quickly enough. The bodies dropped to the ground as the vines retreated to the undergrowth.

When Calen's thoughts came back, he felt the terror building like a ball of ice in the pit of his stomach. The hairs on his arms and the back of his neck stuck out like the spines on a porcupine.

"It's okay." Erik knelt beside him, one hand on his shoulder, staring straight into his eyes. Patches of dirt and mud covered his clothes. Thin streams of blood dripped from newly earned cuts on his face and arms, but he was alive. "Asius is a friend. He is who we are here to meet."

Calen wanted to reply, but the words buried themselves in his throat. The man – or whatever he was – stared at Calen.

He extended his hand, which had to be twice the size of Calen's. "I am Asius, son of Thalm. I am pleased that our paths have crossed, though I apologise for the manner in which it had to happen." Something that resembled a smile sat on his face. At least, Calen thought it was a smile. Without really intending to, Calen extended his hand in return. Asius wrapped his gargantuan fingers around Calen's forearm and pulled him to his feet with unsettling ease.

"Th… Thank you, Asius, son of Thalm. I am Calen Bryer, son of Vars Bryer. I owe you my life," Calen stammered, struggling to pull the words from his throat. He hadn't noticed his heart was racing until that moment.

"You owe me nothing, little one. All that is given will be received, as sure as day begets night."

Calen was not sure what Asius meant, but he nodded anyway. He heard the soft pad of horse hooves pressing into the moss that covered the forest floor. Aeson and Dahlen sat atop their horses, surveying the scene in front of them. Urak corpses were strewn about, Calen and Erik were bruised and a little bloody, and there was an eight-foot man with skin as pale as the thinnest paper and muscles as thick as the hardiest blacksmith. Dann and Rist sat behind them, worried looks on their faces as their eyes searched for Calen's.

"You are all okay. I was worried for a minute there. It was near impossible to count their numbers. Asius, good to see you, old friend," Aeson said. A warm smile spread across his face at the sight of the giant man, who nodded in return, mimicking Aeson's smile.

"It is good to see you also, Aeson Virandr. Far too many years have passed since our paths last crossed. I was excited to receive your message. Do you have it?"

"Yes, they have. Too many to count, old friend. Too many to count. And yes, I have it." There was a pensive look in Aeson's eyes as he stared off into the distance for a few moments, seeming lost in his thoughts. "Come," he said, his eyes snapping back to the group as he finished swimming through his memories. "The camp must not be far if you are here, Asius."

"No more than fifteen or twenty minutes from here. Senas and Larion await us there. There is a fire to warm you and food to fill your bellies. For certain you are both tired and hungry."

It wasn't until the mention of a fire that Calen's body remembered just how cold the night was. A shiver spread through him, and he blew into his hands for warmth. His stomach rumbled at the thought of food. The look on Rist and Dann's faces told him they were much the same.

"Erik, are you and Calen okay to walk? If you are hurt, then we can trade places on the horses." There was a matter-of-fact tone in Aeson's voice.

Erik looked at Calen, who nodded with a grunt. The fire burning at the base of his spine disagreed, but it was nothing a bit of rest couldn't fix.

"Yes, Father. We can walk. It is not far."

"Good, let's be off. The quicker we move, the sooner we will have food in our bellies." Aeson gave a slight tap of his heel into his horse's ribs, urging it into a slow walk.

Erik elbowed Calen in the ribs to get his attention, a mischievous grin on his face. "Now you've fought Uraks twice."

Calen frowned. He wasn't sure how Erik was laughing

after what had just happened. It took all the strength Calen had to not empty the contents of his stomach. His heart still pounded in his chest. And his mind flitted between the monstrous Uraks and the look on the soldier's face as he died, the way the light in his eyes had faded. They continued in silence.

After about fifteen minutes of walking, Calen saw the warm, orange-red glow of a fire, flickering shadows through the gaps in the trees. As they got closer, he heard voices, one male and one female, but he couldn't make out what they were saying.

The trees opened into a small clearing. A large fire burned at its centre, with a massive cast iron pot suspended over it and four large logs arranged about its perimeter.

Calen, Rist, and Dann all stopped in their tracks when they saw the owners of the voices. They were both the same height as Asius, with skin just as pale. Just as icy blue. Though, unlike Asius, they were not bare-chested. They wore matching leather jerkins, well-made, with steel toggles. The others walked straight into the campsite without a second thought, leaving the boys standing there, gawking.

"Larion, Senas, it is fantastic to see you again!" Aeson's voice rang with sincerity. He clasped them both on the forearm, his smile extending from ear to ear.

"As it is you, Aeson Virandr," Senas replied, her voice soft and warm. It almost didn't suit her massive frame. "And who are these fine young men? Not all your children. No, but these two are. They have your eyes." She was looking over towards Erik and Dahlen as she spoke. Calen could see a kindness in her eyes.

"You are correct, Senas, as always. These are my children, Erik and Dahlen. The other three are new companions of ours. To be honest, I haven't properly been introduced. It was Erik who brought them onto our path."

All eyes were suddenly on Calen, Dann, and Rist. A swift elbow from Dann hinted that it was Calen who would have to do the talking. "I am Calen Bryer. This is Dann Pimm and Rist Havel. We are from The Glade. We're not quite sure how we ended up here either, but it is our pleasure to meet you."

"Well met, Calen Bryer, Dann Pimm, and Rist Havel of The Glade. It is a pleasure to share our fire with you this night. I am Senas, daughter of Iliria, and this is Larion, son of Olin. Come, all of you, sit. You must be hungry. We have a soup here and some warm blankets."

Except for Aeson and their new companions, the conversation was non-existent while they ate. Calen was not sure he had ever seen Dann eat that fast in his life.

"Would you like some more?" Senas asked, laughing. She stood up to stir the soup in the pot with a long cast iron ladle. Calen tried not to stare. She was handsome, in a way. Her eyes were a deep green that stood stark against her pale whitish-blue skin, and her silvery-blonde hair was tied up at the back of her head. All three of them – Asius, Senas and Larion – were like nothing Calen had seen before.

"Yes, please. It is delicious," Dann said. He joined her by the pot, holding his bowl out to be filled. He looked like a small child next to her.

"So, Aeson, tell us of your journey so far, and of Milltown. Were you successful?"

Calen had not heard Larion speak until then. His voice was deep and measured, as if he pondered each syllable with the utmost of care. Aeson gave a quick sideways glance towards Calen, Rist, and Dann before answering the question. "Yes, my friend. We were successful."

Aeson gestured towards Dahlen, who reluctantly handed over the large satchel he had been cradling for most of the night. Larion took it into his hands with the caution of a mother handling a newborn babe. His eyes lit up when he peeled back the opening and gazed upon whatever was inside.

"It was truly quite amazing," Aeson said, a glimmer of excitement on his face. "We waited for three days and three nights and almost froze to death in that icy wasteland, but then, on the fourth day, just as we had given up hope, they returned. The journey back was a bit choppy. We ran into some issues with the empire, but we managed to get away, by the luck of the gods. We arrived at the dock in Milltown yesterday afternoon, though not without *complications*."

"I see. And have any of you heard it?" Asius asked, his head stooping down.

Aeson shook his head, letting a sigh escape. They spent the next while discussing the events in Milltown; the soldiers approaching them, and the fighting, right up until Asius had found them in the woods. More questions floated through Calen's mind than he knew what to do with, or how to approach. Where did he start?

"Asius, do you mind if I ask… what are you?" Rist had been quiet, but Calen recognised the look on his face. He had been chewing on that question for a while now. A deep laugh emanated from both Asius and Senas. Larion just frowned for a moment, then peered back inside the satchel, running his hand along the outside with what seemed like affection.

"Well, little one," Asius said when the laughter subsided, "your kind have always called us giants. But to our own, we are Jotnar. Do not think us rude for laughing. It is a laugh of joy. It has been a long time since we have met new friends. Sometimes we forget that you have never seen one of our kind before. The world is not as we once knew it." There was a quiet reflection in Asius's eyes.

Giants. The word echoed in Calen's head. From every story he was told as a child, the giants were hunted and killed to the last by the empire. They were shrouded in such mystery for so long that he had never considered them more than legend, old wives' tales. Yet here they were, right in front of him. He had always imagined that they would be... different? Some bards and storytellers, like Therin, told stories of how the giants were great city builders, shipwrights and scholars. But most painted them as savages; ten-foot-tall monsters with gnarled teeth and a vicious bloodlust – more similar to Uraks.

"I thought the giants were gone. They have not been seen in centuries. Where have you been?" Calen couldn't help but throw Rist a dirty look. Rist never cared much for sensitivity when his curiosity was involved. And the more of his questions were answered, the greater his curiosity became. It seemed counterintuitive to Calen. Surely an answer should sate your curiosity, not stoke it?

Asius noticed Calen's glare. "No, no, it is okay. The questions are natural. We have had long enough to ponder the answers. There are few of us left – not that there were ever many of us at all. We Jotnar are not like you humans. There are a lot less of us than you, but we live a lot longer. It is true—" Asius paused for a moment, clasping Senas's hand. He cast an eye towards Larion, who had a melancholy look on his face. "Fane and his armies hunted our kind to near extinction. We were a strong and proud people, but even we could not withstand the force that was thrown at us. Many of our closest friends and family are now part of the earth once more. As we were, so we will always be."

"As we were, so we will always be," Senas and Larion repeated in a hushed whisper.

"However, there were a few of us who survived by hiding and seeking aid from old friends." Asius smiled faintly towards Aeson. "In truth, I do not know how many of us are left. We stay in small groups and do not communicate often – it would be too dangerous to do so. But with luck and hope, that will not always be the way. When the time comes, the others will answer the call."

"I see," Rist replied, deep in thought. "Why risk showing yourselves to us? We could tell everyone we met."

Calen had to suppress the urge to curse. These were creatures of legend. It was not right to question them so.

"In truth, little one, nobody would believe you." Asius's smile was mirthless.

There was silence for a long moment. "May I ask you one more question?"

Asius nodded. "Of course, little one. If we do not ask, then we will never know."

That seemed to encourage Rist. The village elders usually

shut down his curiosity without a second thought. "*Curiosity killed the kat*," Calen heard Verna Gritten's voice echo in his head.

"Earlier, when you saved Calen and Erik, was that *magic*?" Rist leaned forward in his seat, his eyes glittering in the firelight.

Aeson raised a questioning eyebrow towards Asius, who waved him away.

"Yes, little one. That is what you know as magic. Although, we refer to it as the Spark." Asius's eyes lingered on Rist, a knowing smile on his face. "You—"

"The axe?" Calen threw his hand over his mouth. He wanted the ground to swallow him whole. He had not meant to say that out loud. He was as bad as Rist.

Asius turned to him, still smiling. "Your curiosity is warming, little one. Most humans shun what they do not understand. What you refer to is a *nithrál*. In the common tongue, it would be 'Soulblade'. It is a powerful weapon, created through the threads of the Spark, unique to whoever summons it. It takes many years of focus and learning before one can summon their Soulblade. It is an ability that most never achieve."

Soulblade. Images of the giant – Jotnar – swinging the axe of glowing red light flashed through Calen's mind. He felt the power radiating from it as it sliced through the Uraks chest. It was a weapon, the likes of which he had never seen. How could any man stand against such a thing?

As the night grew older, Rist's questions seemingly had no end, and neither did Asius's enthusiasm for answering them. Dann, Erik, and Dahlen slipped into the world of dreams, lying unconscious around the fire. Larion and Aeson had their own conversation, mostly in hushed whispers. Calen couldn't make out anything they were saying, but it all seemed to centre around whatever was in the satchel that Larion cradled.

Calen wanted to know the answers to Rist's questions. They were questions he himself wanted to ask. Though, the one question that subdued all others in his mind, was the subject of Aeson and Larion's conversation – what was in that satchel. What was it that the empire soldiers wanted to find so desperately? Or more importantly, what was it that Calen had killed a man for. He shivered at the thought of it. He had taken a man's life, and he didn't even know why. *I need to know why.*

Calen shuffled closer to Aeson and Larion, careful not to make too much noise as he inched himself along the ground. He leaned his head over as subtly as he could, straining to make out what Aeson and Larion were saying.

"It is incredible," said Larion in a hushed whisper, "The Valacian—"

All of a sudden, the voices were gone. He could hear the crackling of the fire, and the waft of the nights breeze as it drifted through the trees, but not Aeson and Larion's voices. Calen turned his head to see if they were still talking, and he nearly leapt out of his skin when his eyes locked with Aeson's. Calen spun his head back around so fast he made himself a little dizzy. *Shit.*

He didn't dare look back to see if Aeson was still watching him. He wanted to keep trying, but the voices remained gone. He couldn't even make out the tail end of a whisper.

He felt his eyelids grow heavy as the fire radiated warmth. It had been a long day, and a long night. How long had it been since he had slept? He let himself slide down onto the ground, resting his head against the log behind him, the heat from the fire warming his bones. He felt sleep taking over.

Draleid n'aldryr.
N'aldryr. Draleid.
Draleid.
Draleid.

Calen jumped awake, clasping his hand to his chest. His heart beat with such ferocity, he thought it was trying to escape his body. He used his other hand to wipe the forming droplets of sweat from his brow. He tried to slow his breathing, letting his lungs fill with air, holding and then releasing slowly. His thoughts were a whirlwind. The voice felt so real.

He looked around the camp, his pounding heartbeat returning to something resembling normality. The fire smouldered away, crackling every few seconds. Plumes of ember and dust shot up into the air as bits of wood gave way and collapsed. But the fire wasn't giving off enough heat to explain why Calen's skin was so warm; it felt like it could catch fire.

It was hard to see in fading firelight, but it looked like most of the group were asleep. Senas and Asius were awake. It was impossible to mistake their huge frames, even in the darkness of the forest. They spoke in hushed voices as they sat in front of the fire. Senas's head rested on Asius's shoulder. Her eyes were closed, but Calen could see her lips moving.

Another hulking silhouette was splayed out on the ground, with its head resting against one of the wooden logs, only a few feet from the two giants. Larion's chest rose and fell with a slow, steady rhythm, the satchel he had been holding earlier still wrapped in his arms.

Draleid.

A whisper echoed in the back of Calen's mind, a shadow from his dream. He shook his head, rubbing his palms into his eyes in an attempt to shake off the grogginess. A low grumbling snore let him know that Dann was most definitely asleep.

Something kept drawing Calen's eyes to the satchel in Larion's arms. As his eyes adjusted to the dark night, everything became a little clearer. The satchel was made of thick leather, with extra stitching along the seams and strong iron buckles at the top. He felt *something* emanating from within. Something pulled his eyes towards it.

Draleid n'aldryr.

The words echoed in his head over and over. A fog filled his mind. The forest and the camp faded from view, swallowed by the fog. All he could see was the satchel and a dim glow pulsing from within.

Draleid n'aldryr.

"Draleid n'aldryr," Calen whispered, repeating the words out loud.

"What did you say?"

The fog vanished in a snap. Everything was back to

normal, with the camp washed in a yellowy-orange glow from the fire.

Aeson was perched on the log that Calen's head had been resting on. He had a notebook on one knee, a pen in hand, and a small inkpot on his other knee. He stared down at Calen, his eyes un-blinking.

"I… uh, have you been there the whole time?" Calen stuttered.

Aeson nodded. "For a while now. Just making a few notes before we journey to Camylin. What was that you said a minute ago, when you were half-asleep?" His eyes did not move from Calen.

Calen felt a lump in his throat when he tried to speak. "I don't know. Just something from a dream I was having. Camylin? Is that where you are heading next?"

"Yes." Aeson narrowed his eyes, holding his gaze on Calen for an uncomfortable moment, as though he were going to probe further into Calen's dream. But he didn't. He folded his notebook over and closed the lid on his ink-well, clicking the latch into place. "Asius has given us what we came for, and now we must set off for Camylin in the morning. With the fresh horses Asius has arranged, we can be there in a few days if we ride hard."

Calen nodded. It took him a second to understand what Aeson had said. "Wait, what do you mean? We are not going with you to Camylin. We need to go home. I've already left my father's horse and wagon in Milltown. That's going to be impossible to explain as it is."

Aeson's expression did not change. He placed his pen into a small wooden box, the inside of which was lined with a soft purple material. "I thought we agreed that you going back was not a good idea. Those soldiers are going to come looking for you, and The Glade is the first place they will look. Surely, somebody in Milltown knows you well enough to inform them of where you are from. Friend or not, Calen, money talks."

"We agreed that we would decide in the morning." Panic set into Calen's head. "If they're going to The Glade, then we need to go back. What if they hurt my family because of what I did?" He couldn't bear the idea that those soldiers might do something to his parents or Ella because of what he had done. He didn't mean to kill that soldier.

Aeson rested his hand on Calen's shoulder. "Get some rest, sleep on it. We can talk in the morning. There are not many hours of darkness left either way. We can work out a plan in the morning once we've all had some sleep."

Calen gave a half-nod. "Yeah, I suppose that makes sense. I am pretty tired. We can decide in the morning." A yawn escaped his throat.

"Good," Aeson said, lifting himself to his feet. "If you're not awake by first light, I will wake you and your friends." He gave a thin smile, then walked over to where his blankets were laid out.

As soon as Calen was sure that everyone was asleep, he tiptoed over to where Rist and Dann were sleeping. He moved as quietly as he could, careful not to step on any branches or brittle leaves. "Rist, Dann, wake up," he whispered. "We need to go. Now."

The embers of the fire popped and crackled. Aeson stared into its heart, running his hands over and back across each other. He wasn't cold, but he had decisions to make. The boy was stronger willed than he had given him credit for.

"You know they are on their way back to The Glade?"

Aeson didn't lift his head from the fire. "I was wondering when we might see you, Therin."

The elf stepped out of the darkness and into the dim light of the crumbling fire. He drew back the hood of his greenish-brown cloak. Aeson winced as Therin's silver hair coruscated in the burning light. Therin stood on the opposite side of the fire, pretending to warm his hands.

"I know." Aeson sighed. "They waited until they thought I was asleep and took three of the horses."

Therin tossed a twig he had been fiddling with into the flames, then made his way around the fire until he stood in front of Aeson. "And you let them go. Why?" His tone was not judgemental – that was not Therin's way – but there was more than a hint of irritation in it.

"I hold the same question," Asius said. Aeson hadn't noticed the giant approach. "It is good to see you, Therin Eiltris, son of Alwin Eiltris."

"As it is you, Asius, son of Thalm. It has been too long."

Aeson lifted his gaze from the fire. "I believe it is time that we signal the others. I can arrange for some hawks to be sent from Camylin. Asius, I'm sorry to say this, but how soon can you, Senas, and Larion leave?"

Therin raised an eyebrow at the question.

Asius tilted his head to the side, his eyes narrowing in curiosity. "We can be on the move within the hour, but why? After so long, why now?"

Aeson huffed loudly, lifting his head to meet Asius's curious gaze. "Because, old friend, I think we have found our Draleid."

CHAPTER 13

Everything Changes

Calen pulled on the reins, bringing the horse to a harsh stop. An agitated neigh let him know that he could have been a little gentler. "Sorry, boy. I'm just tired," he said in a hushed tone as he ran his hand along the horse's neck.

Dann and Rist pulled their horses up either side of Calen. They gazed down over the valley of rolling hills that led to The Glade. It really was a beautiful sight. Plumes of smoke drifted from chimneys, blowing in the early morning breeze as the dim glow of the dawn light came over the crest of Wolfpine Ridge, at Calen's back.

"I can't believe we stole horses from three guys who kill imperial soldiers for fun – and three giants," Dann said, a wide grin spread across his face. He laughed a little with satisfaction. "Giants… I'm telling everyone."

Rist shot him a look of incredulity. "Dann, you are telling no one. Nobody would believe you anyway. They would just figure it was another one of your ridiculous stories, like that time you told everyone that you saw a horse with a horn growing out of its head."

Dann gave Rist a downtrodden look. "That happened…." he murmured, defiant yet barely audible.

"Are you two done?"

Calen slid down from his horse. He hadn't meant to be curt, but he was not in the mood. "I figure that if they come, they don't need all of us." A knot twisted in the pit of his stomach. "You go down to your families and stay there. I'll tell mine what happened, then I'll come back here and take the horse. I'll make enough noise that they'll follow me. Aeson said they were going to Camylin. I might ride there and try to find them. If they'll have me."

The idea had come to him as they rode through Ölm Forest. If the empire soldiers came to The Glade, there was no sense in all three of them paying the price. As long as his family were okay, that was all that mattered. And if he could make it to Camylin, and find Aeson, that was what he would do. But if it came to it, he would pay the price for what he did – that was all there was to it.

"Yeah, that's not happening," Dann scoffed. "Firstly, they know we were with you. Secondly, no."

Rist, who had dismounted while Calen was talking, placed his hands on Calen's shoulders. "As Dann so poetically explained," Rist said, throwing a sideways glance towards Dann, "that is not how we do things. You are our family. Maybe not by blood, but water becomes just as thick as blood if you go through enough shit together. Simply put, we are not letting you do this alone. You go, we go. We will tell our families we are safe but that we need to leave, and we will meet you back here. Shouldn't take much more than an hour or two. We can leave the horses tied to one of the trees."

"Exactly," Dann chimed, that familiar mischievous look in his eyes. "We're not letting you have all the fun."

Calen rummaged for the sincerest smile he could muster. He placed one of his hands on Rist's shoulder and the other on Dann's. "I…"

"Don't say anything sappy. Don't ruin it. For the love of the gods, don't ruin it." Dann held a straight face for a few seconds, then grinned ear to ear. "Let's get going."

Calen wanted to argue, but he knew there was no point. He could tell by the look on their faces they had made up their minds.

Once they had the horses tied up, they made their way down the hills, towards The Glade. The sun had only barely crested over the mountaintops, and an icy chill still inhabited wherever the shadows extended. There were quite a few more lights coming from the village than Calen would have expected so early, but he brushed it off as him simply being a little on edge.

When they approached the edge of the village, Rist glanced at Dann and Calen. "Back at the horses in no more than two hours. Understood?"

"Understood," they replied as they split up and set off their own way.

Calen made his way through the streets at a brisk pace. His mind was constantly telling him not to run, while his thumping heart chastised him for moving too slowly. *What are they going to say? I killed someone. I took someone's life.* He kept running through everything in his head. He was about to turn the corner around Tach Edwin's house, towards his home, when he heard the voices.

"You are sure he hasn't returned?" said a voice that Calen recognised. His heart sank into his stomach.

"He hasn't been here. What is this about?" Vars asked in an unyielding tone.

Father.

Pressing his body up against the wall of the house, Calen peeked around the corner. His mother and father stood just outside the front of the house, with a group of soldiers circled around them in an enclosed formation. Two soldiers stood out of formation, in the middle of the semi-circle, questioning Vars and Freis. A crowd of villagers had gathered around them.

"Look, we don't want to cause trouble any more than you would welcome it, but the problem is, I don't believe you." The soldier spoke with a charm in his voice, but there was an edge to it, a warning on the end of every word. "You seem like good, responsible people. Good parents. I can't imagine you would let your children roam free, so you must not be telling me the truth." He held his helmet in the nook of his arm, resting his hand on his hip. His red cloak fluttered lazily in the wind. *Red Cloak.* "Either you tell us what we need to know, or today will not end pleasantly for you – or your wife."

A deep scowl set into Vars's face. "If you so much as lay a hand—"

The soldier swung the back of his hand, clad in a polished steel gauntlet. It connected heavily with Vars's cheek. Vars stumbled backwards from the force of the strike. He raised his hand to wipe at the fresh cut that had just opened, a thin stream of blood trickling from it like a crimson tear. His eyes. Calen had only ever seen that look in Vars's eyes once before, with Rhett. He was ready to kill. The soldier watched him with anticipation, waiting. He was playing with him.

The taller of the two soldiers was silent. His thick black cape flapped in the morning breeze.

Clink.

A golden coin flipped through the air, rising a foot or two, then fell back down into the man's open hand. It was the man who fought Aeson. Farda. A chill ran up Calen's spine. The hair on the back of his neck stood on end. He could not escape this man since seeing him at the docks.

Vars straightened himself, pulling his shoulders back. He let out a long calming breath. "I cannot tell you what I do not know. He is not here, and I do not know where he is. What need have you of a young man like him? Why is the empire at my door?"

Calen heard whispers coming from the gathered crowd, all of which knew his family. They knew Vars, but there was as much fear of the empire in the villages as there was hatred.

"I am not here to explain myself to you, *blacksmith*. I consider myself a fair man, but my patience is wearing thin. Now, tell me where your son is, or I will cut that indignant scowl from your face and take your wife as a serving girl. She still looks capable, despite her obvious years."

The man drew his sword, gripping it in one hand. The

soldiers in the circle did the same. Farda continued flipping his coin, paying as much attention to the conversation as a child would to drying paint. Calen had seen enough. He couldn't stand there, hiding, while his parents were punished for his actions. He would own up to what he did, and he would pay the price, whatever it would be. He stepped out from behind the wall. "Leave them alone," he shouted. "I am here."

Farda snatched the coin out of the air and turned his head towards Calen. His eyes burned brightly into Calen's own, the skin around his mouth twisting into a satisfied grin. He did not speak.

"Come here, young man," the other soldier said. "My name is Rendall." He gestured for the surrounding soldiers to break rank and allow Calen into the centre.

Calen approached one step at a time. The two halves of his brain tore at each other as they argued whether this was the single stupidest thing he had ever done. He had already established that it was stupid. His stomach was in knots. A hand rested on his shoulder. "Calen, what is happening, my boy?" came the whispered voice of Jorvill Ehrnin.

Calen tried to respond, but his mouth felt wired shut. He heard others calling to him in hushed tones. Mara Styr. Ferrin Kolm. His heart skipped a beat as he thought he saw Anya's red hair, but his feet kept moving.

"Calen, what are you doing here?" Vars's voice broke through the noise. There was a look of agony on his face at the sight of Calen.

The soldier in the red cape, Rendall, scowled at Vars

for talking out of turn. "I am an imperial inquisitor, sent from Al'Nasla. You got yourself into a bit of trouble last night, didn't you?" He paused for a moment, not to let Calen speak but to let him stew in his own fear. And fear did grip him; the inquisitors were just scary stories. They did not truly exist. Then again, neither did giants. "What was it he did, Farda? Interrupted imperial questioning, disobeyed a direct order – oh, and what else was it? That's right – murdered an imperial soldier."

A wave of shock rang through the crowd. The commotion burbled with hushed whispers and exasperated sighs. An accusation like that was far from commonplace in The Glade. It was far from commonplace anywhere, Calen reckoned.

Every hair on Calen's body stood on end at the sight of his mother's face. Freis's eyes were swelling pools of loss. "Calen... I..." She stumbled over her own words.

"Son, is this true?" Vars's voice did not waver, his eyes fixed on Calen.

"Excuse me, blacksmith. Are you calling me a liar?" Rendall asked. "Your son attacked my men, in aid of wanted murderers. In doing so, he took the life of at least one young initiate. Oren Harstead – correct, Farda?"

Wanted murderers? Is that what Erik is? And Aeson? and Dahlen? A knot twisted in Calen's stomach. The taller man nodded, an amused grin on his face. Like a kat watching two rabbits fight. Calen wanted to speak, but he was not sure what he could say. He killed that man. He watched the light fade from his eyes...

"Now," Rendall said, "I am in a good mood today, and

as I said, I consider myself a fair man. If you lead us to these murderers, then I will grant you amnesty for your misguided acts, for that is the generous man I am. But if you refuse, I will have no choice but to seek the emperor's justice in claim of your crimes."

Calen heard gasps from the crowd. His father's face was set into a hard stare.

"What… what is the emperor's justice?" Calen asked. He had a feeling he already knew. A weightlessness entered his stomach.

His mother sobbed. "Please…"

Rendall glared at Freis.

"The emperor's justice is true justice; an eye for an eye, a life for a life," Rendall said, his tone level. "Now, if you will kindly tell me what I need to know, then we can be on our way." Rendall raised his eyebrows, opening his arms out to the air. Calen had no idea what to do. On one hand, he had no doubts that whatever Rendall would do if he found Aeson, Erik, and Dahlen would not be pleasant. On the other hand, he didn't even really know them. Were they murderers? They had certainly killed men… he watched them do it. But so had he… was he a murderer?

"I…."

"Spit it out, boy!" Rendall snapped. Cracks spread through his falsely charming demeanour. Calen felt the tension building in the gathered crowd. Everybody was on edge. His mother still sobbed softly, his father's arm around her shoulder. Vars's glare burned through the side of Rendall's head.

"I… I don't know where they are. I left them in Ölm

Forest." Calen tried desperately not to vomit as his stomach twisted in on itself. "I swear."

Rendall's face twitched in irritation. "You see, boy. Like father, like son." In a slow, steady motion, Rendall placed his helmet back onto his head. "It must be hereditary, because I just don't believe either of you." Rendall looked towards Farda, who flipped his coin high into the air, letting it fall perfectly into his open palm. Farda glanced at the coin and nodded to Rendall.

Rendall sighed. "It is a pity to take a life before the sun has even risen to its fullest, but these are the things that must be done." The wicked smile that touched his lips betrayed his words. Calen had a feeling the man delighted in taking a life, no matter where the sun sat in the sky.

A din of disgruntled noise spread through the crowd. The soldiers in the circle turned to face the gathered crowd, which had grown significantly since Calen had first arrived.

"Back! Get back, or there will be more than one dying this morning!" one of the soldiers shouted.

Rendall's grip tightened on the handle of his sword as he stepped towards Calen.

Sobbing, Freis threw herself towards Rendall. "Please, leave him be. He is just a child! This is all a misunderstanding! I—"

Rendall caught Freis with the same vicious backhand that he had given Vars, sending her spiralling to the ground with a scream. "Know your place, woman!" Rendall scoffed, spitting on the ground. Vars roared and lunged at Rendall, connecting with a powerful left hook on Rendall's cheek.

Rendall stumbled a few feet backwards. He touched his hand to his cheek and recoiled slightly as he touched a tender spot.

"Give me a sword and fight me like a man," Vars hissed. Fury burned behind the blue of his eyes. "You go around bullying children and hitting women. Is this what the inquisitors do now? Inquisitors used to be men of honour, at least enough honour to face a man. Put a sword in my hand and show me who you are."

Rendall's eyebrows peaked in surprise. He looked at Farda, who shrugged with disinterest. In a blur of motion, Rendall leapt towards Vars, closing the gap between them in fractions of a second. A look of shock spread across Vars's face as Rendall drove his sword up into his chest, right to the hilt.

"Now, why," Rendall said as he dragged the blade free of Var's chest, staring into his eyes, "would I do that?"

A deep wail filled the air. Freis collapsed on the ground in a crumpled, sobbing heap. "No, no, no…" Her usually warm and welcoming eyes were raw and red. She shook uncontrollably. "Why…"

Calen leapt towards Vars's body as it fell, lifeless, to the ground. He felt empty as he crashed to his knees beside his father's body, grabbing at his shoulders.

"Wake up! Wake up!" He shook him, harder and harder, until his arms felt like they couldn't work anymore. He felt numb, hollow. "Please, please, for the love of the gods, wake up! Dad…" He pulled Vars's body into a tight embrace and sobbed.

"Oh, get up." The disgust was evident in Rendall's voice as he wiped the blood from his sword with a cloth.

Calen felt the numbness melt away. Rage shot through his veins. It burned so hard that his head ached.

The villagers had fallen into a quiet shock when Rendall drove his sword through Vars, but that shock had worn off. Outrage took over. "Keep them in line," Rendall shouted to the soldiers surrounding them.

Calen dragged himself to his feet. Everything seemed to move in slow motion. His heart thumped against the walls of his chest. A low humming blocked out all other sound. Villagers pushed at the lines of soldiers, their mouths moving unintelligibly as they roared profanities, kicked, and pushed. Rendall had his back turned, shouting instructions to the soldiers.

Calen dropped his blood-soaked hand down to his waist. His fingers fell on a thick metal coin that led into a handle wrapped in leather. He had forgotten about his sword. He was so unused to carrying one. His body shook with rage and his fingers wrapped so tightly around the handle he thought it might crumble in his grip. He pulled the blade from its sheath and threw himself at Rendall. The only thought in his head was of his blade piercing through that wretched creature's excuse for a heart.

A jarring vibration shot up through his arm as his sword bounded backwards. Farda had stepped across his path, deflecting his strike with ease.

"Silly child." Farda swung his blade back around towards Calen's head. Calen just managed to parry the blow at the last second. Farda moved faster than any man he had ever seen. His face barely showed any signs of effort as his blade danced through the air. It was nothing like the sword fighting he was used to. It took every ounce of strength and will for Calen to match his strokes, but Farda hadn't even broken a sweat. He barely looked interested. There was no way Calen could keep this up.

Farda's outstretched boot caught him in the chest like a hammer. Calen thought his heart had stopped as he was lifted into the air. Pain wrenched in his chest as he crashed down into the hard ground. His sword clanged against the dirt beside him. His head was a daze. He coughed violently, splatters of blood landing on his shirt. He struggled to draw air back into his lungs.

When his eyes came back into focus, he saw Farda standing over him with a flat expression. He flicked that coin into the air, then let it drop back into his hand. He took a quick glance at it, then raised his sword up over his head.

"No!" Freis leapt at Farda, using all her body weight to push him backwards.

He looked genuinely surprised for a moment, then stood up straight and collected himself. "I am sorry for the pain that must be caused today, but it is simply that, *it must be.*"

With a look of regret on his face, he lifted his hand up into the air, as if swatting away an annoying fly. Something unseen lifted Freis off her feet, sending her flying backwards. She crashed through the wall of their home. The wall splintered in all directions as it collapsed inward. Farda clenched his hand into a fist. Screams and shouts rose above the din as Calen's home erupted in flames.

"No!" Calen's breath caught in his throat. He felt a deep, implacable pain in his chest when he tried to breathe again.

How did he… Mother…

He heard the harsh metallic noise of steel crashing against steel all around him. The village folk had finally snapped.

Gone.

The pain in his chest hurt so deeply, he thought he might die where he lay. He watched, unable to move, as Farda approached him. Farda took one slow step after another until he again stood over Calen's crumpled body. "None of them had to die, but you had to play the hero, and fate made its choice. You, though, you have to die. For this, I do not need to ask."

Once more, Farda raised his sword up over his head. He paused for a moment at the top of his swing. Through the chaos, Calen heard a low whistle. An arrow sliced through the bicep of Farda's sword arm, sending the blade bouncing off the ground in a series of metallic rings.

Calen felt hands wrapping around his chest as someone heaved him to his feet.

"Get up!" Sweat streaked Dahlen's face as he dragged Calen from his slumped position. Calen stared past Dahlen, a hollow void in his chest. His eyes were lost in the roaring flames of his home and the lifeless body of the man who had raised him and loved him. *Mother… Father… Ella!*

"Ella!" Calen lunged towards the blaze. His heart wrenched in his chest with the realisation that Ella would still be asleep in her bed. Dahlen grabbed him by the scruff of the neck, shoved his sword into his chest, and stared into his forlorn eyes. "They are dead. If you don't move, I am leaving you here to die too. Snap out of whatever dream you are in and run!"

They're dead. Because of me. I killed them.

Dahlen grasped a clump of Calen's shirt and shoved him onward into a run. Calen felt his feet moving, but he didn't remember telling them to. He was not in control. *It's my fault.*

Another arrow whizzed past his head. He looked up to see the slight figure of Therin. The bard stood upon a rise in the ground about forty feet away, a large curved bow in his hand. His mottled greenish-brown cloak flapped in the wind as he nocked another arrow. *What is he doing here?*

Calen snapped his head back over his shoulder and followed the flight of the arrow. It slammed into Farda's shoulder. Two other shafts protruded from his bicep and leg. A burning fury was etched onto his face as he glared back at Calen. He flipped that coin again. Whatever the result of the flip, he turned his attention away from Calen. He snapped the shafts of the arrows off with the blade of his sword and joined the soldiers. He wasn't even limping.

Dahlen bounded into view. "Calen, if you don't run, I swear to the gods I will put a sword through you myself!"

Calen stumbled, unable to collect his thoughts. "My mother… Ella…" His voice trembled. The pain in his chest threatened to take away his consciousness.

"They are dead, Calen. I am sorry." Dahlen looked solemn. He sighed. "If we don't run now, then we will all be dead as well. I need you to run. The villagers will not keep them distracted for long, and those arrows will not stop Farda. He is not natural."

Calen took a mournful look at the scenes just a little below him. The soldiers had already overpowered most of the villagers, who were bloody and bruised. They were forced to throw down their weapons. He wanted to help them, but he knew there was nothing he could do. He brought the soldiers. It was his fault. *My fault...*

He looked back at Dahlen and nodded half-heartedly.

Therin had already slung his bow back over his shoulder by the time they reached him. He cast a concerned eye over Calen, searching for injuries. Calen wanted to speak, to ask Therin what he was doing there, but he didn't.

It only took a few minutes before the others came into view. Rist and Dann sat on the two horses they had stolen from the camp that night. Dann had a hold of the third horse's reins. Aeson and Erik were beside them, astride two large brown geldings. They each held the reins of another, similar horse. When they reached the group, Therin leapt onto the back of one of the horses without breaking stride, pulling the reins to his chest as he got up. Dahlen mounted the other spare horse. He reached his hand out and dragged Calen up behind him, sighing with effort as he heaved Calen upwards. Calen felt like nothing but a useless dead weight. He was not in control of his limbs. Just taking in air was a struggle.

"Calen?" Rist's voice was tentative. "Calen, what happened?"

Calen just stared at his blood-soaked hands... his father's blood.

"Are you okay? We heard the fighting."

Calen did not respond. He could not respond. He had as much control over his voice as he did his legs. It all just kept replaying in his head. The moment Rendall drove his sword through Vars's chest. His mother sobbing, then being thrown through that wall. The flames. Ella.

Aeson and Dahlen exchanged looks. Dahlen shook his head. Aeson nodded solemnly, bringing his reins up to his chest. "Ride hard and do not stop until the sun sets."

CHAPTER 14

A New Path

The heavy air of Ölm Forest had become somewhat of a comfort for Calen. He took a deep breath in, letting the heavy air swell his chest, then released it in an exasperated sigh. The sun had set an hour ago, and the group made camp in an opening about halfway into the forest. They had ridden faster than Calen would ever have thought possible through such a dense wood. His new companions looked as if they were almost born into a saddle. He, on the other hand, was not. Every bone in his body ached from riding. His thighs were rubbed raw, and the muscles in his stomach burned from keeping himself upright. One look at Dann and Rist, who sat either side of him, told him they were in the same condition.

Both of them were speechless when Therin told them what happened. The soldiers hadn't come for their families. Therin, Aeson, Erik, and Dahlen had followed them through Ölm Forest and back to The Glade. When they caught wind of the soldiers, they separated and went to find the three boys. It seemed that Calen's name was known to the soldiers from the incident in Milltown, and they discovered where he lived. Somebody must have given them his name.

Calen still wasn't sure how or why Therin was there. He hadn't had time to talk to him, nor the will. He hadn't spoken at all since The Glade. An aching hollow filled his chest. He found it impossible to not become lost in his innermost thoughts. He sighed and tossed a loose twig into the crackling fire.

"Calen…" Rist's voice was tentative, probing. "I…"

Calen sighed. "It's okay, Rist. You don't need to say anything."

"To hell we don't," Dann scoffed, sitting up straight. "Calen, you can't just bury it deep down and never speak about it. It will eat you from the inside out until there is nothing left of you." His shoulders sank a little, the flash of temper subsiding. "Remember what Rist said – family."

Calen sighed and gave a feeble smile. He said nothing, fiddling with a small twig. His emotions washed through him in waves. They flipped from anger to sadness to a hollow emptiness as quickly as the flames of the fire flickered through the air; the embers swallowed by the night. He hadn't even thought about any of the others. How many others died in The Glade because he had to be a hero? It was his fault. *Mother… Father… Ella…*

"Faenir…" Calen suddenly snapped upright; his eyes open wide. The empty hole in his chest filled with an urgent fire. He grabbed Dann by the shoulders. "Dann! Did you see Faenir? He wasn't outside the house. At least, I didn't see him there. He has to be okay…" His words trailed off as the emptiness took hold once more.

Dann sighed and shook his head. "I didn't see him, Calen…"

Calen nodded absently. The image of the blazing fire consumed his thoughts. *I'm sorry.*

Therin leaned against a towering oak tree, deftly flipping a small steel knife across his fingers. The hood of his mottled cloak was drawn up, covering the usual coruscating glow of his silvery hair. He was set on first watch. Calen intended to talk to him, ask him why he was there. Why he saved him. He just couldn't, not yet.

Aeson, Erik, and Dahlen sat at the opposite side of the fire, resting after the hard ride into Ölm Forest. Only a few occasional words passed between them. Calen couldn't help but think that everything started when they appeared. The empire was looking for *them.* The empire was in The Glade because of *them.* If they hadn't been there, none of this would have happened. His family would still be alive. "Why is the empire after you?" Calen surprised himself by the firmness in his tone.

Erik and Dahlen's faces twisted in confusion. Aeson raised his eyebrow, his expression contrasting with those of his two sons. He didn't offer any response.

That ignited a fire in Calen. He pushed himself to his feet. "My family were just killed by men who were looking for you! Now you answer my damned question!" The fire had completely consumed him. His heart raced. Blood drained from his fingers as he clenched his hands into fists. He wanted to explode and shrivel up all in one moment.

"Just calm down a second, and we can talk. We're all friends here." Dahlen's voice was calm and measured. He got to his feet and reached his arm out to Calen.

"Don't touch me!" Calen roared, swatting Dahlen's arm away. "We are not friends. They are dead because of you!" Calen lashed out, shoving Dahlen backwards. His hand fell to the hilt of his sword, which hung from his hip.

Erik leapt to his feet.

Dann rushed to Calen's side and grabbed him from behind by both shoulders. "Calen, stop."

Calen's entire body shook. A ringing noise sounded in his ears, shrouding all other sounds in a dull haze. He tugged hard against Dann's grip, but his friend didn't budge.

"This is not the way to do this," Rist said in his usual level voice, his eyes locked on Calen's.

Just as quickly as it had appeared, the fire ebbed away from Calen's body. Exhaustion took over. He let out a long breath, and his shoulders sagged. The anger was gone, slowly replaced by that familiar emptiness. Tears formed at the corners of his eyes.

Dahlen's face suggested that his anger, however, was only beginning. Before he could say anything, Aeson was standing next to him with his hand across his chest, a stern expression on his face.

"You have suffered a great loss today, Calen, and that is not to be taken lightly. I will look past this outburst, as I have felt the type of pain that is currently washing over you." Aeson directed a soft look towards Erik and Dahlen. They backed away with reluctant expressions, returning to their seats beside the fire.

"With that," Aeson said, "you are also correct. You are owed an explanation as to why they died and why you have been dragged from your home. Please, sit back down. I will tell you everything."

Dahlen and Erik exchanged a sideways glance, uncertainty painted on their faces, but Aeson ignored them.

Once Calen, Rist, and Dann sat on the hard-packed dirt around the fire, Aeson returned to his position atop the tree stump. He reached behind himself and produced the worn leather satchel that had been the cause of everything. Calen still felt *something* emanating from within.

Therin now stood only a few feet away, leaning against another tree. His eyes were fixed on Aeson and the satchel.

Aeson ran his hands over the satchel, hesitation flitting across his face. "In this satchel is the cause of all of this," he whispered. "I'm sure, as you have been raised on Therin's stories, you know how the empire came to power – not the lies the empire spread across the rest of Epheria." Aeson paused for a moment and sighed deeply. "In the four hundred years since the rise of the empire, some of us have sought its downfall. We have aided in uprisings, incited rebellions, and fought in many wars. Unfortunately, we have been beaten back at every turn. Every time it appeared that a victory had been won, the Dragonguard would appear, or Fane himself. Though, in the past few decades, he has not been seen outside of Al'Nasla."

Aeson clutched the satchel a little tighter.

"We could not stand up against the Lorian Empire, with their Dragonguard and their mages, not while the lands stood fractured and divided. They hunted the giants to near extinction. The elves scattered, retreating into the woodlands of Lynalion. The dwarves shut the doors into their mountain kingdoms. And the Lorian Empire ruled over the lands of men with an iron fist. Those remain who would oppose the empire, but most of us hide in the shadows – waiting. We needed something to unite the old alliances, something to rally behind. Finally, after everything, we have found it."

Calen felt the anticipation burning in everyone around the fire. Even Therin tilted his head up to glimpse what was inside the satchel. The flames of the fire flickered across his sharp cheekbones as he feigned disinterest.

Aeson held the satchel between his knees and undid the buckles. He hesitated for a moment before his hands disappeared into its depths. What was it that could cause such pain and misery?

Calen's breath caught in his throat. He turned his face away sharply, bringing his hand up to protect his eyes from the sudden glare that emanated from the satchel. The others in the group did the same.

He pulled his hand away from his face as his eyes adjusted to the shimmering light. The answer he had been craving only resulted in more questions.

It was around a foot long and about half as much wide. Layers of overlapping scales washed over it from top to bottom. The bone-white tips of each scale reflected the blinding light from the fire. The white faded into jet-black at the base of each scale. It looked like an egg. An armoured egg.

Therin stared unashamedly now. The reflected light illuminated his eyes and caused his hair to shimmer, even beneath his hood. "Never in my days…" he whispered; his voice was barely audible amidst the gasps of awe from the others.

Aeson stared straight at Calen. There was something in his expression that unsettled Calen. It wasn't malice or ill intentions, but almost… expectation. Calen shuffled uncomfortably under Aeson's unwavering eye contact. He desperately wanted to break the silence. Fortunately, he had many questions. "What… what is it?"

"It is a dragon egg," Therin said, startling Calen. He stepped closer to the group. He seemed to get taller. Light drew inward around him as the fire dimmed, making him seem almost ethereal. "More specifically, it is a dragon egg from Valacia, the northern icelands across the Antigan Ocean. We were never even sure that they existed. They were just legend." There was a sense of awe in his voice. As he spoke, it seemed to Calen that even the insects in the undergrowth ceased their noisy night-time rituals just to hear his voice.

Therin hunkered down in front of Aeson, his hands hovering inches away from the egg. "Nomadic dragons of the Valacian icelands, with scales as white as snow and as black as the darkest night, able to grow as large as any dragon in Epheria. It is said that their connection to the Spark of magic is as raw and as old as the light from the sun. No elf, human, or giant has ever been bound to a Valacian dragon. I don't believe one has ever even been seen in this part of the world – until now." His eyes momentarily shifted from the egg to Aeson. A smile crept across his face as he clasped Aeson's shoulders in his hands. "You did it, old friend. You actually did it."

The sounds of the forest crept back into Calen's ears, and the firelight once again filled the camp. Therin sat in front of Aeson and the egg, his legs splayed out in front of him. A beaming smile perched upon his face, his eyes now back on the shimmering black and white egg.

"How the hell does he do that?" Dann whispered into Calen's ear. "Is it me, or did he actually glow a little?"

Calen nodded. He couldn't drag his eyes away from the egg. It was beautiful. Harsh – but beautiful.

"What good will one dragon do against the empire? They have the Dragonguard," Rist said abruptly. "How is one dragon to stand against a dozen?"

Aeson sighed, running his hand along the outside of the egg. "It is not what one dragon can do, Rist. It is the symbol it creates. It is what it represents. Hope. Give people hope, and they *will* fight." Rist's expression twisted into a frown. Calen knew that face. It was the face that Rist pulled every time an answer didn't satisfy him.

Draleid.

A shiver ran up Calen's spine at the voice. It was an echo in the back of his mind. It wasn't his own voice, but it was. He didn't recognise it, but it was familiar. A whisper. He tried to ignore it.

Draleid.

The voice drowned out all the sounds around him. The rustle of the leaves, the incessant buzz of the insects, and the occasional nocturnal birdsong all ebbed and faded away. He tried desperately to snap himself back into the real world, but all he could focus on was the voice.

Draleid n'aldryr.

Draleid.

The voice grew louder, echoing throughout Calen's mind. Every hair on his body stood on end. He wasn't sure how much time had passed. It felt like seconds, but it was hard to tell. Everything around him seemed almost a blur.

Draleid.

"Draleid…"

"What did you say? Sorry, I didn't hear you," Rist said apologetically. His eyes searched Calen's. Calen didn't even realise he had spoken out loud.

"Nothing. Sorry. Just lost in my own thoughts." The fuzz in his head started to clear, the voice faded.

He looked around the group and found Aeson and Therin peering over at him, curiosity in their eyes. They looked away as he made eye contact. *Did they hear me? What is happening?*

The shimmering light from the egg disappeared as Aeson placed it back into the satchel. He pushed it to one side and stood up. "Okay, okay. Everybody quiet down. It is time we laid out our plans. In the morning, we ride for Camylin, then onward to Belduar." He looked at the young men from The Glade, breathing in deeply as he did. "I think it best that you come with us."

Dahlen tried to interject. "But—"

"This is not a debate, Dahlen. Now remain quiet." Aeson turned his eyes expectantly towards Calen, Dann, and Rist.

Dahlen's face twisted into a scowl. Erik gave him a look as if to say, "Calm down."

Rist was the first to respond. "The Glade is all we know.

All we have ever known. How can we leave the people who raised us after what has just happened?"

"I'm afraid, young Master Rist, that staying is not an option. What I have just shown you is the reason why. The empire knows that we have it; that is why they followed us to Milltown. And they *will* kill you where you stand without so much as a conversation, and that is nobody's fault but mine. I am sorry that you are involved in this. It was not my wish, but the gods intervened, and here we are." Aeson's eyes softened as he looked at Calen, whose gaze had not left the crackling fire. "Calen has lost a great deal today, more than any young man should. By returning, all you do is put your own families in the same danger. The empire will surely remain in and around the villages for some time. You must use your heads. I'm not saying that you join our cause, but for now, at least come with us. Let us take you safely to somewhere else. We have friends in Belduar who can help you."

"I… I don't know," Rist said.

Aeson did not move from where he stood, his eyes fixed on the young men from The Glade. The fire crackled in the night as a wordless silence filled the air.

"I'm going with them." Calen no longer gazed absently into the fire. He turned towards Aeson, a fixed look on his face. "I'm going with them," he repeated, "on one condition."

"Which is?" Aeson raised his eyebrow.

Therin's interest was also piqued as he sat up to listen.

"I want you to train me in the sword. I never want to be as helpless as I was…" His trembling hands twisted into fists. "I'm going to make them pay for what they did. I want you to promise me I will get my chance at revenge."

A smile flitted across Aeson's face. He extended his arm to Calen, grasped his forearm, and pulled him to his feet. "That, my boy, I can promise you."

"Me too," Dann said. "I'm coming too."

"And you too." Aeson nodded. "And you, young Master Rist?"

Rist twisted his face left to right as he mulled things over. He gently patted the dust from his trousers and stood up. "I guess I'm coming too. These two won't last two days without me." He shot Calen and Dann a weak smile.

"It is decided, then. We leave at first light. It's four days' hard ride to Camylin, so get your rest."

Rhett let his shoulders drop. He slouched back into the soft-packed leather couch, sighing heavily. The Riverside Inn was reasonably small as inns went, about half the size of The Gilded Dragon. Circular tables dotted the airy lounge atop thick wooden floorboards. Most of the tables were empty; the merchants and traders having continued on their way at the break of dawn.

The innkeeper was a stout man, with a bald head and a soft welcoming face. He smiled at Rhett as he cleaned out a tankard with a large cloth. Rhett smiled back at him, giving a slight nod, as you do to somebody you don't know particularly well, but still want to appear friendly towards. He fidgeted absently with the cold handle of his tankard of mead.

Ella had gone up to their room to change and would probably be an hour at the least. She took a while getting herself ready, but it was always worth the wait. She was almost as beautiful on the outside as she was on the inside. He allowed himself a deep smile at the thought of her.

It had been two days and nights since they left The Glade. They had slept under the stars those nights. They dared not stop in the village of Ölm. Their families were too well known there. They were not so well known in Pirn. Still, he was nervous. He was nervous about leaving his home and his family. He was nervous about what a new life in Berona might bring. The journey would be long. With the Darkwood and the Burnt Lands bisecting the continent, boat was the only real way to travel from the South to the North. There were only two main ports that docked ships large enough to make that journey from Illyanara: Gisa and Falstide.

Only the wealthy travelled from Gisa – merchants and traders, lords and ladies travelling to the island city of Antiquar or the capital, Al'Nasla. In all his life, Rhett had not seen enough coin to afford a single ticket from that city. He most likely never would.

Everybody else journeyed from the port of Falstide. It was a longer journey, more dangerous, but it was all they could afford. It would be two months by horseback, at least, to reach Falstide. It would be tough, a lot of rough nights, with cutthroats and purse-snatchers. Then they would either have to face the Burnt Lands or find a captain stupid enough to sail along the Lightning Coast. He knew he did not need to worry about Ella. She was a lady, all right, but her strength of will outstripped his own on many occasions.

"Hello there, stranger."

She was a vision in a floral cream dress, her hair flowing down over her shoulders in a waterfall of gold. Her ocean-blue eyes looked down over him, searching. There was nothing he wouldn't do for her. They would make it to Berona.

"Well, aren't you a sight for sore and tired eyes?" He gazed up at her, a warm smile on his face. "Come on, take a seat. Have a drink with me. We have the place to ourselves."

Ella laughed and sat down next to him, then shoved his shoulder playfully. "Oh, shut up, you."

They gestured to the innkeeper for two more meads. They sat there, talking about the next few days, steering conversation away from their long journey across the plains of Illyanara.

Ella took a timid drink of her mead, then bounced in her seat and turned towards Rhett, her eyes full of excitement. "I'm excited to see Camylin. I've never been. Calen went with Dad when he was younger, but I didn't get to go. I hear the markets are amazing."

Rhett heard the jubilance in her voice. She was incredibly cute when she got excited. He reached into his travel bag beside him and pulled out a small purse. It made a clinking sound when he dropped it on the table. "Well, I've set aside a little bit of coin. We can't pass through Camylin and not shop in the markets."

Ella's eyes lit up. "Really? Are you sure we can afford that?"

"Of course," Rhett replied. "I made sure to set it aside."

Ella placed a small kiss on his cheek.

I'll just have to ration my food a little for the next few days.

Valacian Dragon Egg.

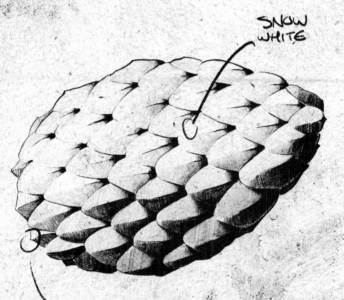

SNOW
WHITE

SHARP POINTED
Ridge

Jet BLACK
Base.

CHAPTER 15

Shadows Don't Sleep

They travelled from sunrise to sunset, only stopping to rest the horses and eat some dried meat and cheese. Calen couldn't remember the last time his body had been free of pain. He had never thought riding a horse could cause so much agony, but he was wrong. The insides of his legs were chafed to a raw red colour, and a constant ache ran from his rear up through his spine and all the way to his neck.

It wouldn't have been so bad if he had the chance to rest properly, but every time they stopped, Aeson took Calen and Dann to practice the sword while the others watched. Sometimes Erik or Dahlen joined in if Aeson requested. Therin and Rist mostly stayed by the horses, splaying themselves out on the ground. Rist was buried in the book he had purchased in Milltown.

Each time, Aeson ran them through a series of forms. Some, Calen recognised from training with his father; most, he did not. Learning each new form was slow and repetitive, but once he got the hang of it, it began to flow. Although his body ached, Calen found comfort in the sword forms. A familiarity that settled his mind.

As the sun sank into the horizon and the birds began their night song, Dann frowned. He wasn't as quick to pick up the forms as Calen was, which frustrated him to no end. He never liked not being the best at anything. There would be no practice that night, though. Camylin would provide a reprieve. But that didn't stop him from sulking, as he had done every night since they started training.

"Camylin," Erik said as he pulled his horse up beside Calen's at the top of the hill.

The city of Camylin sat nestled against the mountainside. The sun setting down over the ocean washed the red slate rooftops with a warm orange light. It was even bigger than Calen remembered. Massive walls encircled the city. Their sprawling lengths were broken at regular intervals by thick cylindrical towers. Even from a distance, the keep stood head and shoulders above the rest of the city. It backed up against the north-eastern wall, just below the mountainside. The Glade would have fit inside the city walls a hundred times over, with room to spare.

"Wow…" It wasn't often that Dann's breath was taken away. Calen had forgotten that Dann had never been to Camylin. Ölm was the farthest east that he had ever been.

Dahlen laughed. "A little bigger than that village of yours? This is only half the size of Berona and half again of Antiquar or Vaerleon."

Dann mouthed to himself, "'A little bigger than that village of yours?' Asshole."

Neither Calen nor Erik could help but laugh at Dann, much to Dahlen's irritation.

Once the laughter died down, Rist turned to Calen. "You feeling okay?" Calen heard the hesitation in his voice. He knew he meant well, but Calen wasn't ready to talk. He wasn't ready to believe what had happened. It was best to roll it into a tiny ball and hide it somewhere in the back of his mind. He would come back to it, but not yet. It was too painful. It would break him if he let it.

"Yeah, I'm good," he lied. "Just trying not to think about it. Have you ever been to Camylin before?"

Calen was aware that Rist knew he was trying to change the subject. Calen knew very well that Rist had been to Camylin on many occasions with Lasch, but he let it go.

"I have, actually," Rist said, playing along. "I've been several times with Father, when he sourced rugs and paintings for the inn."

Calen nodded in acknowledgment. Both young men were aware that the answer was not needed, but it was appreciated.

Therin pulled his horse to a halt just before they joined the main road into Camylin. "This is where I leave you. Camylin is no place for an elf. Not one that wants to keep his head, anyway. I will meet you tomorrow at midday, at The Wilted Leaf Inn, just a couple of hours east of Camylin." Moving his horse closer to Calen, Therin leaned in. His voice was a whisper in the wind. "Your father was a great man. I will mourn him with every passing day. He deserved a better death."

He did not wait for a response. Therin pulled his cloak tighter around himself and ensured the drawstrings were tied firmly. He kicked his horse into a canter, heading down the southerly road that drew down and around Camylin, ignoring Calen's shouts.

"Wait, Therin!"

What did he mean?

Camylin sat at the base of the Wolfpine Ridge. It was the funnel through which all people from the villages travelled to reach the mainland of Illyanara. It was the only major city for hundreds of miles. That meant the main road into Camylin was a busy one. Everywhere Calen looked were merchants and their horse-drawn wagons, laden down with everything from wheels of cheese to casks of cider and ale. The more elaborate and ornately carved wagons belonged to the silk and wine merchants, their elevated status obvious by the height of their noses in the air.

There were young people searching for employment, or a chance at a busier life than their villages could provide. Hardy-looking men with swords and axes belted to their hips and backs walked side by side with families on a rare trip to see the city. Calen had to stifle a chuckle of amusement at the strange mix of people.

Calen pulled up his hood when he saw men and women from the villages, some he recognised, some he didn't. Even the ones whose faces were unfamiliar to him could be marked out by the wide-eyed, expectant stares on their faces. Most would never have seen anything like Camylin. A shot of panic ran through him as he felt a hand grabbing the back of his head, pulling his hood down over his shoulders.

"Get that damned thing off you," Aeson whispered, his annoyance evident even in his hushed tone. "How do you think the city guard will react to a hooded rider with an elven blade strapped to his hip? Think with your head, not your ass."

With that said, he trotted on, bringing his horse to the front of the group. He didn't think the others had noticed, or at least they pretended not to. Feeling a twinge of embarrassment, Calen drew his cloak up around his sword. The last thing his father gave him.

The city guards barely even noticed them as they rode in through the massive arched gateway. They rode just far enough apart from each other so as not to entice any questions. On their own, none of them drew even half the attention that the mercenaries or cutthroats would draw, with their battered armour and motley collection of scars and war wounds.

As they passed through the gate, the road widened to over twice its original size. There was a split in the middle, occupied by a long row of peddlers' stalls, interspersed with large elm trees, carefully pruned to allow just the right amount of shade. On either side, the street was framed by large stone buildings and an ever-flowing network of side streets and stairways as the city fanned out and upwards.

It was even more spectacular a sight than Calen remembered. Up close, he felt like an ant next to the giant buildings.

Calen had always thought that nothing could match the

buzz and grandeur of the Moon Market, no matter how far he travelled. In Camylin, it was as if the Moon Market took place at every corner, at all times, and this was not even a day of note.

"The inn is just up ahead," Aeson said. "We will bring our horses around the back, to the stable yard, and arrange some rooms for the night. I will be meeting our acquaintance there in an hour or so. It would be best to be settled in by then. Also, no names when we're inside."

Aeson pulled his horse to the right to avoid stepping on a small child, who tottered about aimlessly, oblivious to the fact that he had nearly become paint on the bottom of the gelding's shoe.

The stable yard of the Traveller's Rest was reasonably small, with only three or four horses tethered up outside. It was to be expected. With the size of the city, there was not much room to spare for extravagant stables.

The inside of the inn was a different story altogether. The common room was enormous. It was easily three times the size of The Gilded Dragon's, and it smelled of wine, incense and tabbac smoke. Private booths were built into all the walls except the wall behind the bar, which was fronted by large casks of wine and ale. All the furniture was made of the most exotic wood and the finest velvet and leather that Calen had ever seen. The bar was a long slab of oak, ornately carved to such a degree that it easily matched the craftsmanship of the two dragons that sat atop the staircase of Lasch's inn.

Calen couldn't help but tap his foot along to the tune the bard was playing on his flute. It seemed familiar, though he didn't recognise the words that the other patrons were singing.

The clientele were the oddest mix he had ever seen. There were merchants dressed in fine silks of audacious reds, golds, and greens; shifty, weasel-like men with circles under their eyes and dirt melted into their clothes – cutpurses and pickpockets, by the look of them – and grizzled men in heavy leather armour, with more scars on their face than hairs on their head. There were even some women – ladies, by the cut of their clothing. Calen really wasn't sure what to make of it all. Not one of them looked like they should be there, yet not one of them looked out of place.

"What is this place?" Calen whispered to Erik.

"It's a… private meeting area?" Erik said, as if he were not quite sure himself. "Father often uses it to meet *acquaintances.*"

Calen nodded as he looked around the common room. He could see why Aeson used it to meet *acquaintances.* Which he figured was a nice way of saying, "anybody he didn't want to be seen meeting."

It didn't take long for the rooms to be sorted. The inn-keeper had only two left, each with three beds. Calen, Rist, and Dann would take one, and Aeson, Erik, and Dahlen the other.

"Five minutes," Dahlen said as they separated. "We'll see you in the common room."

It was clear to Calen that the room they had been given was only intended for a single occupant. All three beds were so closely jammed together that there was not enough space between them to stand sideways. The room was sparse besides. The only form of decoration on the wall was a badly patched hole, and an oil lamp that looked as though it had long since broken.

"Remind me again, why are we here?" Rist said, tossing his bag onto the bed on the far right of the cramped room.

"We don't exactly have much choice," Dann said with a shrug, running his hand along the damaged patch of wall.

Calen dropped his bag on the floor beside his bed and turned back towards the doorway. "Come on, it's been a long few nights. Let's just get a drink."

We're here because I'm going to find the men who took my family from me.

Erik and Dahlen had already secured a large circular table in the western corner of the room by the time Calen, Rist, and Dann got down the stairs.

"Where's… you know?" Dann asked as they approached the table. His voice trailed off when he registered the sharp look from Dahlen. Aeson had warned them not to use names in there.

"He's sorting business." Erik nodded towards one of the private booths, with the curtain drawn all the way across. "He'll be done in a few hours," he added, playfully elbowing Dahlen.

"A few hours? What are we supposed to do till then?" asked Dann, incredulous.

Erik shrugged. "I don't know about you, but I plan on drinking."

"Well," Dann said, "now you're speaking my language." As they sat down, Dann gestured to a slightly overwhelmed looking serving girl to have three more ales brought to the table. She nodded sheepishly before disappearing into the mass of people around her. "One copper, she forgets the drinks," Dann whispered in Calen's ear.

"Done."

Rist looked up from the book he had just pulled from his pocket. "If I end up waiting the rest of the night because of you two playing a stupid little game, I swear to the gods I will throw water on you in your sleep."

"Oh, relax," Dann said, waving Rist away. "Read your book and stop ruining our fun."

Rist twisted his face into a disapproving look. He licked the tip of his finger and turned the page, his eyes returning to the words within.

"I've never been to Camylin before. It has to be ten, maybe twenty times the size of The Glade. In fact, I don't think I've ever been farther east than Pirn. How much farther is it to Bel—"

Dahlen was frowning at him again, his eyebrows raised. Dann wasn't great at keeping his mouth shut. It was only going to get worse with ale.

Out of the corner of his eye, Calen spotted the serving girl passing by the table, wandering around like a headless chicken. She had already forgotten. He waited until Dann launched into another tirade of verbal diarrhoea, then caught her eye with his, gesturing at the table. Recognition crossed her face. She nodded again and bolted towards the bar, picking up her skirts into her fists as she dodged in and out of the drunken crowd. Within a few minutes, she was back at the table, full of apologies. She placed three tankards of cold ale down in front of Dann. He smiled at her, paid her for the drinks, then slid one each over to Calen and

Rist. He was raising the tankard to his mouth when Calen coughed loudly, one eyebrow raised.

"Oh, fine. You're such a bad winner." Dann dug into his pocket for the coin. He scowled, then tossed it, a little stronger than necessary, to Calen. Rist looked up from his book, a knowing smile on his face. He missed nothing.

The drinks continued to flow as the night wore on. With each drink, Dann talked more and more horseshit. He claimed the bear they killed during The Proving was easily as big as a dragon.

"… it was huge! Easily twelve… *Hic*… maybe fourteen feet…"

By the time Aeson emerged from the booth, Dann had successfully exaggerated every story Calen had otherwise known to be true and also invented some rather dubious other ones.

Rist had rarely looked up from his book. Dahlen, to Calen's surprise, was quite enthralled in Dann's stories, matching him ale for ale as well. Although, that probably explained the former.

Calen had also managed to get Erik to agree to a rematch with the axe throwing, seeing as it was obvious that he had purposely missed the last throw.

Calen's back roared with relief when he finally collapsed onto his bed. It was a welcome respite from the aching throb he had felt for most of the day.

He stretched out his legs and arms as he lay there in the bed. They burned in that delightfully painful way they did after they had been overused. Even Dann's drunken snoring wouldn't stop him from sleeping tonight.

Creaking floorboards on the landing just outside the room woke Calen from his light sleep.

"Dann," he whispered, attempting to channel as much urgency as the situation would allow. No response. Dann continued to snore rather loudly. Calen sighed, throwing his eyes to the sky. "Rist…"

"Yeah?" Rist's voice was groggy, not entirely awake. He rubbed the heel of his palm into his eyes and sat up in the bed.

"There's someone outside the room," Calen said, nodding towards the door.

"Calen, don't be so—"

Thud.

"What the fuck was that?" Dann shouted as he shot up from his sleep.

The door swung open, cracking violently off the wooden wall. Erik stood in the open doorway, a body at his feet. Blood flowed freely across the floor. "Get dressed and get your things. We need to go, now."

He was met with blank stares.

"Now!"

The chill from the wind was bitter and harsh, lashing at Therin's face as he rode through the night. He pulled his cloak tight around himself and signalled Vaen to ride faster. Something didn't seem right. He was not sure what, but he knew there was something, like a feeling scratching in the back of his mind.

It was less than a half hour's ride to The Wilted Leaf. He knew the innkeeper there, and if he kept to himself, there wouldn't be any trouble. It was amazing how accepting people became when coin was involved.

He could use a warm meal and a good night's sleep. The ache in his back spread as he rode. The stiffness in his wrists throbbed. It had been a long while since he'd had a proper rest. Far too long. Gritting his teeth, he urged Vaen on faster.

He was loath to leave the egg now that Aeson had finally found it – and Calen. It was a strange twist of fate that they spent centuries searching for an egg, only to find its Draleid by pure serendipity. The fact that the Draleid was Vars's son... what he would give to know the odds of that. *Rest well, my friend. I will watch over him – at least you saw fit to pass him on my sword.*

And the other one, Rist, had the Spark in him. Finding the Spark in people from the South was a rarity these days. There was, at least, some truth in the old wives' tales of inquisitors roaming the lands, snatching up children who misbehaved. The inquisitors sought all those who even showed a glimmer of the ability to touch the Spark and stole them away, off to the High Tower in Berona. It left the lineage diluted in the South. Every year, there seemed to be less and less with the potential to wield the Spark. It truly was sad. Until now, the villages must not have seen an inquisitor in generations. *Living at the edge of the continent could have its perks.*

Therin cursed as Vaen lurched forward. He thrashed wildly, nearly throwing Therin from his back, head-first into the packed dirt below. Vaen stomped his feet and neighed anxiously as his head spun from side to side.

It took Therin a second to regain his composure. The sudden jolt broke his train of thought.

"Strange to see an elf in these parts." The voice echoed in the night, as if it came from everywhere, and nowhere, all at once. Therin knew that voice, or at least the sound it made. It was harsh, like steel dragged across a gravel path. An uncontrollable shiver ran up Therin's spine. He reached for the Spark, pulling on threads of Fire and Spirit. *Just in case.*

The darkness should not have made a difference to his eyesight, not with the Spark flowing through him. The right balance of Fire and Spirit should have given him the night vision of a kat, but the light seemed to pull away from him, shrouding the night in darkness.

"Oh, now, now. You know better than that, *elf.*"

Allowing the Spark to burn through him, Therin pulled deeply on threads of Fire and Air. He sent a plume of roaring flame from the palm of his hand, in a wide arc in front of him. He caught a glimpse of the black robe flapping in the wind, adorned with spirals and swirls of dark blue. Only a flash and it was gone, but he knew what lay under the hood of that robe. Thin pale skin. Not leathery or cracked, like the hide of a desert animal, but smooth like the finest silk from Narvona. Eyes of jet, from corner to corner, so black that they drew in the surrounding light.

A Fade was a creature of innate shadow, a mage sharing their body with darkness itself. Consumed by the need for power. At least, they believed they were sharing.

Therin did not for a second think it was the mage who was in control behind those eyes.

"Ride!" he roared, lashing at the reins. He gave Vaen a firm kick, urging him to move as fast as his legs would allow, steering him back towards Camylin. *The egg. It knows where they are.*

"You are far too late, elf," the gravelly voice called out, as if from all around him. It was toying with him. "You will not reach them in time, or at all."

An arrow whizzed past his head. The darkness was his only saving grace. The soldiers were not protected by the same dark magic as the Fade. He saw them just fine.

He felt the rough grate at the back of his mind as he drew on threads of Earth. He pushed the threads into the earth and dragged the clay from the ground. He formed it into a spike, hardened it to stone, and sent it piercing through the air at the archers hidden in the thicket to his right. They dropped one by one as he rode past, the hardened spike of clay tearing through their armour as though it were a pin through a cushion. Earth was never his strongest, but he could handle himself.

He didn't look back as the bodies fell. He needed to get to Camylin. Therin placed his hand on Vaen's neck, pulling on threads of Spirit. He willed the horse to go faster, drawing the pain out of his legs, pulling the tiredness from his lungs. He would need a lot of rest after this. They both would.

CHAPTER 16

No Place Like Home

The setting sun cast a warm glow over the city. The yellow-orange rays splashing down over the smooth grey stone of the buildings made Camylin look so magical.

Ella had spent the day exploring the endless markets across the city. She had never seen the likes of it. Entire squares of market stalls dedicated entirely to different colours of silks. Broad streets full of merchants selling scarves, dresses, and hats of all varieties. There were packed colonnades of hawkers flogging everything that Ella never knew she didn't need. She could spend days roaming the city streets and never come close to seeing everything there was to see.

The sheer size of Camylin made The Glade seem like the smallest place in Epheria. She wished her father had brought her along with Calen when they visited. She missed them and Mother already. By the gods, she missed her mother. It had only been a few days, but she felt it already. She knew it might be years before she saw any of them again. She gripped the hem of her skirt subconsciously. It was the right thing.

"'Scuse me, Miss," came a little voice behind her. There was a small child, maybe ten summers of age. A rounded cap with a stiff brim at the front sat upon his head, giving shade to his gaunt cheeks, which were blackened with dirt. His clothes dangled about his slight frame, clearly handed down from an older sibling. Dark circles ringed his eyes, and he looked as though he hadn't eaten in days. "Could you spare some food? I'm really hungry... I'm sorry to ask..."

Ella's heart melted when she saw the little boy. "Of course—"

"Oi, you, get out of here. Leave my customers alone!" The merchant's eyes were hard as stone. He was a horrid-looking man with a thick bushy moustache, a furrowed brow and bald head. She had seen pigs in better shape; his big round belly drooped out from under his fine silk shirt, and he looked as though he were out of breath just from standing still. With one last regretful look towards Ella, the little boy bolted away into the crowd.

"Damn street urchins..." murmured the merchant, shaking his head as he fussed over the arrangement of his fine clothes.

"Better an urchin than a pig," Ella snapped. The man looked at her in shock as she picked up the corner of her skirts, turned and headed after the boy. She found him leaning with his back against a wall, a steady flow of tears rolling down his cheeks. "Hey... Hey!" She hunkered down in front of him and dipped her hand into her bag, producing a shiny green apple. "Take it. Go on."

The boy looked at her, caution painted on his face. He clearly wasn't used to someone helping him. He reached out and wrapped his fingers around the green apple. He pulled it back towards himself, as if he thought it was a trick. As soon as it was out of Ella's grasp, he pulled it to his mouth and sank his teeth into it longingly, spraying his cheeks with its sweet juices.

"Thank you," he said, his mouth still full.

Ella gave the boy a weak smile. She looked back into her bag, at the loaf of bread and the block of cheese she had gotten herself and Rhett for later that night, and then back at the boy. He had eaten the whole apple, core and all. "Here," she said, pushing the bread and cheese into his arms. "For you and your brother."

The boy's eyes were a mixture of joy and confusion. "I… I can't take this… how did you know I had a brother?"

Ella raised her hand into the air, with her palm out towards the boy, like she had seen her mother do to Calen whenever he argued with her. "Take it. I won't hear any argument." She stood straight up, brushing her dress down with her hands.

"Thank you."

"You are very welcome. What is your name?" Ella asked.

"My name is Gareth, Miss," the boy said sheepishly.

"Well, it's nice to meet you, Gareth. My name is Ella. You look after yourself, okay?"

"I will, Miss Ella. Thank you."

Ella smiled. Gareth stood up and made his way down a

side street nearby, looking back towards her with a smile on his face every couple of steps.

She laughed to herself as she walked along the market stalls. She would have to find something else to eat for later, but there was no way she was going to let that boy go hungry. *I suppose that is what happens in cities like this. There are so many people that some of them are just forgotten. That would never happen in The Glade.*

Ella picked up another loaf of bread from a bakery nearby but didn't have enough coin to replace the cheese. They would just have to go without. She quickened her pace as the sun got lower in the sky. She hadn't noticed the time passing. Rhett would be back at the inn, and she'd never been in a city on her own after dark before. She had insisted to him she wanted to do her shopping on her own, that he would only slow her down and that he should let a girl do what girls do. She was regretting that as the streets began to thin out. The orange glow faded, blending into the pale light of the moon, and the merchants and hawkers packed up their wares into the carts and cases.

Ella became overly aware that the faces that were left on the streets were not as friendly as the ones she had seen earlier in the day. These faces were hardy. Dark-circled eyes. Rough leathery skin marked with cuts and scars. Each of them stared at her, tracing her from head to toe. Their eyes did not look like there were good intentions behind them. She picked up her pace again. Any faster and she would be jogging. Shadows lurked around every corner and side street, growing as the sun retreated. She brought her eyes down, tracking her feet. *Just walk.* She wasn't sure why her heart was racing. Nothing had happened, but she was scared.

"All right, love, fancy a bit of company?" came a gruff voice from the other side of the street.

Ella glanced over. The voice came from a man at least twenty summers her senior. He had long, greasy greyish-black hair. A horrendous scar ran diagonally across his face. A shiver ran up her spine. She looked back at the ground in front of her and kept walking. *Not far now. Only a few minutes. Why did I insist on going alone?*

She was only around the corner from the inn when she walked into what felt like a brick wall. She looked up to see the face of a reasonably handsome man. He was about an inch or two shorter than Calen, but maybe ten summers older. Despite his disarming good looks, his eyes were different. They unnerved her.

"Well, well, well. Look what we have here, Rufin. Looks like a lost little lady." The man's voice was oily. A pungent smell of cheap spirits wafted from his open mouth. Ella leapt backwards with shock.

"Now, now, little lady. Don't go running away." The other man, Rufin, was a ratty man with a wiry frame. His thick black hair was slicked back against his head, shining in the moonlight. A thin smile painted his face. "We only want to play."

Both men chuckled wickedly.

Ella's heart pounded. Her hands wouldn't stop shaking. "Please, just leave me alone. I don't want any trouble." The words trembled off her tongue.

"Little lady, we don't want no trouble neither. We just want to play. You like playing, don't you?"

The two men circled her slowly, getting closer and closer, teasing and taunting her.

"Come on now. I think we could show you such a good time that you might even want to pay us after," the handsome man said, laughing to himself.

There was a flash of movement that Ella's eyes didn't catch. The handsome man went crashing to the ground with a howl. His left hand pulled up to his face, attempting to stem the flow of blood trickling from his lip.

"The woman said to leave her alone." The man who had thrown the punch had a strong, confident voice. He stood a head above both men. He could not have been more than two or three summers older than Ella, but he held himself like a man who had seen many more than that. His rich green eyes were warm against his porcelain skin. He had near shoulder-length brown hair and a short, close-cut beard to match. A glistening white mantle was draped around his shoulders, and he wore a surcoat of deep green. At the centre of the surcoat was a motif of a sword, pointing downward, set into the image of a sunburst, all painted in white. The surcoat just about covered a polished steel breastplate, and he had a pair of shimmering steel greaves, and vambraces that matched the breastplates meticulous sheen.

"Oh, you are going to pay for that," the handsome man growled. He pushed himself to his feet. The thin ever-flowing stream of blood now marked a line from his lips to his chin. He twisted his hands into fists. The man in the green surcoat tilted his head to the side. A wry smile formed on his lips, as if amused by the comment.

"Kaffa, that symbol," Rufin said, pointing at the sword and sunburst motif on the man's surcoat. His voice only rose above a whisper. "The Knights of Achyron."

Kaffa's eyes narrowed with suspicion. "The Knights? That old cult? You listen to too many fairy tales, Rufin," he scoffed.

"It's not a fairy tale, Kaffa. She's not worth it."

Rufin put his hand on Kaffa's shoulder, tugging at his shirt to draw him down one of the side alleys. His hand was met with resistance, but Ella saw hesitation in Kaffa's eyes.

She became very aware that she still stood between the man in the green surcoat and her would-be attackers. She slowly stepped backwards, towards the edge of the street, her eyes flitting between the two.

"I would listen to your friend. All fairy tales hold truth," the man said. His voice was flat and measured. His hand rested on the hilt of his sword, his fingers tapping on its rounded silver pommel, one after another.

Kaffa and Rufin exchanged a glance. Kaffa let out an irritated sigh. His eyes narrowed, and a growl escaped his throat. He raised his hand and pointed towards the knight. "We'll be seeing you around." The words left his lips like stones being dragged across rusty iron.

"I sure hope you do," the knight called back as the two men skulked away into the shadows. He turned back towards Ella. He puffed out his cheeks and let out a sigh, then his mouth stretched into a tentative smile. "Well, that could have gone worse," he said with a cautious chuckle. He ran his hand through his hair. "Are you okay?"

Ella was completely off-put by how calm he was. Her heart raced like it was running for its life, and her stomach was in knots. But he seemed like he had just broken up a fight between two children.

"I… Thank you for what you did. This is my first time in the city. I didn't know…"

"It's okay. Camylin is a lovely city – by day. By night, it is a bit different, much like any city you will find. It's not safe to walk around by yourself, whether you're a man or a woman."

Ella raised one eyebrow. "But you're walking around on your own."

"Well, it's a little different for me – as you can see." He gestured down the alleyway after the two men who had slithered away.

"Right, well… Thank you. Your kindness is beyond appreciated, but I must go. I'm definitely late, and Rhett will surely be worried." Ella clutched the hem of her skirt, her nerves still in a fluster.

"You don't have far to go, do you? I can walk you where you need to go."

"No, no… it's okay. I need to be going. Thank you again. Please be safe." Ella walked away so fast that she was almost running. She heard him calling after her, but she couldn't make out the words. Her heart still pounded on her chest like it was a door that desperately needed to be answered.

As she walked, she felt a tear trickle down her cheek She broke into a soft sob, never slowing her pace.

She couldn't tell Rhett. She didn't want him to worry. He would never let her go anywhere alone again.

Rhett tapped his fingers on the old oak table. It had seen better days. He pulled a strip of wood off the edge; it crumbled and flaked at his touch.

He had been back in the Twisted Oak for about an hour or so. The innkeeper, Forn, approached him as soon as he came in to let him know that someone had left a letter for him, a big grin on his bony weathered face. Rhett had told his uncle where he would be, but he still only half-expected to receive the letter.

He took a pensive sip of his ale. He wasn't sure he would ever really get used to the harsh, bitter taste. It always clung to the back of his throat for far longer than it was welcome. It was nothing like the sweet taste of Lasch Havel's mead. He could almost taste it on his tongue. He was going to miss that. He sighed longingly to himself, then picked up the letter with both hands and read over it again.

> *Rhett,*
>
> *I hope this letter finds you well.*
>
> *The Twisted Oak has seen better days, but Forn Blackwell is a good man. He will look after you while you're in Camylin. As we've discussed, I have arranged a position for you in the City Guard here in Berona. It's nothing glamorous, but with time, you will do very well here.*
>
> *Now, in your previous letter, you mentioned that you and your lady would be travelling via the port at*

Falstide. Rhett, Falstide is not a safe place to be, no matter how well you think you can handle yourself. And the journey across Illyanara is long and hard on even a hardened soldier.

I have reached out to my contacts at the port in Antiquar, and I have secured you two tickets through Gisa. I know you don't have the money for that right now, but I have paid them in full. You can pay me back over time once you arrive. I just want to see you here safe, or my brother would never forgive me.

When you arrive at Gisa, go to the port and ask for a man named Jack Narys. Tell him I sent you.
Look after yourself, Rhett. I'm looking forward to seeing you and meeting your lady.

Stay safe,
Tanner

It was the fourth time that Rhett had read the letter. When he and Ella first thought about leaving The Glade, it was Tanner whom Rhett first contacted. His uncle was a good man. Rhett had only met him a handful of times – it was always difficult to get from the South to the North – but every time they had met, Tanner treated him as if he were his own child. *Gisa?*

Gisa was one of the wealthiest cities in all the southern lands, despite it being isolated from the rest of the mainland. Gisa was the principal port between the North and South, where the Lorian riches flowed into the southern land. It was also where the gold from Aonar was transported to Loria.

His uncle must have paid a small fortune for those tickets. It was an incredible act of kindness, but Rhett also cursed him, for it backed him into a corner. It left him with no options. He despised the idea of starting his new life on the back foot, paying back his uncle for a ticket he had never planned on getting himself.

Ella would not be happy. He would have to tell her. Pretending they had more coin than they did so she could enjoy the markets was one thing, but this was different.

Were it anyone else, he would just ride to Falstide anyway, and they would work out the issue when they got there. But he couldn't do that to his uncle.

He sighed, exasperated. He sat back in his chair and took a deep draught of his ale. He grimaced as it hit the back of his mouth. *It is a taste to be acquired.*

His uncle was right. The Twisted Oak had seen better days. He could tell that it used to be a place of some esteem in its day. The ceilings were nearly twenty feet high, tall enough for three men to stand atop each other's shoulders. The legends said that Camylin used to be a city of the giants, but Rhett had always assumed they were just that – legends.

All the tables were made of solid oak, which was expensive, even if they were now as worn as if they had been recovered from a sunken ship. The chairs were fitted with red velvet cushions, embroidered with fine weavings of gold. At least, he was sure that they were fine weavings at some point in time. They were now tattered and falling apart.

Massive slabs of stone decorated the bottom half of the walls, layered atop one another. It was probably the only thing in the inn that had stood the test of time. The top half was another story. Mould peeked through the layered scraps of peeling paint. He was sure that at some point, this inn was as grand as the city in which it resided, but right now, he could not wait to leave in the morning.

He jumped, broken out of his pensiveness by the chesty, phlegm-filled cough of an old man who sat in the other corner of the common room. He looked like he had been sitting there so long that he had been painted into the chair.

Rhett reached into the pocket of his coat and pulled out his coin purse. He set it down on his lap, just below the table, so as not to attract any unwanted eyes. There were not many people in the common room – the old man who sounded like he was about to lose a lung, the drunk at the bar who was struggling to keep his eyes open, a handful of tired merchants, two serving girls, and the innkeeper, who was a nice man, if a little past his best. Rhett didn't think any of them would be paying him much attention.

He opened the drawstrings of the purse, taking a quick count of his coin. He had half-hoped to magically find more than he expected. He was not pleasantly surprised.

The trip to Gisa would be far shorter than the trip to Falstide, maybe only a week and a half by horse. Their money would go a lot further. They wouldn't have to ration the food. They could stay in nice beds every night. It would be safer.

He picked out a coin from his purse; a copper mark. Rolling it across his fingers, he looked over at the letter and then up nodding at the innkeeper, who nodded back and started pouring another tankard of ale.

"Here you go, young man. This one's on the house. Just give my best to Tanner. I'm sure I owe him one at this stage." Forn placed the ale down in front of Rhett. He picked up the empty tankard, his bony hands wrapping around the metal handle. Rhett looked closer and realised that, although his skin looked old and worn and his hair was thin and grey, the man's eyes were bright and full of life. How did his uncle know this man so well?

"That is not necessary but very much appreciated, Master Blackwell. My uncle mentioned your kindness in his letters. He did not overstate it one bit." Rhett smiled and raised his tankard to the older man, who nodded thankfully in response.

"May I ask," he said, "how are you getting to Berona? Is it by Gisa or Falstide?"

Rhett hesitated. He truthfully wasn't sure himself.

"I… I only ask as I've heard some bad news out of Falstide as of late. Large number of bandits along the road from Baylomon and in the Argonan Marshes. I've heard stories of other *things*, coming down from the Marin Mountains. It's no place to be travelling, not now. The Blood Moon don't be far away. And it does be stirring up all sorts of trouble. I'll tell you that much for free." The older man shook his head, absently wiping the inside of the tankard with his cloth.

"Well, the original plan was to travel through Falstide, but Gisa might be an option. We haven't decided yet. Won't have to decide until we reach Midhaven. The Blood Moon?"

Forn nodded and turned back towards the bar, still absently

wiping away at the inside of the tankard. "Gisa would be my choice, young man," he called back over his shoulder, "if you have the coin." He ignored Rhett's question about the moon. *Poor man. The years are eating away at his mind. Just as they are eating away at his inn.*

Rhett stared down into his purse. He took a deep draught of the bitter ale. *It's going to take a long time to acquire this taste.* He sighed heavily as he rolled the coin across fingers, back and forth.

CHAPTER 17

Divided

The echoes of hurried footfall bounced off the high walls of the narrow street, chased by the voices of men shouting commands into the night. Shockwaves vibrated up through Calen's legs as his feet pounded on the cobbled steps. His chest burned as they ran.

They had thrown what they could into their bags. Calen strapped his sword belt on. Dann threw his bow over his shoulder. Rist stuffed his book into his bag. They followed Erik down the stairs and out the back of the inn. Dahlen and Aeson were waiting for them, both of whom had their armour on and their swords drawn. Dahlen spun his two blades around, loosening his hands for what was to come.

All the horses in the stable were dead. Their throats had been slit while they were still tethered to their posts. The man who had tried to sneak into their room hadn't risked the chance of them escaping by horseback.

"Here, down this street. Oliver's Apothecary has access

to the tunnels." The words escaped Dahlen's mouth between puffs of breath. They had been dashing through the streets at a full sprint since they left the stable yard, mostly down backstreets and staircases. It was tough on even the hardiest of lungs. They had been lucky enough not to run into any of the men chasing them so far, but their voices were never far from earshot.

"Who—" Dann stopped to take a breath. "Who the hell is after us? Who was that at the room?"

They made their way down another cobbled staircase, with tight walls on either side. A quick right at the bottom was followed by a sharp left. Calen had no idea where they were. If he lost the others, he would be dead in a matter of minutes.

"It's the empire," Dahlen whispered. "Whoever was outside the rooms was hired, but the men chasing us right now are definitely soldiers. There's too many of them, and they're organised. How they found us, I'm not sure."

"We can discuss it later," Aeson snapped, "for now, we need to move."

"They're here!" came a yell in the night. The soldiers came bursting out of a side street. The cover of night made sure that they were on top of the group before they saw them.

Calen pulled his sword free from its scabbard just in time to block a heavy downstroke. He tried to focus on his forms, but his brain was racing. *Stay alive. Just stay alive.*

He swung his blade across again, parrying blow after blow with more luck than skill. Dann had an arrow nocked and stood back-to-back with Dahlen. The two of them fared much the same as himself. Aeson and Erik both had the upper hand, by the looks of it. The silhouettes of three corpses were draped at their feet.

Calen panicked for a second, unable to find Rist in the chaos. A metallic ringing chimed through the air as he met another overhead blow. He let out a breath. Rist was behind Dahlen and Dann, standing over the body of a fallen soldier. Something seemed a bit off, but Calen just couldn't put his finger on it.

He needed to focus.

The soldier in front of him swung for Calen's head, then tripped over something obscured by the night. Calen caught the soldier's blade with his own, sweeping the backswing across the man's torso. The soldier fell to the ground, his hands grabbing at the wound that had opened his stomach. Blood spluttered from his open mouth. The air caught in Calen's chest. He thought he was going to be sick.

"Calen… Calen!"

Calen barely even noticed Rist calling him. He hadn't felt the din of fighting ebb away. The look of panic on the man's face as he died was burned into his mind.

"Calen, we need to go. Now. Come on!"

He had to focus, but his eyes remained fixed on the corpse that lay sprawled on the ground. *Three.*

He wasn't sure whether to count the Urak. He had watched the life drain from its eyes. It knew what was happening. It counted.

He eventually moved, and his chest burned again as they continued through the maze of streets.

"Only about ten minutes," Erik called. "I think."

"You think?" Dann shouted.

"Look, it's dark, okay? Ten minutes. Just try to keep up."

Dann grunted in agreement.

A weight crashed on top of Calen, throwing him against the wall, knocking precious air straight out of his lungs. Calen grabbed the soldier with his free hand, pushing him back just far enough to drive his sword up into his ribcage. He felt the body go limp as he slid the sword back out.

Four.

"You okay?" Dann called.

"Yeah," Calen replied, sighing. "Let's keep going."

The spiralling twists and turns continued. They ran through back streets, up and down staircases, around corners, and down back alleys. Their pace didn't slow. The burning in Calen's chest was joined by an ache in his legs. The city felt endless.

Calen heard a howl behind him, followed by the ringing of swords colliding. He twisted around. Rist was on the ground, face-down, the contents of his bag strewn out across the cobbled stone. Calen didn't think he could take losing anyone else.

Rist moved. Calen allowed himself to release the breath he wasn't aware he had been holding. Dahlen had gone back for Rist and was surrounded by three soldiers. His twin swords spun in a blur as he weaved between them like a dancer.

Calen looked pleadingly towards Aeson and Erik. Their eyes were fixed on Dahlen.

"Go! We'll catch up." Dahlen ducked out of the way of

a blade that swung through the air where his head had been, driving a deep gash across one of the soldier's legs.

Calen tightened his grip on his sword. He was about to break into a run for Dahlen and Rist when a hand caught his shoulder.

"No," Aeson said firmly, his eyes locked on Calen's.

"I—"

"*No.* You will do none of us any good by ending up at the pointy end of a Lorian sword."

The shouts of more soldiers echoed through the city, closing in on them.

"Dahlen can handle himself," Aeson continued. "And he can look after Rist. We need to keep going. There is no sense in risking us all. There are other ways out of the city, and Dahlen knows them."

A hundred thoughts raced around Calen's mind. Every fibre in his burning body told him to run to Rist, who had just gotten himself to his feet, but what Aeson said made sense. He had never seen someone handle a sword in the way that Dahlen, Erik, and Aeson could. Maybe his father. The thought put knots in his stomach. Images of Vars's lifeless body flashed through his mind. Calen pushed them away. "Okay." Calen sighed and looked back at Dahlen and Rist. Two bodies lay at Dahlen's feet now, but fresh soldiers replaced them.

"Calen, we can't just leave him!" shouted Dann. His knuckles were white, wrapped around the grip of his bow.

Calen looked over at Dann, then back at Rist. Aeson sighed and then nodded. Calen let his eyes rest on Dann's. If they tried to help, they might all get hemmed in. Dahlen and Rist were working their way towards an empty side street.

"We have to, Dann. Aeson is right. Dahlen will look after him. We need to trust them." Calen saw the struggle in Dann's face. He and Rist always poked fun at each other, but the three of them were like brothers. No matter how annoying they could be at times, they would all die for each other.

Dann's gaze fixed on Rist for a second. He had a sword in his hands now, which he must have taken off one of the fallen soldiers. Then Dann looked back at Calen and nodded begrudgingly. They set off in a sprint.

"It's only a few minutes now," Erik said. It was obvious he was trying to reassure himself as much as he was Calen and Dann. Calen had forgotten that as close as Rist was to being his brother, Dahlen was actually Erik's brother. Calen felt a pang of guilt for hesitating when Erik didn't.

"Here it is," Erik said as they approached a small building, nestled against the city wall, connected to a large inn on one side and a small alley on the other. A hand-painted sign hung above the front door, which read, 'Oliver's Apothecary: Happiness and Health'. They followed Erik around to the side of the apothecary. He crouched down and tilted a half-rotted wooden barrel on its side, revealing a heavy iron key. "Well, good news at last. The key is here," he said with a half-hearted chuckle.

"You weren't sure it would be here?" Dann said. "We ran halfway across this city, nearly died more than once, and you weren't even sure the key would be here?"

Erik shrugged. "We didn't have many options. I tossed a coin."

Dann's eyes widened. "You tossed a fucking coin?"

Erik shrugged again. "Yup."

Dann's face twisted in disbelief as he muttered, "A coin… he tossed a fucking coin."

Calen had to stifle a laugh. The occasion didn't really call for laughter, but he found that was often when he struggled to suppress it the most. Dann saw it on his face and threw a filthy look in his direction.

Erik slotted the key into the rusty lock on the side door. It took a push to get it into place, but once it was in, it turned with little difficulty. The door drifted inward on its own, revealing a staircase that descended into blackness.

"Well, you all coming?" Erik said, stepping through the doorway. Dann followed Erik down the stairs. His head twisted around, attempting to find some light. Aeson gestured for Calen to go next, then followed, closing the door behind him. It was as black as pitch. Calen had to feel his way down the staircase with his hands, one running along the damp stone wall and the other along the splintered handrail. The heavy smell of mould and rotted wood filled his nostrils.

"So, how do you know about this place?" Dann asked.

"Oliver is a contact of ours. His grandfather built this tunnel a long time ago. He used it to smuggle Altwied blood into the city."

"Altwied blood? I've heard that stuff can do miracles. Pity it's illegal."

"It can. With just a few drops, I've seen men survive injuries they had no right to survive."

Calen's mother had mentioned Altwied blood before. Petals from the Altwied flower, ground up and mixed with

water. The empire outright banned it in the South. Calen
had heard rumours from travellers that this was not the case
in the North.

"Dad, could you give us some light?"

Give us some light?

Calen heard a hesitant grunt from Aeson.

"I think we're past the point of secrets, Dad, and I don't
want to trip over something in this dank tunnel. We have
a ways to walk."

Aeson replied with another grunt.

"How do you expect him to—"

Dann's words were cut short. Tiny fragments of light
appeared in front of Aeson, coalescing into a small orb. It
floated in the air, illuminating the tunnel with a clear white
light.

"What in the name of The Mother and The Father is
that?" Dann yelped, pushing his back up against the moss-
covered stone wall of the tunnel.

"Calm yourself, boy," Aeson said. There was no patience
in his voice. "It is a *baldír.* We don't really have time for questions about it now. Ask your questions once we've safely
made it to The Wilted Leaf. For now, just accept it. We have
about another twenty minutes of walking before we get to
the hatch at the other side."

Calen had a hundred questions that each led to a hundred
more. He suppressed them. Dann opened his mouth to speak
but closed it again. Calen saw it in his eyes; his mind was
doing cartwheels. Calen's mind was doing the same.

Magic? Actual magic? For some reason, it seemed almost
acceptable that a giant could use magic. But not a man.

Now that there was light, Calen could see that the tunnel was barely three feet wide at any point. It looked like it hadn't been used in years. Moss coated the walls, with a stone poking through here and there. The wooden support beams looked as if they would collapse any second from rot. The ground was soft and pliable; his boot sank in with every step.

They walked in silence for what felt like hours. The only noises came from the squelching of the soft mud below their feet and the squeaky chattering of rats, barely aware of the intruders in their tunnel. An abrupt loss of light signified the end of the tunnel, as the orb disappeared. It was quickly replaced by a sliver of moonlight, which flowed in from the gap in the hatch that Erik had just pushed open.

"There're no stairs here. We'll have to pull ourselves up," Erik whispered. A loud puff of air let Calen know that Erik had just followed his own instructions.

Calen felt a slight flash of relief when he pulled himself up and out of the tunnel. It was nice to have enough space to reach out his arms and stretch his legs. He was happy that the light came from the sky and not a small floating orb.

"Come on, this isn't the time to stop. We need to make it to The Wilted Leaf. Therin will be waiting for us there, and that's where the others will be heading."

"The others?"

Everyone's head swung around to see Therin slumped on his horse about twenty feet away. Dark circles ringed his eyes, and he looked as though he was about to fall from the saddle.

Dahlen swung one blade overhead and blocked the downward strike from the soldier, then plunged his second blade straight through the man's belly. *One more for the gods.*

Ignoring the aches in his shoulders and back, he looked over at Rist. The boy wasn't as useless as he had initially thought. Two bodies lay at his feet, and he was holding his own against the third. He looked tired, though – far more tired than Dahlen would have expected. His shoulders drooped from the unfamiliar weight of the blade, his steps were laboured, and his eyes looked glassy. He wasn't going to last long.

A ferocious shout came from Dahlen's left. He sidestepped the incoming strike by the skin of his teeth. As he did, he stuck his foot out, sending the soldier barrelling down the cobblestone staircase to the left. He wouldn't be getting up from that for a while.

Without hesitation, Dahlen lunged at the man who was attacking Rist.

Leaning in with his shoulder, he hit the man hard in the ribs, sending him crashing into the stone wall at his back. Dahlen followed through with his sword, up through the jaw. The man slumped, sliding down the wall like a snail.

Dahlen paused for a moment to catch his breath. "Are you okay?" he asked Rist, trying to fill his lungs with air. That tackle hit him almost as hard as it did the soldier. Rist's eyes looked heavy. He fell to his knees, letting his sword fall. The clanging of metal on stone rang out through the now eerily silent street.

"Whoa!" Dahlen's muscles screamed in protest as he leapt to support Rist's slumping shoulders. "Rist, look at me. Are you okay?" Dahlen checked Rist's body for wounds. Confusion set in when he could not find any. "Are you hurt?"

"I… I'm okay. I just feel so weak. I can't control it." Rist could hardly catch his breath. There were dark circles under his eyes, and Dahlen would swear to the gods that he looked fifty shades paler than he did before.

"Can't control what?" Dahlen asked. His breath was starting to return, but with it, stiffness began to set into his joints. He couldn't wait for the response. They needed to move; he could hear the shouts getting closer. "Can you walk?"

Rist didn't respond. He stared off into the distance, his eyelids drooping and his mouth agape. Dahlen was certain that if he let go of his shoulders, Rist would collapse. His eyes were open, but he was lost in a dream. *What's wrong with him?*

Dahlen dipped his arm under Rist's and wrapped it around his back, heaving him to his feet. Dahlen's entire body groaned in pain. The shift in balance almost sent them both crashing down onto the cobblestones. Dahlen attempted to keep Rist's dead weight upright. His knees ached with the strain. The last few days were catching up on him. He needed to sleep.

"Come on, Rist. We're not far." Dahlen sighed heavily as he struggled to push one foot in front of the other. "There's more than one tunnel out of this city." Dahlen muttered to himself.

He grimaced as he tossed his shoulders, shifting Rist's weight to a more comfortable position. *It could be worse. At least his feet are moving on their own.*

He was fairly sure they were going the right way, but

it was hard to tell. He had never actually been through the tunnel under the Blind Goat before. His father had only ever let them use the tunnel under Oliver's, but the other routes out of the city were most likely guarded, so that was their best bet. Letting out a slight groan, he tossed his shoulders again. His legs were beginning to fold, and Rist wasn't getting any lighter.

A slight breeze whistled through the empty streets as the pair hobbled along. Rist was barely conscious. The pale wash of moonlight caused the long, cobbled streets to blend in with the grey stone walls of the buildings on either side. The reverberation of their footsteps echoed after each step, sending a slight shiver up Dahlen's spine.

He turned to look over his shoulder every few seconds, checking down side streets and stairways. It was too quiet for his liking, far quieter than it should have been considering the commotion they had made. The city should have been ablaze with activity, but it wasn't. There was almost no noise at all. He pushed through the aching pain, picking up his pace.

The Blind Goat wasn't far away now. *Just a few more minutes.*

"How noble of you," a harsh, gravelly voice echoed.

Dahlen stopped in his tracks. The momentum of Rist's limp body nearly toppled them both. Dahlen twisted around to find the source of the voice. It seemed to come from everywhere and nowhere at the same time.

"What do I do with you, child? You do not have what I came for, but the one you carry is… *interesting.*" The voice trailed off, hissing like a snake.

"Who are you?" Dahlen shouted, panic etching its way into his voice. It seemed as if the night had become darker. The light ebbed from the edge of his vision. He immediately looked towards the sky, but he saw the moon as clear as day. The hairs on the back of his neck stood on end.

"I will make you a deal." The voice now came from behind him. He turned as swiftly as his body would allow.

A man stood in the middle of the street, only a couple of feet away. At least, Dahlen thought it was a man. He looked around six feet tall, with an average build, although it was hard to tell with his body covered in that black hooded robe. The robe seemed darker than the depths of any shadow, almost as if it pulled the light out of the air. In a stark contrast to the light-drinking black, the robe was detailed with swirling brush strokes of vivid blue. Dahlen's eyes strained the longer he focused on it, a sickly feeling bubbling in his stomach.

The man's face would have looked as ordinary as any, were it not that his skin was almost translucent, like a thin sheet of parchment stretched over a candle. His lips were thin and brittle, the usual red supplanted by an icy blue. Dahlen let out an audible gasp when his gaze settled on the man's eyes. They were as black as tar. Dahlen felt that if he were to stare at them for long, they might pull his soul straight out of his body.

The man's needle-thin lips began to move. "Well, if you're quite done staring?"

Dahlen's voice was caught in his throat.

"I will make you a deal, child. For this world can be terribly tedious if you follow the rules." His attenuated lips twisted into something resembling a grin. "Give me the boy. I will take care of him, and you can just go on your way. It is as simple as relieving yourself of a burden."

It took a second to register exactly what the man had said. *Give him Rist?* Dahlen barely knew Rist. He had only met him a few days ago, but to abandon him? That was not in his blood. There was also not a doubt in Dahlen's mind that whatever this man would do to Rist, he would not *take care of him.*

Dahlen steeled himself, fighting the knot in his stomach, and forced his mouth to obey him. "I can't do that," he said with a lot more strength than he felt.

The man laughed. At least, Dahlen thought it was a laugh. It was similar to the rumbling noise that a wolf makes when threatened. "You know, I hoped that would be your answer. The hard way is invariably more entertaining." Without warning, the man swung his hand in an arc. An invisible force crashed into Dahlen from head to toe. It knocked the air from his lungs and sent him crashing into a stack of wooden crates. His head spun. He didn't think there was a single part of his body that wasn't in pain. He pushed himself to his knees, panting.

The hooded man's footsteps echoed through the streets. Dahlen followed the sound to see the man standing over Rist's prone body, his robe flowing in the breeze.

Dahlen reached over his shoulder, feeling relief when his hand tightened around the grip of his sword. He was worried he might have lost them when he was knocked through the air. He was only going to have one shot at this.

Pulling on his last vestiges of energy, in one smooth

motion, Dahlen dragged himself to his feet and pulled one of his blades from its sheath. He launched himself at the robed man, clearing the distance between them in one leap, then drove the sword straight through his chest. The blade passed through the cloak as if it weren't there, slicing into the man's flesh. He felt the release as it came out the other side, where the man's heart should have been. Nobody could survive that.

Dahlen collapsed to his knees, his legs unable to hold him upright any longer. His chest heaved up and down, working hard to fill his lungs. He needed to rest. He let his muscles relax.

The harsh sound of a blade sliding free of flesh caused Dahlen to release a defeated sigh. *No. That's not possible.*

He lifted his head to see his sword being pulled from the man's back on its own. He watched as it floated in the air above his head. There was not a single drop of blood along its blade.

Dahlen's heart sank into his stomach. His throat became as dry as if he had rubbed it with cotton. *What is this creature?*

It laughed again, the laugh of a wolf. "You humans never do learn, but I like you. You may live." The creature turned towards Dahlen, its voice like jagged rocks. Rist still lay on the ground a few feet away.

"However," it hissed, "I cannot let your behaviour go unpunished."

Before Dahlen could understand what was going on, he was hurtling through the air, thrown around like a rag doll. He felt his back crash into something hard. A wall.

Everything went black.

CHAPTER 18

Cracks

"Calen?" Dann repeated, his eyebrows raised. "I said, are you okay?"

Calen shook his head, attempting to loose the grogginess from his mind. "Yeah, I'm okay, Dann. Just got lost in the fire there for a minute."

"Be careful. Stare too long into the fire and it will take pieces of you. Well, at least that's what Dad always said. Look, there is no way you're all right. These past few days have been insane. Especially..." Dann trailed off, his eyes becoming heavy.

Calen sighed through his nose, turning his attention back to the fire. That feeling hit him again, as if his heart were about to fall into the pit of his stomach. It still wasn't real for him, and he would do everything in his power to keep it that way. His entire family. Gone. A piece of him held out hope that Ella hadn't been in the house, but he knew he was only fooling himself.

"They'll be back soon." Calen hadn't heard Erik

approaching; the crackling of the fire covered his footsteps. He sat down on a log beside Calen and Dann, then opened his bag and produced two small wraps of cloth. "Dahlen will see the sign we left him." Inside the first wrap were strips of dried meat. He tossed some to both Calen and Dann, who thanked him hungrily.

"Hold on. There's some bread to go with that. It's a little stale, but it's better than nothing."

Dann looked at Erik apologetically as he swallowed half of his dried meat in one mouthful. He reached out his hand to take some of the bread. Calen thanked Erik for the bread, and the three of them sat in silence as they ate.

As he struggled through the stale, bark-like excuse for bread, Calen realised that it had been quite a while since he'd eaten. He didn't have lunch the day before, and he had eaten nothing in The Traveller's Rest either. His stomach rumbled. He choked down the rest of the bread and dried meat without complaint.

The sounds of the forest settled into Calen's mind as the group waited for Dahlen and Rist to traipse through the trees. The birdsong collided with the incessant buzz of insects. The leaves rustled as the night's breeze brushed shoulders with the trees. A nearby brook burbled. But all of it could not match Therin's rumbling snores. He was worse than Dann. He had been sleeping since they set up camp, which didn't surprise Calen. When they found him waiting for them at the tunnel entrance outside Camylin, he had looked like he was about to fall off his horse. Calen didn't think he had ever seen anyone look that way. It was almost unnatural. There were deep recesses under his eyes, his breathing was laboured, and his already pale skin looked as though it were porcelain. It was as if the energy had been dragged, kicking and screaming, from his body.

Aeson sat behind Therin, his back propped up against the base of a tree. The satchel that sheltered the egg was nestled into his lap, both arms draped around it. His eyes were closed, but Calen was sure he was not asleep. The man never seemed to let his guard down.

Calen turned to face the fire, stuffing his hands into his coat pockets as he did. That's when he felt it. The scarf he had bought his mother in Milltown. He didn't have to take it out to see it. Autumn red. Vines of gold and cream woven through it in the pattern of leaves blowing through the wind. The hairs on the back of his neck stood up as he ripped his hands out of his pockets. He felt the tears welling up behind his eyes. Everything flashed through his mind. His father's lifeless body laying still, the packed dirt stained with blood. His mother sobbing. His home in flames. The screams. His stomach twisted. His hands trembled. *No. Not now.*

Dann leapt to his feet, snatching his bow from the ground beside him. He had an arrow nocked faster than Calen could turn his head. "Dann—"

"Quiet," Dann whispered. He narrowed his eyes as he attempted to see farther into the dark of the forest. Calen followed his gaze but saw nothing except the haze of night, thick with an endless sea of trees. Then he heard it. Someone – or *something* – was making its way through the under-growth at the northern edge of the clearing.

Aeson's eyes opened. He stood, slung the satchel around

his back, and drew his swords. Therin joined him, tiredness still set into his face.

"I live by day and die by night. I can fly, I can walk, and I can swim, but I do not get wet. What am I?" came a voice from within the obscurity of the forest.

Erik asked a question with his eyes. Aeson answered with a nod. It was Erik who spoke. "You are the shadow of a bird," he responded, laughter touching the end of his words. "Now get over here, brother!"

Dahlen stumbled into the firelight. He limped on his right leg. He had a few cuts and bruises on his face, and his clothes were caked in dried blood.

"They made it…" muttered Calen, a smile widening across his face. *I can't lose anyone else.*

Erik pulled Dahlen into a tight hug, then drew back and grabbed him by the shoulders, checking him over for injuries. "Well, you didn't make it easy on yourself, did you?" He laughed. "Don't worry. I'll teach you a few things."

"Oh, fuck off, will you!" Dahlen scoffed.

Aeson put his swords back in their scabbards and smiled. He gave an approving nod towards Dahlen, who returned the gesture in kind.

"Where's Rist?" Dann asked, his tone curt. He peered off into the darkness. Dahlen didn't reply, but his facial expression changed. The hairs on the back of Calen's neck stood on end. *Not Rist. Please, not Rist.*

"I'm sorry," Dahlen said, his voice meek. He stared at the ground. "I did everything I could. We fought our way through. He held his own, but—"

"What happened?" Calen shouted. His anger surprised him. He hadn't felt it rising.

"A Fade – I think. I couldn't do anything, I put my blade right through its heart, but it did nothing. It just tossed me aside." Dahlen's voice was vacant, his eyes pleading.

"A Fade? What in the void is a Fade?" Dann asked.

"What would a Fade be doing here, in Camylin?" Aeson said, ignoring Dann's question.

"It came for the egg – I think," Therin said. All heads turned to him. "I ran into it on my way to The Wilted Leaf. It had soldiers under its command. I only just escaped. It knew you were in Camylin, so it had to have been after the egg."

"Fuck the egg," Calen said. A shiver ran through his body as he took a step closer to Dahlen. "Where is Rist?"

For a few moments, there was silence.

"It took him."

"It took him?" Dann and Calen repeated at the same time. "What do you mean it took him?"

Dahlen nodded solemnly. "There was nothing I could do. It threw me around like I was just a plaything. It knocked me unconscious, and when I came to, it was gone, and so was Rist. I'm—"

"You left him?" Calen leapt at Dahlen and shoved him in the chest, causing him to stumble backwards. A droning noise filled the back of Calen's head. It rose to a crescendo as it tried to outmatch his thumping heart.

Dahlen's empty stare gave way to anger. "Do that again and I'll put you on your back. I'm sorry that it took him, but there was nothing I could do."

"You just fucking left him there? On his own?" Calen shouted, his eyes drawing up level to Dahlen's. "You're a coward. You ran when he needed you!" He pushed his hands into Dahlen's chest again, his blood boiling over.

Dahlen stumbled for half a second, then dug his back foot into the ground. He pivoted and landed a punch on Calen's nose. Calen felt a sharp pain, and a thump as he hit the ground. "At least I was there. Where were you?"

With his head still spinning, Calen leapt to his feet, anger burning through him. Before he could react, Dann put his arm across his chest. "Let it go, Calen. This is not the time."

"Let it go?" Calen scoffed, wiping the blood away as it trickled from his nose. "He left Rist to be taken! He left him, Dann!"

"I know." Dann gripped Calen's shoulders, touched their foreheads together, and looked him straight in the eye. "And we will find him, Calen, but now is not the time to be fighting… okay?"

Calen's hands trembled and his breathing was shallow. His heart hammered in his chest. He sighed. "Okay…" his voice dropped to a whisper. "I shouldn't have left him, Dann. I shouldn't have left him…"

Dann sighed and pulled Calen into a tight embrace. "We both did, Calen."

"That was not necessary," Aeson said, turning to Dahlen.

Dahlen was incredulous "What? He shoved me. I—"

Aeson raised his hand in the air and turned away, returning to where he was seated. He slung the satchel around to his lap once more, as if nothing had happened. "Come, son. Tell us what happened, and we will decide what is to be done. Dann, would you see if there are any rabbits caught in the snares we set earlier? I think we could all do with some fresh meat."

Dann took a deep breath in, then pulled away from Calen. "Yeah, sure." He snatched up his knife and a length of rope, then placed his hand on Calen's shoulder. "Come on, come help me with the snares."

"I think—"

"Calen, help me with the snares."

Dann was right. Calen's emotions were all over the place. One minute, he felt like he was at the bottom of a dark pit with no help in sight; the next, he felt like a bull let loose in a sea of red. He had never been so quick to anger. He should not have lunged at Dahlen, even if he did leave Rist to be taken by that creature. But he was never going to say that out loud. The thought of losing Rist just made him explode. They needed to get Rist back. They had to.

Most of the snares were empty, but the four rabbits they found dangling from their hind legs would be enough for a small dinner for the group. It was better than nothing – and definitely better than stale bread and dried meat.

Dahlen was at the end of his story when Calen and Dann returned to the camp. Aeson listened intently and stroked his grey-flecked beard, his eyes focused on something in the dark canopy above.

"Did it give any indication of why it wanted Rist?" Therin interjected, sitting forward.

"No." Dahlen sighed and shook his head. "It just said that he was… *interesting.*"

Erik gestured for Calen and Dann to join them.

"Go ahead," Dann said, "I'm just going to skin these and get them prepped to set up over the fire before I sit down. My stomach is rumbling. I'll be able to hear fine."

Calen nodded and sat on the ground beside Erik.

"Interesting?" Erik said. Aeson and Therin exchanged a flash of recognition.

"Rist is connected to the Spark," Therin replied. "He has the power to wield magic. And if what I sensed initially is anything to go by, he has to potential to be quite powerful."

Calen stared at him in disbelief, unable to stop his mouth from opening wide. *Rist? Rist is…*

"Rist is a mage?" Dann said, dumbstruck, halfway through skinning one of the rabbits.

Calen wasn't sure what to say or even what to think. Rist had been one of his closest friends ever since he could remember. They did everything together. He was not a mage. Mages – or at least, people who could use magic – they were fairy tales. They were the heroes and villains of Therin's stories. *Therin.* There was somebody else who wasn't who Calen thought he was.

"How are we getting him back?" Dann's voice cut through the silent echoes in Calen's mind.

"I'm not sure that will be possible," Aeson replied, his tone flat. "If that Fade was working with Lorian soldiers, then he will be taking Rist to the High Tower in Berona. That is where the inquisitors bring all young men who can wield the Spark. And if he is strong enough, he will be inducted into the Circle of Magii. The empire would not let a wielder with his potential roam free. And unless I am mistaken, nobody here is in the position to march into the High Tower and demand they release him."

"But…" Calen's voice was brittle, even to his own ears. Helplessness permeated his entire body. He couldn't let that feeling consume him. He would not. "No."

"Calen, I truly am sorry, but Aeson is right. We simply don't have the ability to help him. Not yet, at least." Therin's eyes showed genuine concern.

"I can't just leave him!" Calen shouted. The burning in his veins caused his voice to rise a touch louder than he intended. "I… I can't just leave him. He would never leave me. Dann, your bags. Make sure you have everything."

Dann had fallen silent for the last few minutes, which was unlike him. He looked up from his feet when Calen spoke. "What? Why?"

"We're going to Berona. We're going after Rist."

CHAPTER 19

Bound

Aeson and Erik spent the majority of the next hour trying to explain to Calen why it was madness to go after Rist.

"Even making it to Berona is a near impossibility," Aeson said, "The empire keeps a strict hold on the travel between the north and the south of the continent. Only two ports in Illyanara make the journey to Loria, and neither of them are an option. Sailing from Gisa is impossible unless you have more coin than common sense, not to mention that you and Dann would stick out like sore thumbs in that crowd. Falstide is worse. It's cheaper to travel, for sure, but it's cheaper for a reason. It's a den of smugglers, thieves, and murderers."

Therin had been silent for a while. He had produced a small notebook and a short tin box of charcoal sticks from his bag and had been sketching something. He looked up from his notebook, folding it over as he did. "Even then," he sighed, "the journey across the province would take nearly two months. The journey by ship would be another few days, and then you would have to travel through the Burnt Lands or brave the Lightning Coast to make it to Berona. The Darkwood is not even an option. It would be suicide."

"We're going after Rist. We leave at first light."

It didn't take long for Calen's mind to drift into the world of dreams. His body ached in places he never thought possible, and his head beat like a drum. Aeson had insisted on continuing their sword practice that night, regardless of whether Calen left in the morning. He did not take it easy on him either. Calen lost count of the new bumps and bruises that sprang up long before they had even stopped practicing. It seemed like Aeson was trying to make a point of how helpless they would be if they left to go after Rist.

He longed for some respite from the physical world. His mind melted away.

Draleid.

Calen's eyes shot open. He bolted upright, sweat glistening as it streamed down his face. He felt warmer than the heat from the crumbling embers of the fire should have made him. He wiped the sweat from his face with the back of his hand and tried in vain to steady his breathing.

His dreams did not provide him the relief he had hoped they would. As soon as his eyes shut, a voice tormented him. Words echoed in his head, reverberating down every corridor in his mind.

Draleid n'aldryr.

Again and again, the voice rose to a crescendo. The only image was of the egg. The dragon egg. Its bone-white scales faded to a shadowy black at their roots. It was wreathed in plumes of billowing fire, but somehow Calen knew that it would be cold to the touch. He sensed it calling to him, like a heartbeat pounding in the darkness, his ears its only destination.

Everybody else was sound asleep. The dim glow from the fire illuminated the rise and fall of their chests as they slept. The satchel sat beside Aeson, the egg within. Calen heard it echoing.

Draleid.

Was he losing his mind? What would someone say if he told them that an egg was calling to him? It called out words that he did not understand, and only he could hear it.

He stared across the makeshift campsite. He stared at the large leather satchel, beaten and travel worn. He stared at its iron buckles, rusted and tarnished from the salty sea air of the journey from Valacia. More than anything, he stared at what it held within.

On a passing glance, nobody would have thought that such a worn vessel would carry something so important. It was legend that when Fane defeated The Order, he hoarded every surviving dragon egg in the vaults beneath Al'Nasla. None had ever hatched. The empire still had the Dragonguard and their dragons, of course, but not one new hatchling in all that time. It was one of the few things all the bards agreed on.

Calen hadn't thought about what it might mean to

Epheria – a dragon. A dragon not controlled by the Lorian Empire. It could change everything.

Draleid.

Draleid n'aldryr.

The voice was incessant, blocking out all other sounds. The embers of the fire should have crackled, slowly, like a rumbling river. The trees blowing back and forth in the night's breeze should have rustled as they brushed against each other, and whistled as the wind swept through them. He should have heard the insects. But he heard nothing – except for the voice.

Draleid.

Calen buried his face in his hands. He ran his fingers through his hair and let out a sigh. His head pounded, like somebody was beating it with a stick from the inside out. He pulled himself to his feet. The ache in his muscles and the raw skin on his thighs felt dull compared to the hammering in his head – it was a silver lining; he supposed. It was impossible to tell if he made much noise as he walked through the camp. The voice consumed all sounds.

Draleid.

Nobody moved in their sleep, but it was only a matter of time before he woke them. He could not focus on anything other than the egg.

He stopped a foot from where Aeson lay. He seemed to still be fast asleep, but that didn't comfort Calen much. He saw how quickly Aeson leapt to his feet when Dahlen had stumbled into the camp.

Calen crouched down onto his haunches and inched his way closer to the satchel. The voice got louder the closer he moved to it. What would he say if Aeson woke up? He let the question float in his mind. He had no answer. He just hoped that it wouldn't come to that.

The voice was so loud now that Calen found it hard to focus at all. He felt the vibrations of each heartbeat pulsating through his body. He felt so hot that if he didn't know better, he would have sworn that he was on fire.

"You hear it, don't you?"

Calen's heart stopped. The sound of the voice calling to him was gone. His skin rolled in a cold sweat.

Aeson's eyes were open. He sat up with his elbows resting on his knees, his eyes staring directly into Calen's. Searching.

There was a lump in Calen's throat. Every hair on his body stood on end as fear soaked into his bones "I… what…"

"You hear it calling you. The voice. What does it say?" Aeson's voice was calm and level, as if he hadn't just found Calen reaching across him in the night, his arms outstretched towards a satchel that contained the egg of a dragon. How did he know about the voice?

"It… I just… How can I hear you? It…" Calen mumbled. His brain was not capable of forming coherent sentences. Even breathing normally was difficult. The voice that called to him had been so all-consuming that simply hearing Aeson's words had surprised him.

Aeson smirked. "Calm yourself, my boy. No harm will come to you. I am not angry. As for you being able to hear me, that is a little trick of mine. It is called a ward. I will explain it some other time. For now, all you need to know is that nobody outside of this circle," he said, gesturing his hand in an imaginary circle two feet in diameter, "can hear anything that either of us say. It also has the added side effect of blocking out that voice you have been hearing, which is why you can now hear me speaking."

Calen sat there, dumbstruck.

"I'm not angry, but if you just sit there, staring at me with your mouth open, then I might become angry fairly quickly."

Calen's throat felt dry. He gulped. "I… I don't know what it is. It just keeps saying words that I don't understand. I… I think it's the egg?"

If that meant anything to Aeson, he did not let it show. His face remained as stony as ever. "What does it say?"

"It says 'Draleid,' and um… 'n'aldryr?'" Calen's nerves began to settle.

"I see."

"Do you know what those words mean?"

"I do." Aeson nodded slowly. "They are words of the Old Tongue, Calen. *Aldryr* means fire. 'Draleid,' well… that word is something you should recognise. You have heard enough of Therin's stories, have you not?"

Calen nodded, tilting his head. The word did ring a bell, but he couldn't quite place it. It was like there was a block in his mind.

"Calen, the word 'Draleid' is one that you should know quite well. It means 'Dragonbound.' It was the name given to those whose souls were bound to that of a dragon by a magic older than time itself. The Dragonguard of the empire were once known as Draleid, but they bring shame to that name. Together, roughly translated, 'Draleid n'aldryr' means 'Dragonbound by fire.'"

"Yes…" Calen whispered, his memories flooding back to him. He couldn't understand how the word had not registered with him. All Therin's stories about the fall of The Order, Fane Mortem's betrayal, and the rise of the empire – the Draleid were part of it all.

"Sometimes *the Calling* can dull your mind. It often happens."

"I remember now. Alvira Serris, she was a Draleid."

"Yes, she was. One of the greatest to have ever lived."

"But… wait. What does any of this have to do with me?"

Aeson paused, his eyes locking on Calen's. He twisted and grabbed the satchel with both hands, moving it between himself and Calen. "Calen, I'm going to lower the ward. Therin is awake, and I feel him probing at it."

"Therin? What do you mean?"

"Therin is a mage, Calen. A powerful one. From a time long before that title was claimed by the Circle of Magii."

Calen wasn't sure what to say. He should probably have expected it. His entire world had been turned upside-down in a matter of days. What was one more thing? *Therin is a mage.* "I—"

Therin's voice cut straight across Calen. "I see you finally decided to let us in."

Calen twisted his head around to look at Therin. Just a foot or so behind him were Dahlen, Erik, and Dann. Dann looked about as confused as Calen felt. Erik and Dahlen were unreadable. They stared past Calen at their father, an impassive look in their eyes. Although, for a second, Calen thought he saw an irritated frown flash across Dahlen's face.

"I did. I believe it to be time."

"Time for what?" Calen asked. "What are you talking about?"

Aeson looked at Therin, then back at Calen. He pushed the satchel towards him. "Calen, I believe that you are to be a Draleid."

Dann and Erik gasped. Every hair on Calen's body stood on end. A knot twisted in the pit of his stomach. *Has he gone mad?*

"You have heard the Calling, the ancient magic that binds the souls. It can mean nothing else."

A lump caught in Calen's throat. "How… that can't be possible. There is a mistake. You've gotten it wrong."

"I do not believe so." Aeson pushed the satchel along the soil, closer to Calen. "Open the satchel and hold the egg. If I am wrong, then that will be that."

Calen stared back at the man. *Hold the egg? A dragon egg? He has gone mad.* "How do you even know—"

"Just touch the egg," Therin interjected. There was a firmness in his voice that Calen hadn't heard before. Calen hesitated for a moment, unsure. But in the end, as had seemed to always be the case recently, he didn't have many options. With more care than was necessary, Calen undid the two rusted iron buckles that kept the satchel sealed. They were stiff, and they creaked, but they gave way to his fingers.

The glare from the egg wasn't as blinding as it had been the other night. The light from the fire was a far cry dimmer, and the canopy overhead was thicker, blocking out a lot of the moonlight. Even so, the egg gave off a glow of incandescent white light, just enough to make Calen squint. It was a strange kind of beautiful. The flowing snow-white scales, fading to black at the roots, were sleek and pleasing to the eye, but there was something about it. Something made it seem harsh – dangerous. Calen dragged his eyes away from the egg. "What do I do?"

"Touch it."

Calen puffed his cheeks out, taking a deep breath inward. *How did I end up here?*

His fingers hovered inches from the surface of the scales. He could feel something. A steady thrum, something unseen that pulsed through the air. He steadied himself and extended his fingers. As soon as he touched the egg, everything flooded back. The voice boomed like thunder. Resounding cracks of sound that echoed through every chamber in his mind.

DRALEID N'ALDRYR.

Everything else melted away. It was just him, the voice, and the egg. Even his own heartbeat felt as though it belonged to somebody else. The surface of the egg felt cool to the touch, as if it had been left to sit in the snow for hours. That sensation spread up along Calen's arms, washing through his body, filling him from head to toe. The voice etched itself into the back of his mind.

DRALEID N'ALDRYR, it boomed.

The words repeated, again and again. Each time, it was louder than the last. Every time he thought it would not be possible, it got louder, beating his brain like a war drum. The cool sensation built up in his body, like steam trapped inside a kettle, unable to escape. He felt like he was turning to ice.

DRALEID N'ALDRYR, it repeated, cracking like thunder.

DRALEID N'ALDRYR.

The cool sensation turned to pain. The voice was like a hammer, his mind the anvil. He screamed. *"DRALEID N'ALDRYR!"*

The egg erupted in swirling plumes of orange-red fire that snaked around its exterior, covering Calen's hands. The flowing tendrils of flame thickened as they moved, encasing the egg in a shell of roaring fire. In his head, Calen screamed at the top of his lungs, but nothing escaped his mouth.

Suddenly, it hit him. His hands weren't burning. He did not feel the pain that he should have felt. His skin wasn't peeling from his body, charring and crackling in the flames. Instead, the cool, icy sensation that had permeated his body was replaced with a warm feeling, as if lightning pulsed through him. He felt strong, full of energy, like he had been asleep for a lifetime but finally awoken. And he was oddly aware of… something. Something that wasn't there before. A feeling that scratched at the back of his mind.

As suddenly as the flames had appeared, they were gone. The world snapped back to reality as Calen dropped from balancing on his haunches. His knees crashed into the ground. The egg sat there, just as it had been, except now it sat in a small, charred crater. The ground around it was as black as night, the twigs and leaves burnt to a crisp. The smell of charred ash wafted in the air. *What just happened?*

The voices flooded in. Dann's was the first to reach his ears.

"Calen! Are you okay? What in the gods just happened?" Dann knelt beside Calen and grabbed his hands to assess the damage. A look of utter confusion spread across his face when he saw that there wasn't a mark anywhere. "How in The Father…"

"It is done," Aeson said.

"The first free Draleid in four hundred years." There was a warmth in Therin's voice.

Calen did not know what to say. His brain felt fuzzy, and his eyes were hazy, as if he had drunk one too many meads in The Gilded Dragon.

Out of nowhere, that sensation that had scratched at the back of his mind erupted to the fore. It was like a second voice in his head, but… it wasn't a voice, not really. It was more of a feeling – or an emotion. He felt it so deeply, but at the same time, he knew it wasn't his own. It was a need to escape – not a panicked or a frantic need, but a determined one.

He heard Dann and Erik talking to him, asking him questions, but he couldn't make out the words. His brain just wasn't interested. That feeling required all his attention.

Then he heard it – a sharp crack, followed by another and another.

Calen looked down at the egg, his eyes snapping into focus. A series of deep fissures marred its pearlescent scales. It was breaking.

Calen's heart skipped a beat.

Dann leapt to his feet. "Is it me, or is that egg… hatching?"

Calen didn't hear anyone respond. He wasn't listening.

All his attention was focused on the egg and that feeling in the back of his mind. That determined need to escape.

The fissures in the egg's armoured surface lengthened, spreading out from the tip of the egg like the roots of a tree. Finally, a loud crack emanated from the egg's scaly armour. A small fragment split off, tumbling down the side and landing with a *clink* on a nearby stone.

Calen had experienced a lot in the last few days. He'd felt emotions on levels that he never thought possible. He'd done things that he was still worried might swallow him whole one day, things that he would have to face eventually, whether he wanted to or not. This… this was different.

His throat was dry, his breathing deep. It felt like small butterflies fluttered around in his stomach. He was excited and terrified in a way he could never describe, and he wasn't sure which of the two emotions was the more prominent.

He leaned forward, stretching his neck out to get a better look at the small gap left by the fragment of fallen eggshell. There was a thin membranous layer underneath the outer shell. There wasn't much light, but he was sure he saw something wriggling around inside.

The thin membrane spiked upwards, out of the confines of the shell. It stretched as whatever was inside tried to force its way out. As it did, more cracks appeared, and more fragments broke off as the armoured shell gave way to the life that it had been protecting.

Calen's eyes widened in awe as the membrane began to tear. It gave way to a small, scaled snout with two thin slits for nostrils. The snout was covered in tiny, thumb-sized scales that flowed into each other, exactly how the scales had covered the egg. And just like the egg, the scales were a brilliant white, like the purest snow, growing darker at the base.

As the snout pushed its way farther out of the membrane, Calen found himself staring into a mesmerising pair of pale lavender eyes. They coruscated in the dim firelight, each one bisected by a black slit, like the eyes of a kat. They glimmered with intelligence, momentarily freezing as they studied him. That feeling scratched at the back of his mind again, but this time, it was different. It was a rumble of recognition.

Following the snout, a small head and neck emerged from the shell, pushing its way through the thin membrane. Its head was not dissimilar to a lizard's. Ridges of small horns framed the edges of its angular face, running along its jawline and back down along its slender neck.

Two forelimbs followed, pushing free of the membrane and clasping onto the cracked frame of the eggshell. As the small dragon heaved itself free of its shell, Calen saw that its forelimbs were joined to its torso via a thin but sturdy layer of skin that fanned outward as it extended its arms. It was pure white, with veins of black running through it that extended back to the dragon's forelimbs. Calen remembered seeing a similar feature on the bats that made their homes in some of the caves near Milltown. *Wings.*

Once its forelimbs were free of the shell, the rest of the small dragon's body followed within seconds. Its legs looked strong and oddly muscular compared to its spindly forelimbs. At its rear, a long tapered tail swished back and forth in the air, spreading out into a barbed spearhead-like tip. Two sets of frills ran the length of the creature's body, stretching from the back of its neck and right down its spine.

It cocked its head to the side, its pale lavender eyes still fixed on Calen's own. For a creature of legend, feared and awed by so many, it seemed oddly… vulnerable.

"Beautiful…" Therin said. The words sounded muffled, as if they had come from underwater.

Calen couldn't shake the feeling that kept scratching at the back of his mind. It was ever-changing, growing clearer by the second. It was a need to escape, followed by a sense of recognition, a sense of longing.

The dragon suddenly stepped forward, finding its feet. At first, it was unsteady, swaying from side to side. It shifted its weight, dropping its forelimbs to the ground for balance. It didn't take long before it moved with confidence. Satisfaction warmed at the back of Calen's consciousness.

The dragon stepped clear of the remnants of its shell. His fear told him to run, but there was something else that told him not to. A feeling of familiarity with this creature – of kinship. It was not something he could explain. It was like… like he could *feel* what the dragon felt.

It extended one of its spindly forelimbs towards Calen's knee, then used it as leverage to pull itself into Calen's lap. It was larger than Faenir was as a pup; maybe about a foot from head to tail. Turning in circles, the small dragon padded its feet, as if testing out how sturdy Calen's legs were. Then it finally curled and twisted itself into a ball, rested its head down, and closed its eyes.

CHAPTER 20

Twist of Fate

F arda shifted his weight in the leather chair, pushing his shoulders backwards to soften the firm cushion that lay underneath. He cracked his neck from side to side. The resulting sound provided satisfaction, even if it didn't provide any relief from the aches that made themselves at home in his bones. That had been born from many lifetimes of blood and violence. Even when everything else was taken from him, those aches remained. A memory of a time long past.

Giving up on softening the cushion, he sat forward, leaning his elbows on the arms of the chair. The steel breastplate was heavy, and his vambraces irritated the skin on his arms. He was sick of them and just wanted to pull them off and toss them in the corner, but he needed to make an impression, and for that, he had to weather a little discomfort.

His right hand instinctively fell to his trouser pocket.

His finger traced the outline of the coin that lay within.

It had been a few days since the commotion in the village streets. If it had been up to him, it would have been handled differently, but it was Rendall's charge, and he was impulsive. He supposed impetuosity was a common trait among inquisitors. It taught people to give the right information the first time because they might not get a chance otherwise. Every method had its place.

Still, the boy's father didn't need to die, nor his mother. Farda didn't consider it honourable to use threads of Air to hold an unarmed man in place and drive a sword into his chest. But Rendall was not Farda, and 'Honour is not efficient,' as Rendall had so eloquently put it.

Farda was far from innocent himself. He had done things that would have made his younger self spit on his own grave, but they were things that needed to be done. He had learned that over time. There were things required by fate, and he was simply a conduit.

He pressed down firmly on the edge of the pocketed coin. He twisted his wrists around in circles, trying to relieve the stiff aches that had bedded into them. He would have to see a healer soon, or it might start to become a problem.

Farda let a soft sigh escape his throat as he leaned back into the stiff leather chair. The crackling of the fireplace filled his ears. The room was quite nice for what it was, not what he had expected from a small village on the wrong side of the Burnt Lands.

Although, the innkeeper was more than hesitant to let him a room at all. Not that Farda blamed him. There were a few villagers killed that day. It couldn't have been avoided after Rendall's outburst, but the empire's servants weren't exactly welcome in The Glade.

On top of that, it appeared that the innkeeper's child had left on the same day, along with the boy, if the rumours were true. He must have been one of the two that was with him in Milltown. It could be worth looking into those two, but the boy was the priority. Both Aeson Virandr and Therin Eiltris came to his aid. That told Farda enough. He was curious to find out what made the boy so special as to bring those two out of hiding. If it had anything to do with the egg they had discovered on Aeson's ship, then things were about to get a lot more interesting. A firm knock on the door interrupted Farda's pondering. "Enter."

The door creaked open, and the soldier tentatively pushed his head into the room. Farda heard a croak in his voice as he spoke. "Sir. The, erm... The boy, he's here as requested, sir."

"Well, send him in, then," Farda said, not even turning his head, the impatience obvious in his tone. It was difficult to remember the last time that he had slept. The Spark could only sustain him for so long. And blood magic left an awful taste in his bones.

Even on the old carpet, Farda's attuned ears heard the boy's footsteps clearly, as if he were striding along the wooden floor of an empty temple. His pace did not slow, and it did not falter. There was no caution. *Curious.*

Farda had seen battle-hardened soldiers stutter and trip over their words, never mind their feet, after seeing what he could do. Use of the Spark wasn't common in the southern lands. The emperor made sure of that, especially in these isolated villages. Here, it was nothing more than legend. But with the Circle of Magii in Berona, mages were far more common in Loria, and even then, if you were smart, you knew to watch your step around a mage.

Either the boy was incredibly brave or incredibly stupid.

Without a word, he strode past Farda's chair, dropping himself lackadaisically into the twin chair on the opposite side of the fireplace. He had a wiry frame, but by the way he carried himself, Farda was willing to bet that it bore a bit more strength than it appeared. The boy's features were sharp and angular, with a slightly hooked nose. His light brown hair was slicked back up over his head with some kind of oil. His eyes were shrewd. Farda believed that eyes were the measure of a man's intent. He did not speak. He looked into the boy's eyes, unblinking. He let himself sink into the chair, ignoring the complaints of his back as it battled with the stiff cushion. There was silence as they stared into each other's eyes.

Farda tapped his fingers impatiently on the arm of the chair. He was beginning to think that the boy was going to land on the stupid side. He might just need some incentive. Raising one hand, Farda pulled on threads of Fire and Air. The fireplace erupted in a blaze. Orange and red flames twisted and turned over themselves as the fire tripled in size, bathing the room in a harsh orange light. The boy almost leapt out of his seat, fear shimmering in his eyes. *Good. Maybe you're not stupid after all.*

The boy's gaze flitted back and forth between Farda and the roaring fireplace. Farda savoured an entirely different type of silence now. Satisfied, he made a noise as if clearing his throat. Its intention was clear.

The boy's eyes were fixed on Farda now. Farda could see the lump in his throat.

"… Fritz, sir. Fritz Netley," the boy said, shifting anxiously in his chair.

"I am Farda Kyrana, Justicar of the Lorian Empire," Farda said. He leaned forward, his elbows again resting on the arms of the leather chair. Judging by the boy's reaction, he had not expected the words that had just left Farda's mouth. "Inquisitor Rendall said you were helpful in locating Calen Bryer's residence. And that you might be of use in tracking him further?"

Anger flashed across the boy's face at the mention of the name. *That could be useful.*

"Yes," Fritz said. "Sir," he added almost immediately.

Good. He is learning.

"Calen is a lying coward, and we have unfinished business," Fritz said. Contempt burned in his eyes.

Farda shifted in his seat, narrowing his eyes. "Well, it is good to hear that our desires are aligned. Now show me that you are of use. How do you think we should find him?" Farda held his gaze on the boy, making sure not to break it. The boy shifted in his seat. Farda thought that he saw the moment the idea struck. An eerie grin crept across his face.

"His sister."

"Sister?" Farda repeated, attempting to hide the surprise in his voice. That weasel Rendall had ensured him he had questioned the villagers, and that the boy's entire family had perished that day. It seemed that Rendall was either not as thorough as he would like to believe, or he underestimated the villagers' contempt for the empire. Either way, it was an interesting development.

Rendall could wait, but this incompetence would be dealt with. He was long overdue for a lesson in respect.

"Yes, sir. His sister, Ella. There are rumours that she left The Glade the night before you arrived, sir. Despite what they may have thought, her little affair with Rhett Fjorn was common knowledge. It's a small village. From what I've heard, Rhett has family in Berona. I would bet the skin on my back that is where they are heading."

Farda tapped his fingers on the arm of the chair. "And this helps me… how? What do I care for the boy's sister?"

"Well, sir," Fritz said, gaining confidence, "if you can find her and take her, just let it be known that she will face the noose if Calen does not make himself known to you. Simple, sir."

The boy is not stupid. "And you are sure that Berona is where she would be going, boy?"

"Yes," Fritz said, nodding. "To the North, at least, but I would reckon Berona."

"Hmm…" Farda bit the bottom of his lip as a plan formed in his mind. "There are two ports in Illyanara that head north. Gisa and Falstide."

Fritz stifled a laugh. "Gisa? Those weasels couldn't afford a ticket from Gisa… sir."

"Nevertheless," Farda said, "we must account for all possibilities. I will send men to both Gisa and Falstide. You will go with the men to Falstide, seeing as you are so un-convinced on Gisa. Understood?"

Fritz's head twisted in confusion. "I—"

Farda cut him off, tossing him a purse full of coins. "This is yours. The journey to Falstide is a long one, so use it wisely. There will be more if you bring her back alive. Captain Mormun is waiting for you in the lounge downstairs. You will report to him, and you leave at first light."

The boy's eyes lit up. *That is probably more coin than he has seen in his lifetime.*

Farda gave him a few moments to enjoy his newfound wealth, then raised his eyebrows and signalled towards the door. The boy got the message. He stuffed the coin purse in the pocket of his coat like a hungry urchin would an apple. He jumped to his feet, patted down the creases in his shirt, straightened his back, and cocked his chin up. "Sir, thank you, sir."

Farda gave a curt nod and sat back in the chair, turning his attention towards the far corner of the room. As the boy made to leave, Farda picked his opportunity. "And – Fritz, is it?"

"Yes, sir."

"If you ever strut into my chambers like you just did today, I will cut out your tongue and set it on fire in front of your eyes." Farda waited to hear the silence that he knew would follow. "Are you still here?"

The door slammed shut, not in anger but in haste. Farda allowed himself a satisfied grin and stood out of his chair. He had an idea what Rendall saw in the boy. He was rough around the edges, but with a little work, he could be moulded into a half-decent inquisitor. It was one of the few lines of work that catered to a short temper and a sadistic nature. *The boy would fit in fine.*

Farda let out a sigh of relief as he pulled on threads of

Air. He slid his vambraces off and unfastened the buckles on his armour, then tossed them on top of his cloak, which lay neatly folded on the long couch at the end of the room. He sat down on the bed, closed his eyes, and emptied his lungs in one deep puff.

His fingers trailed down to the coin in his pocket, a habit that would never leave him.

"What are you doing here?" Farda sighed, opening his eyes again. The light from the fireplace had dimmed, shrouding the room in shadow.

"Not happy to see me?" the Fade hissed. It sat in one of the leather chairs by the fire, its light-drinking cloak draped over the chair's leather arms.

"Just say what you have come to say."

"The troops you requested have arrived, and the blockade has been set. Are you sure that Belduar is their destination?" There was a twist of irritation in the Fade's voice.

"No," Farda said, standing up from the bed. He could see the Fade more clearly now. Its bone-white fingers were wrapped around the arm of the chair, and it stared into the roaring flames of the fireplace. The fireplace should have bathed the room in warm light, but instead, it barely gave off a glow. The Fade drank its light. As it always did. "But the ship we found them aboard at sea was Narvonan. And Arthur Bryne is the only one who would have the kind of gold needed to pay for a Narvonan vessel. It is the smart choice. Either way, we will need more troops in the South from now on."

"*We?* I do not serve your emperor," the Fade snarled.

"Do you not? Did you not just report to me like a little messenger boy?"

Farda didn't see it move, but in a flash, the Fade stood in front of him, its eyes level with his. "I serve the one *true* god. As does your master. You would do well to remember that. I should teach you to remember."

"Try it. I will rip you from that body."

"You would die first."

"I would welcome death."

There was a silence as the Fade's cavernous eyes stared into Farda's.

"Do not fail," it hissed before stepping away from Farda and moving towards the door. "I look forward to hearing your screams if you do."

Farda dropped back down onto the bed. His heart beat with a slow, methodical thump. He did not lie; he would welcome death. But it was not his time to die. He lay back down into the bed, his finger falling back down to the coin in his pocket. "Fate is my only master."

Looking out along the open plains of Illyanara, Ella was more than happy to finally be out of Camylin. The city was beautiful, but she couldn't escape the sickly feeling that occupied the back of her mind every time she thought about the events of the night before. She shivered to think what might have happened if that stranger hadn't shown up. It didn't bear thinking about.

On top of that, there were riots in the city during the night as well. She awoke, well past the stroke of midnight, to men shouting and the ringing noise of swords colliding against one another. She wasn't sure she liked cities. The fighting from the night before was all people were talking about in the markets that morning as well.

"Rebels looking to seize the keep," she heard one woman whispering to another.

"No, no. Spies from Varsund, looking to steal correspondence from the High Lord," the other woman said, with a sly wink and a nod. "My Tamwell knows a man who works in the blacksmith around the corner. He's friends with a maid who serves under Lord Karnel, and she's heard things."

Whatever it was, Ella was overjoyed when Rhett told her that there was a merchant travelling to Midhaven who would take them in his cart for a reasonable fee.

She let out a deep breath of air and nestled herself back into Rhett's chest. He smiled down at her, then turned his eyes back to the fading silhouette of the city, which had become barely a speck on the horizon. Ella closed her eyes and took in a deep breath as the cart bounced over a particularly rough patch of road. She was going to have a sore back by the time they got to Midhaven. She would be almost as happy to get out of the cart as she was to leave Camylin.

CHAPTER 21

A Change of Plans

Well, this changes things," Aeson said. The small dragon was still curled up in Calen's lap. It twisted and turned as it slept, nuzzling its head into his leg. It was hard to believe that it could ever become anything like the creatures of legend. Calen had never seen one himself – the empire's dragons hadn't been seen south of the Darkwood since long before he was born – but it was said that they could grow as large as ships, with teeth as long and as sharp as swords. Their fire could burn entire cities to the ground and turn nations to dust. It was hard to see that in those curious, lavender eyes. It took a moment to register what Aeson had said.

"What do you mean?" Calen replied, looking up from the small creature slumbering in his lap.

"You cannot go chasing after your friend, Calen. Not now."

"I—"

There was a firm, immovable look on Aeson's face.

"Calen, my sons and I risked our lives to bring that egg across the ocean from Valacia. That dragon – and now you – are more important than you may *ever* know. We need to get you to Belduar. It is the safest place right now. The empire cannot find out that you exist. An egg is one thing, but a Draleid is another thing entirely. You can't just go traipsing off across the continent. What do you think will happen if you show up at Gisa or Falstide with a dragon?"

Calen's voice was stuck in his throat. He couldn't just leave Rist. Abandon him. It was his fault the empire had Rist. He never should have left him.

"We can go after Rist, but not now. We must get to Belduar, and we must keep you safe. You saw what the empire did to your village – to your family."

A shiver ran up Calen's spine.

"This might not have been your cause, Calen, but it is now. You are part of this. You said you wanted revenge for what they did. You will not get that revenge if a knife is slipped into your back while you go chasing the wind."

Dann's voice was probably the last one that Calen expected to hear. "He's right, Calen." There was a solemn look in his eyes. "Not that I want to admit it, but what can we do if we go after Rist? We wouldn't know the first place to look, and even if we found him, what good are we against a Fade? Against the empire? What could we even do?"

Calen gazed at the dragon curled up in his lap. The feeling that had been scratching at the back of his consciousness did not stir. The small dragon just yawned in its sleep, revealing rows of small, razor-sharp teeth.

"Calen." He turned his gaze from the sleeping dragon to Therin, who was staring straight at him. "You are a Draleid now. To be a Draleid is one of the most sacred callings in all of Epheria. Your soul is now bound to that creature by a magic older than the mountains and the skies. For nearly three thousand years, the Draleid and The Order were the protectors of the free peoples of Epheria, until they were betrayed by the man who now calls himself Emperor, and his followers. You do not understand yet what it is to be a Draleid, but you can be taught. Come with us to Belduar and help us right the wrongs that have ravaged these lands."

Calen's heart sank low in his chest. He never asked to become a Draleid. He was happy in The Glade. He sighed heavily. It felt like the weight of a mountain was on his shoulders. He was only fooling himself, thinking that he had a choice to make. All his options had been taken from him. They were right, he couldn't go after Rist. What good would it do? He would never find him. Even if, by some divine intervention, he managed to find him, he didn't stand a chance against a Fade. Calen let his head droop. He gazed over at the small creature that had just changed his life even further. *And then there is you.* "Okay," he sighed. "To Belduar."

"It is decided, then," Aeson said. "Erik, Dahlen, will you saddle the horses? We will get moving as soon as they are ready. There is no point in dallying. The sun will be up soon, and it is best that we are already clear of the woods by then."

It took three days of riding before the outline of Midhaven came into view. Its multitude of towers pierced upwards into the sky, with the near twilight sun bouncing off their red slate rooves. Calen had never seen Midhaven, but travelling storytellers often told of its picturesque white walls and sprawling city streets.

The massive towers had walls as thick as Calen's arm was long, with wide open platforms on each side – landing towers for the dragons of old. That was what the storytellers said, though Calen had a feeling that they may have been making their own truths to suit their tales. It was yet another question he could ask Therin.

Calen glanced over at the elf, who rode only a couple of feet in front of him. He didn't look old – forty summers, maybe – but then again, Calen had never seen another elf. He didn't know what an *old* elf would look like. Aeson had said that Therin was a mage since long before the title was claimed by the Circle of Magii in Berona. That meant Therin was at least four hundred years old. That couldn't be possible.

Calen squinted his eyes as he examined Therin more closely. As if he had eyes in the back of his head, Therin's neck snapped around. He stared straight back at Calen, who nearly leapt out of the saddle. Calen twisted his head to the north, pretending that he had been gazing out at the Lodhar Mountains.

"I think you and I were thinking the same thing," Dann said as he pulled his horse up alongside Calen's, before whispering. "He seems in good shape for a walking sack of bones."

Calen glimpsed back at Therin. He could have sworn

he saw the elf throw an unimpressed look towards Dann before turning back to the landscape in front of him.

The journey had been longer than expected. Aeson had decided that it was best for them to stay clear of the roads and villages. Not only would the empire be searching for them along the roads, but it was also difficult not to draw attention when Calen had a baby dragon riding on the front of his saddle. It was worth taking the extra time. Calen didn't fancy running into any more imperial soldiers anytime soon.

The dragon didn't move much as they travelled. It mostly slept, curled up at the front of the saddle at the nape of the horse's neck, only waking for food.

Calen had no idea what dragons ate, but he soon found out that the answer was anything that used to have – or still had – a heartbeat. It didn't eat too much at once. A few chunks of rabbit meat a few times a day seemed to keep it happy, but Aeson said that would change as it grew. It was already starting to look bigger. Aeson also said that it would probably sleep for most of the first week or so as it started to grow, but that would change once it got hungrier. Calen was not sure where Aeson's knowledge of dragons came from, but it seemed to have no end.

To his left, Calen saw the foothills of the Lodhar Mountains creeping away into the distance. From the maps that his father used to show him, he knew that the mountain city of Belduar lay just over that ridge. He never thought he would see it with his own eyes. The city of legend that withstood siege after siege and repelled imperial armies time and again, through dragonfire and catapults.

The world just didn't seem like the same place anymore. Everything had changed. Only a few weeks ago, he had spent his days helping his father in the forge, drinking mead in The Gilded Dragon with Rist and Dann, and pining after Anya Gritten. He didn't suppose he would ever see her again, nor anyone from The Glade, for that matter. The smell of honeysuckle drifted through the back of his mind as he remembered dancing with her that night. It was a memory he would hold on to.

He looked down at the small dragon curled up at the nape of the horse's neck, then at his companions. All of that seemed inconsequential now. It wasn't something that he asked for, but it had found him.

The idea of leaving Rist, abandoning him, still clung to Calen's conscience. They would find him as soon as they were able. They just couldn't do it right now. *I will come for you.*

Aeson's informant in Camylin had mentioned some troubling rumours of a Lorian blockade at Belduar. After a bit of discussion, they decided that only Aeson and Erik would venture into Midhaven. If they couldn't find any reliable information, Dahlen would scout the northern plains between the forest and Belduar. Between them, they would know for sure by the end of the day. Taking an elf or a dragon into Midhaven was not an option, so Calen and Therin were left to set up camp for the night.

"Okay, we will see you all in a few hours. Stay within the tree line and don't go wandering. Dahlen, scout only. Do not engage." Aeson nodded at Erik, and both of them broke off into a gallop towards Midhaven, their black mantles billowing in the wind as they rode.

"I will be back as quickly as I can," Dahlen said as he turned north, towards the plains. He and Calen hadn't really talked since Dahlen came back without Rist. Everyone else had noticed the atmosphere between them, whether or not it was spoken about. Calen knew it was mostly his fault, but he couldn't help it. He wasn't sure if he was angry at Dahlen, or at himself. He had left Rist just like Dahlen did. Just like he wasn't there for Haem. Just like he couldn't help his family. *Not now…*

"You know," Calen said to Dann, trying to pull himself out of his own thoughts, "you can go with them. Neither of us have ever been this far from The Glade, and before Camylin, you had never even seen a city. I would go if not for…" Calen gestured towards the sleeping dragon that lay curled up on the saddle.

"No."

Calen raised a questioning eyebrow.

"Calen, we just lost Rist. We have no idea where he is, and it's killing me that we can't just go and get him. I'm not letting you out of my sight. We're in this together. Plus, if anything happened to you, Rist would never let me live it down, and he's already a bit of an ass as it is."

Calen couldn't help but laugh. Dann did always have a way with words. The journey through the forest would have been a silent one, were it not for his ramblings.

"Where do dragons come from?"

"Why do elves have pointy ears?"

Or Calen's personal favourite: "Can mages use magic to make people taller?"

Therin did not answer a single question. The elf seemed

a bit lost in thought, but Calen was sure he saw an amused smirk more than once. Therin's silence didn't deter Dann, even in the slightest. "You'll answer, eventually. I know you will. I'm like a weed – I'll grow on you."

Calen shook his head and laughed to himself as Dann continued.

"Can you grow a beard? I heard Elves can't grow beards."

This is going to be a long night.

"Here, this spot will do fine," Therin said as they entered a small clearing of level ground. The forest wasn't as dense as Ölm. The air was lighter, with a sweet twinge of fresh pine leaves. The warm orange glow of the setting sun sprayed through the tall, slender pine trees to create a crisscross of shadows along the ground.

"Okay, while you two set up, I'll see if I can catch anything before the sun goes down completely," Dann said, grabbing his bow from the saddle of his horse.

"Well, thank the gods for that," Therin said with a sigh when Dann was out of earshot. "Does he ever stop talking?"

The change in Therin's demeanour caught Calen off-guard. He struggled to stifle a laugh as he dismounted. "Wait, why did you not just answer his questions?"

The look of disbelief on Therin's face answered Calen's question. "Can elves grow beards?"

"Okay, okay. I understand." Calen laughed. "He can be a bit much, but he means well."

"I'm sure." Therin chucked his saddlebags to the ground, then fished out a bowl and a flask of water for his horse.

Calen shifted his attention to the dragon. It still lay curled up on the saddle of his horse, its white scales a stark contrast to the dark green and mottled brown canvas of the forest. The feeling at the back of his mind when the egg hatched had only grown more noticeable over the past few days. It slept most of the time, but as soon as its eyes opened, Calen knew. Whenever it was hungry, he just knew. It was just… *there.*

Just as he had done each time they had stopped for the night, Calen slipped his hands under the sleeping creature's belly. Being careful not to wake it, he scooped it up and off the horse's back, and lay it down on a set of blankets he'd folded on the ground. The spines and horns that framed its face and ran down its back were small and rounded, but Aeson and Therin had insisted they would lengthen and sharpen.

"Therin… Can I ask you a question?"

"Of course," Therin said. The elf had just finished piling a mound of wood for the fire and was dragging a log out from under a bush to use as a seat. He moved the log into place, then dropped himself down onto it. "What was it you wanted to ask?"

Before Calen could answer, the elf waved his hand, and the pile of wood erupted in a plume of roaring flames. *I don't think I'm ever going to get used to that.*

"I…" The elf's magic had taken Calen out of his train of thought. "Sorry," Calen said, shaking his head. "How do you and Aeson know so much about dragons?"

It was not the burning question that he wanted to ask, but it was a start.

The elf paused for a moment. "To be honest, I'm surprised you haven't asked more questions already, but I suppose you've had enough to process." Therin shuffled in his seat. "When someone is connected to the Spark, they age differently than other people. I have lived to see entire nations rise and fall and cities burned to ash, only to be rebuilt and razed once more. Many lifetimes. A long time ago, when The Order was at the height of its power, dragons roamed all over these lands. From the walls of Eselthyr to the towers of Ilnaen; from the Rolling Mountains of Valtara to the Sea of Stone.

"In this time, I was the Elven Ambassador to The Order. I counted many of the Draleid among my closest friends. I have had more than one lifetime to learn of dragons, my boy." Therin looked down at the dragon that had now crawled back up onto Calen's lap. "Though until the other night, I never thought I would see one again. At least, not one that I would be happy to see. As for Aeson, that is a story for another time."

Calen nodded. "My father, you—" The sound of footsteps drew Calen's attention. Dann strolled into camp, two rabbits slung over his shoulder, already skinned and ready to cook. Calen sighed to himself, letting his question hold in the wind. He turned his head towards the fire and let his mind get lost in the chaos of the flames.

"There wasn't much choice, I'm afraid," Dann said. He knelt in front of the fire, preparing the spit. A pang of hunger washed over Calen, from almost nowhere. Then he felt it. He looked down. The dragon was awake. It tossed its sleepy head from side to side, making a short, metallic chirping noise as it lifted itself to its feet.

"Holy shit. The thing's awake again!" Dann yelped and fell backwards onto the ground.

"You are such a baby," Calen said. He ran his hand down the back of the dragon's neck. The scales had much the same texture as a coarse stone, but were a lot softer than Calen initially thought they would be.

"A baby?" Dann scoffed. "That thing wakes up every time I bring food back into the camp. It nearly took my hand off last night!"

"Well, learn your lesson then."

As if to back Calen up, the dragon stood up straight, fanned its wings out, and let out a high-pitched screech towards Dann. Even at the size of a small dog, it looked fearsome.

"Oh, fuck off!" Dann cut the leg off one of the rabbits and tossed it on the ground in front of the dragon. It screeched again, then shook its head from side to side as it tore into the meat. "Little savage..." muttered Dann. Calen saw Therin smirking out of the corner of his eye.

Calen coughed as he choked down a lump of stale bread, following it up with a draught from his waterskin.

Rabbit meat and stale bread was becoming a staple of his diet. It was better than nothing, which is what Calen would be eating if he had been out there on his own. "Therin, why Belduar?"

"Belduar has been a thorn in the empire's side since the fall of The Order. It was the only independent city of men in all Epheria that withstood Fane's advances. The king of Belduar, Arthur Bryne, is by all accounts a good man. He is a friend of mine and Aeson's and probably one of the few people who we can trust right now. Arthur is the one who sent Aeson to Valacia in search of the egg. Well, I suppose he is not an egg anymore." Therin gestured towards the dragon. It now lay contently at Calen's feet, its tongue flicking back and forth as it picked pieces of meat from its mouth. *He.*

"At Belduar," he continued, "we will find sanctuary. A place to rest without having to look over our shoulders, and then we can decide what is next."

"I see," Calen said. "And then? When can we search for Rist?"

Therin sighed. "I don't know, Calen. That is the truth. Rist can touch the Spark. That much we know. That is probably why the Fade took him, and if that is the case, then he will be on his way to the High Tower. But to guess the reasons a Fade would do anything is like trying to catch the wind in your hands. They serve the traitor god, Efialtir, and in doing so, their interests align with Fane Mortem. Beyond that, I know as much as you do." Calen looked at Dann, who was staring absently into the fire. His chest rose and fell in heavy sweeps. Therin must have noticed. "If there is one thing that the emperor appreciates, it is the power of magic. Rist will be safe. They will want to train him, recruit him – not kill him. That means we have time. I told you that I don't know when we can search for him, and that is the truth, but we *will* search for him. That, I promise you."

The conversation left a sour taste in Calen's mouth. Everything Therin said made sense, but that didn't make it any easier to hear. They sat in silence. The only sound was the snapping and crackling of the wood as it was consumed by the flames.

Dann's eyes darted from side to side at the *clip-clop* sound of horse hooves approaching the campsite.

"No," Therin said when Dann reached for his bow. Dann shot him a questioning look, but Therin did not respond. After a few tense moments, Aeson and Erik strode into the clearing. The light from the fire illuminated their faces. "What news?" Therin tossed Aeson a hunk of now-cold rabbit meat as he hopped down off his horse.

"Not good," Aeson replied as he sank his teeth into the meat. "The talk in the taverns is that a Lorian force began a blockade of Belduar not more than four days ago. The numbers range from two thousand to fifty thousand strong, depending on who you ask. I'd wager somewhere closer to ten thousand."

Erik dropped himself down beside Calen, his eyes transfixed on the now-sleeping dragon. "That really is all it does, isn't it?" he laughed. "Eat, sleep, eat, sleep."

"More or less," Calen replied. "But your father said that will change in a few days. I'm not sure whether that's a good thing."

"Have you thought of a name?"

"A name? What do you mean?"

"I mean a name. As in, what are you going to call him?"

The thought of naming it – *him* – hadn't even crossed Calen's mind. It had not dawned on him that he would be the one to choose the dragon's name. "I wouldn't have the slightest idea. What do you call a dragon?"

"Don't look at me," Erik said. "Maybe ask Therin or my dad. I'm sure they might have an idea." Calen nodded, his mind already pondering it. *What kind of names do dragons have?*

"How about 'lazy pile of scales?'" said Dann. He poked at the sleeping dragon with a small stick, almost leaping out of his skin when it gave a short shriek in response, its eyes never opening. Both Calen and Erik threw their heads back in laughter.

Aeson sat himself down on a log beside the fire. "Dahlen has not returned yet?"

"He has not," Therin answered.

Aeson shifted uncomfortably. "I see. I thought he would have returned sooner than us."

"I wasn't far behind you, in fairness."

Calen twisted his head around, a frown setting into his face as Dahlen dismounted from his horse. He couldn't help it. Every time he looked at Dahlen, a ball of anger knotted in his chest.

"The news isn't good, I'm afraid," Dahlen said. "There is a blockade. The campfires are spread for miles. I would say maybe ten or eleven thousand men. Difficult to tell from that distance at night, but I wouldn't think I'm far off. They must have been signalled when they found our ship at sea. There is no other way they would have gotten here so fast. Is there any of that left for me?" He gestured towards the rabbit leg that the dragon had half-devoured. Dann tossed him the last scrap that had been resting by the fire. Dahlen thanked him as he sat down beside Erik.

"We know," Aeson said. "That was the talk in the city.

We just needed you to confirm." There was a pensive look on the warrior's face.

"How did they know we were going to Belduar?" Dann said, leaning forward.

"Maybe they don't," Aeson replied. "The empire has tried to take Belduar more times than I can count. This could simply be another attempt. But it is more likely that Farda has worked out where we are going."

"What now?" Dahlen asked as he stripped the bone clean of meat.

Aeson did not speak but looked at Therin, who shifted uncomfortably.

"I do not know, old friend. It would not be my choice."

"Choices are not something we have many of right now," Aeson said.

Therin furrowed his brow. Calen had not seen him take it from anywhere, but Therin flipped a small silver knife between the fingers of his right hand as he stared into the fire. "Okay."

The reluctance in Therin's voice was difficult for Calen to ignore. "Can someone please explain what is going on?"

The towers of Midhaven were even more impressive from up close. Ella weaved her way through the passing strangers who shuffled about the city. Her eyes moved between the path ahead of her and the skies above her. If the towers were any higher, they might pierce the clouds.

Their colouring was striking. Whatever had been done to cast the stone in such a white hue, she did not know, but the way the orange glow of the rising sun bounced off the buildings created such a soothing, warm light in the city streets. It was almost as if whoever built the city had painted it instead of constructed it. It was a masterpiece on a canvas of stone. When she saw it from a distance, it was spectacular enough, with the red slate rooves striking against the snow-white buildings. But up close... it was breath-taking.

"Oh! Sorry!" Ella dragged her eyes from the sky and swerved out of the way of an on-rushing peddler.

"Fool girl!" he shouted back, shaking his hand at her as he dragged a small cart behind him, filled with odd bits and trinkets.

"Maybe we should keep our eyes ahead of us instead of in the clouds?" Rhett said, laughter touching the edge of his words.

Ella smiled, a slight blush spreading on her cheeks. He always did that to her, no matter where they were. It was his eyes, she thought. Or it could be his smile.

Rhett narrowed his eyes. "Stop looking at me like that." He laughed.

The merchant who brought them to Midhaven gave them the name of an inn that was "both cheap and cheerful." The Golden Bow. Not that Ella was in any rush to find it. She could have wandered the streets all day without a care in the world. They weren't as busy as the streets in Camylin, but that was probably because the day had barely even begun. Even then, as the morning sun sprayed down over the cobbled stone streets, Ella could almost *feel* the day's excitement in the air.

The magical plethora of aromas that wafted through the air added an entirely different dimension to the city. Midhaven was famous for four things: its high towers, white walls, flowers, and bakeries. The first two made it a visual spectacle; the second two allowed you to float around the streets on the waves of aroma.

Her eyes almost jumped out of her head as she passed the window of the largest bakery she had ever seen in her life. It was at least ten times the size of Madame Gourna's in Milltown. There was everything she could think of. Loaves, cakes, tarts, pies – the list went on and on. It pained her to continue walking.

Rhett wanted to get to the inn first and make sure that there was room. Summer was one of the busiest seasons in Illyanara for travellers and merchants, but in Midhaven especially, as it was commonly used as a midway point for all travel in the province. "There, up ahead. By the butchers."

Sure enough, about twenty feet ahead, on the right-hand side, was the butcher. Next-door, a large sign hung over the building with 'The Golden Bow' printed above the intricately painted image of a bow in gold and silver.

Just as the merchant had promised, the inn was a lovely little place. It was smaller than the inn in Camylin but had a much nicer atmosphere, and there wasn't mould growing on the walls, which was a positive. The innkeeper was an upbeat fellow, slightly plump with a balding head and a beaming smile. His bleached white apron was immaculate; not a speck of dirt could be seen from top to bottom. *That definitely won't last the day.*

To Ella's pleasant surprise, not only did they have rooms available, but the room that he offered them was so lovely and quaint. A comfy-looking double bed lay nestled into a nook at the far end, just below a slanted wooden roof. A small antique mirror hung on the wall in front of an ornate wooden desk. *Perfect.*

Ella threw herself onto the bed, closing her eyes as she sunk into the soft mattress. She exhaled contently, then let her eyes open again. Rhett stood two feet away with a letter in his hand and a concerned look on his face.

"I have something to show you."

CHAPTER 22

Valerys

So, just one more time. Why is it exactly that we're going to the most ominous-sounding place in all Epheria? *The Darkwood.* I mean, besides the legends, it just doesn't sound very welcoming, does it?"

Dann, as expected, hadn't stopped talking to take a breath for more than five minutes over the past few days. It was at the point where Calen thought Therin might just kill him in his sleep and drag the body away. The elf glared at the back of Dann's head. His lips moved, but he was too far away for Calen to hear what he was saying. Calen wagered that it wasn't anything pleasant.

For the fourth time, Aeson answered Dann's question with more patience than Calen would have been able to muster himself. "There is an old mountain pass in the Darkwood, at the foot of the Lodhar Mountains. It is not a pleasant journey, but it should see us to Belduar safely and allow us to skirt the blockade."

Dann was silent for a moment, pondering. "I see. And

why is it that Therin is so opposed to going this way?"

Therin did not even acknowledge the question.

"He has his reasons," Aeson said. "Now if you can stay quiet until we reach the Darkwood, I will answer three questions that Therin has refused to answer for you, but only if you don't speak from now until we arrive."

Dann went to open his mouth almost immediately, but paused when Aeson cocked his head and tilted one eyebrow upwards. He gestured as if he were tying his mouth closed with string.

I don't see that lasting.

Therin and Aeson had not had any verbal disagreements about their new path, but it was clear to everyone that Therin did not approve. His mood had deteriorated since the Darkwood was mentioned. Calen wasn't too keen on the idea either. There was not a story he had heard that involved anyone walking into the Darkwood – and then walking back out again.

Calen felt a burst of excitement coming from the dragon, combined with a rather loud shriek as it spread its snow-white wings. It leapt from the back of the saddle and up onto his right shoulder. Calen couldn't help but smile. It had been sleeping a lot less over the past few days and nights, and its appetite had increased twofold. It had also grown by almost half its original size, which Calen felt as its claws dug into his shoulder. "I think you might be getting a bit big to be standing on my shoulder." Calen felt a rumble of disagreement as the dragon chirped harshly. It understood him, he knew it did. Just as he understood it.

He still hadn't given it a name. He had talked to Aeson

and Therin to find out what kinds of names were usually given to dragons. It hadn't helped. They just kept rattling off names of past dragons, lost in the nostalgia of days long gone. "Well, Vyldrar was the name of the dragon to which Alvira Serris was bound. Tinua, Xarden, Anaia, Salina, Purlon…" The list just went on and on. He had hoped to narrow it down a little.

"We will settle here for the night," Aeson said. They approached a small alcove set into the side of a rock face, beside a slow-running stream. "Bathe, eat, and then sleep. We will set off as soon as my eyes are open again. We will not wait for the sun."

They hoped to reach the Darkwood by nightfall of the next day, and at the pace they were going, that was a certainty. Aeson had been running them ragged. Calen figured they had to have covered at least fifty miles a day. The horses were close to collapse. They marched each day relentlessly, stopping only once for food and water. Then they set up camp. Dann hunted, Dahlen built the fire, and Dann and Calen practiced the sword with Aeson. It was routine. Regimented.

At first, when they practiced, Aeson only allowed them to run through the different forms. They had to do it, he said, "until moving between them was as effortless as breathing." Calen had felt silly the first time; they were more intricate than the forms his father had taught him, and he kept tripping over his own feet. But that changed over time. He felt more powerful, confident in his movements. He quite enjoyed it now. It was relaxing; it reminded him of being in the field with his father and Haem.

After a while, Erik joined them. Despite how flawlessly

he flowed from one form to next, Aeson always found something wrong. A misstep, a sword held too high, a slight hesitation. Even so, Erik never complained. He simply nodded and continued. Aeson never had to make the same criticism twice.

Calen felt the dragon watching him as he practiced. Its pale lavender eyes were awash with interest. Sometimes, when they sparred, he swore he *felt* a warning right before a strike landed. It confused him at first, putting him off balance, but when he listened to the feeling, he realised that it was always true to its word. More than once, he had drawn strange looks from Aeson when he pivoted and blocked a strike that he had no right to know was coming. He couldn't help but smirk as he glanced at the dragon, who simply tilted its head from side to side, watching.

Calen ambled down to the stream. He had bathed already, before they ate, but his throat was dry and his waterskin empty.

He found Therin sitting on the edge of the bank, his eyes closed and his shoes off, with his feet dipped into the gelid water. "Mind if I sit?"

"Not at all."

Calen dropped down beside Therin, pulling his knees up to his chest. He stared out over the water. "What you said, outside Camylin... How did you know my father?"

Therin sighed. He opened his eyes but didn't turn to look at Calen. "I met your father many years ago. At the start of a war."

"The Varsund war?"

Therin nodded.

"Why… why did I not know this? Why only now?"

It didn't make sense. Therin had been coming to The Glade for as long as Calen could remember. He had never been anything more than friendly with Vars.

"We all have our secrets, Calen. Even your father. He made a choice, and I honoured that choice."

"But—"

"There will come a time. But that time is not now."

Calen felt the anger rising at the back of his mind. It wasn't only his. It was shared. He didn't have to look to know the dragon was staring at Therin. Calen took a breath.

Fine. For now.

There was a silence that held in the air as they sat there. Its only opposition was the sound of the stream as it meandered its way through the land. Therin broke the silence. "Have you thought any more on the young one's name?"

Calen nodded. "I have… But I still am not sure." Calen looked back at the dragon, who was now curled up by the fire. The anger had dissipated. The mixture of pale moonlight and warm firelight caused its scales to shimmer in an incandescent glow. "It is a Valacian dragon, you said?"

"Yes, *he* is from Valacia. The Icelands."

Calen nodded, dipping his waterskin back into the stream. "Is that how you say 'ice' in the Old Tongue?"

"Not quite," Therin replied. "Valacia means 'Icelands.' It comes from the words *valerys*, meaning 'ice,' and *cia*, meaning 'land.'" Therin reached down into the stream, touching his fingertips to its surface. "Valerys," he whispered.

Calen's eyes opened wide as the water around Therin's hand began to freeze. Tendrils of icy white spread slowly outward in a circle, thickening as they travelled, until it was as if clouds began to form beneath the water's surface. Then it stopped. Therin removed his hand from the water, a warm smile on his face.

"How…" Calen let out a delayed sigh of relief. "I don't think there will ever be a point where that will seem normal to me."

"You should try," Therin said. There was no hint of a joke in his expression.

Calen just stared back at him with incredulity. "Me? What would be the point? I'm no mage."

A wry smile spread across Therin's face. "That is correct. You are not, but you *are* a Draleid. Calen, some people are born with the ability to touch the Spark and to wield its power in this world. Others are not. Many people will go their entire lifetimes, never knowing what they are capable of. When things happen around us that we can't explain, most people just put it down to chance. This is not always the case. Rist did not have an inkling as to his strength, yet he has the potential to be one of the most powerful mages I have encountered for a long time.

"Dragons are magical creatures, to the core of their being. The Spark is in the very fire that they breathe. When someone becomes bonded to a dragon the way that you have, it changes them. The bond created transcends everything that you can see and touch. Pieces of who you are become bonded to each other. You will see. Both Draleid and dragons gain many things from the bond; the most important of these *gifts* for a Draleid is the ability to touch the Spark."

It took Calen a moment to understand. "You mean...me?"

"Yes." Therin laughed softly. "You, Calen. Don't question. Just do. You will see."

"What do I do? I just... touch the water and say the word?"

Therin scrunched up his mouth and tilted his head to the side. "The words are not necessary. Often, when a young mage begins their training, speaking the word is helpful. It allows them to focus. The power of the Spark is not in the words we speak, nor is it in your fingertips. It is in your head and your heart, it is... everywhere.

"It is difficult for people, especially your kind, to understand what they cannot see and feel. This is why using your hands is helpful. It's like a totem – a conduit. Touch your fingers off the surface of the water. Take the heat from the water and push it outward. Picture it freezing, slowly moving, like the roots of a tree."

Calen puffed his cheeks out as he exhaled heavily. He felt that familiar twist form in his stomach, and his heart picked up its pace. He had no idea why he was so nervous. *What does it matter if it doesn't work?* He was not convincing himself.

Exhaling again, Calen pulled himself up onto his knees. He reached his hand down over the flowing water. The chill bit at his fingertips as they grazed the surface of the stream. "It's half-frozen already," he joked, swallowing nervously.

The elf smiled, but he did not laugh. His eyes were fixed on Calen's hand.

Okay, I can do this.

Calen turned his attention to the stream, where his

fingertips rested against the running water. He tried to clear his mind, imagining the water turning to ice, spreading like a ripple after a rock had been dropped in a lake. He slowed his breathing and felt the vibrations as his heartbeat slowed in his chest.

"It's not working."

"Patience. There are five elements, Calen: Fire, Earth, Water, Air, and Spirit. The Spark consists of all of these. Imagine energy. Just power, raw and untamed. Now, from that energy, take what you need. Pull from it like a thread of yarn, slowly. Treat it with the same caution you would treat a roaring fire or a razor-sharp blade. Do not take too much. The Spark has consumed those who ask for too much too soon. Focus on the elements of Water, Air, and Fire."

"Fire?" Calen asked.

"I know it seems strange, but you need something to control the heat that you take from the water. Feel it. You will understand."

Calen's nerves were only getting worse. *What did he mean, "it has consumed those who ask for too much too soon?"*

He slowed his breathing again and closed his eyes. He could see an empty blackness. It touched every corner of his mind. The only source of light came from a ball of energy – right at the centre of the darkness – that pulsed, turning in on itself as it floated in his mind. The more he focused, the more he realised that the ball of energy was not smooth or solid. It was made up of interlaced strands of light. He watched them in his mind, pulsating. They were separate from each other, but at the same time, they were not. They twisted and turned, constantly moving, changing. Each strand was unique. He could not explain what it was, but each thread *felt* different as he touched them with his mind. Power emanated from them; he could feel it. It washed over his skin and filled his bones. It pulled at him, tempted him. He wanted to reach out and let the Spark consume him.

Focus.

He reached out with his mind. He plucked at two of the strands, drawing thin threads into him. Air and Water. He wasn't sure how he knew, but he did. He could feel the strand of fire. Its pull was stronger than the others, as if it were calling to him. Air, Water, and Fire. It yearned for him. It made him cautious. Therin's words echoed in his mind.

Calen reached out for the Fire strand, drawing a thin thread of its essence into him. He was careful not to draw too heavily. Not to take too much.

A sweet, warm glow flooded through his body from head to toe. It was the same glow he felt when the egg became wreathed in fire. He felt it now, and he knew what it was. The Spark.

His breathing steadied. He drew the threads through him, using them to shape and mould the water to his will. He watched in amazement as the water around his finger-tips began to freeze, spreading out in a concentric circle. *"Valerys..."* he whispered, a soft smile touching his face.

"Calen... Calen!"

Calen was mildly aware of Therin's voice floating in the back of his mind, tapping at the edge of his focus. The touch of his hand on Calen's shoulder took him by surprise. Calen felt the warmth leave his body, losing the Spark. He pulled his hand away from the water and shook his head, trying to erode the grogginess that had set in.

"Sorry. I just… I got a bit lost in it. It feels—"

"Addictive," Therin said abruptly. "That's because it is. The power to change and bend things to your will is something that will always be addictive. The warmth as you pull the Spark through you can entice a man to take more than he needs or can handle. You need to be aware of it. You need to learn to focus. It will come with time." Therin gave a reassuring smile. "And with *time*, you will find that you can handle more of it. With time, and practice."

Calen nodded. His arms felt heavy, and his breathing was laboured, like he had spent an entire day working in the forge.

Therin's hand clapped him on the shoulder. "Don't worry. Drawing from the Spark can be exhausting, especially for those who aren't used to it. It is called the drain. It can leech the very life essence from your bones. Its effects will grow less over time, as you grow stronger. For now," he said, lifting himself to his feet, "you will have a fantastic night's sleep. Come. Aeson won't keep his eyes closed for long, and you will need the rest."

Calen looked back at the stream as they walked back to the camp. It was still frozen solid where his fingertips had touched. Steam wafted from its surface as the warmth of the summer night eroded away at it.

The dragon lay curled up by Calen's saddle bags when they got back to camp, still awake but eyes drooping. It poked up its head to watch Calen and Therin approach. Calen set himself down on his haunches in front of the dragon, running his hand along the side of its head with the utmost of care. The comfort that pressed at the back of Calen's mind matched the purring noise that emanated from the dragon's belly. Calen stooped his neck down to look into its eyes. He smiled.

"Valerys…"

CHAPTER 23

Not as it Seems

The downpour came upon them without warning. Within minutes, Calen's hair was matted to his face, and his skin had begun to shrivel as the water soaked him through to the bone. He lifted his hand to cover his eyes from the onslaught of rain as he stared up at the sky. The thick, charcoal-black clouds looked as if they would cave under the weight of the rain they held within their fragile frame. He dropped his eyes to survey the sight in front of him. He had never seen anything quite like it.

Just as they planned, the eerie ocean of woodland that was the Darkwood had come into view just as the sun retired beyond the horizon. As far as Calen could see, and farther beyond again, the landscape was painted in muddled brush strokes of dark green and blackish-blue. The only thing illuminating the eldritch woodland was the cracks of lightning that tore through the sky above, momentarily exposing the flocks of jet-black birds that weaved in and out of the deluge.

Calen had heard many tales of the Darkwood. Terrifying stories of monsters and voidspawn. Of a forest that consumed souls and stripped flesh from bones. Even those stories did not compare to the sinking feeling in his gut as he looked down over the sinister woodland.

"Keep moving," Aeson shouted. "The canopy will break the rainfall."

Calen felt irritation from Valerys. The dragon cocooned himself in his wings and shuffled around on the back of the saddle. Calen gave his horse a tap on the ribs with his heel, urging it into a fast canter. The rain stung Calen's face as they picked up speed, making him wince. His eyes were more closed than open.

He only realised that they had reached the edge of the forest by the sudden relief he felt on his skin and the change in sound. The harsh cracking of rain on his coat gave way to a duller sound as it barrelled down on the canopy above. It gave him the same familiar, calming feeling of sitting inside when the skies emptied rivers down upon The Glade, of being sheltered as the rain drummed on the walls and windows.

Calen sighed, wiping the water from his face. He rolled his shoulders back and surveyed the dense canopy above. He had underestimated the utter blackness that would consume them in this forest. Even if the moon wasn't imprisoned by the wall of charcoal clouds above, its light would not have been able to penetrate the aphotic roof of the dense wood-land. The darkness made him feel trapped.

It was disorienting how the absence of sight heightened his other senses. He could not see past the ears of his horse, but even the soft susurration of the branches felt heavy in his ears. The overpowering scent of loam and decomposing leaves mixed with the mouldy dampness of tree bark permeated his nostrils.

A sigh of relief escaped his chest when the glow of white light illuminated the space in front of him. The small floating baldír pulsated as it held its position about four feet in front of Calen. A similar orb hovered in front of each person in the group. *That is a handy trick.* It was not something that he wanted to try on his own. He hadn't tried to touch the Spark since the river. He would have to ask Aeson to show him how it was done.

"The path to the mountain pass is less than a day's ride from here," Aeson said. There was a twist of irritation on his face as he squeezed firmly on his coat sleeve, releasing a stream of water that had soaked into the fabric. "Within this forest, day or night matters not. There are few places where the light penetrates the canopy, but we still need sleep and to dry out our clothes, or else the cold will set into our bones. We will carry on for another hour or so, and then we will stop. I think the horses have that much left in them." He patted his horse on the neck with affection and received a soft neigh in response.

Calen felt the occasional chill on the back of his neck as small droplets of rain dripped through the dense canopy. The deeper they went into the forest, the heavier the air became – not in the ethereal way it did in Ölm Forest, but in a more tangible sense. Although the canopy held the deluge above at bay, it also kept the dampness of the soil and the bark from escaping. He could taste the thickness of the moisture in the air as it hit the back of his throat with each breath.

There was something about a forest, especially one so devoid of light, that caused time to pass differently. Everywhere Calen looked was indistinguishable to what he had seen five minutes before, as if he hadn't moved an inch. He heard the occasional flapping of wings amongst the branches, often drowned out by the cracks of thunder that followed the lightning strikes in the sky above. Had he been on his own, he did not think he would ever find his way out.

"This looks like as good a place as any," Dahlen called, hopping down from his horse. "We could walk for hours here and not find anything different."

There was a murmur of agreement amongst the group.

Valerys yawned and lifted his head to survey the area. He leapt down from the back of the horse and stretched out his wings, as if they were groggy from sleep.

"Calen, Dann, sword forms," Aeson said firmly. He tossed his saddle bags to the ground and drew one of his blades from across his back.

"Now?" Dann sighed, "Can't we sort a fire first, dry ourselves out a bit? These clothes feel like a sack of stones."

"No," Aeson replied. "We rarely fight on our own terms, so *that* is how we must train. Sword forms. Begin from Striking Dragon."

Dann sighed heavily, then threw back his head and pulled his sword from its scabbard. Calen did the same. His thighs and back were a mixture of numbness and agony. He had never ridden a horse so much in his life. The rain didn't help. He took a deep breath as he entered the starting position for Striking Dragon. Some of the forms' names were beginning to stick in his head. Not all of them, but some of them. It was a start.

"Again."

The word shook Calen's resolve. They had been practicing sword forms for over an hour while the others sat by the fire, awaiting the warm meat of a small boar that Therin had found skulking around the campsite. His shoulders cried out in pain as the sword grew heavier and heavier. It felt as though his muscles were on fire. Calen focused on his breathing. He swung the blade downward in one long sweep and sidestepped an imaginary strike. He brought the blade back up for a parry and then drove it into the ghostly attacker's abdomen.

"Stop."

His knees dropped into the damp ground. A wave of relief flooded over him. Pangs of hunger punched at his stomach. His skin burned from where the damp clothes had chafed the inside of his legs.

"Dann, go warm yourself and eat." Aeson turned towards the campfire, a glint in his eye. "Dahlen. You will spar with Calen. Now."

Dahlen responded with a look of confusion as he rubbed his hands over each other in front of the flames. "What, now? Look at him. He needs to rest—"

"Now."

Calen dug the point of his sword into the ground and dragged himself to his feet. He didn't speak. He didn't have the effort left in him to argue. *Is he trying to kill me?* He felt concern tipping at the back of his mind. Valerys's lavender eyes watched him from atop the trunk of a fallen tree.

"Yes, sir," Dahlen replied. He pulled one of his swords from its scabbard, which stood propped against his saddle-bags. Calen stood up straight and heaved his sword upright. He didn't stand a chance. Dahlen raised his sword up in front of his face. "Ready?"

Calen responded with a nod. He wasn't wasting his energy on speaking.

Dahlen's first strike was heavy. The shockwave jarred Calen's forearms. His shoulders burned as he parried the blow. Calen didn't have the strength to counterattack, and his fingers loosened on the handle of his sword with every deflected blow.

Dahlen swung a vicious sideswipe, and Calen leapt backwards to avoid it. His left leg collapsed from exhaustion under his own weight. His knee crashed into the muddied ground. He was done. He had no strength left. It infuriated him. The last person he wanted to concede to was Dahlen. Anybody but him.

A warm feeling washed over him. He felt Valerys at the back of his mind, pushing him, willing him strength. He noticed Therin and Aeson exchange a look. Calen risked a glance over at the young dragon. He stood fully on his hind legs, his eyes fixed on Calen, his teeth showing as his mouth twisted into a snarl. Calen heard the rumble coming from Valerys's throat.

Dahlen's downstroke swept through the air. Calen brought his blade up to meet it mid-swing. The newfound strength flooded relief through his muscles, and he sprang to his feet. A confused look set into Dahlen's face. He thought Calen had given up.

They traded blows back and forth. Calen pressed, running through the forms, his sword a flurry of movement. Then Dahlen pressed, pushing Calen onto the back foot. It went like this for several minutes, but even with the new push of energy, Calen knew that he wasn't a match for Dahlen. He already felt exhaustion creeping back into his bones.

He couldn't lose, not to Dahlen.

Calen pushed away one of Dahlen's blows and leapt backwards, urging him to follow. He took the bait. When Dahlen attempted to make up the ground between them, Calen reached out to the Spark, doing as Therin had said. He could see the ball of energy floating in a sea of black. Twisting and turning in on itself. The elemental strands called out to him.

He drew on threads of Water, Earth, and Fire. Calen drew the moisture from the damp soil, freezing it in place. Unable to halt his momentum, Dahlen's foot slid across the ice. He hit the ground with a thud. Calen stood over him, the tip of his blade resting against Dahlen's chest, a satisfied smirk on his face.

Dahlen's face furrowed in fury. He swatted Calen's sword away with his hand. "What the fuck was that?" he roared as he leapt to his feet.

Calen felt a pang of guilt in his chest. "I…"

"No, seriously, you think that's okay?" Dahlen shouted, pushing Calen. Anger replaced the guilt. Calen heard Valerys shriek as he glared at Dahlen. Their anger was shared.

"Stop this. Right now!" roared Aeson. "You are both no longer children. Have you not seen your eighteenth summer? Have you not seen death?" His voice flowed with authority as he stepped between the two young men. "You," he said, pointing at Calen, "this was a test of swordsmanship, not of a new gift that you do not understand. Do that again while practicing and consider this arrangement null and void."

Calen hung his head in shame.

Aeson turned towards Dahlen. "And you," he said, "you know better. Situations change. Circumstances vary. Your environment can be your friend one second and your enemy the next. If that were a real battle, you would be dead. We will face enemies who can do far worse things than that with the Spark."

Aeson stormed off towards the fire. The anger in Calen's chest did not subside entirely. It flickered, like a candle running out of wax, but it endured. He stomped past Dahlen and took a seat between Erik and Dann.

"Don't hold it against him," Erik said. He handed Calen a hunk of boar meat and some small slices of cheese wrapped in a cloth. Erik shrugged. "He doesn't like losing."

Calen nodded absently. He took a swig from his waterskin, panting heavily. "Yeah…"

"So… you're a mage now too? Am I the only one who isn't?" Absorbed in his own dark mood, Calen had forgotten that Dann was there. He realised that with everything that had happened in the past few weeks, he hadn't talked to Dann properly. The anger faded, and the guilt returned.

"I'm sorry. I haven't been myself. I should have told

you. I'm not a mage… Therin said that it has something to do with the bond between Valerys and me."

The young dragon made his way over to the three young men, dropping himself in a curled ball in front of the fire. The glow of his snow-white scales was almost hypnotic.

"You named him?"

Calen felt another pang of guilt. One more thing he hadn't thought to tell his friend. "Sorry, Dann. My head has been up in the sky. I only decided on it last night. It means 'ice' in the Old Tongue."

Dann smiled. "It suits him." He nodded and looked at Valerys, who was now tearing into one of the boar's legs. It didn't seem to bother him whether or not the meat was cooked. Although, he attacked it with more enthusiasm when it was cooked.

Calen felt a rumble of anger when he saw Dahlen sitting on the other side of the fire, glaring at him as he ate. He quashed it. He was too hungry to be angry.

"You're getting better," Erik said. His tone was not condescending, but sincere. "You could hold your own when we met you, more than I would have guessed. But now you are starting to understand the sword, instead of just holding it. I don't know if that makes sense, but—"

"It does. Thank you," Calen interrupted, giving Erik an appreciative smile. Erik had been nothing but friendly to him, even though Calen had a frayed relationship with Dahlen. He was a good man.

Calen, Erik, and Dann chatted for a while, sitting around the fire until the cold was drawn from their bones and their clothes had dried to a point that they no longer sloshed when they walked. It was the first time in what felt like a lifetime that Calen could step out of his own mind and just relax. That was why, when he felt sleep tugging at his eyelids, he tried to fight it as much as he could.

"I'm going to get some sleep now," Aeson announced. "Dahlen, Erik, you two can take first guard. I will leave the baldír around the perimeter, so you can see better. If anything moves, wake us. There are few things in this forest without sharp teeth. The rest of you, I would advise getting some sleep."

"I will stand guard with them," Therin called. "I am not so tired, and an extra pair of eyes will not hurt. Especially in this place."

Aeson shrugged his shoulders softly. "Okay. Wake us in a few hours, so you can get some sleep yourselves." With that, he lay himself down by the fire, pulling his blanket roll up around him.

Erik grabbed his swords from atop his saddle bags and slung them over his back, along with his bow and quiver. "I will see you in a few hours," he said, clapping both Calen and Dann on the shoulders. He moved off to take up position at the edge of the camp.

"I'm going to follow Aeson's lead," Dann said. "I get the feeling that this journey isn't going to get any easier. I, for one, am going to need some sleep to get through it."

Calen felt a nudge at the side of his leg. "I know, I know. I'll get some sleep."

He ran his hand down the spines on Valerys's back, receiving a rumbling purr in reply.

"Uraks!"

The shout pierced through the night, jolting Calen awake. It took half a second for the grogginess to clear from his mind. His eyes were still in a hazy blur. The ringing shrieks of steel colliding with steel brought him back to the waking world. He leapt to his feet, only just stopping himself from tumbling to the ground as he tripped over a loose tree root. His brain was still in a scattered daze.

Calen saw flashes of fighting everywhere. Erik and Dahlen stood back-to-back twenty feet away. Uraks, their hulking forms illuminated by the light from the baldír, surrounded them.

Aeson weaved through a stream of leathery grey skin, the ground around him wet with blood. Calen couldn't see Therin, but there were far too many bodies on the ground filled with arrows for Dann alone.

My sword.

Calen ripped his sword from its scabbard just in time to block the first blow that nearly caught him in the head. Only a warning in the back of his mind from Valerys allowed him to spin on his heels and block the blow. The force sent him stumbling backwards, cursing as he tried to stabilise himself.

The Urak turned its attention to Valerys, whose shriek in response was more that of a wolf cub trying to howl than it was a war cry. The young dragon didn't stand a chance.

Calen launched himself through the air, catching the Urak off its guard when he crashed into its side. There was a moment when he thought the massive creature would not budge. It was like trying to knock over a wall. But luck was on his side. The creature lost its balance, and they both tumbled over Calen's saddlebags and down onto the damp forest floor.

It took Calen only a moment to react once they hit the floor. He did not wait for the Urak to regain its bearings. Throwing himself up onto his knees, he grasped the hilt of his sword with both hands and drove it down through the creature's chest. He felt the crunch of bone as the sword found home. He pushed down harder. Blood spluttered from the creature's mouth.

It's dead. Get up!

Calen heaved the sword free from the Urak's limp corpse. His heart boomed claps of thunder. The camp was in chaos. Uraks were everywhere.

Snap.

Calen spun around, not hesitating as he drove his sword straight through the belly of another onrushing Urak. He didn't wait to see the body drop. Pulling the sword free, he looked down to make sure Valerys was by his side. Hatred pulsated from the dragon.

A guttural roar dragged Calen's attention to his left, just in time to block the Urak's thick, blackened blade. Again, twice, three times. The beast kept coming. The strength of its strikes jarred Calen's arms. He blocked another blow, only to be caught off-guard when the creature planted its leathery grey shoulder into his chest.

He hit the ground faster than he understood what was happening. His head hit off something. Hard. It erupted in a piercing pain. He saw stars. A blurry haze clouded his vision. The only thing he could see were the crimson eyes of the creature as it stood over him, its blade in the air.

"Calen!"

Something plunged into the Urak's neck. Blood spurted in all directions.

An arrow.

Calen shook his head, blinking furiously as he tried to clear his vision. The Urak coughed and spluttered, choking on its own blood as it staggered forward. Even with the shaft of the arrow buried in its neck, the creature lifted its jagged blade back to full height; its hate-filled stare was fixed on Calen.

A piercing shriek sliced through the air. Calen just about made out Valerys's silhouette as he leapt at the Urak's face, rending bone with its claws and tearing away chunks of flesh with its teeth. Fury consumed the dragon.

Calen pushed himself to his knees as his vision cleared. He felt Valerys's fury pulsing through his veins. The dragon stood on top of the Urak's now prone body, his claws still tearing away at its torso. The red of the creature's blood stood stark against Valerys's white scales.

"Calen." Dann now stood over him, his arm out-stretched. Calen took it, heaving himself to his feet. "Are you okay?" Dann panted as he tried to catch his breath.

"I'm okay. What happened—"

Dann howled as a jagged black spear pierced through his right shoulder, lifting him off his feet. Calen swung himself around Dann, bringing his sword down across the shaft of the spear. He snapped it clean in half, allowing Dann to fall to his knees.

Without hesitating, Calen swung his blade in an upward arc towards the Urak holding the now-broken spear. It deflected the blow with its thick iron vambraces, then stabbed the shattered spear shaft at Calen.

Calen felt himself subconsciously reaching for the Spark. His lungs burned and chest pounded. Sweat streamed down his face. He drew heavily on threads of Fire, embracing the warmth as it flooded his body.

Burn.

A column of flames erupted from Calen's left hand as he thrust it towards the towering beast. The flames burst forward, consuming the Urak from head to toe. The whole campsite lit up like a signal fire. He felt the Spark flooding through him; it touched every corner of his mind. The Fire called to him, yearned for him to take more. *No. Stop!*

Calen let go of the threads of Fire as the energy leeched from his bones. His knees shook as they struggled to hold his weight. The putrid aroma of charred flesh filled his nostrils in seconds.

He turned back to Dann, unable to look at the blackened remains of the Urak. The sound of its skin crackling and popping filled his eardrums. Dann was in a heap on the ground, the tip of the spear still jutting from his shoulder. Fear bolted through Calen's heart. "Dann!" He dropped to his knees beside his friend, hitting the ground far harder than he had intended.

"I'm okay," Dann coughed, his lips coated in a thin layer of blood. "Go, help the others. I'm not much good right now." Calen began to protest. "Go! You can't do anything for me. I'll be all right."

Calen nodded reluctantly. He had to try twice before he could drag himself to his feet. His body was not cooperating with him. Therin wasn't joking when he said using magic could leave him drained. Every movement felt heavy and laboured, as though he had been working in the forge from sunrise to sunset.

By the time he made it over to Erik and Dahlen, his body was littered with small cuts and scrapes. He swung his blade downward, parrying a stabbing strike from an Urak spear, then swung the blade back up the spear shaft to send the creature to the void. Sword forms ran through his mind as he flowed from one to next. Striking Dragon to Charging Boar, falling back into Crouching Bear.

A searing pain ripped through his thigh, forcing him to collapse to one knee. He looked back just in time to watch Valerys's claws tear through the creature's neck. Calen was almost scared to see what the dragon could do when he was bigger.

His heart jumped as an Urak caught Valerys in the side with a swinging hammer, sending him soaring through the air. He hit the ground with a thud. He didn't move.

Something burned in Calen as he leapt to his feet. He pulled on threads of Air, screaming as he catapulted them at the Urak. He sent the unsuspecting monster hurtling through the air, snapping the trunk of a tree clean in half with the impact.

Calen felt the drain again. He dropped to one knee momentarily, fighting to stay conscious. Blood rushed down the inside of his leg, accompanied by a burning pain that ran along the length of the fresh wound. Ignoring it, he pushed himself to his feet and stumbled over to Valerys. He felt the dragon's heartbeat even before he reached him, but that didn't stop him from placing a hand on Valerys's side, just to feel the rise and fall of his lungs. Relief flooded through him.

Another blood-curdling roar burst through the din of battle. He turned and saw a towering Urak with a plate of iron across its chest swinging a wicked double-bladed axe above its head. Calen tried to move, but he barely had the strength to keep his fingers wrapped around the handle of his sword. He sighed and stretched his body across Valerys, closing his eyes.

Calen heard a *whoosh* and opened his eyes. The Urak stumbled back and forth, an arrow tip jutting from where its left eye had been only moments before. A second arrow exploded from its neck. Calen looked around. Dann was still on the ground. Therin was now in sight, but he was holding his sword, limping heavily as he fended off two Uraks.

Just as Calen saw them, both Uraks dropped, arrows jutting from multiple places on their bodies. Surprise coated Therin's face. The slicing sound of arrows cutting through the air filled the campsite. Raining death. Calen spun his head around to see where they were coming from, pulling Valerys in closer to shield him.

The largest stag Calen had ever seen burst through the brush at the edge of the camp, the light from the baldír bouncing off its bone-white fur. The stag's body rippled with muscle. Its powerful neck held up a head adorned with ferocious antlers, black as coal, with veins of gold rippling throughout. A man sat on its back, with a moss-green cloak draped around his shoulders and a hood obscuring his face. The man drew a sleek arrow from his quiver, nocking it and loosing it in a flash. An Urak dropped to the ground.

More warriors in green cloaks burst into the clearing, each wielding massive bows of stained white wood. Uraks dropped wherever their arrows flew. The fighting was over in a matter of moments. Those Uraks not lying motionless on the ground, arrows protruding from them like spines in a hedgehog, stumbled, crawling and limping away into the forest abyss.

The muscles in Calen's legs seized, and he struggled to hold himself upright. He tried to fight it, but he felt himself drifting in and out of consciousness.

Someone was approaching him. They were running. At least, he thought they were running. It was hard to tell. His vision blurred as if he were underwater. He felt a crack of pain as his other knee gave way. He fell to the flat of his back, hitting his head off something solid. The figure had almost reached him. They were definitely running.

He couldn't fight it anymore. He let his eyes close.

CHAPTER 24

One Who Survived

Calen's head pounded as a ringing noise pierced his ears. He felt himself shaking. A pair of hands wrapped around his collar.

"Calen! Calen!"

The voice was familiar. He tried to open his eyes, but the little strength he had was ebbing.

"Calen!" The voice was louder, clearer. "Calen?"

Pulling every drop of strength he had, Calen willed his eyes open. Everything was fuzzy at first, but it began to clear.

"He's alive!"

Calen tried to form words, but his mouth felt like it was full of cotton. The coppery taste of part-dried blood coated his tongue. "Therin?"

"It's me, child. Just breathe."

A hand pressed against his shoulder. A shiver ran the length of his body as a pulsing wave of energy flowed into him. The burning pain from his wounds faded to a dull ache, and the ringing noise in his head cleared. As his eyes focused, he could just make out the sharp features of Therin's face.

"Therin, I—"

"What in the gods were you thinking, you idiot child?" Therin shouted. His hands shook as he held the collar of Calen's shirt with one hand. "I told you! I warned you not to take too much. You could have killed yourself! It is only by the miracle of the gods that you didn't."

Calen hadn't seen the elf angry before. Guilt picked at the back of his mind.

Therin let go of Calen's collar with an exasperated sigh. "Don't do that again," he said, shaking his head. He got to his feet and ran his hands through his silver hair, digging his fingers into his scalp in frustration. "Stupid fucking child…"

Calen felt Valerys's heartbeat, in sync with his own. The dragon whimpered as it licked at a cut on its side. It was not life threatening, but it hurt.

"Come here," Calen said, as he got to his feet. He reached out his hands, scooping up Valerys into his arms. He rested him on his shoulder, with his tail draped across the back of Calen's neck. The whimpering did not stop, but Calen felt comfort coming from the dragon.

"Draleid." The man who rode the stag stood in front of Calen, his hood pulled back. Aeson flanked him on one side, and one of the hooded warriors stood on the other. He was an elf. He stood about the same height as Calen, with short, cropped blonde hair and a motley array of scars etched into his face. He had the same tapered ears as

Therin. One of his eyes was a milky white all over, with no iris or pupil. "Draleid, I am Thalanil, High Captain of the Aravell Rangers."

Calen found it nigh on impossible to determine the age of an elf. They may have seen three hundred summers or twenty. Therin looked youthful but was older than some of the trees in The Glade, while Thalanil looked as if he had lived through a thousand battles but may well be Therin's junior many times over, were it not for the scars that raked his face.

"I am Calen Bryer of The Glade." A rumble came from Valerys's chest. "And this is Valerys of Valacia," he added.

"It is an honour to meet you, Calen, Valerys. Never in my lifetime did I think that I would be welcoming a Draleid and a dragon to Aravell. It would be an honour if you were to allow us to escort you to the city."

"The city?" Calen replied. "There is a city... *in* the Darkwood?"

"I'm sorry, Thalanil, but we can't," Aeson interrupted before the elf had a chance to respond. "We are on our way to Belduar, to commune with King Arthur Bryne, and we must move with haste. I'm sure you must understand now that you see who we travel with?"

"I see," Thalanil said. There was a twinge of hurt in his voice. "Are you sure you cannot come with us? We can provide you safe haven in Aravell. Nobody who wished us harm has even set eyes upon its walls in the three hundred and fifty years that they have stood. It would be our greatest honour to provide sanctuary to the first free Draleid in four centuries. You know this, old friend."

Aeson sighed. "You know as well as I do, Thalanil, that there is more to it than that. You have my word that we will return here if we are welcome. But we must go to Belduar first. There are oaths to honour and people awaiting us. Surely, you understand?"

The elf took a moment to respond. "I do. But the Uraks have been acting strangely of late. The Blood Moon is not far away, only a year at most. I would be hard pressed to remember a time where they came this far into the Aravell in such large numbers. I will provide you with an escort of five rangers, as an honour guard for the Draleid. The elves of Aravell have always stood by the Draleid and The Order, even before this place was our home, and that has not changed."

A smile touched the corners of Aeson's mouth. "The honour would be ours, High Captain. Calen?"

"Yes," Calen stuttered, "it would be our honour."

The warm smile on Thalanil's face grew wider. "The honour will be shared, Draleid." The elf turned to the warrior to his left. "Faelen?"

The woman drew down her hood. Calen tried his best not to stare. She would have been considered beautiful in any part of the world. Her long brown hair was tied at the back of her head, pulling it off her face. She looked as youthful as Therin, while somehow also seeming younger. She had the same sharp features and high cheekbones. Her white-wood bow was slung across her back. Calen saw what the elves had done to the Uraks with those bows; it was ruthless. "Yes, High Captain?"

"I will need you to select five rangers, at least one of

whom must have a connection to the Spark. Do not dally."

Faelen nodded. "Yes, High Captain." Before she left, she turned to Calen, bending one knee slightly as she tilted her head. "Draleid, Valerys."

Did she just bow to me? Before Calen could ask her to please not do that again, she took her leave, marching over to a group of rangers that were sorting through the Uraks' bodies. Aeson must have seen the surprise on Calen's face. He smirked.

Suddenly, a thought struck Calen. "Aeson! Dann... Where is Dann? Is he okay?"

"He is okay," Aeson said. "The spear missed anything important, and one of Thalanil's rangers is an excellent healer. His shoulder will likely be stiff for days, but he will be okay."

Relief washed over Calen. "Thank you."

"Excuse me." Faelen had returned. Five elves stood behind her, each wrapped in their moss-green cloaks, with their hoods pulled down onto their shoulders. "These are five of our best, High Captain. They all expressed a desire to swear the oath. This is Vaeril," Faelen said, gesturing towards a youthful warrior with shoulder-length blonde hair and a serious look in his eye. "He is young, but his connection to the Spark runs deep, and he is particularly adept at healing."

Did she say oath?

The young elf gave a short bow from the waist. "Draleid, Valerys, *Rakina*, High Captain."

"Vaeril." Thalanil nodded. "All of you, you are willing to swear the oath?"

"Yes, High Captain," the group of elves chorused.

"With honour," Vaeril added.

"Then you may do so now. We will not keep the Draleid and the Rakina. They must make haste."

Without hesitation, all five of the elves dropped to one knee. They placed one hand atop their standing leg and the other across their chest.

"Wait. Aeson, what—"

"I hereby swear oath, by witness of those here and the six who watch over us, to protect the Draleid, Calen Bryer, and the dragon, Valerys. To go with him wherever he may lead, to the void or beyond."

With the completion of their oath, the five elves rose to their feet and turned expectantly to Thalanil.

"It is with honour that your oath has been witnessed by those here and by the six who watch over us," Thalanil replied. "It is done. Draleid, these rangers will protect you with their lives. Your bond is not that of blood or magic but of honour, and it is stronger than steel."

Calen couldn't be sure, but it looked as if Thalanil glanced at Therin as he spoke. The elf had been keeping his distance.

"Thank you for everything. If you had not found us, then I fear we may not have lasted the night," Aeson said. He reached out his arm and wrapped his fingers around Thalanil's forearm in a tight grasp, which Thalanil reciprocated.

"Aeson Virandr, it is always a pleasure to set eyes upon you, old friend, but to see that you bring hope with you." Thalanil paused, directing a warm smile towards Calen. "The first free Draleid in four centuries. If I am to be honest,

I had given up on that hope a long time ago. If I could, I would march all of Aravell out of these woods alongside you."

"That day may well come," Aeson responded sombrely. Thalanil twisted his mouth, nodding his head in agreement. "For now, we thank you for your aid and your oath, but we must be on our way. It is a long journey to Belduar through the mountains."

Thalanil made to bow towards Calen. Instead, Calen mimicked Aeson's gesture, extending his arm out towards the elf. "I owe my life to you and your elves, as does Valerys and everyone here. Thank you."

The look of shock on the elf's face gave way to one of appreciation. He grasped Calen's arm. "It was my honour, Draleid, as I hope it will be again."

With a quick nod, Thalanil rounded and walked back towards his men. Faelen followed him, though Calen couldn't help but notice her mouth turn as she glanced sideways at Therin. Her gaze lingered, but he seemed to do his best to pretend he didn't see her.

Erik, Dahlen, and Dann approached, with Dann clutching his arm close to his chest.

"You okay?" Calen asked.

"Yeah, just a scratch, really." Dann shrugged, a wry smile on his face. He winced as his attempted shrug pulled at the healing wound in his shoulder. "We got new friends?" Dann's head tilted towards the five elves who still stood in a straight line, their stances rigid. "Wait, I know you," he said, nodding towards Vaeril. "You're the one who fixed my shoulder. Thank you."

"It was my honour," Vaeril replied. A satisfied smile spread across his face.

"Okay," Aeson said, looking around the group. "It is time that we are on our way. We will march towards the pass, breaking only when we catch first sight of the moon. It is impossible to tell the cycles of day and night in this place." Aeson turned towards the elves, addressing them alone. "Do any of you need to gather anything before we leave?"

It was Vaeril who replied, speaking for the group. "No, *Rakina.* We have everything we will need." He gestured to a satchel slung across his back, with a blanket roll tied to its side. Each of the elves carried similar.

"Horses?" Calen asked, unsure himself whether he had intended to speak aloud. "Do you not need horses?"

"No, we will keep up just fine," one of the elves replied, whose name Calen did not yet know. His response seemed unnecessarily curt to Calen.

Calen nodded. "Before we leave, your names. You cannot swear oaths to protect me without me even knowing your names."

"Oaths to protect you?" Calen was convinced that Dann would have laughed at him if it would not have caused him so much pain.

Vaeril was the first to step forward, "As you know, Draleid, I am Vaeril. Vaeril Ilyin, ranger of Aravell."

The other elves stepped forward in turn, presenting themselves in the same way.

The firmness in Ellisar's eyes led Calen to believe that he had seen many a summer, which belied his youthful face. If they could look past his tapered ears, many women in the villages would have considered him incredibly handsome. His short black hair was similar to Rhett Fjorn's, as was his build, and women often swooned over Rhett.

Alea and Lyrei were twins. At least, in Calen's mind, that was the only explanation. Even if he had hours to examine their faces down to the most minute detail, he did not think he would have the slightest chance of telling them apart. They were both beautiful – perhaps not in the conventional sense, but they were most certainly beautiful in Calen's eyes. Both had short blonde hair with fringes that hung to one side and shimmering golden eyes. He had never seen golden eyes before; it must be a uniquely elven trait.

The last was Gaeleron, the elf who was curt to Calen. His long brown hair was tied up at the back of his head, giving his face a harsh appearance. A thin scar on his right cheek ran horizontally, just under his eye. Calen couldn't quite put his finger on it, but there was something about the way the elf spoke and looked at him that made him uneasy. There was contempt in his eyes.

Therin approached the group, already on horseback, eying the elven rangers uneasily. "Are we ready?"

"We are," Aeson replied.

"Wait, what about the bodies?" Calen asked.

"The forest will take them."

By the time they reached the edge of the treeline, the crescent moon was shining like a beacon in the night sky. They had marched through the entire day. Calen was sure he had fallen asleep in the saddle. Whatever Therin had done to him had eased the pain of his wounds and relieved some of his fatigue, but it certainly hadn't cured him of sleep deprivation.

The elves, true to Gaeleron's word, kept pace with the horses without breaking a sweat. In fact, the twins had remained in front of the group for the entire journey, insisting on scouting ahead. Their cloaks allowed them to fade into the forest, almost at will.

The first night at the mouth of the mountain pass was rather uneventful. They went through their usual routine. Calen complained at first when Aeson had told him to grab his sword, but the man had a way of staring wordlessly until he yielded. There was no sparring that night, just forms. There had been enough fighting already.

Calen couldn't help but notice that all the elves stopped eating to watch. Their eyes followed him with every movement, every swing of the blade and twist of his body. It made him feel uneasy.

There were few words exchanged when Aeson and Calen sat down for their supper. Dann lay unconscious by the fire, his empty bowl of broth on his stomach, moving up and down with his breathing. The elves did not allow the hunting of deer, for whatever reasons they had. The broth of rabbit and potatoes was perfect for Calen, who smiled ear to ear when Vaeril revealed a loaf of fresh bread from his satchel. It had been so long since Calen had eaten bread that didn't have the consistency of stone.

Vaeril also healed Valerys's wounds as much as was possible. The dragon was still in a bit of pain, but the whimpering had stopped, and he was strong enough to go searching for his own rabbits.

"So, have elves always lived in the Darkwood?" Calen asked as he held his palms over the open fire. "I didn't think that anyone could live here."

Vaeril looked up and held a short silence before answering. It was only the two of them. "No. We came to the Aravell about four hundred years ago. After the Fall, we tried to fight back, to resist the Empire. We failed. It was before my time."

"Why do you call it the Aravell? Is it's name not the Darkwood?"

"That is what it has always been known to my people. The Darkwood is a name that was given to it by your people."

"Why did you come here? I've always heard that the elves retreated into Lynalion when The Order fell. But never anything about the Darkwood – the Aravell."

A melancholy smile touched the corners of Vaeril's mouth. "We believed different things. So, we followed different paths. Does every human always think the same way?"

"No. I don't suppose they do." Calen sighed. He fiddled with a piece of long grass that he plucked from the ground. "What is it they believe? The elves of Lynalion."

"That the troubles of men and dwarves do not belong to them. That the empire was born from human arrogance. And that the blight on these lands is naught to do with elves."

"And what do you believe?"

Vaeril pondered for a moment. There was a softness in his eyes beyond his serious expression. "That this world is all of our responsibility. That all races were involved in The

Fall. We occupied the Aravell to act as a wall between Loria and the rest of Epheria. To do everything we could to weaken the Empire's grip. We make sure that nothing that enters the forest ever leaves. Either we take them, or the forest does."

"The forest?"

There was a loud pop as part of the fire collapsed, sending Sparks spiralling through the air.

"There is old magic in the woodland," Vaeril said. "Older than stone in the mountains and the songs in the wind. Even we elves thread lightly when we roam its depths. You were lucky to have only found Uraks last night."

Calen nodded, letting out a short sigh. "Vaeril, why did you swear an oath to protect me? You don't know me. You owe me nothing."

The elf gave a weak smile as he leaned towards the fire. "My people didn't always live in the Aravell. We used to live in sprawling cities of beautiful white stone. With sweeping walls, breath-taking towers, and domes of gold that would shimmer in the sun's light. My elders told me stories of these cities. I have never seen them for myself. Maybe with your help, what once was, might be again, and I may see for myself. It is a dream that I am willing to give my life for."

The group had already packed up their things and were over an hour in their saddles by the time the sun rose the next morning. Aeson was determined to reach Belduar within two weeks' time, which meant marching during every second of light that the sun gave them.

As the sun rose over the crest of the mountains, splashing light into the valley, Calen could see the truly epic scale of the Lodhar mountains that was impossible to see the night before. The group walked along a small dirt track, framed on either side by sheer rock faces that disappeared into the clouds. In the distance, Calen saw nothing but mountains and clouds, stretching far off into the horizon. Up. That seemed to be the only direction the path could lead – up and then up again. Calen had no idea how the elves were still standing. He even felt his horse struggling, but the elves loped through the pass like wolves, not a hint of fatigue on their faces.

They had to have been walking for six or seven hours before they reached the first flat. They stopped for no more than fifteen minutes to eat and drink. Therin used the Spark to draw pools of water up from the ground for the horses. Calen thought he could almost *see* how he did it. The threads of Water mingled with threads of Earth.

"Therin." Calen drew his horse closer to Therin's. "I'm sorry." The elf hadn't spoken to Calen since he had stormed off in the forest.

"It is okay. I, too, apologise… for my anger." Therin paused for a moment, staring off into the sky above. "You nearly died, Calen. You would have if I hadn't been there. Drawing so heavily from the Spark with as little experience as you have is dangerous beyond words. With Valerys at your side, you have the potential to be powerful, but right now, you are not. It is my fault. I should not have shown you the path without first teaching you how to walk. From now on, after your training with Aeson, you will train with me. Understood?"

"Yes," Calen replied with all the enthusiasm of a pig facing slaughter. Just the thought of touching the Spark again made his knees quiver. He had never felt a weakness like that before, as if his body were too weak to keep a hold on his soul. "Therin, can I ask you a question?"

Therin's eyes narrowed. He nodded reluctantly.

"What does 'Rakina' mean?"

Therin sighed. He seemed uncomfortable at the very mention of the word. "Why do you ask?" Calen got the impression that he already knew.

"The elves all refer to Aeson as 'Rakina.' What does it mean?"

Therin hesitated, leaving Calen uncertain whether he should have asked at all. "'Rakina' is a word of the Old Tongue. It means 'broken,' or more correctly, 'one who is broken.'"

Therin's answer only led to more questions in Calen's mind. "Why would they—"

Therin interrupted Calen with a hand in the air. "It is Aeson's story to tell, but I feel it is something he may never do. It may anger him for me to tell it, but so be it. You deserve to know the people to whom you have given your trust."

Therin pulled his horse in closer to Calen's. He watched as Therin drew from the Spark, but he was too quick for Calen to follow what he did.

"A ward of silence," Therin explained when he saw Calen's curious face.

Aeson and Vaeril's heads spun as soon as Therin erected the ward. When he realised that it was Therin, Vaeril flicked his head back to the road ahead of him, not wishing to pry. Aeson was not as quick to ignore the ward. His gaze lingered on Therin and Calen for longer than was comfortable before feigning disinterest. It was apparent to Calen that they felt when Therin drew magic from the Spark. He felt something too, just a tickle at the back of his mind, but it was there.

"Now we can talk," Therin said. "I will likely have to explain to Aeson why we are warded, but I will deal with that later." There was a moment's pause. "A long time ago, Aeson was a Draleid."

Calen felt like his heart had stopped beating.

"Aeson is a Draleid?" He couldn't stop the words from leaving his mouth. He hadn't realised it until that point, but even surrounded by friends, he felt alone. He had Valerys, who gave a rumble of objection at the thought of Calen feeling alone, but it was not the same. He needed someone who could talk to him, guide him. Tell him what to do next. Ever since Valerys hatched, people looked at him differently. Not Dann – he was still the same – but everyone else did. Therin, Erik, Dahlen. These elves, whom he had never met before, swore an oath to protect him with their lives. It was as if when people looked at him, they saw someone different than he did when he looked in a mirror.

"He *was* a Draleid, Calen." Loss consumed Therin's eyes. "Aeson's dragon, Lyara, was killed in the years following the collapse of The Order. She was hunted by Fane and his *Dragonguard.*" Therin spat out that word, as if it left a foul taste in his mouth. "Aeson barely escaped with his life. Even then, parts of him died with her. That's what it means to be Rakina, Calen. To be broken." Therin wiped a tear from his left cheek. "The bond between a dragon and their Draleid runs far deeper than could ever be explained. I'm sure you feel it by now, Calen, but your souls are not just entwined; they are as one. Who you are as a person changes Valerys, and who he is changes you. At your very core. I see it in you already. But when you blend something so completely, it is impossible for it to return to what it once was. Two souls blended together are not the sum of their parts, but something new entirely."

Calen couldn't help but look back at Valerys, who sat behind him, curled up in a ball, his head resting against Calen's back. Had Valerys changed him?

"When a Draleid loses their dragon," Therin continued, "or a dragon loses their Draleid, they lose parts of themselves. They can lose the ability to draw from the Spark. They can lose fragments of their personality, emotions, connections. They can lose the will to live." Therin exhaled deeply. "Rakina may mean 'one who is broken', but among the elves, it is a mark of respect. It also means, 'one who survived'."

CHAPTER 25

A Deep Cut

A shock bolted up Ella's back as the wagon hit yet another stone. She rubbed her back, attempting to provide herself with some kind of relief. Rhett smiled at her. She jolted forward as he dug his thumb into the aching muscle, arching her back in a mixture of pain and relief.

"Not long now," he laughed. Whenever he laughed or smiled, he did it with his eyes.

When Rhett showed her Tanner's letter in Midhaven, she had no idea what to think at first. They didn't have the money. They had talked about it before. That was why they chose Falstide; tickets from Gisa would cost an arm and a leg. *Or more.*

The idea of arriving in a new city already indebted to someone was not an idea that she liked to think about. This was meant to be a new start for them, somewhere to build their lives. How could they do that if they always had money looming over their heads?

However, Tanner was a good man. At least, from everything Rhett said, she believed him to be. Rhett was a good judge of character.

In truth, she was backed into a corner. Despite her spine feeling like it was days away from snapping from the vibrations of the damned wagon and the fact that they were running out of coin, Falstide would still be her preferred choice. She didn't want to owe anything to anyone. She was more than willing to put up with another month or so of travelling to truly start anew.

Unfortunately, Tanner had already paid for the ticket from Gisa. No matter what they did, when they arrived in Berona, that fact would remain. Ella knew Rhett well enough to know that he would not be able to live with himself if Tanner paid out that kind of coin on Rhett's behalf, in good faith, and it was never returned. There was only one true option. She cursed the man in her head.

Ella looked out the back of the wagon. The open plains were behind them, and the foothills of the Lodhar Mountains were on their left. She had never been so far from home. It had only begun to hit her in the last few days of travelling. That sickness in her stomach, a longing for home.

She was happy – moving to Berona was mostly her idea – but that did not mean she didn't miss her parents. The way her father looked at her whenever he saw her, like she was a shining star fallen from the night sky. The way her mother sat up with her at night, just talking about the world, the stars, boys. She even missed Calen. He really was a thorn in her side most of the time, but he had a good heart, and he always did right by her. She put her hand on her stomach, as if it would do something to alleviate the sinking feeling.

Ella turned her head to look over the front of the wagon. The city of Gisa came into view just as they crossed the Irnell river. Its massive grey walls wrapped around the city in a semi-circle, stopped only by the coastline. The Beacon Tower rose high above everything else within the city walls, famous for its eternal flame that marked the city for ships far and wide. There were, of course, other beacon towers across Epheria, but this was the first. Her father had told her that. He always thought she wasn't listening, but she was.

Ella leaned into Rhett, resting her head on his chest. *Not long now.*

Decisions aside, it didn't matter to her what they did. It was Rhett who mattered. They would work it out.

The merchant – Master Harson Link – had not charged them anything for the transport. He had sold most of his wares in Midhaven and was meeting a supplier in Gisa. "No sense in taking an empty cart," the wiry old man had said, the teeth he had left spread wide in a friendly grin. The kindness of strangers was not something Ella had come to expect in life. Most people were good at heart, but that didn't always translate to kindness when nothing was offered in return. Harson Link, however, was a kind man.

Ella looked around at the people they shared the back of the wagon with. One other couple, and a father and his son. Neither pair looked wealthy. Their clothes were not torn or dirty, and they did not look hungry, but they also did not carry the aura of someone who could afford to live in Gisa. Although, she supposed to herself, the simple fact that they were riding in the back of a merchant's wagon could have told her that. Perhaps they had family on the other side, like Rhett did. Maybe they were going to Gisa in search of work. They did not talk, so she would never know. They all rode in silence.

Only Rhett's arm catching her shoulder saved Ella from being thrown forward into the small child when the wagon stopped abruptly.

"Are you okay?" he asked, waiting for her disgruntled response before he stood up.

Ella heard voices at the front of the cart, but it was almost impossible to see what was happening.

"Oi, all of you in the back of the wagon, out now. By order of the emperor." The voice belonged to a man. His gruff tone suggested that he was not one who liked to be kept waiting. Barely more than a few moments passed when a soldier marched around the rear of the cart, the black lion of Loria emblazoned across his crimson breast plate. His face looked like he had been beaten off a rock as a child. His nose had clearly been broken in several places, and deep pock marks painted his cheeks. "Did you lot not hear me?" he growled, the impatience in his tone deepening. "Get your arses out o' this wagon, *now* – fucking Southerners."

Ella was about to say something, but Rhett squeezed her shoulder, just enough to let her know that now was not the time. He was the first to jump off the back of the cart.

"Of course. Right away."

The soldier grunted, looking him up and down as he walked past. Rhett was easily half a foot taller than the man.

Ella and the rest of those in the wagon followed Rhett's lead, jumping down from the back of the cart and making their way around to the front. Harson Link had come down from his seat at the front of the cart, and his bony old fingers fidgeted with the straw hat that he now held clutched to his chest. He stood beside Rhett, with five soldiers lined out in front of them. It all seemed odd to Ella. What was the empire doing stopping random carts on the road to Gisa?

"Is there something I can do, sir?" Harson said, stumbling over his words. "I haven't done anything wrong."

Amusement was painted on the face of the soldier with the broken nose. "And I'm just to believe you, old man? You ain't done nothing wrong, and I should just let you go without being sure?"

The old merchant looked like he was about to answer, but then he thought better of it.

"Don't put yourself in an early grave, old man," the soldier said. He laughed and looked over towards his men, who all laughed in kind. It was the kind of laugh that you did when you didn't think a joke was funny, but you knew what was expected of you. "We are looking for someone. All we need are some names, and then you can be on your way. Easy enough?"

The old man nodded.

"Easy enough?" the soldier repeated.

"Yes, sir."

Another soldier stepped forward. He was young, definitely not more than twenty summers. He carried himself with the walk of a man who was trying to make a name for himself. Though, his armour looked as if it had been made for a taller man – passed down through family, maybe – which did not help him in that regard. The soldier moved up through the group, asking each their name in turn. He started with the other young couple. He stared at the man as if he were not nearly a foot taller than the boy. "Name?"

"John Tarnell."

The soldier lingered for a minute, looking John up and down, as if a few more moments of nervous waiting might change his answer. When he was satisfied that John's name wasn't going to change, the soldier moved on to his partner. The father and his young son received a similar treatment, even the boy, which seemed unnecessary to Ella.

Everything seemed fine until Ella gave them her name. "Ella Bryer."

It was as if the wind changed. Ella might not have caught it, were it not for the surprise in the soldier's eyes. He had been trying so hard to seem intimidating that he couldn't hide the way his eyes turned. It was a mix of surprise and nerves. He looked over to his captain, the man whose face looked like the wrong side of a horse's ass. His stony expression offered nothing but the slight twist of a smile at the corner of his mouth. He nodded.

The young soldier's stance shifted slightly wider as he turned back towards Ella. "Ella Bryer, we're going to need you to come with us, by order of the emperor." The other soldiers moved, surrounding the group of weary travellers, who had all expected to be wheeling through the gates of Gisa before sunset.

"Excuse me?" she blurted out. She attempted to catch the words with her hands before they left her mouth, but it was an exercise in futility.

"There must be some mistake here. Please, we are on our way to catch a vessel to Antiquar." Rhett was as surprised as she, as well he should be. The idea that anyone outside the villages would know her name at all was surprising, let alone a group of imperial soldiers on the merchant's road to Gisa. It had to be a mistake.

"We don't need any trouble. Just come with us, and the others can be on their way," the soldier repeated firmly. He reached out to grab Ella's shoulder. Instinctively, she tugged her shoulder away, out of reach of the man's hand. His hand immediately fell to the pommel of his sword.

"Whoa!" said Rhett. Ella heard the nervousness in his voice, which only served to make her nervous as well.

What is happening?

Rhett stepped forward with his arms open. "Can we please just talk?"

Two of the soldiers immediately dropped their spears to hip height, their tips aimed at Rhett's stomach.

"Do not step closer," one of them called. Again, he had to be less than twenty summers.

Rhett raised his hands in the air, backing away slowly. Ella felt the situation slipping out of control. The soldiers were jumpy. Something was very wrong.

"Okay, we'll go with you, but can you please just tell us what this is about? And just let these other people go. We don't even know them." Ella did her best to keep her voice calm and level. Her father had always told her that she could change the tone in a room with the tone in her voice. He was not often wrong. She stepped closer to the soldiers and raised her hands in the air, just up to her shoulders, to show them she wasn't carrying anything.

"Just you," the soldier barked. Keeping his hand over the pommel of his sword, he grasped Ella by her shoulder with his free hand, pulling her in closer to him. Ella batted at him with her hands, but it was no use. Even if they were the same size, her palms did nothing against his armour.

"You let her go, right now!" roared Rhett. He whipped his sword from its scabbard in a blur. There was not so much as a tremble in Rhett's blade as he held it out in front of him, but his eyes were on fire.

"Rhett, no!" Ella might as well have been screaming at a stone wall, for all the good it did.

"If you harm a hair on her head, I will take your head from your shoulders." Rhett's voice was flat and measured. He meant every word.

The cocky young soldier pulled Ella in tighter. He wrapped the inside of his arm around her neck and held out his sword. "I dare you to try, Southern scum!" The soldier spat on the ground.

The other soldiers pulled inward, tightening the circle around the group of travellers. The boy whimpered as he hid behind his father's legs. A worried look was on the man's face. The other couple had barely moved an inch, the woman's head buried in her partner's chest.

"Just let her go."

"You are in no position to be—"

The man's words were cut short as he cried out in pain.

That was something her mother had taught her, not something her father would approve of. *"If you ever find yourself in that situation, Ella... Praise the gods, you won't. But if you do..."* Her mother had said, pointing to her heel, as she gave a swift kick backwards, a smirk on her face.

It worked just as Ella had hoped. The young man rolled around on the ground with his hands between his legs. Ella's heart felt like it was about to explode. She immediately ran towards Rhett. A shriek escaped her mouth as something caught her by the foot, sending her hurtling towards the ground. A shooting pain erupted in the side of her head when she landed.

"Stupid bitch!" the soldier spat as he heaved himself to his feet and sent a swift boot into her rib cage. The coppery taste of blood sprinkled her mouth. She coughed viciously. It felt like her lungs would come out of her chest.

Before she could collect her thoughts, something landed on the ground beside her with a *thud.* She turned and screamed as the soldier's cold eyes returned her gaze, blood streaming from where his neck had been attached to his body. Within seconds, screams and shouts filled the air. The shriek of steel on steel rang harshly in Ella's ears.

She clamoured to her knees, still dizzy from hitting her head. She reached out with her hands. Finding purchase on the wheel of the wagon, she used it to heave herself up to a hunched position. Her ribs ached with every breath, and blood rolled over her lip, trickling down her chin.

A sinking feeling enveloped her when she saw Rhett standing in the middle of the three remaining soldiers, long cuts along his thigh and shoulder. Aside from the young soldier who had grabbed Ella, there was another, crumpled in a heap at Rhett's feet, blood streaming from his neck.

She looked around quickly. The boy and his father were gone; they most likely bolted in the chaos. She would have done the same. Harson Link – may the gods harbour his soul – was strewn out in the dirt, soaking in his own blood. Ella's heart ached. He was such a kind man.

Wailing caused Ella to spin her head. The other man from the cart launched himself at the soldiers, taking one of them to the ground in a bouldering tackle. Tears rolled down his partner's eyes as she screamed after him.

In the confusion, Rhett slid his blade through the heart of one of the other two soldiers, then rounded quickly to block a blow from the other. The captain. His already horrid face was contorted in fury. He swung wildly at Rhett, roaring unintelligibly into the air. Rhett side-stepped one of his haphazard swings, ducked under it, and cracked him around the back of the head with the pommel of his sword. The soldier fell to the ground with a heavy thud.

"Ella!" Rhett ran over to her, his hand outstretched. She grasped it with all her strength, so much so she saw him wince momentarily. "We need to go, now!"

"What about the others?" She hadn't even noticed that she was screaming. Her heart was beating so loudly in her chest that it drowned out everything else. She saw the reluctance in his eyes. He didn't turn his head, just kept his gaze fixed on her own.

"Ella, we need to go. Now—"

He spat out the last word, snapping his mouth closed as blood trickled out and over his lip.

Every hair on Ella's body stood on end as her heart dropped into her stomach. "Rhett! Rhett, what's wrong?"

His lips tried to move. More blood spilled over them like wine from a cup. He looked down, holding his hands around his stomach. A polished steel spear tip jutted out from just below his belly button, dripping thick red blood onto the dry dirt below. "Ella?"

He dropped to his knees as the spear was yanked backwards, pulled free of his body.

"No! No, Rhett…" She could hardly see. Her eyes welled with tears. She couldn't breathe. "No, no, no…."

Ella cupped her hands, pushing them against Rhett's stomach, but the blood just poured through her fingers. She couldn't stop it.

He fell onto his side, then rolled onto his back. He tried to talk, but every attempted word summoned forth spurts of blood.

Ella's head pounded. Her eyes were raw, and her stomach sank into the depths of the void. She was going to be sick.

"Don't you dare!" she roared. "Don't you dare leave me! Rhett Fjorn, *do not* leave me alone!"

Rhett reached up and rested his hand on her cheek. The slightest of smiles touched the corner of his face, just short of his eyes. "I… would… do it all…" He was cut short as he coughed up more blood.

"Rhett… please… I can't do this, not without you. I can't…"

He rubbed his thumb against the side of her cheek, like he always did. She did everything she could to burn that feeling into her mind, to etch it into every crack and crevice.

"Rhett…"

His hand dropped to his side. His chest fell. Ella's throat dried up. She wanted to scream, but her entire body had lost feeling. Her tears dried up, along with her throat. She felt her heart ripping.

"Get on your feet, or I swear to the gods, I will run you through as well." The soldier's voice was like a rusty nail being dragged across steel. It was the younger of the two. The captain stood behind him, his hand pressed against a bloody gash on the back of his head.

Ella filled her emptiness with rage.

It was like something had possessed her. Ella leapt to her feet, screaming so hard that her lungs burned. The soldier didn't even have the time to swing his spear. He howled as she crashed into him. Grief and rage consumed her. She clawed at him, feeling the skin peel away under her nails. His screams washed off the back of her mind.

Something hard hit her in the side. The force of the blow sent her spinning to the ground. She landed on her back with a crash. Her ribs howled, as if someone had struck her with a hammer.

Something sharp nicked a cut into her neck as she lay there.

"Oh, you better be able to give me a reason why they want you alive, because if you don't, I will just slit your throat now and pretend we never found you. And I would smile while I did it." The man with the battered face stood over her – the captain. She pushed her neck forward, only stopping when she felt the sting of the blade cutting into her skin. She stared at him, rage burning in her eyes.

"Oh, has the kat got your tongue?" The man's laugh was wicked. It made Ella's skin crawl.

"Just gut the bitch!" screamed the young soldier, still lying on the ground. He held his hands to his face to hold back the cascade of blood that streamed from where Ella had torn strips from him. She hadn't noticed him stop howling in pain.

"Will you shut—"

A low rumbling growl cut the captain's words short. The next sound that filled Ella's ears were the howls of the man as something tore him from his standing position. His sword clattered against the dirt beside Ella's head.

Ella pulled herself up onto her elbows, just catching sight of the grey flash of fur as it bounded across the dirt, leaping onto the younger soldier.

The screams turned Ella's stomach. She closed her eyes. The only sounds were the thumping of her heart as it pulsed through her body and the crunching of bones snapping like twigs. Ella took a deep breath in, holding it for a moment before she released. *I'm coming.*

A long moment passed. She heard cautious steps, muffled in the dirt, making their way towards her. Something pushed up against her stomach and gave a rumble of familiarity. Ella peeled open her eyes, unsure if she wanted to see what it was that tore apart those men so easily.

"Faenir!" she shouted, overwhelmed by shock and surprise. "What are you doing here?" She immediately dragged the wolfpine into a tight embrace, ignoring the blood that matted his ashen grey fur. "Wait, if you're here… Where's Dad and Calen? Did you all come after me?"

All she got was a nuzzle in response.

Ella looked around, scanning the landscape, hoping to catch sight of her brother or father. Her heart skipped every second beat at the idea of seeing them, but all she saw was emptiness. Swirls of dust whipped across the ground, and there was the occasional cluster of trees.

She pulled Faenir in close. His warmth comforted her as she sobbed uncontrollably.

CHAPTER 26

Fading Light

Calen let out a heavy sigh as he rested his elbows on his knees. His arms burned. His legs burned. And if he were left alone, he could easily sleep for an entire week. The training and the journey had begun to take their toll.

Every night, when they broke for camp, Calen was the last to eat. First, he went through forms with Aeson. Then they sparred. Aeson did not take it easy – not that Calen had expected him to. Sometimes he sparred with Erik instead, but that was not any easier on his body. They were not allowed to draw blood intentionally, but that did not stop the bruises.

With a groan, Calen dragged air into his lungs, rubbing his hand across his ribs where Aeson had hit him with a particularly nasty side kick. Out of the corner of his eye, he saw one of the elves approaching.

Gaeleron had watched Calen's sparring sessions every night, as had all five of the elves. But Gaeleron was different.

It wasn't simply curiosity in his eyes. It was as though he were analysing and judging every movement he made. Calen felt heavy under his gaze. More than once, he was on the end of a particularly vicious strike from Aeson or Erik because he allowed his attention to drift to Gaeleron.

"Spar with me," the elf said. He unclipped the latch that held his cloak around his shoulders, allowing it to drop to the ground, revealing the thick layers of overlapping leather armour that covered his torso. A set of heavy spaulders protected his shoulders, and his arms hung free.

Calen couldn't hide the surprise on his face. The elf's blank stare was unnerving. He unsheathed his blade before Calen could respond.

Gaeleron sometimes sparred with the other elves after they ate. It wasn't every night, but it was enough for Calen to see that it would be a short fight. Gaeleron was as skilled a swordsman as Calen had seen. He moved like the wind. Each step he took, every swing of his blade, flowed into the next effortlessly. He never hesitated or faltered, at least not while Calen's eyes were on him. He was not small either; his frame was dense with lean muscle, and square shoulders to rival any blacksmith's.

"I would," Calen said, not exactly eager for another sparring session that would leave him limping, "but unfortunately, my training must continue with Therin now."

Ever since the Urak attack, after sword forms and sparring, Therin began taking Calen for lessons in controlling the Spark. They were not any less tiring. He taught him to control the threads as he pulled at them, how to control their flow and their strength, how to twist them and weave them together in the exact ways that he had wished. He was getting better. With each passing day, it tired him less. Therin said that it was like a muscle; the more he used it, the stronger it would become.

Therin showed him how to create the orb that Aeson had used to light the tunnel – the baldír. It surprised Calen how simple it was. Small amounts of Fire and Air weaved carefully together with Spirit. The hardest part was learning how to sustain them without constant attention and a drain on Calen's energy. He hadn't quite gotten there yet, but he was determined.

Without responding to Calen, Gaeleron sought out Therin with his eyes, finding him by the fire with a rabbit leg in his hands. Gaeleron simply raised an eyebrow, opening his arms out towards Calen.

Calen let out a resigned sigh when he saw Therin nod, not even bothering to speak as he returned to his food.

"Right then," he puffed as he dragged himself to his feet. "First to yield?"

Best just to get on with it.

Gaeleron nodded, raising his blade up in front of himself. With no warning, he sprung off his back legs, launching himself at Calen.

Calen was immediately on the defensive. Twisting and pivoting, he swung his blade wildly to try to stop the elf's barrage of ferocious blows.

One got through: a back swing with the pommel of his sword. Calen saw stars as it cracked him in the side of the head. He fell forward and dropped to one knee. He attempted to spring back to his feet, only to feel a boot catch him in the ribs. He coughed as he gasped for air, spinning onto his back. It was only a warning in the back of his mind from Valerys that allowed Calen to sling his sword up into the air in time to stop Gaeleron's downstroke.

What if I hadn't stopped that?

Calen rolled to his side, then bounded to his feet. Without time to take a breath, he was back-stepping again. Gaeleron probed his defences. In the middle of a forward step, the elf lunged. Another warning from Valerys allowed Calen to deflect the blow downward. He slid his sword up and caught Gaeleron on the chin with its hilt. The elf looked jarred.

Everybody was watching them now. Even Therin cast a sideways eye as he feigned disinterest. Dann was perched atop a large stone, an excited grin on his face. Calen certainly didn't feel as confident as Dann looked.

Gaeleron recovered from that surprise blow and redoubled his barrage. His sword flashed, far too quick for Calen. The empty feeling in Calen's hand was shortly followed by a metallic ringing as his sword crashed against the stones at his feet. The tip of Gaeleron's blade pressed against his neck.

The elf tilted his head curiously at Calen, as if measuring him, weighing him up. The blade did not move. Calen felt a slight sting as it pressed into his skin. He breathed a sigh of relief when the elf finally lowered the tip of the sword from his neck, sheathing it in one motion.

"From now on," Gaeleron said, "you will spar with me.

I will talk with Aeson. You can still practice your forms with him, but when it comes time to spar, it will be with me."

Calen raised his eyebrows, not quite sure what to say.

Gaeleron must have read his mind. "If you are going to carry an elven blade at your hip, you will learn how to use it." The elf did not wait for a response before returning to his seat by the fire.

"Don't worry," Dann said as Calen sat down beside him, grabbing his waterskin. "You'll get him next time." Calen wasn't sure whether Dann's wink was meant to be mocking or reassuring; it was almost certainly mocking.

As expected, it did not take Calen long to get to sleep. His lack of energy overrode the aches and pains that plagued his body. He wondered if that was what life was going to feel like from now on – constant pain followed by the loving embrace of dreams. He hoped his body would get used to all this training, eventually.

It was the chill that woke him. The hairs all over his body stood up as a shiver ran from his head to his toes. It seemed a darker night than usual. Even with the fire still spitting embers, Calen struggled to see more than two feet past his face. In his mind, he knew Valerys was still fast asleep at his side, a slight rumbling noise escaping his mouth as he dreamed.

Calen wasn't quite sure what it was, but something wasn't quite right. Slowly getting to his feet, he reached out to the Spark. He saw the elemental strands. Pulsing, twisting, forming the spiralling ball of energy that was the

Spark. It radiated power. The warmth licked his skin as he drew on thin threads of Fire and Air, shrouding them in Spirit as Therin had taught him. He formed the baldír just in front of him, careful to control its glow. He didn't want to wake everybody up.

He let out a sigh of frustration. No matter how much energy he pushed into the baldír, it didn't get any brighter. It was as if everything he pushed into it was drawn into something else. It should have been bright enough to light up the whole campsite, but it barely gave off a glow to rival a dying flame.

"Interesting..." hissed a voice, like nails dragged across stone. It did not seem to come from any one fixed place.

Calen almost leapt out of his skin. "Who's there?" he whispered, a little louder than intended. The darkness pulled back, revealing the outline of someone standing only a few feet away, in the middle of the path they had come down that day.

"Who are you?" Calen whispered, stepping towards the figure.

As he got closer, he saw the silhouette of a black cloak adorned with pale blue spirals and shapes. A step closer and the man's face came into view. It was as pale as the porcelain from Vaerleon, almost as white as Valerys's scales, but as thin as the finest paper. Calen stopped in his tracks as it clicked into place. Set in the middle of the man's sickly pale face were two bottomless wells of black.

The Fade!

Panic set in. Calen screamed at the top of his lungs. "Wake up! Therin! Aeson!"

His shouts were met with silence.

A wicked laugh echoed through the cavernous space. "They cannot hear you," it cackled. "You must be very raw if you cannot detect the warding. Peculiar to find two so connected to the Spark in one place, both so unlearned." The Fade paused, considering. "He talks about you, you know. Your friend. You left him. Left him to die."

A knot formed in Calen's stomach. "Rist? Where is he?"

A low, mocking laugh rumbled from the Fade's throat. "I will make you a deal, boy. I do like deals. Those treacherous outlaws you travel with, the ones who got you wrapped up in this, the ones who caused the death of your family…" The Fade gave a twisted grin when he saw the pain on Calen's face. Its thin, pale lips looked terrifying in the fading light. "Well, they have something I want. An egg. A large, scaled egg. If you bring it to me, I will release your friend."

Valerys's egg…

Calen was frozen on the spot. He didn't know what to say. Even if he wanted to betray Aeson, Therin, everyone… He couldn't. There was no more egg.

But Rist…

"I… I can't do that. Please… please just let him go. He has done nothing to you."

A flicker of irritation crossed the Fade's face. It stepped closer to Calen. His pitch-black eyes were like caverns. "Bring it to me, boy. *Now*," it hissed.

"I can't!" said Calen, his voice rising. He stepped backwards.

The Fade wrapped him in threads of Air, fixing him in

place. Everything in his body began to panic. He reached out to the Spark, but there was nothing. He couldn't feel it. He couldn't see the strands. Panic set in. He was helpless.

The Fade stepped closer again. "Oh, You are quite strong. But you most certainly do have a lot to learn. I will take you with me once I find the egg. He will be pleased to have found two of you with this kind of strength."

The Fade reached out to touch the side of Calen's face. A piercing shriek sliced through the air. The creature clapped its hands to its ears, writhing in pain. Calen felt a fury rising as Valerys leapt into the space between him and the Fade. A sound halfway between a shriek and a roar cascaded from his mouth. The frills on the back of his neck stood at full height, with his wings spread as wide as they could go. Even at that size, the dragon looked ferocious.

"No!" hissed the Fade. His eyes flitted back and forth between Valerys and Calen. "You are bound…"

Calen shuddered at the sound of its voice, scratching at his ears. The Fade took another step back, hissing at Valerys. The dragon continued his shriek, baring rows of razor-sharp teeth.

"Your friend will suffer pain, the likes of which you could not conjure in your nightmares." The black wells for eyes narrowed as he glared at Calen. "We will meet again."

Calen felt the threads of Air holding him in place tighten, then he was launched through the air, crashing to the ground with a thump. Ignoring the new pain in his lower back, he leapt to his feet, immediately drawing threads of Fire into his hand.

The Fade was gone. Valerys still screeched into the

night sky, but Calen knew it was gone. Something just *felt* different. And he could see properly again, almost blinding himself with the baldír before he extinguished it.

"Calen, what's going on?"

Calen hadn't noticed Therin stepping up beside him, his bow drawn and an arrow nocked. Everybody in the group was there. Valerys's screeching must have woken them.

"Valerys, stop. It's gone."

Calen felt a rumble of disagreement from the dragon as it halted its screeching. A slight growl still emanated from its chest.

"Calen, what is gone?"

"The Fade," Calen replied, allowing himself a breath of relief. "It was here. It came for Valerys's egg."

"It was here?" There was a hint of panic in Therin's voice.

Aeson was suddenly standing at Calen's side as well, framed by Erik and Dahlen.

"I'm sorry. I—"

"It's okay. You're all right, Valerys is all right, and it's gone. To say you were lucky is an understatement. I just don't know why it left so easily. I've not known a Fade to leave without what it came for."

"Valerys!" said Aeson, an urgency in his voice. "Calen, did he see Valerys?"

Calen did not need to answer.

"We need to move, now. If he saw Valerys, then he knows the egg is hatched, which means Fane will soon know." Aeson turned to the elves, who had already fanned out across the campsite, bows in hand. "We will need you to scout ahead and behind. Gather your things and begin as soon as you can."

The elves nodded in response, flitting about as they gathered their sparse possessions into their satchels. The twins and Vaeril headed west to ensure the path up ahead was clear, while Gaeleron and Ellisar moved to make sure that nobody followed them. It took fifteen minutes for the rest of the group to be on the road. The sun would not replace the crescent moon in the sky for at least a few hours, but Aeson did not plan on waiting for it.

"We are to be in Belduar in three days. We rest only for sleep and to refill our waterskins. During the day, we will eat in our saddles."

He did not wait for an acknowledgment. Instead, he snapped on his reins, and his bay broke into a trot.

Farda had just about gotten to sleep when the Fade's voice scratched at his ears. "The egg has hatched."

"Must you always come when I'm trying to sleep?" Farda let out a sigh as he sat up in the cot. If the egg had hatched, it would change everything.

The Fade stood at the opening to his tent. It had its back to him and was staring out at the camp, its black cloak draped around its shoulders.

The way the creature seemed to swallow the light irritated Farda.

"I come when I please," it hissed, turning back into the tent. Even in the dim light, the creature's cavernous black eyes were clear to see.

"What do you want?"

"I need soldiers."

"For what?"

What Farda could only describe as a growl emanated from the Fade's throat. "You were right." The words left its mouth like chains dragged across stone. Farda couldn't help but grin. *They must be heading to Belduar.*

"And what, may I ask, was I right about?"

"Enough games. I grow tired of them," the Fade said, dropping into the chair opposite Farda's cot.

Farda didn't reply immediately. He reached over to the bowl of water at his feet, placed it on his lap, and then splashed its contents on to his face. "I thought you enjoy games?" he said, wiping the water up his face and through his hair.

The Fade didn't reply. It simply stared at him. Its attenuated lips were drawn into a brittle line. Its near translucent fingers tapped on the arm of the chair.

"Okay," Farda sighed. He needed sleep, and he'd had his fun. "I don't have enough soldiers for you to take Belduar. The empire hasn't been able to break through its gates in four hundred years."

"I don't intend on taking the gates. I only need a thousand men."

Farda raised a curious eyebrow.

The Fade's thin lips pulled into a wicked grin that set an uneasy feeling into Farda's stomach.

CHAPTER 27

Worlds Apart

Calen shook his head as he did his best to stay upright in the saddle. He stifled a yawn. His eyelids began to lose their fight against gravity. Ever since the Fade showed up that night, Aeson pushed them harder and harder to reach Belduar. They barely slept four hours a night, and every waking moment was spent in the saddle. Calen was certain that there were entire stretches of the journey where he was completely unconscious while riding his horse. How the horses kept up the pace was a mystery, although Calen suspected the Spark was involved. He had seen Vaeril and Therin tending to the horses each night before they ate.

Every part of his body ached. His back and his legs were stiff from all the riding, while his inner thighs felt like they had been stripped bare, and the muscles in his stomach burned with a fury. Over the last few weeks, his body had begun to get used to the pains of the saddle, but the last few days had taken that to a whole new level.

Even at Aeson's new rapid pace, he still managed to find time for Calen to practice his sword forms. Calen also continued his lessons with Therin and sparred with Gaeleron each night. He was not sure what he had done to make Gaeleron hate him so much, but the elf seemed to take pleasure in leaving Calen to nurse new bruises and cuts. It was the only time Calen saw him smile.

"How's the head?" Erik asked, yawning as he pulled his horse up alongside Calen's. There were dark, drooping circles under Erik's usually alert and vibrant eyes.

"Yeah," Calen replied, twisting his mouth. He absently rubbed at the lump on the back of his head where he had taken a nasty blow from Gaeleron the night before. Even then, it throbbed. He felt a puff of annoyance from Valerys at the mention of Gaeleron's name. A growl came from the young dragon's chest as he padded along beside the horses. "I think it will feel better after a good night's sleep."

"Aye," Erik said, laughing. "I know that feeling, all right. And you, Dann. How goes *hunting* with Alea and Lyrei?"

Dann blushed when Erik followed up his question with a sly wink. Dann had been spending a lot of time with the twins over the last few nights. He had even taken to hunting with them and joining them on guard when he could. He had insisted that it was to learn more about the craftsmanship of elven bows, but Calen had a feeling that there might be a bit more to his intentions.

"It goes well. I am learning a lot." Dann kept his reply short, probably trying to avoid any teasing.

"I'm sure you are," Erik said with another wink that made Calen burst out laughing.

"Oh, fuck off." Dann gave his horse a tap in the side and kicked on ahead, which only made Erik and Calen laugh harder.

Up ahead, Ellisar stood with his hands on his hips. "This looks like a dead end."

The path ahead closed off into a small alcove, with rising rock faces on all sides.

"Looks can be deceiving," Aeson replied. He dismounted, took his bay by the reigns, and led him over towards the rock face on the right-hand side of the alcove. Aeson reached into his bag and pulled out a smooth green stone, with veins of white that rippled just under the surface. It looked as if it were made of glass. A slight shimmer bounced off its surface whenever it caught the sun.

Therin had been teaching Calen to identify the different threads when other wielders drew from the Spark. He was not particularly good at it, but Therin had insisted that it was the quickest way to learn. It was difficult to tell, but it looked like Aeson drew threads of Spirit into the stone.

The stone began to pulsate in a green glow. Calen blinked and wiped his eyes with the heels of his palms. Where there had been a wall of stone, as solid as any Calen had seen, only moments before, there now stood the mouth to a cave. It was over ten feet wide and eight feet high. It seemed to stretch onwards forever into the mountainside.

"Okay... I've seen a lot of things in this last month or so, but somebody is going to have to explain this," Dann said. He sat there on his patchy grey horse, his arms folded across his chest in protest, with a stubborn look on his face.

"It is a glamour," Therin said. He dropped down from his saddle, joining Aeson at the mouth of the cave. "It is old magic, not something you would find common in these lands. It mostly disappeared with the giants. The stone is the key?"

Aeson nodded, tucking the stone into his coat pocket. "Come on," Aeson said. "Off your horses. We will have to walk them from here. The roof gets lower the farther you go in."

Calen swung his leg over and hopped down off his horse. He nodded to Dann, laughing at the grumpy look on his face.

"What?" Dann barked. He furrowed his brow. "He just made a tunnel appear in the side of a mountain!"

"Technically," Erik interrupted, nudging Dann with his shoulder, "the tunnel was already there." Erik scrunched up his nose in a 'just saying', kind of way, which earned him a glare from Dann.

"He is right," Lyrei and Alea chimed at the same time, with a giggle at Dann's expense. Calen didn't blame Dann for trying his luck with them.

"Yeah, yeah," Dann muttered as the two elves walked on ahead into the tunnel.

As soon as they had all passed through, Aeson produced the stone once more. Calen watched closely as he drew threads of Spirit to replace the glamour, then pocketed it and took his place at the front of the group.

Aeson wasn't lying. The farther they got into the cave, the lower the ceiling became. It almost brushed the top of Calen's head, and the horses had to bow their necks to fit through comfortably.

Torches rested in cast iron sconces, fixed into the walls on either side of the tunnel at regular intervals, just enough so that their light overlapped. The tunnel looked as if it had been cut by hand. The stone face was smooth, almost polished. Calen reached out with his hand, running his fingertips along the surface of the stone.

"It was cut with the Spark." Calen turned to see Vaeril walking beside him. The elf wasn't looking *at* him but *past* him, studying the walls of the tunnel. "We used similar techniques when constructing our home in the Aravell. In the histories I've read, it was common for dwarves to employ mages for this very purpose. It made constructing cities and tunnel networks far more efficient. Though, I have never seen it done myself."

"It's incredible."

Vaeril nodded, a soft smile on his face.

It was at least an hour's walk through the torch-lit tunnel before they came to a cast iron portcullis fixed into an alcove in the wall. A stone staircase on the other side led steeply upward. Once more, Aeson pulled the polished green stone from his pocket. He slipped it into a tiny groove in the wall, which it fit into like a hand in a glove. Immediately, it lit up, pulsating that emerald green glow.

"Now what?" Dann said after about one minute of waiting.

"Now we wait." Aeson leaned his shoulder against the wall of the cave. "That stone has a sister, which should light up when our stone has been placed in its groove."

It wasn't long before Calen heard footsteps echoing down the stone staircase. "Who goes there?" came the gruff voice of a man, echoing over the sound of his footsteps.

"It is me, Ihvon. Aeson Virandr."

The pace of the footsteps increased. "Aeson, you old dog! Get in here!"

The man before them looked as though he had seen more than his fair share of battles. The lack of hair on his head was fully compensated for by a thick beard that jutted out from his face, looking as though it had been carved from stone. His nose zig-zagged down his scar-latticed face; it had definitely been broken more than once. A short stump of mottled flesh remained where his left ear had once been. He was a little shorter than Calen, but his shoulders looked like they could take the weight of a horse. The navy doublet he wore seemed out of place on him, like a wolf trying to masquerade as a fox.

Out of his pocket, Ihvon pulled a pulsating green stone, the twin of Aeson's. He slid it into a similar groove on his side of the portcullis. As soon as he did, Calen felt a tremor reverberate from the walls as the cast iron portcullis receded into the ceiling.

"Get over here," Ihvon guffawed. He pulled Aeson into an embrace that was reciprocated with a similar but more reserved warmth.

"It is good to see you, Ihvon. How is the king? Is he well?"

"Aye, aye, he surely is. He wishes to see you as soon as he can. He will be eager to know that you have returned. I see your party has grown larger since last we met."

Ihvon looked around the group, his affectionate smile masked a calculating look in his eyes. Calen hadn't realised how strange his group might look. Five humans and six elves marching around, armed to the hilt. It almost made him laugh out loud.

Ihvon's eyes widened and his jaw slackened as he saw Valerys, who now stood at Calen's feet. A slight rumble let Calen know that the dragon was hungry.

Ihvon turned his gaze to Aeson, back to Valerys, and then back again. "That isn't…? It couldn't be."

He rubbed his fists into his eyes in an exaggerated manner before looking down at Valerys again, who shrieked in response. Ihvon took an involuntary step backward, caught by surprise. A deep laugh came from the man's stomach as he clapped his hand down on Aeson's shoulder.

"There will not be a day that you do not surprise me," Ihvon said, shaking his head in disbelief. "Come. Arthur will want to see you now more than ever, if that were possible. You can leave the horses here. I will send someone for them shortly." Ihvon turned and walked back up the staircase, waving for the group to follow. "A dragon…" Calen heard him mutter. "The bastard actually did it."

At the top of the staircase, the pale blue sky was the first thing Calen noticed. He stepped out into a massive open courtyard. The cool light of day bounced off the walls, and the breeze kissed his face.

He wasn't sure what he had thought a city built into the side of a mountain would look like, but this wasn't it. The smooth stone courtyard was immense, easily as large as the entire Glade. It was hemmed in all around by stone-grey walls, as thick as Calen was tall, with large square towers set into every bend.

Long purple and gold banners hung from each of the towers. Each banner was emblazoned with a crossed axe and a sword, with a lonely mountain in the background. On top of each tower was what Calen could only describe as a massive crossbow, fixed into the ground with large steel plates and bolts. He had never seen their like before.

To the right of the courtyard stood a massive keep, embedded in the climbing rock face, rising high up into the sky. Set into the front of the keep were a massive set of thick wooden doors, arching into a point towards the top. They were easily fifteen feet wide and twenty feet tall at their highest point.

It took a minute for Calen to notice the two parallel columns of soldiers that occupied the courtyard, framing the pathway out of the tunnel. They wore shimmering plate armour, with pauldrons on each shoulder and billowing purple cloaks. Their helmets covered most of their face, leaving only two almond-shaped openings for their eyes and a narrow slit from their nose to their chin. It was an impressive sight. They looked very much like they had walked straight out of Therin's stories. Calen's first instinct was to reach to his sword, an instinct that he had to actively stave off.

These are friends. We are safe here.

Calen felt the same sense of awe – and caution – from Valerys. The young dragon padded around Calen's feet, taking in the sheer size of the courtyard. He had grown quickly during their travels, although he was still about half the size of Faenir.

"The royal courtyard," Ihvon said, opening his arms and

gesturing outward. "This is the inner circle of the city. It has the thickest walls and the tallest towers in all of Epheria. It has never been breached, not in the over two thousand years since it has stood." There was a look of gleaming pride on Ihvon's face. "Do you want to see the city?"

Ihvon marched off towards the walls before anybody even had the time to answer the question. The column of soldiers fell in either side of him as he walked, hemming the group in between them.

"Don't mind them," Ihvon chirped. "They are the Kingsguard, and you are guests of the utmost importance.

"The machines you see mounted atop the towers are Bolt Throwers. They have been installed here, with the help of the dwarves, since the fall of The Order. They are a large part of why the empire was never able to take the city. The bolts they fire are eight feet in length and nearly two handspans wide. Even dragons hide from them," Ihvon explained as they ascended the zig-zagging staircase to the top of the walls. "And this," he said, gesturing out over the ramparts, "is the city of Belduar."

Calen felt it as the breath was taken from his lungs. Never in his wildest dreams had he imagined something like this.

It felt like they stood on a sheer cliff edge at the end of the world. So far was the fall that Calen could not see the bottom. To the west were the gargantuan mountains of Western Lodhar; to the east, the plains of Illyanara rolled off as far as the eye could see.

Hundreds of feet below, the sprawling city of Belduar was separated from the Inner Circle by a heavy-set stone bridge that spanned a cavernous gap between the two areas of the city. Calen could not help but think that if he fell off that bridge, he would keep falling until the end of time.

The city itself fanned out in tiers of concentric circles. Each circle was ringed by more walls, each set with countless towers, with a Bolt Thrower nestled into its centre. The lowest tier, which touched the plains down below, was so far away that Calen could only just make out the brown spots atop each tower.

Just past the outermost city walls was the fabled lake of Haftsfjord, where the people of Belduar first broke bread with the dwarves. All Therin's stories flushed through Calen's mind as he looked out across this city of legend. It was the last bastion of freedom in Illyanara, the only place that the empire's hand did not extend freely.

Calen peered over the ramparts. He rubbed the disbelief from his eyes as a pair of eagles glided through the air, not thirty feet from where he stood. They strafed sideways and nosedived down the sheer face of the Inner Circle walls. He knew that his mouth was open wide, but he did not care.

"Not many people get to see the world from where you are standing right now," Ihvon whispered. He leaned his arms down on the stone walls, gazing out at the spectacle in front of him.

Calen couldn't help but allow a smile to creep onto his face. The view from those walls was one of the most incredible things that he had ever seen. He knelt down to Valerys. "You will fly over this city as soon as you've grown."

The dragon shook his wings, a low rumble escaping his throat.

"Now that is something I would pay some silver to see!" said Dann, grinning from ear to ear. "How long until he can fly?"

"It depends," Aeson replied. "Some dragons can fly as early as a few weeks old. Some can take a couple of months. It will depend how he grows and how soon his wings can support his weight. By looking at him, I don't think it will be too long. It appears that Valacian dragons grow faster than Epherian ones."

Dann nodded. "And breathe fire?"

That same question had been lingering at the back of Calen's mind for a while.

"Fire is a tricky one," Therin said, stepping up beside Dann. "Some dragons find their fire as young as a week old, though it is barely a trickling flame at that stage. Others are nearly a year old when they find theirs, but it can pour forward like a cascading river, capable of turning plate armour into molten steel. There is a lot we don't, and will never know about dragons."

"Come," Ihvon said, breaking the pensive silence. "We'd best be getting on. I am sure the king is eager to see you."

It was only when they crossed the courtyard again that Calen truly realised how massive it was. Such a large, open space carved into the side of a mountain – it was incredible.

"It is a kill-box," Ellisar remarked, as his eyes combed the wide-open space.

"That it is, elf," Ihvon said matter-of-factly. "It was designed that way. Every archer on the keep walls would have a clear line of sight across this whole yard if it were ever breached. The Bolt Throwers on top of the keep's towers have a wide range of motion, capable of aiming straight down into the yard. It is not somewhere that I would want to find myself, were I an enemy to the king."

As they scaled the stairs leading up to the entrance of the keep, Calen appreciated the true size of the hulking wooden doors. He could not imagine that there was anything capable of busting them open. Just as he was lost in thought, there was a thunderous creaking as the two gigantic doors began to part.

The soldiers who flanked them picked up their pace, pulling ahead of the group. They formed an honour guard into the keep. Calen watched as each of the soldiers attempted not to get caught gawking at Valerys, who craned his neck upwards as if he were a show pony. They may have looked like soldiers of legend in their polished plate armour and streaming purple capes, but they were still only men – men who had never seen a dragon.

The inner hall was almost as breath-taking as the view from the walls. The ceilings were nearly forty feet high, held up by a sprawling network of colonnades, with swooping arches in between them – Purple and gold banners dangled from every second one. At the end of the long hall was a raised podium, atop which stood an ornately carved granite throne.

"Aeson Virandr," the man who sat on the throne bell-owed. His voice boomed through the wide-open hall.

Despite the fact that he was no more than six feet in height, and his frame was as wiry as Dann's, Arthur Bryne oozed authority. He seemed to almost glide across the floor, a deep purple cloak draped around his shoulders. His greyish-black hair was streaked with wings of white on either side, and a simple crown of winding gold sat on his head. He was by all definitions a handsome man, even in what seemed to be, at the least, his fiftieth summer.

"Your Majesty," Aeson said, dropping to one knee as the king approached. Erik and Dahlen followed Aeson's lead, with Dann giving Calen an unsure look. The elves stood as they were.

"Get off your knee, you fool," the king said. He reached out his arm and clasped Aeson's forearm, in much the same way that Aeson had done to Thalanil, pulling him to his feet. "It is good to see you. When you left for Valacia, a part of me feared we would never set eyes on each other again. And your sons – my, how they have grown yet again!"

Arthur took it in turn to grab both Dahlen and Erik by the shoulders, admiring their growth like a fond uncle. Then the king's eyes fell on Calen – and Valerys. He gazed at Valerys in disbelief, then looked back at Aeson, as if to confirm that his eyes were not deceiving him.

"By the gods… Not only did you retrieve an egg… but it is already hatched and bonded. How is that even…" Arthur turned his gaze to Calen, taking his arm in the same acknowledging grasp. "My boy, I am delighted to meet you. To say that I have waited a lifetime would be an understatement."

There was something sincere in the way Arthur Bryne spoke. He didn't break eye contact, and that smile never seemed to leave his face. The man was so charismatic that every word that came out of his mouth felt like it was plucked straight from his heart.

"And you," he said, focusing solely on Valerys, "you are one of the most breath-taking creatures I have ever laid eyes on. His scales are a thing of beauty. And those eyes…" The king was in a world of his own as he fawned over Valerys, who was happy for the attention. "What is his name?"

"Valerys, Your Majesty."

Arthur waved Calen away. "Enough with the 'Your Majesty.' Even if you were not a Draleid, I can't stand all that formality. Valerys, you say? That is a very suitable name indeed."

Arthur rose back to his full height.

"Okay, I will indulge myself later. For now, you all must be tired and hungry. We will show you to your chambers, and I will arrange for a feast. My son, Daymon, is around here somewhere as well. Come, come."

The kiss of the setting sun felt warm on Calen's back as it trickled in through the window. He was more than thankful for the warm bath he had just soaked in. His muscles felt as though they were brand new. He did not think he would ever get used to bathing in cold river water.

His weak smile was one of relief as much as it was satisfaction as he pulled the linen shirt over his head. It was like wearing a cloud compared to the leathers he had grown used to. Arthur had provided each member of the group with their own private chambers, as well as fresh clothes for the feast, while the clothes they had travelled in were washed by the maids.

"Maids!" laughed Calen to himself. *If only you were here to see me now, Dad. You would slap me across the back of the head for even saying the word out loud.*

A touch of sadness crept into Calen's heart. He dropped himself onto the edge of the bed. In that moment, as he sat there, alone for the first time, everything came crashing onto him like a waterfall.

They were all gone. His mother, his father, Ella, Faenir… Haem. His entire family. He didn't even want to guess how many others might have lost their lives in the chaos that day. Faces flashed through his mind. Jorvill Ehrnin. Mara Styr. Tach Edwin… Anya. A sickly weightlessness filled his body.

The next face he saw was Rist's. He had left him. Left him with Dahlen. Left him to be taken, and he was too scared to go after him. Anger mingled with his sadness, bubbling through it. Anger at Dahlen, anger at himself, anger at the world.

Once I'm stronger… I'll find you.

The sound of smashing pottery reminded Calen that he was not truly alone. He puffed out his cheeks, wiping the nomadic tear from the side of his face. He allowed himself a subdued laugh. "Get over here!"

Valerys's head poked up from amidst the rubble of two flowerpots that had previously held tulips and daisies. Like Faenir would do when wet, Valerys shook his body from head to tail, sending bits of shattered ceramic darting around the room.

"Hey!" shouted Calen as he shielded his eyes. "Watch it!"

The dragon puffed back at Calen in response. He spread his wings and leapt from the ground, up onto the bed.

Calen stood, his eyes falling on his sword that lay in its scabbard, resting against the far wall. Instinctively, he reached for it. But he knew well enough that it would be insulting to bring a sword to a king's table. He felt a moment of hesitation as his hand touched the leather scabbard. *We're safe here, I don't need it.*

"Come on." He scratched under Valerys's neck, producing as close to a purr as the dragon was able. "Let's go. We don't want to be late for supper. It's been a while since we've eaten anything decent."

As the porter guided him through winding staircases and maze-like hallways, Calen thanked the gods that Arthur had sent someone to show him the way back to the main hall. He would have wandered haplessly for hours otherwise.

The young lad, fifteen or sixteen summers at most, continually peered over his shoulder to gawk at Valerys, who padded along at Calen's feet. Calen allowed himself a wry smile. He often forgot what a strange sight it must be. Only a month ago, he had never even seen a dragon, and now Valerys was as normal to him as the morning sun.

"Thank you, Conal," Calen said, as the young porter brought him to the entrance of the hall. In truth, he wasn't much younger than Calen. But he *seemed* younger.

"My pleasure m'lord," the boy said. He bowed around a corner before Calen could correct him. He was the furthest thing from a lord that someone could possibly be.

Calen took a deep breath before he entered. The hall was much the same as when Calen and his group had arrived earlier, with one exception. There was now a massive rectangular table right in the centre.

The table was piled high with fruit in all sorts of shapes, sizes, and colours. Some he recognised: apples, oranges, pears. Others, he could not even imagine what they might be called. Curved, yellow fruit with leathery skin sat beside a small fruit with brown skin that was covered in fur. Calen had just picked up one of the furry fruits when Dann made his way into the hall.

"By the gods!" called Dann, his voice echoing through the hall. "I'm never leaving here, Calen. I could have sat in that bath for hours. And these clothes!" He lifted his arms up in the air, rolling his eyes back in his head. "Do we sit?"

"I'm not sure," Calen replied, still rolling his thumb across the surface of the hairy fruit. "Look at all this fruit. I don't think there would be as much in all the market stalls in The Glade combined." Calen found it hard to match Dann's enthusiasm. He couldn't help but think how much that amount of food would cost back home.

"I know!" exclaimed Dann, his voice muffled as he bit deeply into an apple.

It wasn't long before the rest of the group found their way to the hall. Everyone looked so different with the dirt scrubbed from their faces and hair, and clean linens on their backs.

"I don't know about you," Erik said, wrapping his arms around Calen's and Dann's shoulders, "but I'm starved. I intend to eat until I can no longer fit in these trousers!"

Dann muffled out the words, "Me too," through a mouthful of apple, which earned him a laugh from Erik.

"Calen, Dann, Erik, Dahlen. I would like you to meet

my son, Daymon."

Calen had not even seen Arthur enter the hall. The young man now standing beside him was the spitting image of the king, only about thirty summers his junior by the looks of it.

"Pleased to make your acquaintance," Daymon said, bowing slightly at the waist. "My father tells me that you have all come a long way to be here. I hope your journey has not taken too much of a toll on you."

Daymon did not yet possess the effortless charisma that oozed from every word that left his father's mouth, but Calen figured that was something earned, not something you were born with.

"It took what it needed to," Erik replied, with a solemn twist in his lips.

"That it did," Arthur said, a regretful look in his eyes. "Okay, now that we are all acquainted, why don't we eat?" Arthur must have read the expression on Calen's face, changing the conversation in an instant.

Once they were all seated, Arthur called over the same porter who had shown Calen to the hall. "Conal, can you please inform the kitchen that they may send up the food?"

"Yes, my king. I'll fetch them now."

"Thank you."

That was one thing about Arthur that stood out to Calen, the way he acted towards people.

In the villages, the village elders always spoke with an air of superiority – even Erdhardt, whom Calen considered to be a kind and just man. Yet, here they were in the great hall of Belduar, at a table with its king. Not the elder of the village or a local lord, but a *king*. He did not treat anyone as though they were less. He did not command. He asked. His authority was clear, and he was not weak, but he knew that he did not need to command.

Calen had not met many kings – or any – but something told him that this was a rare quality among those with power.

"Send up the food?" Dann whispered, leaning over into Calen's ear. "How much more food could there be?"

Just as Calen was about to agree, a stream of serving men and women swept into the hall. Some of them held large silver trays of steaming hot meats, potatoes, and vegetables. Others held jugs of wine and ale. By the time they all left the hall again, there was not so much as an inch of space on the wooden table to be seen through the mass of food and drink.

"Well," Arthur announced, "do not wait on my account. Eat, eat!"

Calen watched as everyone piled their plates, talking and joking between them. He felt a warm smile sneak its way onto his face. This was the first time in quite a while that they were actually safe.

Maybe he could allow himself some contentment. He wanted to, but it was almost impossible to push the images of blood and death from his mind. It felt strange to not have the familiar weight of his sword hanging at his hip.

Erik must have seen the look on his face. "We have to allow ourselves the small things," he said with a thin smile.

Calen nodded. Even Valerys was having the time of his life. He sat just behind Calen, tearing into a leg of lamb that Arthur had arranged for him.

"You not going to eat?" Dann raised a questioning eyebrow.

"I am, I am. Sorry, just got lost in thought there for a minute. What's good?"

CHAPTER 28

Brother

R ist jumped at the knock on the door. He folded over the corner of the page and slipped his book under the covers of his bed. He wasn't sure why he felt the need to hide it. He just did.

There wasn't much in the room. A small bed with a wooden frame. A desk for reading and writing, adorned with a single candle. Two wooden chairs, a small dresser, and a woollen rug. There were no paintings, decorations, or ornamentations. It was simple. In honesty, he didn't mind it too much.

The man who had knocked did not wait on an invitation to enter. He never did. He looked middling in his years, with a plain enough face, a strong jawline, and short, cropped black hair. A black robe adorned his shoulders and flowed down over his body. As usual, he carried a covered silver tray with that evening's dinner.

Roast lamb, by the smell of it.

Rist had been there nearly two weeks, by his count.

Every day flowed in much the same way. He woke with the sun to an empty room and a locked door. He ate one meal a day, which was always delivered by the same man. When he needed to wash or relieve himself, he did so under guard. That was it.

"Are you well?" The man's voice was firmer than Rist had expected. There was an authority to it. He caught Rist off-guard. This was the first time he had spoken. Two weeks. He brought him his dinner every day for two weeks and had never said a word.

"I… I am. Thank you."

A hint of a smile sat on the man's face as he lifted the lid from the silver tray, showing two plates of food. Lamb, carrots, potatoes, and a small pitcher of meat gravy. The food had been like this every night. It was better than home. But there had never been two plates.

The man took the plates from the tray and lay them down on the desk, then placed the tray and lid on the floor under the table. He scooped up the pitcher of gravy and bathed his plate in the sweet-smelling brown liquid.

"Gravy?" he asked.

"Em… yes, please." Rist was still unsure. It could be a trick. He had not been mistreated while he was there, but nor had he been free to leave. Not one person had spoken to him.

Rist had been angry at first, when he woke up. It had done nothing. He was barely even given a second look. So, he decided to try a different tack. A horse often responded better to a carrot than a stick. "Excuse me… Why am I here? Where are my friends?"

The man waved his hand, calling Rist over. "Come and sit. We will talk."

Rist's stomach rumbled. It was not like he had many options. He had been trying to get this man to talk for the last couple weeks. Now was his opportunity.

Rist got up from the bed and took the empty chair. The food smelled amazing. He had tried not to eat it the first few days, but they simply replaced the old full plate with a new full plate. Eventually, the hunger became too much. If they wanted him dead, they could have done so with ease. There was no need to poison him.

He looked up at the man, who chewed away on a piece of lamb. There was nothing about his face that would make him stand out. With an inward sigh, Rist took up the cutlery that the man had set out beside the plate and joined him in eating dinner. It tasted as good as it smelled.

"You are in Al'Nasla," the man said out of nowhere, as if they had been in a free-flowing conversation. "The embassy of the Circle of Magii in the palace, to be exact."

Rist's fork dropped to the ground, clinking off the silver tray below the table. "I'm... I'm in Loria?" His mind raced a hundred miles a minute. "I can't be... How is that even possible? I was in Midhaven, in Illyanara. How did I get to the North?"

Rist stopped. He needed to collect himself. He had no idea why this man had finally started talking, or if he would ever talk again. He needed to be smart and ask the right questions. "Who are you? why am I here?"

The man chewed his food meticulously, swallowing before he answered. "You may call me Garramon. I am your… guide." The man pondered for a moment. "You are here because we found you on the side of the road just outside Al'Nasla. I do not know how you got there, nor did I care. You were filthy and half-starved to death. We took you in."

Rist raised one eyebrow. "Took me in? Took me captive, more like. I am locked in this room, unable to leave unless I am under guard, and even then, only to bathe and relieve myself. That sounds like a captive to me."

How did I get to the North? Calm down. Focus. Breathe.

Rist struggled to think. He tried to remember what happened, but the only thing he could remember was fighting in the streets of Midhaven, and Dahlen carrying him. Then everything went black.

"Captive? You are fed, are you not? Clothed? Have you been harmed?" Garramon did not wait for an answer. The begrudged look on Rist's face was enough. "Well, I have given you my name. It is only fair that you do the same in return."

Rist had not realised that the man would not know his name. "My name is Rist Havel."

"It is nice to meet you." Garramon swallowed another piece of meat, washed down with gravy. "Rist, there is a reason you are here and not in a tavern somewhere, and I think you might know what that reason is. It is the same reason that you have not been allowed to roam the grounds freely. And for all I know, it is the same reason that you ended up on the side of the road."

"I don't know what you're talking about." Rist's back stiffened. *He couldn't know.*

Garramon sighed through his nose as he finished his mouthful. He wiped his knife and fork with a cloth that he produced from inside his cloak, then set them down on the desk beside the plate.

"You are among friends," he said after a long moment of silence. Garramon turned his gaze to the candle on the desk and twisted his hand upward in the air, ending with a flick. The wick on the candle burst into life with a flame that flickered back and forth.

"You…"

A satisfied smile flitted across Garramon's face. "Yes, me. You are no longer alone, Rist. We had to keep you under lock and guard. A fledgling mage can be a danger to both himself and those around him when he is untrained. We needed to watch you. And we did not know you enough to trust you. Surely, you understand?"

Rist's pulse quickened. This was not how he had expected this day to go.

A fledgling mage.

"I… I think I do…"

"Good." Garramon clasped his hands together and leaned forward, his elbows resting on the arms of the chair. "Rist, I want to teach you to use your gifts. To not fear them, but to embrace them. To not let the fear in the hearts of others stop you from being who you were destined to be. We must never dim our light so that others may shine."

Rist felt a sense of warmth flowing through him. It was as if Garramon's words were the remedy to something that he didn't know was ailing him. "Yes. I would like that very much. Truly, I would."

"Fantastic!" said Garramon. He clapped his hands together as he rose to his feet. "We will start tomorrow. I will send for you at first light." Garramon turned towards the door. "And from now on, please, call me Brother Garramon."

"Yes, Brother Garramon," Rist said, a touch of hesitancy in his voice. "Brother Garramon?"

"Yes, initiate. What is it?"

A lump formed in Rist's throat. He held his breath for a moment. "My friends… my family. They will be looking for me. I need to see them or contact them. Let them know I am okay."

The mage stood in the doorway for a moment, considering. "I will have someone drop a pen, ink, and some parchment to you this evening. If you write them, we can dispatch hawks."

"Thank you, Brother Garramon."

The morning after the feast, Ihvon brought Calen and Aeson to speak with the dwarven emissary in Belduar. With the Lorian blockade only a few days' march from the city, a meeting with the Dwarven Freehold was to be held as soon as possible. Arthur had asked Calen if he would be part of the embassy. It was the least Calen could do, considering Arthur had welcomed them into his home.

Calen was not sure what he was expecting, but he was most definitely surprised to find that Oleg Marylin was, in fact, a human, and not a dwarf at all. He was a heavy-set man, with a bit of a belly, a bald head, and a short beard.

"Not at all," Oleg said, laughing, when Calen apologised for the surprised look on his face. "Many people are surprised when they find that the emissary to the Dwarven Freehold is not a dwarf himself. The dwarves of the Lodhar Mountains have not been above ground in hundreds of years, so I take care of their interests up here."

Oleg stood up from behind his desk, patting down his wrinkled linen shirt. "May I just say, it is an honour to meet you, Calen Bryer. Word has been spreading around this city since your arrival yesterday morning. I have been eagerly awaiting the opportunity to meet you – a Draleid."

"Now, Oleg, don't be swelling the boy's head," Ihvon said, his friendly demeanour yielding to an authoritative tone.

"Yes. Please excuse me, Lord Arnell," Oleg said, raising his hands outward in apology.

"Not at all," Ihvon replied. "Now, have you sent word to the freehold to arrange the meeting and to inform them of the Draleid's arrival?"

"Not yet, m'lord. I was waiting to hear from the king, but I can send a messenger immediately, if it pleases you."

"It does," Ihvon replied, raising his eyebrow.

With a jolt, Oleg moved back around to his desk. He pulled a sheet of blank parchment from a stack behind him and an inkwell and pen from a drawer to his left. He began drafting a letter. When he finished, he folded the parchment and slid it into a small cream envelope. He dripped wax on the lip of the envelope using a deep purple candle that had been burning on the side of his desk.

"If you please."

"One moment." Ihvon dug around in his pockets, then produced a small brass stamp. He pressed it into the cooling wax, leaving the impression of a crossed axe and sword with a mountain in the background. It was the same emblem that adorned the banners in the courtyard and great hall.

"Thank you, m'lord," Oleg said. He picked up the envelope and slipped it into his coat pocket. "On second thought, I think I will deliver this myself. That should impress the desire for a swift response. You know yourself the way the freehold operates. It will be at least a week or so before I return, but I will make haste as much as is possible."

"See that you do, Oleg. The king will be watching this closely."

The stout man nodded and grabbed a satchel from behind his chair. "I'll leave now, my lord. If you'll excuse me."

Calen, Ihvon, and Aeson followed Oleg out of the room. He swung his satchel in front of him, searching through it as he double-timed his way down the corridor. In his haste, Oleg kicked the extended foot of a short table, almost sending himself spiralling to the ground, only to catch himself at the last moment.

"Strange man," Aeson remarked.

"That he is," Ihvon said, "but he's a good man."

CHAPTER 29

The Skies Above

Sweat dripped from Calen's brow as he parried a downward strike from Erik.

"Good. Keep your guard up," Gaeleron said. Since they had arrived in Belduar, the elf had stopped sparring with Calen and instead had taken to observing him spar with others. It would be easier for him to assess Calen's progress that way.

A metallic ringing chimed through the courtyard of the Inner Circle as Calen and Erik's blades met in a flurry of blows. On the surface, they seemed evenly matched, but Calen knew that he was always only one mistake away from a new bruise.

There was a knowing grin on Erik's face as the two men circled each other.

In a flash of movement, Erik lunged, like a viper who had cornered a hare. Calen dropped back into Patient Wolf.

Erik's blows came in hard and fast; as they always did.

Calen counted his heartbeats, waiting for an opening.

One.

Erik struck high, twice. The vibrations jolted up Calen's arm as he parried both.

Two.

Calen just about brought his sword down in time to block the understroke that followed. It really should have landed; only a warning in the back of his mind from Valerys had allowed him to stop it.

Three.

He leapt backwards, willing Erik to follow.

Four.

Erik dove after him.

Five.

Calen saw his opening. He lunged.

It happened too fast for him to see. Erik turned with the speed of a kat, and brought his blade down on top of Calen's, knocking it to the ground with a crash. A roaring pain burst through Calen's face as Erik's elbow flew backwards and slammed into his nose, sending him sprawling to the ground.

"You must be aware!" shouted Gaeleron as Calen hit the stone. Calen didn't even move to get up. He just lay there, staring up at the sky above. His head pounded, there was a ringing noise in his ears, and he could taste blood on his tongue. If he lay there a little longer, maybe he wouldn't have to do another round.

A shadow blocked out the light from the sun. "Do not strike only to leave yourself open. That is enough for the day," Gaeleron sighed, standing over Calen's sprawled body.

"I will not have Therin complaining again that you are too exhausted to listen to his spells and stories."

It had been two weeks since Oleg left for the Dwarven Freehold. In the meantime, Therin had decided to not only instruct Calen on the ways of magic but also to educate him on the history of Epheria. He taught him the customs and cultures of the many races that inhabited Epheria and what the land was like before the rise of the empire. He insisted that if Calen were to be of use to anyone as a Draleid, he would need to understand more than just the people of the villages in western Illyanara.

Gaeleron's humour deteriorated whenever Therin was mentioned. He took on a mocking tone every time he spoke of Therin's teachings – 'spells and stories', as he called them. Calen did not feel right to bring it up with Therin directly, but there was a strange tension between him and the elves from Aravell – all but Vaeril, who was almost the opposite. His attitude towards Therin stopped just short of reverence. Calen had no idea what to make of it all.

Calen propped himself up on his elbows. He blew the air from his lungs up over his face in exhaustion and let the sweat roll down his forehead. Erik hunched down beside him in much the same state.

"That was good," he panted, resting his elbows on his knees. "Sorry about the nose. Just try not to over-extend yourself. Gaeleron seems to be warming to you, at least. He's a bit stiff, isn't he?"

Gaeleron raised an eyebrow.

"I think he may have heard you," Calen whispered, ignoring the pain that throbbed in his nose as he tried to laugh.

"Ah, he's fine. Good lesson, Gaeleron!" Erik gave Calen a cheeky wink as he stood up from his haunches. "I'm going to get some water. Want some?"

"Please."

Just as Erik walked away, Calen felt something stir in the back of his mind. He turned his head to see Valerys stand up from where he had spent most of the afternoon bathing in the sun. Calen wasn't sure if it was because Arthur had been letting him take his pick of whatever goats or sheep he wanted each day, or if it was just the way dragons grew, but Valerys had nearly doubled in size in the last few weeks.

He was easily the size of Faenir; at least seven feet from snout to tail. His jaw had widened, his snout had elongated, and his chest was deeper. The ridges of horns that framed his neck and face were longer and sharper. His neck was thicker, more muscular, and the frills that ran the length of his body were more pronounced. Where his forelimbs had once been weak and spindly compared to his hind legs, they had grown strong and powerful. As Calen watched Valerys approach, his white scales glistening in the sun, he couldn't help but stare in awe. He was still a far cry from the dragons of legend, but he was no longer the vulnerable creature that had crawled from that egg.

Valerys's pale lavender eyes drew level with Calen's as the dragon stopped in front of him. Warmth flooded the back of Calen's mind, a conscious recognition. Comfort. Calen closed his eyes and placed his hands either side of Valerys's head, touching his forehead against the tip of the dragon's snout.

"Draleid n'aldryr," Calen whispered. He wasn't sure why he said it, the words had touched his tongue without ever passing his mind; but they felt right. *Dragonbound by fire.* He felt an acknowledgement from Valerys, a mix of emotions and colours that somehow mimicked the words. Then there was something else – a longing. For something that Calen didn't recognise. But then he felt a sudden flash in the back of his mind – he understood. Calen opened his eyes. "Go."

Without waiting for another word, Valerys shook his body from side to side as if throwing off imaginary chains that held him down. The frills on the back of his neck stood on end as he moved forward, towards the walls of the inner circle that looked out over the city below. Calen felt it as if it were his own – the urge, the *need.*

Valerys spread out his wings. If he had doubled in size, they had grown even more so. They were as white as the purest snow, with veins of black that streaked from Valerys's forelimbs, giving them shape.

There was a *thump* as Valerys cracked his wings against the air. A gust of wind swept across the courtyard. The need that Calen felt at the back of his mind only grew stronger. It burned through him, as it did Valerys. Another *thump* carried Valerys forward, lifting him off the ground. Calen felt his feet moving, following Valerys as his wingbeats carried him higher – towards the walls. *Thump.* Valerys's powerful wings lifted him into the air.

Gasps of shock came from the precisely one hundred armoured men who stood guard along the outer rim of the courtyard. Arthur had insisted upon their presence anytime that Calen practiced there, as though the empire would suddenly swarm the Inner Circle if he were alone.

He ignored their open-mouthed stares. His feet moved faster, bounding over the stone of the courtyard, towards the stairs that led to the ramparts. Valerys was almost twenty feet above him and had almost reached the walls. His heart hammered in his chest as his feet pounded against the stone steps. Then it lurched as he watched Valerys lift higher into the air, clear the wall, and then plummet over the other side. Gone from sight.

Left foot. Right foot. The vibrations shot through his body as he scaled the stairs. Just as he reached the top and threw his hands onto the parapet, a white blur shot past him, followed by an immense gust of wind. The noise that tore through the sky was like nothing Calen had ever heard before. It was a visceral roar that rippled through the air, like a howling clap of thunder booming forth from Valerys's jaws.

Something pulsed inside Calen as Valerys soared through the air. He felt Valerys's mind in a way that he never had before. He closed his eyes; he didn't need them. The emotions, the thoughts, feelings, sensations – he felt everything. The power that flowed through Valerys's wings as they hammered against the sky. The cool air as it swept over his scales. The soft susurrations of the wind with every slight movement of his wings. The warmth of the afternoon sun on his back. The raw, primal emotion as it coursed through both of their minds at once.

Every hair on Calen's body stood on end. It was the

most intensely free feeling he had ever experienced. Even with his eyes closed, he could see every movement Valerys made.

He stood there for what felt like hours before he eventually forced himself to open his eyes. Reluctantly, he pulled himself back into his own thoughts. He still felt Valerys, as he always did, but the overwhelming intensity was gone.

He almost jumped when he saw that Dann and Erik were beside him. He hadn't heard them approach, they must have heard Valerys's roar.

"Incredible…" Erik's hand rested against the parapet and his eyes were fixed on the swooping figure of the glistening white dragon above.

Dann stood beside him, wordless.

Calen watched as Valerys twisted and turned in the sky. It was a thing of beauty the likes of which Calen never imagined he would see. A dragon soaring through the skies above the city of Belduar. He felt as though he were right in the middle of one of Therin's stories.

A feeling of tired satisfaction scratched at the back of Calen's mind as Valerys looped back towards the Inner Circle.

"He's coming back." Calen's sudden announcement startled both Dann and Erik, who hadn't noticed him open his eyes.

Without waiting for a response, Calen made his way down the stone staircase to the courtyard of the Inner Circle.

A shadow spread over the ground in front of Calen as Valerys swooped down into the courtyard, his powerful wingbeats whipping spirals of dust into the air as he alighted on the cool stone ground. The dragon craned his neck from side to side and walked over to Calen, spreading his wings wide in what felt like a celebration.

"Show-off," Calen said. A warm smile spread across his face as he reached out and rested his hand on Valerys's snout. A sense of pride emanated from the dragon.

"That was amazing," Dann said, breaking his silence. "I never thought…"

"Never thought I'd see the day when you were speechless," Erik laughed, nudging Dann in the ribs as he stepped up beside him. "But I agree. That was something else."

The heavy sounds of Ihvon's footsteps echoed across the empty courtyard. At least, the courtyard could be considered empty if not for Calen, Erik, Valerys, and the guards who stood, staring in awe at Valerys, their purple cloaks billowing in the wind.

"Calen, Erik, Dann. It is time. Oleg has returned. The king requests your presence in the drawing room."

By the time they entered the drawing room, it was already tight for space. It was not Therin, Aeson, Oleg, Dahlen, or Arthur who sucked the space from the room. It was the hulking form of Asius, who most likely dared not sit on any of the furniture for fear of breaking it. Instead, he leaned lackadaisically against the wall at the back of the room. Were he to stand at full height, he would have to take care not to crack his head off the low-hanging chandelier that hung in the middle of the room.

Considering the sheer vastness of everything else in the city, it surprised Calen that the king's drawing room was so quaint. The small space was decorated simply. The room itself was centred around a low, solid wooden table that was framed on all four sides with plush couches of red velvet. The eastern wall was occupied entirely by an impressive bookshelf that stretched from floor to ceiling. *Rist would love this.*

It was Asius who spoke first. He shifted his weight off the wall and closed the distance between himself and Calen in four long strides.

"Calen Bryer, son of Vars Bryer." The giant's enormous hand wrapped around Calen's arm with unsettling ease. "It pleases me to see you again and to hear that you are now bonded. It would warm my heart if I could meet the one who shares your life – as soon as we are done here, of course."

"Asius, son of Thalm," Calen responded. He bowed his head, which was reciprocated by Asius. "To warm your heart would be my honour."

Calen's response earned him a wide grin from the giant. The giants, or the *Jotnar,* were a race layered in formality and cultural complexity. It had taken Calen an irritating amount of time to memorise their multitudes of greetings and customs, along with their various responses.

Without looking, Calen could tell that Therin was grinning from ear to ear. The elf had insisted that Calen not sleep until he could repeat every one back to him without hesitation. He could almost feel the "I told you so" from across the room.

"Where are Senas and Larion? Did they not travel with you?" Calen asked.

"They had other journeys to travel, but our paths will join again soon."

Erik, Dann, and Ihvon briefly exchanged greetings with Asius, then the giant returned to his position, leaning against the far wall, and the four men took their seats on the couches.

"Asius, I assure you, we can have this meeting in a room that is more considerate to your needs. I simply had not anticipated you arriving with Oleg."

By the tone in Arthur's voice, Calen had a feeling that this was not the first time that this topic had been broached. The giant simply waved him away.

With a light shrug, Arthur turned his attention back towards the rest of the group. "Oleg, please," he said, opening his arms.

Oleg cleared his throat. "The Freehold have convened, and all four kingdoms have agreed that a meeting should take place in the Heart Chamber of Durakdur. They wish us to leave for the Wind Tunnels as soon as is possible."

"Fantastic," Arthur said, clapping his hands together. "We shall leave for the tunnels before the day is through."

Calen saw a look of distaste on Ihvon's face. "Typical dwarves. Take two weeks to make a decision and then expect us to snap to attention at their call." Ihvon's tone disappeared with a sharp look from Arthur.

"If I may, my king. There is more." Oleg shifted in his seat.

"Please," Arthur said, rolling his hands over each other.

"The invite for the meeting extends only to the Draleid, Aeson Virandr, and Asius." Oleg had to crane his neck upwards to look at the giant. "And yourself, my king, of course—"

"Absolutely not," Ihvon interrupted. With his mouth covered by that beard, it was Ihvon's eyes that let Calen know he was scowling. His face softened under Arthur's glare. "You cannot go down there without a guard, Arthur."

"I can go where I please, *Lord Arnell*. The dwarves of the Lodhar Freehold have been good to our people, in case you have forgotten. Besides, I do not believe a guard could protect me from anything that a Draleid and a Jotnar could not."

Ihvon grunted in disapproval, but he did not argue. He folded his arms and sat back into the red velvet couch.

"Aeson, Asius?"

"We can be ready to leave within the hour, Your Maje – Arthur."

"It would warm my heart, King Arthur Bryne, son of Thuram Bryne."

Arthur almost leapt from his seat in enthusiasm. "Fantastic. It is settled, then. Oleg, please inform the Wind Runners Guild that we will be at the tunnels within the hour, requiring transport to Durakdur."

"It will be done, my king," Oleg said. He rose from his seat and made his way to the door.

"Okay. Those of you who will be joining me, please

gather what you may need. We will meet at the Wind Tunnels in an hour's time. Calen, I will send Conal to guide you."

Calen had to hold back a sigh of relief. He would have felt silly asking for Conal himself, but he did not have even a notion as to where the Wind Tunnels were. He still needed Conal's help to find his way from his chambers to the courtyard. The boy never complained, though. He seemed eager to walk with Calen whenever the opportunity arose. Especially when Valerys came with them. Once or twice, Conal had taken the wrong turn, too preoccupied with asking questions and staring at the dragon's shimmering scales. He was rather disappointed when he found out that Valerys could not yet breathe fire.

"Thank you, Your Maje – Thank you, Arthur."

A smile crept onto the king's face when Calen corrected himself.

"Okay, be off with you all. We have preparations to make and only an hour to do so."

As the group were saying their goodbyes, Calen felt a hand drop down on his shoulder. He turned to see Asius looking down at him.

"Calen, it would warm my heart if I could meet the one who shares your life."

It took a moment for Calen to remember that was how the Jotnar referred to the dragons. "Of course, Asius. To warm your heart would be my honour."

Asius seemed to know his way around the city far better than Calen did, which was a relief. Calen did not have a doubt in his mind that he would have gotten completely lost on his own. It didn't take long for them to make their way through the maze-like corridors of the Inner Circle, to the courtyard where Valerys lay sleeping on the smooth stone ground, the warm sunlight shimmering off his scales – it appeared the earlier flight had taken a lot out of him.

"He is beautiful," Asius said, dropping to one knee beside Valerys, a slight tremble in his voice. The giant didn't move as Valerys's eyelids peeled open, revealing a pair of pale lavender eyes.

"Asius, son of Thalm. Meet Valerys." Calen felt a rumble of recognition from Valerys as the dragon lifted its head and extended it towards Asius's now outstretched hand. Asius's pale, whiteish-blue hand hovered just inches from Valerys's scales, as though he feared they might burn him.

"Asius, are you okay?"

A single tear rolled down the giant's face as he ran his hand along the scales on Valerys's head. Calen didn't know what to do. He felt like he was intruding on an intensely personal moment. Asius turned his head towards Calen. The giant took in a deep breath before speaking, allowing the tear to roll freely down his cheek. "Four hundred years, we have waited. My people have been hunted to the edge of extinction. Senas and Larion are all I have left. I have not seen others of my kind in that time. It is safer for us to stay hidden." Asius ran his hand back along Valerys's scaled neck, then stood to his full height, his massive frame making Calen feel as though he were a child.

Taking a deep sigh, Asius stretched out his hand and grasped Calen's forearm. "Thank you, Calen Bryer, son of Vars Bryer. And thank you, Valerys, son of Valacia. For giving me the gift of hope. It is with honour that I stand beside the Draleid once more."

Shards of ceramic sprayed around the room in a crash as Dahlen flung the pot against the far wall. He slammed his two fists down onto the writing desk with enough force to leave two shallow indents in the soft wood.

He tried to slow his breathing. He took deep breaths in, holding them and allowing them to release slowly.

"Fuck!"

He swept his hand across the table, sending its contents crashing to the ground. He stood in the middle of the room, his chest heaving. He and Erik had dedicated every waking moment to his father's cause. Given everything. And Calen had simply fallen into their path and taken what should have been his. He should be by his father's side, going to Durakdur. *He* had fought for that right. He had bled for it.

Dahlen collapsed onto the bed. He rested his elbows on his knees, running his hands back up through his hair.

CHAPTER 30

Pawn in a Game

Dann wasn't happy that he could not go with Calen to the dwarves. *Not happy* might have been a bit of an understatement; but at the least, he understood. Calen hadn't seen much of him in the past few days either way. That tended to be the way when Dann was interested in a girl. Although, Dann might be better off chasing a wild goose than Alea or Lyrei. The two of them were more than a match for him, and they seemed to enjoy making him jump through hoops, which wasn't altogether unenjoyable for Calen.

Vaeril and the other elves were a different story altogether.

"We made an oath, Draleid, to go with you *wherever* you may lead, to the void or beyond. You cannot ask us to disobey that oath." Vaeril was usually a placid person. He and Calen had started to grow close, but Calen saw a touch of anger in his eyes. He knew by the tone in the elf's voice that he would have to be careful with his words.

"Vaeril, I am not asking you to disobey your oath. You left your home and have followed me all the way to Belduar. You saved my life even before that. I am asking you to trust me."

"Trust is earned, Draleid." Ellisar was the one elf that Calen had spent little time around since they had arrived in Belduar. He spent a lot of time with Dahlen, practicing in the yard. That put an unconscious bad taste in Calen's mouth, but what the elf said was not unfair.

"See that Aeson continues to spar with you while I am not there," Gaeleron said. It was not a question.

"Draleid, you *do* understand that if harm were to come to you while you are with the dwarves, and we were not there to prevent it, that dishonour would follow us." Alea was usually bright-eyed, with a bubbly personality to match her quirky smile. But in this, she was as stony-faced as Aeson.

Calen had made the mistake of thinking that they were worried about him, but it turned out all they were worried about was harming their honour. It stung. "Look, I am going. The dwarves have not invited you, and from what I have learned in Therin's teachings –" Therin's name drew a twist of contempt from more than one face, but none of them spoke, "– the dwarves are extremely selective about who they allow into their lands. You cannot come. I will make sure not to die so that your *honour* remains intact."

Calen saw a touch of hurt on some of their faces as he stormed from the room. But he knew they were only hurt because they knew he had figured them out.

Therin had tried to explain the Wind Tunnels to Calen – unsuccessfully. All he remembered was that the dwarves built them a long time ago, and they allowed fast travel between the kingdoms of the Dwarven Freehold and Belduar. "Conal, have you used the Wind Tunnels before?"

The look of confusion on the boy's face told Calen that he should already know the answer, but Conal was quite polite. "No, m'lord. I've seen 'em lots, but I've never used 'em before. Not a lot o' people travel to the dwarven kingdoms, m'lord, and the dwarves never come up 'ere. They say that they helped our ancestors build this place, but I ain't never seen 'em."

Calen still hadn't gotten the boy to stop calling him a lord. He had tried, but Conal was insistent. Calen found it uncomfortable. Most people didn't notice. Dann usually just laughed. *"Ooh, m'lord! Can I fetch you some tea, m'lord?"*

"'Ere we are, m'lord. The Wind Tunnels."

"Thank you, Conal…" Calen's voice trailed off. In front of him was a massive courtyard, which seemed as though it had been hollowed out of the mountain. The ceiling was part of the mountain itself and stood about two hundred feet above the smooth flagstone floor. Six passageways, framed by buildings on either side, cut through the main city of Belduar, acting as entrances to the Wind Tunnels. It was through one of these passageways that Calen had emerged into the courtyard.

At the opposite side of the courtyard, there were five enormous perfect circles cut into the side of the rock face. Each was easily forty feet across, fronted by a stone landing with a set of stairs at the side. Even from where he stood,

Calen could tell that each circular entrance was connected to tunnels that dove into the depths of the mountain.

The others were already waiting for him on the landing that fronted the first tunnel. Therin and Ihvon were there as well, along with a handful of the Kingsguard, in their burnished armour and heavy purple cloaks.

"Come on, Valerys. They're waiting," Calen said as he made his way over to the landing.

Valerys ambled along beside him. The dragon's head pricked up in the air, tilted a little sideways. It was as if he were pressing his ear to the wind, like he heard something that Calen couldn't. When Calen listened, he heard a low whistling sound, like when he held the seashells he found on the coast at Milltown to his ear. It was soothing. In a way, it felt like home.

Calen reached the top of the stairs and stepped out onto the landing. Nestled inside the entrance of the tunnel was some kind of machine with three massive golden rings tucked inside each other. The outermost ring was pressed up against the wall of the tunnel, with a series of enormous ball bearings embedded along its outer rim. In the very centre of the concentric rings was a circular platform made of the same golden metal, framed with low metal walls. The platform had an open space at the centre, while the outer areas had seats fixed onto its base.

Calen could have spent years gazing at it without ever understanding a single thing about it. He had never seen anything like it in his life.

"Magnificent, isn't it?" Arthur seemed to glide across the stone towards Calen, such was the languid confidence with which the man moved. "The dwarves call them Wind Runners. The dwarves are capable of all sorts of mechanical wonders, Calen... but these... there is nothing like these anywhere else in the known world. I'm excited to see how you find the ride."

An uneasy lump formed in Calen's stomach. The thought of being inside that thing while it moved made his knees go weak.

Arthur must have noticed the change in expression on his face. A laugh crept into his voice. "Come on, we're setting off in a few. I will introduce you to the navigator." He patted Calen on the back, directing him towards the rest of the group. "Calen Bryer, let me introduce you to Falmin Tain, navigator of the *Crested Wave* and member of the Wind Runners Guild."

The navigator was a wiry man with black hair slicked back over his head. He wore a simple cotton shirt with the sleeves rolled up past his elbows and thick cotton trousers tucked into rugged leather boots. He had a strange set of glasses strapped around the top of his head; their lenses were dark, almost black, and they shimmered in an array of colours when the light hit them. A sheet of copper was melded into the frames, covered at the end with padded leather. It was held on his head with a strap of leather that had a buckle for tightening. They were strange indeed.

"'Tis a pleasure, Mister Bryer," Falmin said, shaking Calen's hand. "And to you..." he said, turning his attention towards Valerys, who half-bared his teeth in a snarl. "S'long as you don't take me arm off, you'll be the first dragon to ever ride a Wind Runner. Good thing you're small. They didn't make 'em with dragons in mind!"

The man had a sort of endearing arrogance about him that Calen couldn't help but admire.

"If y'all will excuse me, I'm gonna make sure that this little lady here is good to go." Falmin didn't wait for any replies. He headed across a rope bridge connected from the landing to the platform of the *Crested Wave*.

"All set?" Therin asked.

Calen nodded wordlessly.

"Good. Dann didn't mind being left alone then, I take it?" Therin gave a wry smile that implied he already knew the answer.

Calen sighed. "No, he understood. The elves, however… they are not particularly happy with me."

Therin never showed the same contempt towards the Aravell elves that they showed towards him. Instead, there was a twinge of regret in his voice whenever he spoke of them. "They swore an oath of protection, Calen. I know we haven't talked too much on elven culture yet, but honour… honour is everything to an elf. Without it, we have no trust. How can you trust someone without honour? It tells others who you are."

Calen couldn't help but let a trickle of indignation find his words. "That much I understood. Their honour was all they talked about. What is the point in taking an oath to protect me if they won't even listen to me?"

Calen thought he saw disappointment in Therin's eyes. The elf let out a sigh, resting his hand on Calen's shoulder. "Calen, they swore an oath to protect you, not to obey you.

Not only that, but they volunteered to swear that oath. They chose to abandon their home and everything they knew in the Aravell to follow you. They have shown their honour. Now you must show them yours."

Calen found himself searching for something on the ground to trap his gaze. He felt like an idiot.

"Come," Therin said. "The day we stop learning is the day we will be consumed by what we do not know. Do not dally. I have only journeyed on a Wind Runner once before. It is quite an experience."

Therin gave Calen a little push, aiming him towards the rope bridge where Oleg waited for him. The others had already made their way across to the platform of the *Crested Wave.*

"And Calen," Therin called, "the dwarves are stubborn. They are proud, and their tongues can be sharp, but they have always been loyal to the Draleid and to The Order. They are going to test you, but remember, it is not just you who has to prove yourself to them. They have to prove themselves to you. You are a Draleid now. Don't forget that."

Calen allowed himself a brief smile. *I am a Draleid.* He couldn't help but look down at Valerys, who waited restlessly by his side.

He felt the dragon's impatience scratching at him. It was his own impatience. Even when they were apart, Calen *felt* the dragon. His anger. His hunger. Everything. With each day, the bond between them grew stronger – It was getting increasingly difficult to separate his own emotions from Valerys's.

"I will see you when I'm back, Therin. Thank you."

The elf simply nodded, taking his leave of the landing.

"Master Bryer, if you are ready, we are about to set off." Oleg stood at the edge of the landing, beside the rope bridge, a quirky smile on his face.

"Yes, of course. Sorry." Calen stepped past Oleg and onto the rope bridge. He swallowed a shout and clutched onto the ropes for fear of his life as the bridge swayed unexpectedly under his weight. He snapped his head up to the air as he felt a mocking rumble from Valerys, who glided overhead, then swooped down onto the platform of the *Crested Wave*. Calen picked up his pace so as to not spend any longer on the bridge than he had to. "They can build a machine like this, but they can't build a proper bridge?"

Calen looked up from his ranting to see everybody on the platform staring at him. Arthur smirked, while Falmin was outright laughing.

"Quite right, Mister Bryer," the navigator cackled. "I do say it all the time. We often forget the little details, so we do." Calen wasn't sure if the man was mocking him. He didn't think he was, but it was hard to tell. His tone seemed to always hold an undercurrent of sarcasm.

"If it helps at all," Oleg panted, wiping the sweat from his brow as he leapt onto the platform, "I travel on these things more than I do horses, and I'm terrified every time. Both, of the Wind Runners *and* the bridges." The emissary's belly swelled out a bit farther as he let out a sigh of relief, dropping himself into one of the seats that was fastened to the platform.

"I see Valerys has found his wings," Aeson said, as Calen took a seat beside him. "It's a beautiful thing – to see a dragon fly."

Calen turned to look at Valerys, who padded over towards him, his claws clicking on the metal platform. "It was... incredible. I—"

"Okay, okay," Falmin called, who stood at the front of the circular platform, half-swinging off a crossbar that swooped down from the first inner ring. "If e'rybody can please take a seat, make sure to fasten the buckle as tightly as you can, and we'll all have a good old trip. If you feel like vomiting, please aim down." Falmin paused, turning his attention to Asius, who didn't fit in any of the seats. "You might just have to hold on to something..."

The man's ear-to-ear grin was less than comforting, but it didn't bother Asius, who simply nodded and held onto one of the nearby railings.

Falmin's eyes moved over to Valerys, who was curled up on the ground to the side of Calen's feet. He raised his fist to his taut lips. "You... yeah... I'm not quite sure what you can do with 'im. Does he 'ave a leash?" Valerys lifted his head, pulling his lips back in a slight snarl. A deep growl resonated from his chest. "Okay. No leash. Understood. Maybe just hold on to 'im."

Calen heard Arthur laughing as Valerys dropped his head back onto the ground, and he couldn't help but join him.

Falmin pulled his odd glasses down over his eyes. The copper sheet on the side of the lenses fit neatly around his cheeks and nose. He exhaled, cracking his neck from side to side, and turned to face the inner section of the tunnel. Calen felt that tickle at the back of his mind that he had come to know meant somebody near him was drawing from the Spark. He sat up in his seat, his eyes fixed on Falmin.

The man raised his hands slowly, his palms facing upward. Calen could almost see it. The threads of Air weaved their way around, moving in a hundred directions, encasing the entire machine in a sphere of wind. A metallic creaking noise shuddered through the platform as the rings swung into motion. The *Crested Wave* began to move as the rings spun around the platform in alternate directions, faster and faster, until they were almost a blur. Only the inner ring seemed to remain stationary. Calen felt the platform shaking, vibrating ferociously.

Then they were gone, shooting through the tunnel at speeds Calen did not even know were possible. The walls of the tunnel never changed, so their speed was hard to gauge. The rotating rings caused an almost constant haze, blurring anything outside the platform. But when Calen looked back, he saw the dim light of the tunnel mouth, shrinking at a jaw-dropping rate, until it was nothing but a speck.

Calen turned to Aeson, who was seated beside him, the belt buckle fastened tightly across his chest. Something seemed odd, but he couldn't quite put his finger on it.

Aeson turned to find Calen's eyes narrowed, staring at him. He raised an eyebrow. "What are you doing?"

"There is something…" muttered Calen "Something… Your hair!"

Aeson's brow furrowed. "What about my hair?"

"It's not moving! Even when you ride a horse, the wind blows at your hair, yet now, there is not even a ripple. What… what is he doing?"

Aeson followed Calen's eyes to Falmin, who stood at the front of the platform, his knees slightly bent, his arms spread out wide. Calen felt a drop of irritation when he noticed the smirk on Aeson's face. His face was usually so impassive that a smirk seemed even more mocking than it would on another man.

"Follow the threads, Calen," Aeson said. "Read them. Learn."

Calen focused on Falmin. Even though somebody who drew from the Spark did not need to use their body to direct the threads, it was almost like a reflex. Falmin's left hand twisted left, right, up, and down. It directed the *Crested Wave* through the tunnels.

His right hand, however, was constant. It moved repetitiously around the same space, his fingers contracting and expanding. As if he was smoothing down the surface of a ball.

"He's blocking the wind…" muttered Calen. His gaze moved from the navigator to the threads of Air, whirling around the platform in sync with the spinning rings.

"Precisely," Aeson said. His smirk was almost proud. "You are learning quickly."

Calen couldn't help but smile. He wasn't sure why, but a compliment from Aeson held twice the weight that it did from most others.

Without warning, everything shifted. Calen grabbed onto the frame of his seat, unsure. He felt weightless. Then he looked out, past the blurring rings. They had left the enclosed tunnel, and they were now hurtling through an open cavern. His heart fell into his stomach. Its thumping made him nauseous. The cavern extended in both directions until the end of Calen's eyeline and farther. He didn't even need to look down. He knew that he would not see a bottom. It was only for a few seconds, which felt like a lifetime. A heavy thump sent shockwaves through the platform as they entered a new tunnel on the other side of the cavern. Calen closed his eyes for a minute, doing everything in his power to slow his breathing.

We're going to die down here.

Just as he calmed himself to where he felt he could open his eyes again, something slammed into his shoulder, cracking it against the back of his seat. "Fuck..." he muttered. He reached back, jerking forward a bit as his thumb ran over a tender spot just below his shoulder blade.

"Sorry!" shouted Falmin without looking back.

Calen now realised why the man wore his odd glasses. If a gust of wind like that broke through the barrier, he wouldn't be able to see a thing. The thought of colliding with something at that speed put a knot in Calen's stomach.

Finally, Calen felt them slow down. A tiny speck of light in the distance grew larger by the second.

"Don't be nervous," Aeson whispered.

Calen furrowed his brow. "I'm not nervous," he lied.

Aeson nodded, that same smirk on his face.

There was a short jerk as the *Crested Wave* came to a stop just short of the cave mouth. Falmin spun around on the spot, pulled the glasses from his face, and placed them on top of his head. His face still held an arrogance to it, a slight grin that just twisted the corner of his mouth.

"Well, a little wind aside..." He paused, as if expecting a round of applause for his joke. A look of disappointment crossed his face when he didn't receive one. "Here we are, safe and sound. Durakdur. If you give me a moment, I will extend the bridge, and you can be on your way."

The navigator strode past the group, to the edge of the platform. Drawing on threads of Air, he launched the crumpled-up rope bridge across to another stone landing that lay waiting to receive the vessel's passengers.

Calen felt a hand rest on his shoulder. "Well, my boy, I wish that I could see this through your eyes. I remember the first time I saw this place. It was a good five minutes before I could speak again." Arthur smiled and then moved ahead, making his way onto the bridge. His shoulders swayed as he moved. Reluctantly, Calen followed him. He wasn't looking forward to crossing that bridge again.

"I meant what I said, Mister Bryer." Calen hadn't noticed Falmin approach him at the foot of the bridge. The man had a serious look on his face, at least compared to the grin he usually wore. "It was my pleasure to have you aboard – both you and your dragon. I wish you the best of luck, and so does the guild. Should you ever need us, we are at your service." The navigator bowed at the hip, just a short bow, but it was enough to convey sincerity. It was a formality that Calen did not expect from the flamboyant man.

"Thank you, Falmin. Your… *ship?* It's an incredible feat of engineering… as is your skill with Air. It was a pleasure."

There was a touch of recognition in the man's smile. "The pleasure is shared."

Calen extended his arm, grasping his fingers around Falmin's forearm. Falmin reciprocated the gesture, then walked off across the platform, inspecting every square inch of the *Crested Wave.* Calen couldn't help but stare after the man in curiosity. Falmin shook a brass connection, a look of surprise on his face when it came unstuck. He pushed it back in, pursed his lips, gave a satisfied shrug, and walked on.

Calen turned back to the bridge, trying his best to look dignified as he scurried across the wooden planks. "Fucking bridge…" he muttered to himself, nearly slipping as he stepped off the last plank of the bridge. He felt a sense of comfort as his foot contacted the solid stone of the tunnel entrance.

When he looked up, it was exactly as Arthur said it would be. It took away his words.

The platform upon which he stood jutted out from the side of the mountain wall, looking down over the breath-taking city of Durakdur. It looked as though the mountain had been hollowed out, and a city was built in its place. Everywhere Calen looked, stone walkways and bridges weaved through the city, connecting innumerable stone courtyards and platforms. Barely an inch of rock wall had been left untouched. The walkways ran everywhere, with doors and tunnels all along them that led deeper into the mountain.

Lanterns emitting a greenish-blue hue were alight everywhere Calen looked. They were suspended from chains, mounted on walls, and set in doorways. He had never seen a light that colour before. It had a kind of ethereal beauty. Directly across from the platform, on the other side of the cavernous city, a monstrous waterfall cascaded down to the lower levels.

The low, sonorous bellow of horns filled Calen's ears. He had been so taken away by the sheer beauty of the sprawling city that he had failed to look closer to where he stood.

Just below the platform was a huge stone landing. It was connected to the platform by a double staircase adorned with statues of dwarves in heavy, sharp-cut armour, hefting axes, spears, and swords. The landing was crammed. Two columns of armoured soldiers stood on either side of a small group that waited at the bottom of the staircase.

The dwarves were shorter than the average man of Epheria, but not by the distance that Calen knew from legend. The tallest stood at around five and a half feet. Their faces were as gruff and varied as the stories said, though. Some had thick, squashed noses, while others were sharp and thin. Some had skin as pale as the winter snow, while others looked charred and ashen.

All the men had beards, which were as varied as their faces. Some were short and red, kept tidy with meticulous care. Others ranged from a hundred different shades of blonde and brown, to the darkest of jet. Some were braided, some were tied in intricate patterns, some reached their knees, and some didn't pass their chest. All of them – even the women – wore bronze, silver, and golden rings tied carefully throughout their hair.

The soldiers at either side of the staircase wore thick plates of armour over coats of shimmering mail. Their helmets were blocky and sharp-cut, leaving space over their eyes, with a bridge of metal that shielded their noses. Each of them held a ferocious, twin-bladed axe hefted over their shoulders.

At the front of both columns of soldiers, the axes were replaced with long brass horns. Four distinct sets of flags hung from the horns. Calen recognised each one from Therin's teaching. The crimson and gold flag, emblazoned with an intricately crafted hammer, and four stars positioned above it in a semi-circle, was the flag of Durakdur. The green and silver flag with an anvil wreathed in flowers belonged to Azmar. The flag that bore black, crossed axes with a white backdrop was Ozryn's. And the yellow and black flag with a horned helmet at the fore was Volkur's.

Four dwarves stood at the foot of the staircase: three women and one man. They didn't wear plates of armour and mail like the soldiers did. All four wore an odd mixture of leathers and silks. Their shoulders were padded out and a cuirass of leather covered their chests, which flowed down into a silken garment not dissimilar to a skirt. All four heads were adorned with intricate crowns of the finest gold.

The woman at the front of the group stepped forward. Her hair was a flowing straw-blonde, with scattered silver and gold rings laced throughout. She had a beauty about her. She radiated confidence, and her eyes were fierce.

"Welcome," she said, "to the Dwarven Freehold. I am Queen Kira of Durakdur." The sweetness of her voice surprised Calen. She bowed slightly at the hip, though not deeply enough for it to be born of respect. It was more of formality.

"Your presence here is most welcome. I am King Hoffnar of Volkur." The man wore his dark hair short, only long enough to drop down over his forehead. His face was angular and free of cuts or blemishes, yet he moved like a soldier. Were it not for the friendly smile he wore, Calen might have reached for his blade.

"I am Queen Elenya of the dwarven kingdom of Ozryn. Your swords are welcome under our roof." Elenya was a warrior. If her words did not give that away, she was the only one of the four who carried a weapon; a short throwing axe strapped to her belt. Her hair was like a roaring fire, wild and untamed. It cascaded down over her shoulders and back, reaching near to her elbows. The hardness in her face unsettled Calen.

The last of the four was Pulroan, the queen of Azmar. Her blonde hair was tied back behind her head in braids. She was a stocky woman. The furrows in her skin and lashings of grey through her hair clearly marked her as the senior of the other three.

"Thank you for your kind welcomes," Arthur said, bowing at the hip. "As you know, I bring with me today, esteemed guests. Two, you have met many times before. One has never graced these halls. May I present to you Calen Bryer, the first Draleid free of Lorian influence since the fall of The Order and the first new Draleid in four hundred years."

Arthur stepped aside, waving him forward. Calen was not sure what to do. He wished that he were better at listening. Therin had probably told him precisely what to expect four times over. There was so much to take in, so many customs and traditions. It was as if each new piece of information forced something else back out of his mind to make space. Everybody stared at him expectantly. He tried to remember the greeting that Therin had told him. It was in his head somewhere.

"Your Majesties, thank you for welcoming us into your halls. From Valerys and I, may your fires never be extinguished and your blades never dull." He tripped over his words a bit, but he was sure he had gotten it right. Valerys mirrored him with a low rumble. He spread his wings to their fullest.

All the four – except for Kira, who had a twist of impatience on her face – smiled back at him warmly. "May your fire never be extinguished and your blade never dull," they chorused, though Kira's words lacked the verve that the others possessed.

Calen saw a look of satisfaction on Aeson's face, which was mirrored on Arthur's.

"Please," Hoffnar said, catching Kira with a sideways glance, "let us escort you to the Heart. We have much to discuss. Have you eaten? We can arrange for food to be prepared."

"Food would be—" Oleg clamped his lips shut after a glare from Arthur.

The king seldom chastised those who served him, but Calen was beginning to notice a steeliness to him. Although Oleg was the dwarven emissary, he was now in the company of kings and queens. It was his turn to bite his tongue.

"That is quite all right, Hoffnar," Arthur said. "We left for the Wind Tunnels as soon as we received your message. Our bellies might rumble a touch, but we can wait for supper. As we are all aware, ever since our *companions* returned from their voyage, the empire has held a blockade some three days' march from Belduar. With their intentions not yet determined, and with the arrival of the Draleid, I'm sure you can appreciate the need for haste."

"That I can," Hoffnar replied.

The route through the city wound from walkway to bridge and through numerous open squares. Most of the squares were completely cleared ahead of time – armoured soldiers stood waiting on each – but Calen could see throngs of dwarves lining the walkways above, staring down over the procession that weaved its way through the city.

A harsh *whoosh* sound drew Calen's attention to the air above him. A Wind Runner shot from the mouth of a tunnel overhead, soared through the sky, then flew perfectly into the open mouth of another tunnel. The machines truly were incredible.

He remembered Therin saying that no matter how hard they tried, no mage had ever been able to make themselves fly. Nobody was sure why, but it was the way. To Calen, it looked as though the dwarves had come as close as was possible.

The procession stopped at an enormous set of wooden doors. They could have been the twins of the doors that marked the entrance of the keep in Belduar, were it not for the intricate carvings inlaid in the wood.

One of the soldiers stepped from his column and strode over to the doors. "Open the gates!" he bellowed. "Queen Kira has returned." Without waiting for a response, he fell back into his column. A stiff creak rumbled through the air as the doors crept open, struggling under their own weight. The doors gave way to a courtyard. It was at least the match of the inner circle in Belduar, except this one was surrounded by buildings. Each was carved from slabs of smooth stone, gilt lacing their edges.

The entrance to the courtyard was framed by a colonnade of pedestals, with one of those strange lanterns placed on top of each one. It was only then that Calen realised the lanterns around the city did not contain candles, but *flowers*. Inside each lantern were bunches of small flowers, the petals of which glowed with a vivid, bluish-green light.

"Heraya's Ward," the Queen of Azmar, Pulroan, said as she stood beside Calen, a warm smile touching her weary face. "The gods' gift of light in the darkest of places. Little natural light touches the heart of mountains, and although the Wind Tunnels provide air flow, we must reserve open flames for the kitchens and the forges."

"The entire city is lit by—"

"Yes, my child, by flowers. I quite enjoy the notion of it." Before Calen could respond, Pulroan pottered on, joining the other dwarven rulers at the front of the group.

In the very centre of the yard stood a fountain, with a statue of a woman in a long flowing robe, with a circlet atop her head. The woman held a small jug, from which the water flowed. Calen recognised the statue of Heraya – the Mother, the *Waters of Life* flowing from her jug.

Kira turned to the procession. "The Heart of Durakdur."

The Heart was a city all on its own. On the far side of the square, an armourer hammered away at a piece of mail. The orange glow from the forge behind him cast an enmity against the bluish-green glow of the lanterns. Beside the armourer was a fruit seller. The colours and shapes of her fruit put even Arthur's feast to shame. They gleamed in vivid oranges, ocean blues, and one of the oblong fruits was even purple. Servants and officials darted around, dressed in crimson and gold livery carrying silks, scrolls, jewellery, and a wide assortment of other trinkets.

"Captain," Kira said, addressing the armoured dwarf who had ordered the doors open, "please disperse the guard. May your fire never be extinguished and your blade never dull."

"At once, my Queen," the soldier replied, mimicking the salutation.

The sound of so many heavily armoured men moving in unison filled the chamber until they moved far enough away that it was only a faint murmur in the background.

"Please, let us continue. The council chamber is just this way." Kira led the group through the many streets and squares of the Heart. She stopped, passing servants in their livery, doling out instructions wherever she went. It seemed to Calen that she was the unofficial leader of the council – or, at the least, she thought herself to be.

Unlike Arthur, she carried herself in the way that Calen had expected of a monarch. Her shoulders were thrown back, and her chin was just a touch higher in the air than anybody else's. Even for one of such a short stature, she managed to make her strides long and purposeful.

As they made their way through the city within a city, Calen noticed that it wasn't just dwarves that resided within Durakdur; there were elves and humans as well. Though there were not many, there were enough to be noticeable. It was not something that Therin had mentioned.

"Mages," Aeson replied when Calen asked who the men

and elves were. "Far more than all other cultures, dwarves value magic above most other things. They cannot touch the Spark themselves, for reasons unknown to even the most voracious of scholars. Despite this, the dwarves have always embraced magic wholeheartedly. I suppose it is their way. They see the value of things, big and small. Mages are held in high esteem here in the Freehold and in dwarven cities beyond. It is where a lot of young mages come when they are shunned by the world or on the run from the empire. If they are lucky."

Perhaps it was because, up until a few weeks ago, Therin was the only elf Calen had ever met – well, the only non-human Calen had ever met – but to see so many different races in one place seemed odd to him.

Calen had been so engrossed by what was going on around him, he only just realised that everyone they passed in the street stared at them. Not in the way you would expect people to stop and watch a foreign delegation or to admire their queen; they openly gawked, with wide-open mouths and eyes that looked as though they may pop from their heads.

A shriek, growing closer to a deep growl, reminded Calen what they were gawking at. Even there – miles inside a mountain city, surrounded by dwarves, elves, mages, and a particularly hulking giant – Valerys stood apart. They had seen giants before. At least, they had seen Asius. Magic was in their every day. All the things that overawed Calen were normalities to them. Yet, they had never seen a dragon. Calen had to conceal a smile when Valerys shrieked sharply at a dwarf whose eyes had lingered just a touch too long.

It did not take long before they found themselves in front of a large stone building, with a domed roof, set into a sweeping rock face. The building itself stood over fifty feet tall, nearly two hundred feet across, and was cut from smooth grey stone. Two giant square doors, that looked as though they were cast in solid gold, were set into the front of the building. Halfway up the building, on either side of the doors, were a multitude of alcoves. Each housed beautifully carved statues of dwarven men and women in the same dress as the rulers that stood beside Calen.

"The Chamber of the Council," Kira announced matter-of-factly as they entered the enormous building and made their way to a large circular room. In the centre of the room stood a raised, semi-circular dais with four thrones. Behind each of the thrones hung a massive banner, each bearing the colours and sigils of one of the four kingdoms of the Dwarven Freehold.

Six evenly spaced alcoves were set into the wall behind the dais, in a matching semi-circle. In each of the alcoves stood a statue. Each one was at least ten feet tall by Calen's measure. He recognised them all immediately. Statues of the gods.

Their placing was interesting. In all depictions of the gods that Calen knew, Varyn and Heraya, the Mother and the Father, always stood beside each other. But here, it was Heraya and Hafaesir, the Smith, who stood side by side, set into the alcoves directly behind the dais. Achyron and Elyara, the Warrior and the Maiden, stood on either side of them. Varyn and Neron, the Sailor, were set into alcoves at the end.

Calen couldn't help but think that the room was designed in such a way as to intimidate whoever had been granted an audience with the council. As much as he tried to fight it, it was working. He couldn't shake the feeling that he was in over his head. Over the past few days, the more he thought about it, the more he couldn't help but think that he was nothing more than a bargaining chip to be passed back and forth between powerful rulers.

That's all he seemed to be to everyone. Arthur, despite his outward friendliness, only wanted him to help convince the dwarves to come to Belduar's aid if the empire attacked. Despite what Therin had said, the elves were only using him to grow their honour. Aeson had manipulated him from the start, steering him to Belduar at every turn. Calen did not know what the dwarves wanted from him, but he was sure they wanted something. Only Dann, Erik, and Rist had not asked anything of him. He had allowed one of them to be taken, and the other two he left in Belduar.

"Now," Elenya said, her fiery hair rippling in the odd light from the lanterns that hung in the chamber. "First, Arthur, King of Belduar. You have come here to ask something of us. Please, what is it you require?"

Arthur stepped forward from the group, his bravado never faltering. Somehow, even as he stood below the raised dais, the four dwarven rulers looking down over him, he seemed in control. "As you all know, the Lorian Empire has set a blockade less than three days' march from Belduar. This has not happened in over fifty years, and even then, the force was a quarter the size of the current blockade. My scouts report that, in the past few weeks, their numbers have swollen with local levies from Illyanara and now count over twenty thousand strong, with many mages among their number. I believe they are planning to lay siege to the city."

Pulroan and Hoffnar both stifled a gasp. Neither Kira nor Elenya allowed any reaction to touch their faces.

"All I ask," Arthur continued, "is that, should my fears be true, the dwarves of the Freehold aid in the defence of Belduar."

"All that you ask?" Kira remarked in an openly mocking tone. "You know as well as any, Arthur, that no dwarf of the Freehold has left the shelter of these mountains since the fall of The Order. Nearly four hundred years. Why do you think that is?"

"I have my ideas," Aeson muttered.

Kira did not await Arthur's reply. "It is so the empire would not hunt us down and torch our race from these lands, like they did to the giants."

For the first time since they met, Calen saw anger in Asius's eyes.

Kira caught it too. "No offence was meant, Asius, my friend. I am simply trying to be honest."

As quickly as the anger had appeared on Asius's face, it was gone. "None is taken, Kira."

Kira gave a thankful nod. "If we march our armies from these mountains, we open ourselves to the empire's eyes. I am sorry, Arthur, but Durakdur's answer is no. Your city has survived without our soldiers until now. It will continue to do so."

Calen saw a brief flash of anger on Arthur's face, quickly concealed by a furtive grin. His voice raised, not by much but noticeably enough to make the other rulers sit straighter in their thrones. "The empire already knows that you are here, *oh, Queen of Durakdur.*"

Calen couldn't help but wince at the mocking tone in Arthur's voice. He did not know the queen like Arthur did, but from what he did know, she was not the kind of woman he wanted to see angry.

"They do not believe that it was the craftsmen of Belduar who constructed those Bolt Throwers or built the great walls of the city, nor do they forget the past. If Belduar falls, the kingdoms of the Dwarven Freehold will be next." That drew some angry gasps, even from the guards around the outer rim of the chamber.

"I will remind you where you stand, King of Belduar." Elenya's face was fury as the tips of her fingers stroked the head of her axe. Then the fury gave way to a face of calm. "Though, I am inclined to agree. They do not forget our existence, nor do our tunnels and mountain walls protect us. We must simply look to the dwarves of Kolmir to see that is true. May Hafaesir guide them."

"May Hafaesir guide them," the other dwarves chorused.

"Well, what is it you suggest, Elenya? Please, do tell." Kira's taut voice suggested that she and the queen of Ozryn did not see eye-to-eye.

Elenya sat forward in her seat. "Let the Draleid speak." Calen froze.

Kira stroked her chin absently for a moment, then turned to Calen. "Yes. What do you say, Draleid?"

Calen's throat was suddenly devoid of moisture. He glanced at Aeson, whose face was a twisted grimace. He was not going to get help there. There was an expectancy in Arthur's eyes, as though he knew that this is what it was always going to come down to. Calen should have known it too, but he had been naïve. *They planned this.* Anger bubbled over in his belly. If looks could kill, Arthur would be dead where he stood, and judging by the king's face, he understood that.

Calen stepped forward to address the dwarven rulers. He was glad when Valerys moved up beside him, a low rumble emanating from his throat. That put the dwarves off-kilter. "What is it that you want me to say? Your mind is already made up."

"So, you will say nothing?" Kira's eyes narrowed. She shifted in her throne.

"That is not what I—"

"Is this what you hoped for?" Kira interrupted, turning to the other dwarven rulers. "A child with a dragon that is only the size of a goat?"

"What are you—" Calen felt rage swell inside him as Kira cut him off once more.

"How is he to face the Dragonguard, never mind lead our armies? He would flee at the sight of a fully grown dragon. He is but a spoiled brat pretending to be a hero. Look at him now. Look at the petulance."

Calen bit his lip. He could feel the Spark. Touch it. The warmth of it pulled at the back of his mind, urging him.

Something touched his shoulder. It was Asius's hand. Calen looked up at the giant, who simply shook his head, a knowing look in his eye. Calen let the Spark fade away, but the anger remained.

"Did you just call me here to insult me?" he roared. He felt the anger burning off Valerys; it fed his own. The dragon's lips pulled back in a snarl, baring his razor-sharp teeth. The frills on the back of his neck had grown longer in recent weeks and now stood on end. "Is this the honour of dwarves?"

"Now, now!" shouted Pulroan. It was the first time she had spoken. "You overstep."

A sly smirk spread across Kira's face.

"The both of you," Pulroan sniped. She no longer seemed placid. She looked as though she could shatter stone with a word. "You are both children, and you have much to learn." She turned her glare to Kira, emphasising the point.

"Draleid, understand me. There is a lot that rests on your shoulders. A lot that you do not yet understand. These men that brought you here, they did so with the hope that simply your existence would inspire the dwarven kingdoms to return to the surface and aid them in the war they have yearned for since the fall of The Order. It is not that simple. There is no prophecy. Your coming was not foretold, and we will no longer blindly follow those who wield the power you will one day possess.

"It was men and women like you, humans and elves, who brought our civilisation to its knees and drove us from the sun. It was Draleid who turned on their brothers and sisters. It was Draleid who stood behind Fane Mortem. Drove the elves from their cities. Hunted the giants to near extinction. We need to know the depth of your character. We need to know *who* you are. Although, some among us reveal enough about *themselves* in the methods they use."

The elder dwarf sat back in her throne, her chest rising and falling heavily. She sighed and pulled a small cloth from her pocket, wiping the sweat from her time-furrowed brow.

There was silence in the hall. All eyes rested on Calen. He took a deep breath. He remembered what his mother once told him. *You will only know your true friends once they know you truly.*

"I am sorry," he said, and he was. "I am sorry for what was done by those who came before me. For what happened to your people." Calen turned to Asius. "And to yours."

The giant gave a slight bow of his head.

"The empire took my family as well. They killed my mother, my father, my sister. They took one of my closest friends. The first time I killed a man, I felt sick to my stomach. I counted every life I took. I have stopped counting now, but I haven't forgotten. Until now, all I wanted was revenge. I wanted the men who took my family from me… I wanted them dead. In honesty, I still do, but now, I want more.

"Still in Belduar, there are five elves who pledged an oath to protect me, without even knowing who I truly was. I want to become a man they are proud to protect. I want their oath to mean something. I want to earn their trust, as I want to earn yours. I might be a child to you, but I promise you one thing: I will bleed for you. I will not stop fighting until my lungs give way, and neither will Valerys." Calen hadn't noticed his voice rising as he spoke, but he couldn't help it. His heart pounded in his chest, and his blood rushed like fire through his veins. The rumble in

Valerys's throat reverberated through the hall, a deep growl. "I will stand on the walls of Belduar if the empire attacks. I will be there. I didn't want this. I certainly didn't ask for it, but it is what fate has given me, and I will not walk away." Calen paused for a moment, considering. "You want to know my character, show me yours!"

Durakdur

Ozyrn

Azmar

Volkur

CHAPTER 31

All Things Lost

Dann had wandered the streets of the outer circle for what seemed like hours before he happened upon the Old Man's Cellar. It was exactly the type of inn he was looking for; dark, comfy and full of wine.

The packed common room was filled with chatter, and dimly lit by candles of white and red wax that were scattered about so haphazardly that it could only have been done on purpose. The only pieces of furniture were large, red leather chairs arranged around small wooden tables in sets of twos and threes. Dann couldn't help but feel as though he were getting drunk in some lord's lounging area. He didn't mind though; that was his sole intention anyway – to get drunk.

He had managed to nab himself a comfortable chair beside one of the two hearths that sat at either end of the room. The fire never seemed to go past a smoulder, which gave off little light but provided that extra bit of heat he had been looking for, and incensed the room with the familiar scent of burning wood.

Dann leaned back into the softened leather chair, swirling

his wine around in his cup. He'd never tasted wine until he got to Belduar, which he quickly decided was time lost. He lifted the cup to his lips and took a mouthful of the deep red liquid. He sighed out his nose in satisfaction as the fruity flavours coated his tongue and drifted into his nostrils. Lord Arnell had given him a purse full of coin and told him to enjoy the city, and that was fully what he intended on doing.

"Mind if I join you?" Dann looked up from his wine to find Dahlen looking down at him. Droplets of water dripped onto the floor from the ends of his coat, and his hair was matted to his face.

"Sure." Dann pushed himself up into a seated position. He caught the attention of the serving girl who had brought him the wine earlier. Elaiya was the name she had given him; he had made sure to ask – people always remembered you when you asked for their names. He gestured for her to bring a second cup. "Wine?"

"Please," Dahlen said. He draped his sopping wet cloak over a cast iron rail near the fire and dropped down into the chair opposite Dann. "You got left behind too?"

"Thank you," Dann said as he took the second cup off Elaiya and proceeded to fill it with wine from his jug. It wasn't his coin, and it would be a long time before the purse was empty. Why not share? Though, Dahlen's question left a sour taste in his mouth.

"Left behind?" he replied with a raised eyebrow. He handed Dahlen the overflowing cup of wine. Dahlen nodded his appreciation, sipping from the top of the cup immediately to stop it spilling over.

"Sorry." Dahlen placed the cup down on the table and ran his hands through his saturated hair. "I didn't mean it like that. I'm just—"

"It's okay," Dann interrupted. He sank back into his chair and took another mouthful of his wine. "It might be the wine talking, but you're right. I would rather be down there with him."

"You two are close."

"Like brothers. Until we get Rist back, he's all I have out here."

Dahlen flinched at the mention of Rist's name. Dann didn't blame him like Calen did. But it was clear that Dahlen blamed himself.

Dann refilled the wine in his cup and gestured for Elaiya to bring a new jug. "Keep it," he said when she tried to give him his change. Four silver marks. He would have run naked through the streets for that kind of money in The Glade. It wasn't his, anyway. It was better she had it.

"Sir, I can't possibly. This is far too—"

"I'm no sir. Please, keep it."

Elaiya's smile spread from ear to ear as she thanked him profusely. At the very least, Dann was sure that he would be getting the best wine at the inn for the rest of the night. He wrapped his fingers around the handle of the fresh jug and gestured towards Dahlen before realising that his first cup was still full.

"That was kind," Dahlen said. He lifted his cup to his mouth, emptying it in one go, and extended it towards Dann to refill, a smirk on his face.

I knew there was a reason I liked him.

Dann realised that the last time he had sat down and had a drink with Dahlen was in the Traveller's Rest back in Camylin – the night they lost Rist. They hadn't stopped looking over their shoulders since then. The thought made him even more appreciative of the wine in his cup and the coin in his purse, but it set a sense of longing in him for his friend. "Where is your brother? Does he not enjoying drinking away his sorrows as well?"

Dahlen laughed as he pushed himself back into his red leather chair. "Erik enjoys getting drunk as much as the rest of us. But no, not tonight. We deal with frustration in different ways. I drink, he practices."

"I think I'll stick with drinking."

"I will drink to that," Dahlen said, laughing. He raised his cup and tipped it off Dann's. They both emptied their cups. "I'm sorry about Rist."

A silence followed Dahlen's words. Dann was sure that he had been chewing on those words since he sat down. Dann leaned forward, resting his elbows on his knees. He took a long draught of his wine and let out a sigh. "It was not your fault. I don't fool myself thinking that it would have been any different if I had been there."

Dahlen gave a weak nod and refilled both of their cups. A silence held the air for a moment. The din of conversation around them faded into the background.

"I'm sorry about Calen. He can be—"

"Arrogant? Self-centred?"

Dann put his cup down on the table and held Dahlen's gaze. He stilled the anger in his stomach. He came here to get drunk, not to argue. "I was going to say passionate."

I was going to say stubborn, but I'm not giving you that.

Dahlen smiled awkwardly and called over Elaiya. "Can we have two hits of Wyrm Blood, please?"

Dann shivered involuntarily. He had only drunk Wyrm Blood once before. It wasn't actually the blood of a wyrm. It was a concoction created from a mix of pure grape spirit and botanicals that had a vivid green colouring. Lasch had imported some for The Gilded Dragon from Valtara two summers back, and Dann distinctly remembered struggling to use his legs afterwards.

Dahlen passed a small cup of the sharp green liquid to Dann. "Thank you for sharing your wine with me. To friends and family."

"To friends and family." Dann winced as the spirit burned its way down his throat.

Dahlen slammed his small cup down on the table, his face contorted in pain from the spirit. "Shall we get drunk?"

"That had been my only intention for tonight," Dann laughed, as he called Elaiya over again. She was quite beautiful. *I wonder if she would join us for a drink.*

"Have I ever told you about the time that I saw a horse with a horn growing from its head?"

CHAPTER 32

The Hand

W e have heard all we need to hear."

That was all Pulroan said. Nobody else spoke after that, which suited Calen. He didn't think he would have been able to say anything else.

They were brought back to the Heart and shown their chambers. Both Aeson and Arthur came to see him that night, but all he did was roar at them and send them away. He had never been so angry in all his life. He felt it in Valerys too. It burned in the back of his mind like smouldering coals. Aeson flat-out refused to leave until Valerys snapped at him. Had the dragon tried a bit harder, he would have taken Aeson's hand.

Calen sat on the edge of his bed, tears streaming down his cheeks. He knew if he pushed everything down, it would eventually come back up. He just hadn't expected it to come back at a time like that. He felt like a fool. He had roared at kings and queens, lost his temper. He made an idiot of himself. But that was not what hurt him.

When he lost his temper in the chamber, something switched in the back of his mind. It was the first time that he allowed himself to accept the truth. He couldn't hide from it anymore; he couldn't lie to himself. His family was gone.

His heart felt like it had been ripped free of his chest. He would never lay eyes on his mother again. Never feel the warmth of her hand against his cheek. Never hear his father's voice. Ella had always believed in him, always kept his chin up, and she was always there to show him the right way. At least they would be with Haem now. He didn't move to stop the tears from flowing. It would be like a bandage on a broken arm.

He could still save Rist. He *would* save Rist.

For that night, though, he needed to feel everything. He lay back and let himself sob, shaking. Valerys lay at the door, ensuring nobody came in, but Calen felt him. The sadness and the comfort.

Calen lay his scabbard down against the wooden rail of the practice yard, sliding his sword free as he did. He let out a puff of air, spinning the blade around to loosen his arms.

He did not look forward to facing Gaeleron's stony stare when he returned to Belduar. The elf was regimental when it came to Calen's practice with the sword. He would not be happy when he discovered that Calen had refused to spar with Aeson.

He still practiced his forms, at least. It was all that kept him sane while they waited. Four days had passed without a word from the dwarves. Therin had said that the dwarves of the Freehold could take a lifetime to reach a decision, such was the nature of four kingdoms attempting to work as one. Each had their own agendas. Each tried to make sure their own needs were met. That didn't help the sickly feeling that sat in Calen's stomach, though.

He had not spoken to Aeson or Arthur either. They had tried, but he simply walked away. He didn't want to talk to them. They had put him in that situation. They knew what he was walking into, and they just threw him like a sheep to wolves. They used him. But it was his own fault for not noticing it sooner.

The Heart had its own practice yard. It was meant to be for the royal guard only, but every morning, when Calen practiced his forms, a crowd gathered – as it did now. They may not have known who he was when he first arrived, but word had spread that a Draleid was in Durakdur. He heard many things when he had wandered the city streets during the day. Everybody had a different theory as to why the Draleid had come to Durakdur. Everybody seemed to know more than he did.

Calen took a deep breath in as he dropped into Crouching Bear form. *Don't think. Just move.*

He released control as he flowed through the forms that were part of a movement that Gaeleron had been teaching him; the *svidarya*. Burning Winds. There was something about the fluidity of the movement that settled Calen's mind.

The first morning he practiced his forms in the yard, it was just fifteen or twenty servants, trying to pretend that they weren't watching. They walked a little slower or just stopped for a moment, pretending to catch their breath. Calen wasn't sure if it was his practice or the opportunity to gawk at Valerys, but by the fourth morning, the yard was crammed with as many as three hundred people. They didn't even pretend to busy themselves. They gathered in groups, leaned over walls or fences, and some stopped and sat on the ground, watching. There was no fear of the royal guard moving them on either, for the guard made up at least a fifth of their number.

There were easily a few hundred watching him now, as sweat glistened on his face, and his shirt clung to his chest. He brought the blade through in sweeping motions, allowing each swing to carry into the next. The svidarya was a movement of aggression; it involved taking the fight to the enemy. A barrage of powerful, sweeping strikes that would push your opponent onto their back foot. It was exactly what Calen needed.

A bluish-green glow washed over Calen's skin as he ran his fingers along the edge of the luminescent leaf that sat in a glassless lantern mounted atop the low parapet of the walkway. He had taken to walking the maze-like walkways and streets of Durakdur most evenings. He knew them no better than he did the first day. But he wasn't walking them to learn. He was walking them to escape. To get out of his own head.

Calen pulled his hood tighter around his face as two dwarves walked behind him.

"You should have seen him train earlier. I reckon the Draleid could fight a Depth Stalker on his own! And his dragon... Lorik said it will grow bigger than the mountain itself. And he knows things. I'm going back to the yard to watch again in the morning," one of the dwarves said.

"A Depth Stalker? Not a chance. Although, I may join you in the morning. See for myself."

Calen waited until the two dwarves had passed before he continued walking. He took in the wonders of the dwarven architecture. Domes of shimmering gold. Archways that stretched hundreds of feet. Strange machines of which Calen fostered no understanding carried goods and people up and down the outer walls. He hadn't noticed it before, but every piece of hewn stone was sharp and angular, even the archways. There was order in everything. The only exceptions were the magnificent domes atop the larger buildings, reflecting the other-worldly glow of the flowers in a goldish shimmer.

After taking a walk around the city, Calen sat atop a low wall that overlooked the interwoven walkways below. He chose it because it had a perfect view of the waterfall and because it was the quietest spot he could find. The noise of the city was too much. He sat there, his mother's scarf between his fingers, gazing out over the breath-taking cityscape, dotted with the glow of bluish green lanterns. He listened to the ever-present crashing of the water as it cascaded down the inner mountain wall. It drowned out everything else.

"It's beautiful, isn't it?"

"Leave me alone, Arthur." Calen kept his eyes fixed on a point across the cavernous opening, where the light from the flowers glittered through the cascading water.

Arthur sighed. "Calen, I'm sorry. I promise you; I did not know that Kira would attack you like that."

"Save your apologies. She was right. Just because you heard

it in some prophecy or read it in some book. I'm not what you've waited for. It should have been someone else. I'm sorry."

"Prophecy?" There was indignation in Arthur's voice. "You think I pushed you down here and threw you in front of those dwarves because I heard a prophecy?"

Calen didn't know how to respond. "That's how it always is in the stories. Therin—"

"That's where prophecies belong, Calen. In stories and fairy tales. Prophecies and fate are words that are used by kings and queens to send young men and women to their death with smiles on their faces, dreaming of becoming heroes. Fate is fluid. Your destiny is in your own hands – nobody else's. Yes, when I saw that someone had been bound, that someone had become a Draleid, my heart skipped a beat. I dared not dream it would happen. I brought you here because Draleids used to symbolise hope. Because if there was anything that would stir the dwarves from their slumber, it would be a Draleid. But Calen, what you said in that chamber, the way you spoke… You are more than we could ever have hoped for. I'm not here talking to you because you are a Draleid. I'm here talking to you because I believe in who you are."

Calen wanted to speak, but he didn't. He stared out over the edge, letting the waterfall fill the silence.

Arthur's footsteps echoed off the walls. "I'm going back up to Belduar for the night. Ihvon has sent word that Daymon has fallen ill. My wife – may she find rest – would never forgive me if I did not check on him. I will be back in the morning." The only response was the sound of the crashing water. "And Calen, I'm not the only one."

Calen tossed in his bed, like he had done all night. He should have said something to Arthur. He had been unfair. What happened in the council chamber had unleashed a lot inside his head, and he had taken it out on Arthur and Aeson. However angry he was at them, they were good men, and they had done right by him, for the most part. He needed to apologise to them both – Arthur, in particular.

That wasn't the only thing that plagued his mind and stood in the way of his dreams. Had his outburst cost Belduar the support of the dwarves? The last four nights, scenes of Belduar burning had clouded his dreams. Imperial soldiers storming through the streets, laying waste to everything in their path. The inner circle being overrun while trebuchets rained destruction down upon the tightly packed houses of the outer circles. All of it, his fault.

Despite his need for sleep, those were not dreams he wished to return to. Still, he shuffled his hips into the mattress in an attempt to form the right groove. He fluffed the pillow, turning from one side to another.

Every time he stopped moving, the *tick-tock* from the ornate, wrought iron clock on the wall seemed to rise to a crescendo, until it was a battering ram beating at his mind. There weren't many clocks in The Glade. They were expensive and hard to come by. In Durakdur, there were clocks in every room. He had to admit, it was the only thing that gave him any sense of night or day in a city where the sun never rose or set. But now, he wanted to tear it from the wall and smash it against the stone floor.

Tick-tock.

Calen's eyes snapped open as he heard a creaking sound coming from the door. He had locked that door. His heart beat almost as loud as the clock now. He had left his sword in its scabbard, about two feet away, on top of the writing desk.

He heard another creak. This time, it was a floorboard. He was sure of it. Somebody was in the room.

Valerys was still asleep. That was the only time they couldn't feel everything, as if the dream world gave them both time apart. Calen cursed in his head, breathing as quietly as he could.

Another creak. There wasn't a doubt in his mind.

Stilling his fear, he threw his sheets off and leapt the short distance between the bed and the desk. Calen pulled his blade from its scabbard in one sweeping motion and turned to face the intruder.

In the dark, his eyes had barely focused on the intruder's outline when threads of Air cannoned into his chest. They lifted him from his feet and launched him into the wardrobe against the far wall, shattering it to pieces.

Calen shook his head. It was spinning, and he needed to clear his eyes. His hands were empty. The impact made him drop his sword.

A short, gruff laugh drew his attention. His attacker stood over him, a sword pointed towards his chest. All Calen could make out was his silhouette. His eyes still hadn't adjusted.

"Just a child." The man's voice was deep and coarse. "I'll make it quick."

Calen closed his eyes. He reached out for the Spark. Drawing on threads of Fire, Air and Spirit, he formed a baldír as bright as he could, as if it were the sun itself. Once he heard the man gasp in pain, he snuffed it out.

The man stumbled backwards, with his free hand clasped over his eyes. "You bastard! My fucking eyes!"

His howls were cut short as Valerys leapt up across his shoulder. The dragon sank his teeth into the man's neck and tore at his back with his claws. The pair of them collapsed onto the bed in a tangle. As they fumbled, Calen caught sight of a second man lurking in the doorway.

In case one wasn't enough.

Calen didn't need a moment to think. He could see the threads of Fire as the man pulled them towards his hand. Calen was quicker. He reached out with the Spark, wrapping threads of Air around a thick splinter of wood. He sent it straight through the man's heart. A brief flash, and the man dropped to his knees without a whisper, then collapsed on his side. A rumble of satisfaction let Calen know that Valerys's opponent was no longer an issue either.

Calen could already feel the drain from the Spark seeping into his muscles. In his panic, he hadn't controlled the flow as much as he should have. His heart thumped. He heard shouts coming from the hallway outside, but it was only when he made to follow them he realised he was still in his smallclothes. He buttoned up his shirt, dragged a pair of trousers up his legs, and stamped his feet into his boots.

Bounding from the room, he crashed straight into a stone wall. When he looked up, he realised that wall, was Asius. Aeson was with him, and both had splatters of blood on their clothes. It wasn't their blood.

"Someone—" Calen didn't get a chance to finish his sentence.

"We know," Aeson said. "They were in our chambers too. They must have snuck into the city."

"They're—"

"Mages. We know."

Calen frowned as he was cut off again.

"Calen, listen to me. They are the Hand. The empire's assassins. If they came for us, then they are after the Council as well. We need to get to them. You and Valerys go to Queen Kira. Her chambers are only five minutes from here, down the western corridor. You'll know it by the vermilion doors inlaid with the symbol of Durakdur. Asius and I will see to the others. We will meet again at the Wind Tunnels. Calen, if they are here, making this move out in the open, they are doing the same in Belduar. I have sent Oleg to the Wind Runners Guild hall to fetch Falmin. Make sure the queen is okay and get to the tunnels."

"I—"

"Don't argue! Go!"

Calen thought about doing just that. He thought about shouting and telling Aeson that he would go where he chose and not where he was told. He didn't. He furrowed his brow, turned on his heels, and ran. As quick as his legs would take him, he ran towards the queen's chambers. Valerys bounded along beside him. As much as he hated to even think it, let alone admit it, Aeson was right. Everything else could wait.

Calen reached out for the Spark as he approached the large, vermilion double doors, inlaid with the symbol of Durakdur, that marked the queen's chambers. Two dwarves in heavy plate armour and thick crimson cloaks, which marked them as

Queensguard, lay rigid on the floor. Calen didn't check their bodies. Their blood stained the smooth stone.

He crashed through the doors of the queen's chambers, ramming them open with his dropped shoulder. Drawing on thick threads of Air, he used a barrage of wind to send the hooded man spiralling across the room, shattering the window to pieces. The man fell, screaming, into the endless depths on the other side.

He moved to parry the blow from the second man, stopping mid-air as Valerys crashed into the assassin's chest, rending his leather armour like soft butter. Calen shuddered at the shrieks of pain.

In his mad rush, he hadn't noticed Kira standing in nothing but the skin she was born in. She held a long, thin axe in her right hand. Even in the heat of the moment, his chest heaving and the blood pumping through his veins, Calen's cheeks coloured. He took perhaps a moment too long to shield his gaze.

"Now is not the time for modesty, Draleid." Despite the fact that she stood there in her bare flesh, moments from an assassin's blade, her voice was still steel.

Calen couldn't bring himself to raise his eyes. A dark shade of crimson painted his cheeks. "Your Majesty, there are more assassins in the city. Aeson and Asius have gone to check on the other members of the council, but we must go to Belduar. If they are here, then the king is in danger too." Half of him wanted to take a second look, but the other half of him refused to tear his gaze from the stone floor. "Will you be all right?"

"Yes, boy. I will be fine. Go!"

Calen didn't need to hear anymore. With a grunt, he dashed from the room, his eyes never rising above knee-level. It was not right for him to see her like that. She was a queen. Even if she were not, it would not be right.

He cursed himself as he weaved his way through the labyrinth of streets and walkways. Every second turn was the wrong turn. He would die of old age before he reached the Wind Tunnels. The streets were quiet. He had not seen nor heard a trace of any more of the Hand. That could only be a good thing.

"Fuck!" he shouted when he realised he had just spent two minutes running to a dead end.

"Calen?"

Calen did not think that there would be a point for the rest of his life where he would be happier to hear Oleg Marilyn's voice. Falmin was with him. Sweat dripped down both of their rouged faces and Falmin's shirt clung to his chest, revealing the lean muscle that hid on his wiry frame.

"Oleg, by the gods, your timing couldn't be any better! We need to get to the Wind Tunnels." Calen couldn't help but sigh in relief. Five more minutes trying to escape that maze, and he would have descended into madness.

"This way, Calen. We're close."

By the time they reached the Wind Tunnels, Oleg's chest heaved. He bent over double, trying to drag air into his lungs. Calen couldn't help but be impressed. The rotund man had matched both himself and Falmin for pace. Although, he was paying the price for it. "Falmin—"

"Give me five minutes, and she'll be good to go, Mister Bryer."

The gangly man leapt up onto the platform of the *Crested Wave*. Calen had resigned himself to the fact that he would not get to finish a sentence that night. He tapped his foot on the stone platform. *Aeson and Asius should be here already.*

As if he had summoned them, the man and the giant loped around the corner of a high wall. One or two fresh cuts stained the front of Aeson's shirt, but they were otherwise unharmed.

"How long?" Aeson asked as he scaled the stone steps of the landing. He might not have let on, but Calen saw his chest dragging a bit more than it usually would. There was a wound somewhere causing him more pain than Calen had first thought.

"Less than five minutes. Falmin is making sure the *Crested Wave* is ready to go."

Aeson nodded. "And Queen Kira?"

"She is okay. Though, I cannot say the same for her guards. The others?"

"They'll live," Aeson replied. "Hoffnar will have a few new scars, but that's nothing he isn't used to."

Calen wanted to say more, to ask questions, but he knew Aeson wouldn't answer them. The man simply nodded, then turned his attention to Asius, a questioning look in his eyes.

"How bad?" the giant asked.

Aeson shrugged, wincing. "I'll live if I stay here. But I'll die if I take it up there."

The giant's lips made a grim, thin line, but he nodded. He placed his hand on Aeson's ribs, where a large red stain had begun to form through the brown fabric of his shirt. Calen felt Asius drawing from the Spark, pulling at threads. Air, he thought. Spirit. He missed the rest – it was too fast – but he saw the relief in Aeson's eyes when the giant pulled his hand away.

"Thank you." Aeson's next breath was a deep one as he tested out the results.

Calen still hadn't learned anything of healing. Therin had warned him it was dangerous for someone who did not understand it. Even then, he saw Asius's eyes were a bit darker, his breaths longer.

"Falmin, are you nearly ready?" The frustration in Calen's voice was cut short by the thunderous sound of footsteps. How many, he couldn't tell, but there was a tremor in the ground and a ringing in the air.

Coming over one of the four stone bridges that connected to the main platform, ten abreast, were dwarves, armoured from head to toe in that familiar thick plate, with the nose-bridge helmets. Each carried a wicked, twin-bladed axe, with a short sword strapped to their hips. Each wore a thick crimson cloak that billowed behind them.

Queensguard.

Sure enough, marching at the front of the column was Kira, in full plate armour. Silver and gold rings laced her flowing blonde hair. He couldn't tell how many Queensguard she had with her, but they were still pouring over the bridge, and the ground still trembled.

There was a smirk set into Kira's face. "You didn't think we were going to let you take all the fun for yourselves, did you?"

Something about the woman unsettled him. He wasn't sure what it was, and he wasn't sure if he enjoyed it or despised it.

"Your Majesty… What are you doing?"

"Showing you our character." Her smirk deepened, but then her face turned serious. "We are with you, Draleid."

Ihvon stopped for a moment. He closed his eyes, focused on his breathing.

Just a moment. I just need a moment.

The heavy wind nipped at his face and neck, but he did not flinch. He felt as though he had been sitting by the fire for hours. Beads of sweat rolled down his forehead. He kept moving. His steps echoed through the paved streets, accompanied only by the whistling of the wind and the occasional shout of a sentry on patrol. He walked through the merchant's square, under the arch of the bell tower. He fingered his pocket, where the stone had been.

It's too late now. There's no going back.

Arthur had given him no choice. They couldn't resist the empire any longer. And the dwarves were not the answer. They only cared for their own desires. Through his coat, he touched the scar that ran along his stomach. It was a constant reminder of that day. He had screamed at them to go back. To let him go back. But those dwarves were too scared for their own skins. They ran, and dragged him with them.

Alyana. Khris.

Ihvon clenched his hand into a fist. He felt a sting in his palm as his nail cut into the skin, leaving a thin line of blood that trickled along the creases in his hand. Even as his anger burned, he fought the other half of his heart. The guilt that scratched at the back of his consciousness.

He nodded as he passed two sentries, not breaking his stride.

The boy and his dragon, for the emperor's amnesty.

It was a good deal. A fair deal.

He kept one foot moving in front of the other. He couldn't allow for weakness, but his pace slowed. He stopped. His chest rose and fell in heavy sweeps.

"Fuck!" he yelled, feeling a crack as his knuckle connected with the stone wall. The boy reminded him too much of Khris. "Gods curse me, I can't do it."

He turned on his heels. He wasn't long past the bell tower. He could still warn them. He ignored the pain that shot up his weary knees as his feet pounded against the stone.

There is still time.

He ran faster.

CHAPTER 33

Of Blood and Fire

almin was true to his word. The *Crested Wave* was
ready to launch in five minutes, not a minute less or
a minute more. The man knew his craft.

Kira had brought all one thousand of the Queensguard
with her. To bring more would have required the agreement
of the other council members, and that was something they
didn't have time for. She had also sent for more navigators,
but that was something else that they didn't have time to
wait for.

The *Crested Wave* could fit two hundred at the most,
as long as everyone was standing and didn't mind a few
bruises along the way. Even that number sent Falmin into
a flustered temper. He flounced onto the vessel, muttering
to himself, "They always think they know everything…
Never listen… 'Just do it, Falmin.' I'll show you where
to…"

Kira, Aeson, Calen, Valerys, and Asius went first, piling
in as many of the Queensguard as was practical. Asius's size

meant a few less dwarves. The others would follow when the rest of the navigators arrived.

Oleg stayed behind to "coordinate."

The trip back up to Belduar was far less comfortable than the trip down. It was impossible to tell whether they were going faster or not, but it certainly felt like they were. More than once, Calen was lucky to avoid the nick of a loosely held axe as the *Crested Wave* jostled from side to side, bouncing off the smooth tunnels. Valerys nearly tore strips from the platform as he attempted to keep himself steady.

As they approached the landing in Belduar, the din of fighting echoed down the tunnel. Calen felt the atmosphere around him change as everyone on the *Crested Wave* readied their heads for what was to come.

Chaos.

The attacks in Durakdur were quiet and calculated. Belduar was under siege. The courtyard that fronted the Wind Tunnels was a meat grinder full of bodies, dead and alive. Calen couldn't tell Belduaran from Lorian. All he saw was steel and blood. Men howled battle cries, screamed in pain, wailed in death. Calen saw threads of Fire, Wind, and Earth everywhere he looked as mages on both sides reaped maelstroms of destruction.

The dwarves leapt from the platform as soon as the rings ceased spinning. Their short legs belied their speed as they bounded across the rope bridge and onto the landing, leaping into the frenzy of the courtyard below.

"This is madness…" Aeson said, furrowing his brow. "How is it even possible? How did they get past the walls?"

"We can ask them that when they're dead," Kira replied as she bounded off the platform. She sliced through an imperial soldier as she landed, as if he were made of dry paper.

She is insane.

Except for a passing glance, Aeson paid her no heed. "We need to get to the Inner Circle."

Calen was incredulous. "What about here? We can't just leave them!"

"We need to get to the king. If we don't, then these people die for nothing." Aeson held Calen's gaze for a long moment, as if daring him to challenge. When he didn't, Aeson nodded across the courtyard, to one of the six entrances that lined the southern edge of the yard. "That passageway leads to the main street. We can get to the bridge from there and cross to the Inner Circle."

He didn't wait for a response but leapt down from the platform into the yard, expecting the rest to follow. The group cut their way through the fighting, never stopping. But if a blade could be raked across someone, it was. About halfway across the yard, Calen caught Kira's eye as she heaved her axe from the chest of a behemoth of a man. He didn't need to say anything.

"Go!" she roared, separating head from shoulders as she spun her axe in a sideways arc.

They got to the other side of the yard and into the passageway relatively unscathed. Asius was the only one who seemed to earn any new marks. A thin slice trickled blood down his left thigh. He didn't seem to notice.

The passage opened into the double-sided street they

had come down a few days before on their way to the tunnels. It had looked a lot different then. Not tainted by the blood of the dead, and the screams of the dying. Calen sidestepped a frenzied strike, slicing the man across the back as he slipped past him. Something itched at him. Something wasn't right. Out of the corner of his eye, he saw it. "Aeson!" Calen roared over the shouts and screams of the pitched battle. "The walls!"

Aeson looked at him as if he had lost his mind, shrugging wordlessly.

A heavy shield to the chest knocked stars into Calen's eyes. He shook his head as he steadied himself for the second blow. A shimmering white blur took the man by the neck. Calen frowned as he leapt over the man's body. Fury pulsated from Valerys.

"The walls, Aeson! There's nobody on the walls!" Calen grabbed Aeson's shoulder, shoving him into place, so he could look down to the lowest tier of the outer circle. The walls were empty, the gates barred and locked shut. There had been no fighting there. The empire had not fought their way into the city; they had been let in.

Calen saw the moment when it clicked. The man nodded, a coldness in his eyes. "Come on."

Asius carried on, carving his way up the street. His glowing red níthral pulsated in the shape of an axe in his hand. Most stepped out of his way. They had never seen a giant before, but they knew well enough to steer clear.

As they cut their way through the street, Calen's joints ached, and his muscles groaned. Even with his training, he still felt the drain from the Spark. He hadn't thought earlier.

It was the first thing that came to his head. He was growing stronger, though. He could feel it.

Up ahead, two figures stood amidst a mass of soldiers. Dahlen and Erik were unmistakable. The two brothers stood back-to-back, their twin blades drawn, whirling in and out of pockets of Lorian soldiers before slotting back together. They looked tired, though. Calen saw it in the way they stood. They would not last much longer.

One nod from Aeson, and Asius waved his hands, whipping swathes of Lorian soldiers off their feet with threads of Air, clearing the way to the brothers.

"It's about time you got here." There was a cheeky smirk on Erik's face. Even then, with a deep gash along his side, and his face painted in blood, he seemed unphased. It seemed unnatural to Calen. Though, he remembered a time when the idea of taking a man's life turned his stomach. Now…

"What happened?" The coldness didn't leave Aeson's eyes.

Erik shrugged. "We were in our chambers when we heard the bells ringing. By the time we got to the courtyard in the inner circle, it was already consumed. It was like they crept in from the sewers. The others are still up there. We fought our way down with some soldiers to try and clear the Wind Tunnels." Erik panted when he finished.

The fighting around them had begun to die down as the Belduarans gained the upper hand.

"Kira and the dwarves are down by the Wind Tunnels. They need help. Gather these men and go. We're heading up to the Inner Circle. Have you seen the king?"

Dahlen pursed his lips, a frown creasing his brow, but he did not argue. "He must be in the hall." He and Erik turned back to the remaining soldiers. "To the Wind Tunnels! For the king!" Shouts and cries rang out in response.

The fighting had thinned out by the time they reached the stone bridge that separated the Inner and Outer circles. It was gargantuan – two hundred feet across and wide enough for four carts to ride side-by-side. Calen couldn't bring himself to look over the edge the last time he had crossed it, and that hadn't changed. It was deep enough that if he stumbled off, nobody would hear him hit the bottom.

For the most part, the bridge was empty. Anyone unfortunate enough to be standing in Asius's way, though, was wrapped in threads of Air and tossed off the side. Calen didn't hear them hit the bottom, but their screams echoed all the way to the other side of the bridge.

The sound of fighting poured through the half-open gate as they reached the walls of the Inner Circle. The harsh ringing of metal melded with the howls and screams of men who stared death in the face. The waft of air was putrid; sweat and dirt mixed with the metallic twinge of blood.

Calen took a minute to steady himself before he followed Aeson and Asius through to the gate. In the heat of everything, he had pushed it to the back of his mind – the fear of death, the urge to vomit – but standing at the gates, his stomach felt as though it might tear itself from his body. His knees shook. He took a deep breath before he strode through the gate. Valerys was quick on his heels.

The yard was madness. Were it not for the purple

cloaks of the Kingsguard, he would not have been able to tell friend from foe in the mass of bodies that consumed the wide-open space. The Bolt Throwers atop the towers were blazing infernos of orange and red, smoke billowing into the night sky.

Calen arched his head down as he avoided a swinging blade, taking the man's legs from under him as he followed through. He couldn't move five feet without having to swing his blade. He saw the towering figure of Asius about twenty feet ahead. His shimmering red axe swung through the air, slicing limb from limb as if it were the will of the gods itself.

Calen felt the drain in his muscles, the lethargy that soaked into his shoulders with every swing of his blade. Drawing on the Spark, even as little as he did, was taking its toll. Yet, the giant seemed unaffected as he weaved through the mass of men like a maelstrom of death. There was no doubt in Calen's mind that Aeson was right there beside him.

They needed to get to the other side of the yard. The king would be in the hall. Though, it seemed strange that he was not in the yard, bellowing at the top of his lungs, spurring his men on in the battle's heart. Arthur did not seem the type to shy away from battle.

There was a ringing noise in Calen's ears. He yanked his head backwards, but were it not for Ellisar's blade, his head would no longer be fixed to his shoulders. The elf whirled around him. Using his momentum, he sliced through the arm of the man who had nearly closed Calen's eyes.

A nod between the two was enough. The elf had

looked better. His silvery hair was mottled with a mixture of dry and wet blood. Two long cuts raked his right arm, just above his leather greaves, and he carried a limp, though it didn't seem to impede him much.

"The others?" Calen shouted, despite his mouth being almost pressed into Ellisar's ear. The cacophony of the fighting would have swallowed any sound less than a roar.

Ellisar gave a quick tilt of his head, nodding toward the centre of the yard. It was the same direction as the great hall. Calen immediately chastised himself for even considering the idea that he might not have gone to his companions had they not been in that direction. He needed to get to Aeson and Asius – he needed to get to Arthur – but there were certain costs he was not willing to pay.

With Ellisar at his side, making ground was a lot easier. Despite his limp, the elf glided through the madness. His long, slightly curved sword swept death with every stroke. It was strange to see a blade that looked like his own. He hadn't really thought about it until Gaeleron had mentioned it. He had not understood what Gaeleron meant when he said that he needed to learn how to fight with an elven blade. To Calen, a sword was a sword. Even sparring with Gaeleron, he saw little difference. But watching Ellisar, he understood. There was an elegance to the way he moved. If death could be beautiful, this was as close as it could come.

Calen felt a shiver of disdain at his own thoughts. Death could not be beautiful. As he looked around the courtyard, past the contorted faces and howling battle cries, past the whirs of steel and cracking of bodies colliding, the ground was littered with the dead. Some were missing arms or legs, some… more. The stone was stained so thoroughly with blood that no amount of scrubbing could ever wipe it clean. One man dragged himself across the ground by his fingertips, his entrails leaking from his stomach. Spurts of blood muffled his screams, but Calen saw the pain etched into his face.

Death cannot be beautiful.

Calen hardened himself and pushed it down – the sickness, the nausea, the sadness. Death could not be beautiful, but sometimes, it was necessary. He swung his blade in a parry, whirling around and separating arm from shoulder. *Sometimes, it is necessary.*

By the time they caught up to Aeson and Asius, Dann was standing at the giant's side. He looked as though he had been beaten within an inch of his life. Even so, Calen was beyond happy to see him. The idea that something could have happened to Dann hadn't really come into Calen's mind until he saw his friend alive. His clothes were in tatters, there was an open gash on the side of his head, and a reddish stain had spread through his shirt, but he was alive.

He greeted Calen with a tight grimace and a nod.

Calen didn't have to ask.

"The twins are somewhere over there," Dann shouted, tilting his head towards the western side of the yard. "They went after Therin. I haven't seen Gaeleron or Vaeril."

There was a grim look on Dann's face. It was the same look that Calen knew was on his own. The blood on Dann's shirt hadn't stopped spreading.

Aeson caught Calen's gaze. "He'll live. The hall."

"He's hurt! I'm not letting—"

"Calen! Now is not the time for this." Aeson glared at Calen, his cold eyes unwavering. He turned his attention to Dann. "Can you keep going?"

Dann gave a half-hearted nod. Calen wanted to argue again, but his words got stuck in his throat as a Lorian soldier charged him with a spear outstretched. Calen's feet were planted, and he knew he wouldn't be able to move quickly enough. He took in a deep breath.

In a crimson flash, the man's body split in two from shoulder to hip, slopping to the ground mid-run. Calen looked up to see an acknowledging nod from Asius. "You go to the hall. I am needed here. The battle teeters on the edge." The giant did not wait for a response. He waded through the thick of the bodies, swinging his axe in measured strokes.

"I'm glad he's on our side," Dann said, wincing as he puffed out his cheeks.

Calen held Dann's gaze. "Dann, are you sure you can—"

"Calen. I'll be okay."

Slow and steady, the four of them cut their way to the foot of the steps that led up to the great hall. Valerys loped along beside them, clawing at legs and tearing through men who were unfortunate enough to have fallen in his path.

With each foot gained, Calen grew to appreciate Ellisar's presence. The elf was stuck to him, never allowing him to drift more than two or three feet away. At any other time, Calen would have complained; not now. Ellisar had kept Calen's heart beating more than once, where otherwise he would have been lying on the cold stone, having never seen the blow coming.

Bodies littered the steps that led up to the keep. The acrid smell of death was more pungent when it wasn't mingled with the heat of battle. An involuntary heave made Calen catch vomit in his mouth, but he choked it back down.

He twisted his body sideways as a warning flashed in his head from Valerys. A searing pain burned through his side as the blade bit into his skin. Calen stumbled backwards from the shock. His fingers fumbled for purchase on the handle of his sword as he moved to block the next strike. A *whoosh* passed his head as an arrow plunged into his attacker's eye, spurting blood as he fell to the floor. He shook for a moment, then lay still.

Calen's heart hammered against his chest so hard that it hurt. Valerys stood beside the man's head. A deep growl bubbled in his throat as he watched for signs of movement.

Therin bounded up the steps. He pulled another arrow from his quiver and nocked it as his eyes swept the landing. He lowered it ever so slightly when he was satisfied. "Are we going in?"

Aeson nodded.

Calen felt a hand on his shoulder. "What's in there, Calen?" There was a look on Dann's face that Calen hadn't seen before. Fear. His eyes were sunken, his shoulders were drooped, and his hand was clasped against his ribcage.

"The king." Calen tried to sound as confident as he could, but inside, his heart beat like a horse at a gallop, and his sword hand shook every time he lost focus. He needed to be strong for Dann.

The hall looked much the same, except the purple and gold banners fell flat, drooping down from their mounts. The torches seemed dimmer in their sconces. Everywhere he looked, his eyes fell on the bodies of slain Kingsguard. A chill ran through Calen's body. The farther they walked into the hall, the deeper the light retreated.

"There is a dark magic here," Therin muttered, more to himself than anyone else.

The sound of their footsteps and the click-clack of Valerys's claws on the smooth stone echoed through the halls, piercing the otherwise eerie silence. Calen knew that at the end of the hall was Arthur's throne, perched on its raised dais, even if, at that moment, it was shrouded in the absence of light.

"It is about time."

The voice carried through the empty hall, scratching at the air. It hissed from all sides, but Calen knew where it came from. He didn't have to look at Dann to see the fear on his face. It was the same fear that Calen felt when he heard that voice for the first time in the mountain pass.

Even as they drew closer to the dais, it became no clearer. Blackness enveloped everything outside arm's reach. Calen waved away his mind's idea to create a baldír; it was less than useless the last time. They pressed on, but the voice didn't stop.

"You're too late... *Far* too late."

The dais couldn't have been more than twenty feet away, though it was impossible to tell. There was an unfamiliar nervousness in Dann's voice as he whispered, "Calen...

that doesn't sound like the king…"

Calen didn't reply; he didn't get the chance. Without warning, the darkness peeled back, as if it were a shroud of fog retreating with the dawn. Calen gasped as the dissipating darkness revealed even more corpses. The entire hall was covered in the bodies of Belduaran soldiers, those who had come to protect their king.

The Fade stood at the foot of the dais, its black hooded cloak draped over its shoulders. The blue swirls that adorned the cloak shimmered in the firelight, dancing with the flickers from the sconces. Beside the Fade was a young man, suspended by threads of Air that were twisted around his arms and legs. His mouth was forced shut, but his eyes were screaming. Fear muddled with sadness. Tears streamed down his cheeks. It was Daymon, the king's son.

"By the gods…" There was a tremor in Aeson's voice, a weakness that sounded alien coming from that man's lips. Calen's eyes settled on the throne. It was Arthur.

The king sat in his throne. Even in death, he looked every bit the king he was. His golden crown rested on his head, just above the white wings that streaked through his blackish-grey hair. His coat was a deep purple, the edges trimmed with gilt. On the left side of Arthur's chest, where his heart should have been, was a gaping wound the size of a man's fist. The blood that stained the front of the king's coat and trousers was dry.

The Fade stepped closer, drawing his hood back. Its shoulder length-hair was as black as its cloak, as black as its soul-drinking eyes. Its near-translucent skin sent a shiver down the back of Calen's neck. Its brittle lips cracked as they moved. "It seems the Hand could not carry out their task." Irritation flashed across the Fade's face as its black pools cast their gaze across the group. "No matter," it said, flicking its tongue across its teeth. "It is more satisfying to do these things yourself."

Calen couldn't take his eyes off Arthur. His mind was awash with guilt. The man came to him earlier that night, and Calen had ignored him. Arthur had treated him well, and Calen all but spat his apology back in his face. Now he was dead.

"He died quickly," the Fade hissed, a wicked grin on it's face. "I can't say I will do the same with his offspring, though."

The Fade clicked its tongue off the roof of its mouth as it surveyed the scene. "I can give you a chance to save him, though," the Fade said, looking straight at Calen. "What do you say, *Draleid?*" It spat out the word, as if the taste of it was bitter on its tongue. "Do you think you can save the son, like you failed to save the father?"

"Don't listen to a word it says, Calen." Therin didn't look at Calen. His bow was slung over his back, but Calen felt him touching the Spark. He felt that familiar shiver at this back of his neck.

Aeson stood there, a grim expression on his face, each hand fastened tightly around the hilts of his swords. Fear was etched into Dann's face, but still, he held his bow, and his hands did not shake.

Ellisar stepped closer to Calen, both hands wrapped around the handle of his sword. "Stay behind me, Draleid. Do not let it goad you."

"Quiet, *elf!*" The Fade's voice seemed to rise and fall like the wind, booming throughout the hall on demand. "I grow bored of talking. Which of you is to die first?"

Calen felt the anger rolling over inside him as he looked towards Arthur's lifeless body. He was done letting the Fade decide everything. He bounded forward, swinging his sword over his head in a downward arc. It came to a jarring halt as the creature spun and reacted with inhuman speed, a sword wrought of black, pulsing fire held in his grasp.

Calen felt it. It was the same type of weapon that Asius used, a níthral. It looked different though. Asius's axe was smooth, more controlled, as if forged like steel. The Fade's blade was chaos incarnate. The flickers of black flame seemed to blow in a non-existent wind, twisting and spiralling of their own volition.

The creature's brittle lips twisted into a grin. Calen had to fight himself to drag his gaze away from its eyes. Those cavernous wells of black seemed intent on pulling his soul from his body.

Calen felt the Fade pull on threads of Air as he was hit by an invisible battering ram, thrown backwards in the air, then hammered into the ground. A roaring pain erupted through his body. He shook the stars from his eyes just in time to see Valerys launch himself at the Fade.

A single swipe of the Fade's hand, sent Valerys crashing through a nearby pillar. Pain shot through Calen's head.

"No!" He couldn't stop the scream. It was part his own, part Valerys's. He felt it; Valerys was alive, but his body ached in pain.

Before Calen could get to his feet, Aeson and Ellisar flashed past him. They charged straight towards the Fade. The creature moved like a snake in long grass, its flickering blade snapping at them in a maelstrom of ferocious blows. Aeson and Ellisar were two of the most incredible swordsmen that Calen had ever seen – and even they did not have the time to consider going on the offensive. It was all they could do to keep the creature at bay.

Dann dropped to one knee, nocked an arrow, and sent it soaring through the air, where it plunged into the Fade's chest. Two more arrows followed, sinking into the Fade's belly and neck. But they didn't slow the creature; they only irritated it. While deflecting a strike from Therin, it pulled the arrows from its body with threads of Air, then it reached out its hand. Arcs of purple lightning shot from its fingertips, crashing into Dann and launching him into the air. Fragments of stone flew in all directions as the lightning ripped through the ground.

"Go, help them!" roared Therin as he ran to where Dann's body had been thrown.

Calen dragged himself to his feet. His head and his heart pulled him in two directions. His heart urged him to run to Dann, but his head commanded him to help the others. He felt Valerys at the back of his mind, his pain and his anger. He felt his own heart beating – not racing, like it had been, but slow, purposeful. Calen steeled himself and charged at the Fade.

Even with the three of them throwing everything at it, the Fade continued to toy with them, striking them with hammer blows of Air and whips of Fire, turning their bodies into canvases of cuts and gashes. For every two strikes Calen deflected, three fresh cuts appeared on his arms or legs. Each one burned as well as sliced. He didn't want to give the Fade the satisfaction of his pain. But his body held no such grudge. He howled out more than once when the fiery black blade sliced through his skin like molten steel. Ellisar and Aeson did not fare any better. Numerous times, their blades sank into what should have been flesh, only to emerge without a drop of blood on their edge.

How?

Calen tried to strike back. He tried to draw from the Spark, but his mind could not focus. When it could, the Fade sliced at his threads with something unseen, cutting him off as if snipping the strings from a puppet. *How is that possible?*

Without warning, the Fade drew on thick threads of Air and sent both Aeson and Ellisar hurtling in different directions. The creature snapped its neck around, its gaze fixed on Calen. "Fane wants you alive." The Fade's voice slithered off its tongue as it circled Calen. Its blade trailed along the ground, smoke rising where it cut into the stone. "But I think I would prefer you dead. It is cleaner. I have not yet decided."

I need to do something. I can't keep going like this.

Calen took a breath in, focusing his mind. He moved into the svidarya, dropping his legs into the wide stance of the Crouching Bear. As the Fade swung at him with his black-fire blade, Calen pounced. The creature was taken aback by the aggression. It immediately took a back step, sweeping its blade across its chest to block Calen's strikes. Calen moved fluidly through the forms, losing himself in them.

"Keep pushing!" Ellisar leapt up from behind Calen, swinging his sword in a downward arc. Just as his sword collided with the Fade's black-fire blade, Aeson came charging from the other direction. The three of them redoubled their efforts, pushing harder and harder at the creature, not letting up. *Maybe… just maybe.*

"Enough!" The Fade twisted its hand into a fist before slamming it into the stone floor, sending a shockwave in all directions. Calen didn't feel it draw from the Spark, but somehow he was thrown backwards, crashing into one of the sprawling columns that lined the hall. He heaved himself to his feet, pushing the pain to the back of his head. But Ellisar had risen quicker.

Calen's heart sank into his stomach as he watched the black-fire blade arc through the air. He watched as Ellisar parried the first strike, and he dropped to his knees as the second swing separated the elf's head from his shoulders.

Ellisar's body dropped, lifeless, to the floor. He had given an oath to protect Calen. To follow him to the void or beyond. And that was exactly where Calen led him.

Calen's stomach lurched. He lifted himself to his feet. A mix of fury and fear burned through him as his feet carried him towards the Fade. He didn't even move to react as thick threads of Air pummelled into his chest. He hit the ground with an agonising crack.

"I might keep you," the Fade said as it stood over him. It cocked its head to the side, staring down at him with its dark eyes. "You could be an interesting… *project.*"

The Fade carried on muttering to itself, as if Calen weren't even there. When Calen tried to get to his feet, he was slammed back to the floor. Threads of Air pushed down against his chest and shoulders. The Fade barely gave a hint that it had noticed – just an irritated flash of its eyes – but the invisible weight that bore down on Calen's body was evidence enough.

Amidst the chaos, Calen remembered Daymon. The prince still floated in front of the throne, as he had since the darkness had peeled back, but his eyes were no longer filled with fear. They were following something by the corner of the throne.

Valerys.

The young dragon skulked around the dais, its head held low against the floor, like a wolfpine hunting its prey. Calen felt his pain. Every step sent fire through him. Fear filled every crack in Calen's mind. He couldn't lose Valerys. He couldn't lose anyone else, but especially not him. He cried out in his mind, urging the dragon to hide, but Valerys heeded no warnings. He moved closer to the Fade, every purposeful step like a burning knife, but Valerys didn't stop.

Just as the Fade began to turn, it howled in pain as a bolt of blue lightning slammed into its chest. Calen watched as Aeson charged at the Fade, his twin blades spinning in his hands. The two of them exchanged a flurry of blows. If the Fade had been a man, it would have died twice over. But it wasn't. The mortal wounds that Aeson inflicted did nothing more than slow it down. Aeson, on the other hand, was a man. And his wounds were taking their toll on his already weary body.

Calen knew he needed to do something… anything. He reached out for the Spark. His energy was already fading, and his muscles burned, but there was nothing else he could do. The Fade spun on his heels. Even in that cold, dead face, Calen saw the anger. The outrage. As if he were disgusted that Calen would not simply resign himself to his fate.

The threads of Air holding him down pushed even harder. He felt his bones stressing under the weight. They felt as though they would shatter.

Valerys was behind the Fade now, and the creature didn't notice. He was too focused on Aeson and Calen.

Calen felt something in Valerys, something that he had not felt before. It was building, steadily. An enormous pressure. Without thinking, Calen kept reaching for the Spark. He focused his mind. Closing his eyes, he reached out. That ball of ever-moving energy. Its five elemental strands weaving around each other, twisting and pulsating, radiating power, like they had since the dawn of time. Calen reached. He pulled at the strands of Spirit and Fire. He didn't know why, but that was what he needed. He pulled at them, dragging threads into him, then funnelled them into Valerys. Even as the Fade pushed harder and harder, crushing Calen into the stone floor. He kept drawing from the Spark. He felt consciousness slipping from his grasp – his soul drifting away.

He couldn't take much more. Aeson needed to move. Calen screamed at the top of his lungs. "Aeson!"

Aeson didn't hesitate. He threw himself to the ground. The pressure at the back of Calen's mind stopped.

Valerys's head kicked back, and his chest expanded. A river of fire poured forth from the dragon's mouth, a torrent of flickering orange and red flame that consumed the Fade in its entirety. It howled, a piercing shriek like nothing else Calen had ever heard. It was as though its soul was being torn from its body. A feeling of intense power coursed through Calen as the fire cascaded from Valerys's jaws. In that moment, they were one. Calen pushed everything he had into Valerys, feeling the dragon's rage burn through him.

There was no way that anything could have survived, but still, the fear didn't seep from Calen's bones until he watched Daymon fall to the ground. Until the flames lost their vigour and flickered out of existence, leaving only a pile of char and ash in their wake.

Therin's voice drummed on the edge of Calen's consciousness, as if the elf's head were underwater. He had drawn too deeply from the Spark. He knew it. He felt himself slipping away. His vision blurred. Calen felt a hand rest on his chest. A warm glow flooded his body, but Calen knew that he might be too far gone. Either he knew it, or he heard someone say it. It was hard to tell. His thoughts were scattered, wrapped around themselves a thousand ways, muddled and mashed together.

He heard Therin calling, his voice fading in and out. "You are an idiot, boy… a fool…"

CHAPTER 34

Long Live the King

It was a few days before Calen could hold on to consciousness for longer than an hour or two at a time. Even then, his body still ached as though he had been thrown off the side of a cliff. In that time, his room had been a never-ending stream of visitors, though he was unconscious for most of them. Dann even brought his blanket roll and slept on the floor for the first two nights before Therin ushered him out, telling him he wasn't helping.

After Valerys killed the Fade, the fighting in the rest of the city didn't last long. The Fade had not brought enough soldiers with him to take the city by brute force. The polished green stones that Aeson had used at the hidden mountain pass were found nestled in their alcoves, the portcullis open. That was how they had stormed the city, as if from nowhere. If the bells hadn't rung out, everything would have been different. Calen was sure that he wouldn't be drawing breath. How the Fade had gotten the stones was another question entirely.

Calen looked over at Valerys, who rested on the floor by the fireplace. His pale lavender eyes watched Calen with intrigue as he fastened the top button of his gilt-trimmed silk shirt that Therin had insisted he wear. The dragon had recovered a lot faster than he had, but then again, Valerys had not dragged himself to the edge of the void.

A smile touched the corners of Calen's mouth as he watched Valerys. For a moment in that hall, Calen had thought that he might lose him. He had never felt a fear like that. Like half of his soul had come a hair's thickness from being shorn from the living world. Even then, as he stood there in the lavish room, his new scars covered by the fine clothes given to him by Daymon, he felt that sense of loss. It made his stomach weak.

"Calen, it is time." There was a weak smile on Erik's face as he walked into the room, Dann and Therin either side of him.

Calen nodded. He checked one more time that his shirt was buttoned properly before making his way towards the door.

Dann hissed as Calen pulled him into a tight embrace. "Take it easy, *m'lord*," Dann said in a mocking tone. "Some of us didn't get the attention of all the healers in the city."

Therin gave Dann a sideways glance. "I offered to look at your wound, and I was told to leave it because 'women love scars'."

"Oh, shut up, Therin. You're ruining the moment."

Calen couldn't help but laugh as Therin waved Dann away with a dismissive hand and went over to check on Valerys. "Speaking of scars, let me see?"

Dann grabbed his shirt by the neckline and pulled it back across his shoulder, revealing a knotted mess of burnt flesh that spread across his collarbone and up over his left shoulder. "I don't plan on getting hit by lightning again anytime soon."

Calen grimaced as he ran his finger over the twisted skin on Dann's collarbone. "What about the one on your side?"

"Oh, no, I let them heal that one. That one would have killed me."

Calen went to argue with Dann, but instead, he shook his head, pulled Dann in for another embrace, and laughed. Healing one wound, only to leave another solely for the stories he could tell about it, was quite possibly the most *Dann* thing that Calen could think of.

Calen took a deep breath in, then turned to Erik. "Let's do this."

The hallways were empty as they made their way to the courtyard. Every soul in the city would be squashed together to lay witness. Therin turned to Calen as they made their way down one of the long corridors. "Calen…" There was a cautious tone in his voice. "You need to be careful. Arthur was a good man. I trusted him, as Aeson did, and Daymon might well be the same, but—"

Calen cut him short. "But he might not be."

Therin nodded, twisting his lips into a reluctant frown. "Just be careful. There will be few who will not seek to tie a string around you."

"As you and Aeson have?" Calen replied, without missing a beat.

Calen felt a twinge of regret as he saw hurt flash in the elf's eyes, but Therin did not reply. He simply turned his head forward and kept walking. Dann and Erik did not speak either, but Calen felt the tension. That had not been his plan. The words just slipped out.

The elves of Aravell joined them at the end of the corridor before they stepped out into the square. They had stood guard outside Calen's room day and night, but that was the first time he laid eyes on them since the battle.

"It is no loss," Gaeleron remarked when Calen gawked at the stump where his left hand had once been. "I wield my sword with my right, and I am not much with a bow." That was the end of the conversation as far as the elf was concerned. Calen did not think he would be so calm had he lost a hand. He was not sure whether to laugh at the elf's candour. He decided not to.

Calen's heart held heavy in his chest as he looked over the elves. Five had followed him from the Darkwood. Only four stood before him now. "Ellisar—"

"Ellisar died with honour, fulfilling an oath that he believed in," Vaeril said not allowing Calen to finish his sentence, "an oath that we all *still* believe in. We are with you, Calen, now more than ever."

They all nodded in agreement.

Calen felt a rumble of pride from Valerys in the back of his mind. The white dragon stepped up beside Calen, craning his neck in the air.

"Thank you," Calen said. He reached his arm out to Vaeril, who in turn reached out his own. "*Du gryr haydria til myia elwyn.*"

You bring honour to my heart. Therin's teachings had not been going to waste.

Vaeril smiled at Calen's use of the Old Tongue, as did the other elves. "*Du gryr haydria til myia elwyn,*" they replied in unison.

Dann leaned into Calen. "When did you learn to speak elf?" he whispered.

Calen smiled, suppressing a laugh. "It's the Old Tongue. I'll explain later." He turned to the group. "We'd better keep moving, or we'll be late."

The archway that led out into the courtyard was flanked by two dwarves in full plate armour, crimson cloaks draped around their shoulders. Calen wondered how Daymon felt about the dwarves remaining in the city, but he hadn't brought it up. The man had enough to concern his mind with.

"Draleid." The dwarf on the right side of the arch tilted his head ever so slightly. His beard was knotted heavily with gold and silver rings. Calen returned the gesture as he passed under the arch.

The air itself seemed to shake as the cheers of the crowd echoed through the courtyard. The people were crammed together like blades of grass in a field. Calen didn't think he had ever seen so many souls in one place. In fact, he knew he hadn't. He stared out in amazement over the crowd. Therin gave him a slight push, ushering him onto the raised platform at the front of the crowd.

Calen greeted Daymon as he stepped onto the platform. Valerys leapt up beside him to a rapturous applause from the gathered crowd. Daymon had come to Calen's room and asked if he would be the one to crown him in his father's place. "It would be an honour," he had said, "to be crowned King by a Draleid."

Both Therin and Aeson had told Calen, in no uncertain terms that he absolutely could not. That alone might have spurred him on to do it, just so he would not be dancing to their tune, but they were right. To be seen to think that he had the power to crown kings was a dangerous message to send. But he had told Daymon that he would stand by his side to show his support. Therin and Aeson had argued against that as well, but he was set. He owed Arthur that much.

Lord Ihvon Arnell stood at Daymon's right side. The king-to-be's new chief advisor had a grim look on his face, and he was sporting more than a few new cuts and bruises. Ihvon had come to visit Calen while he was recovering. He had said nothing; he had just sat there in silence. He didn't know that Calen was awake. It had seemed odd to Calen that he would visit but not speak. But he was Arthur's good friend, and mourning affected people differently. On this occasion, the man gave him a purposeful nod before turning his attention back towards the soon-to-be king.

The kings and queens of the Dwarven Freehold also stood on the platform – as a sign of unity. Kira's plate armour was replaced with her padded leather cuirass and silken skirts, in a deep crimson laced with gilt. The golden crown nestled atop her star-fire hair. She looked as fair as any woman he had ever seen, with the bloodlust gone from her eyes. Calen thought she gave him a quick smile, though it was too quick to be sure.

"Thank you," Daymon said as Calen took his place beside the soon-to-be king. There was a loss in his eyes. A loss that Calen understood.

"It is my honour, Your Majesty."

The coronation did not last long. Once Daymon was crowned, he spent a few moments waving to his people, who chanted and cheered, voracious for the sight of their new king. Calen and Valerys simply stood there by his side. Calen couldn't help but think that the image would look powerful. The newly crowned king, standing side-by-side with the king and queens of the Dwarven Freehold, and a Draleid. It would be like one of Therin's stories.

Daymon raised his hand in the air, quieting the crowd. It amazed Calen how, with a gathering of so many, that silence could truly be achieved. But it *was* silent. He could have heard a pin drop as the people of Belduar waited on the first words of their new king.

"My father was a good and just man. He was a *true* king. He was the king that I aspire to be. I will miss him, and I will mourn his loss along with you every day. But I will not let it break me!"

A cheer erupted from the crowd.

Calen could see a mage behind the king, pulling threads of Air and Spirit into the king's words, funnelling them throughout the courtyard, above the din of the crowd.

"*We* are the people of Belduar. We have defended this city for thousands of years. From tyrants, from armies, and from dragonfire. We have not – and we *will* not – bow down. And we are *not* alone! When we were in need, our allies came. The dwarves, ever our steadfast brothers and sisters, came to our aid. And we must not forget that dragonfire is no longer owned by the empire. The Draleid have returned! They stand again! They stand with us! This is our time!"

Chants of "Long live the king" and "Long live King Daymon" still boomed through the air as they stepped down from the platform.

The celebrations would go on for days, no doubt. It would be a welcome respite from the mourning. Arthur's death had cast a shadow over the city.

Aeson, Therin, and Asius made their way over to bestow their well wishes on the newly crowned king, no doubt. But as they did, the barrel-chested figure of the new Lord Captain of the Kingsguard, Tarmon Hoard, his purple cloak billowing behind him, pushed his way past them. He stopped in front of the king, his knuckles pressed to his forehead.

Daymon frowned, tilting his head. "What is it, Tarmon?"

"My king, I bring urgent news. The empire's blockade has been lifted."

Daymon smiled for the first time since Arthur's death, but the soldier's brow furrowed.

"Tarmon, *what is it?*"

"They move towards the city, my king. The Dragonguard are with them."